SUNSET

Book III

The Stefan Székely T

SUNSET

Conclusion

to

The Stefan Székely Trilogy

Stephen Swartz

MYRDDIN PUBLISHING GROUP

UNITED STATES · UNITED KINGDOM · AUSTRALIA

ISBN-13: 978-1-68063-029-9

ISBN-10: 1-68063-029-6

www.myrddinpublishing.com

Cover design by Iris Schaeffer

I am the way into the city of woe.
I am the way to a forsaken people.
I am the way into eternal sorrow.
Sacred justice moved my architect.
I was raised here by divine omnipotence,
primordial love and ultimate intellect.
Only those elements time cannot wear
are beyond me, and beyond time I stand.
Abandon All Hope, Ye Who Enter Here.

Dante Alighieri, *The Divine Comedy: Inferno*, Canto III

Part One

1

"THERE! DO YOU SEE IT? THE BLACK STORM APPROACHES!" THE YEOMAN leaned out dangerously from the stone rampart of the turret, high on the palace wall, one of the new additions to the old palace. Dressed in rough brown cassock with crimson sash, he cared little whether he soiled his uniform as he stretched out into the warm, humid night. "I've never seen it so dark. It would blot the sun!"

"It is a sign—perhaps the sign we've all awaited," responded the stout bailiff, dressed in imperial purple with a white rose emblazoned upon his broad chest. With large frame, he dared not lean there. He set down his ceremonial halberd with a heavy sigh. "It may reach us by the time the ceremony begins."

(The words they both spoke were *Magyar*—Hungarian, the official language of the Empire of Europa—yet courtesy demands translation.)

"All the better, Joshua. Our lord will rejoice." The yeoman pointed at the horizon. "The black wave comes! Isn't it glorious? The thunder! The talons of lightning! The acid rain!"

"Yes, Kristóf, it is glorious. Another danger to us. I got caught in it once a few months ago, nearly burned my skin off."

"I know! I got caught in it last week, myself. Still, wasn't worse than this pain in my side, damn lump. And the storm's pressure brings to ache my joints. My poor head is about to explode, too. But, Joshua, to have the Black Storm come over us on this eve, on *this eve*, what an omen! It is like my dreams."

"Only by the whim of the calendar, Kristóf, nothing more. And you best keep your voice down. Words echo in these stone corridors."

Lowering his voice, the yeoman continued: "You're wrong, Joshua. On this millennium eve yet? You should know. You need to read more. It must be a sign of His great transformation. It signals a new era—since His Holiness reset the calendar. This is our thousand-year reign. A new millennia of Europa begins!"

The bailiff exhaled. "A century, Kristóf. Only a century. I read very little these days. How to keep this halberd sharp, all I need to know. No more than what's been happening for the past hundred centuries. It is merely a stormfront, a black stormfr—"

"Stormfront! Yes! His Holiness welcomes such a stormfront!"

"You're clearly mad, Kristóf. And you'd better keep your thoughts to yourself. The Black Storm is only the work of our scientists—"

"But don't you see? The way the black cloud grows, swells like an eager penis, like a famished skyborne cancer? To engulf and enshroud everything? As though He summoned it special for tonight's august occasion. He has the power to—"

"You dream of dark fantasies, Kristóf. Too much reading of the old tales, vague legends, and myth. He is not a myth, not legend, not—"

"Precisely! You know how it began. How our suffering began?"

"A mere man—vampire, I'll grant."

"Yes! Begun more than one-hundred-sixty-thousand years ago, at the very birth of humanity, when genes were cleaved and we were all made anew, a new line, a superior strain, masters of the world!"

"For a time, perhaps. Then shunned, hunted, destroyed."

Kristóf clapped, lifting his hands like steam rising from a cauldron. "Then risen again!"

"You've gotten into some spoiled red again, haven't you, Kristóf? From a low-born vein, I suspect." Joshua offered a tidy smirk. "Better no one catches you in your moment of mirth. If His Holiness should overhear you, then you . . . ."

A shadow appeared on the wall behind the yeoman and crept up the stones, overtaking the yeoman's height, besting his peaked cap, broadening the yeoman's square shoulders, darkening the rampart's torchlight. Joshua pointed at the shadow.

"He approaches," Kristóf uttered, voice stymied as he straightened into his stance.

The bailiff stiffened, held the halberd upright with both his white-gloved hands, his chin raised, salt-and-pepper goatee pointing.

The shadow filled the turret as did the accompanying noise, at first like a huddle of crickets, then a locust army, then legion after legion of enraged bats screeching as the entourage, marching down the corridor, abruptly halted within the turret where the balcony provided an open-air view of the city below and the countryside beyond—dark with night and darker with the Black Storm, Erebus over the fallow soil long stripped of fertility, scourged of life, awaiting the poison of acidic rain to poison it once more.

The monstrous hulk of THE LORD strode into the turret like the raging storm of lava from a shattered volcano, radiating heat ahead of its burning touch—yet, for Him, the reverse: the actual temperature was ice, the forewind a blizzard cutting through the tepid night.

The Lord halted as if a mighty wall stood before him. He turned to the opening in the turret and surveyed the impressive storm rolling loudly toward the palace, shot through with tongues of lightning.

Kristóf the yeoman held his breath, sucked in air as he pressed his back against the wall, praying not to be noticed. The noise caught The Lord's attention. Joshua the bailiff could not hide, standing upright like a granite statue.

The Lord stepped to the rampart, placed his pale, gnarled hands there. The gray stone sizzled, turned bone white, cracking beneath his cold touch.

"THE DARK . . . ."

The vibration of his voice shook the walls around them. The Lord took a long breath, drawing in the scent of the storm.

"The dark consumes the light once more." The words bounded from His mouth like cut timber banging down a ramp. "Like the glove that overlays the hand. Like drapery shielding the window." He gazed at the stormfront billowing before Him. "Like the lid that covers the casket. As it has been since the commencement of measured time."

The Lord gave a laugh, too short for His entourage to notice.

"It is a sign. Soon we shall be completely one."

"Your Holiness . . . ?" queried the chamberlain behind The Lord, appointed in black with gold trim, laurel leaves upon his shoulders, long gray beard tugged by the storm, bald pate beneath gold skullcap.

Kristóf tightly pursed his lips, wishing to speak a clever remark, as was his bent, yet daring not. Joshua, opposite him, caught his friend's desperate expression, understanding how his friend must have been correct after all. The Black Storm had special meaning for this night, the last night of the century. Both turned their heads to follow the gaze of The Lord.

A bank of clouds the color of coal-shafts boiled over the gray stone plaza below, as though the entire world was aflame, spreading beneath the soot-stained marble ramparts and the shadowed city. Silent fangs of lightning stabbed the distant earth, craving its essence: the blood of all creatures that had fallen over a thousand-thousand years. A slice of light like thinned blood cut across the horizon, marking the boundary between ravaged heaven and barren earth, between the storm and the city's dark rooftops.

"How many millennia has it been?" The Lord mumbled, heard only by Kristóf, standing closest to His Holiness. The Lord's eyes suddenly shifted, fell upon the yeoman. "How many?"

"Your Holiness, I—I do n-not—know," Kristóf tried to speak, voice shaking. He bowed his head, chin to chest, held it there.

The Lord returned his gaze to the distant view. "The night arrives in solemn glory, fetid storm winds smelling of sickly steeds struggling to haul carriages overfilled with plague corpses. As they did in 'thirty-three. And yet . . . ."

Seething thunder rushed towards them like a giant black wave, grumbling its warning, then exploded overhead, shaking the turret. All who were there were rattled, half-cringed—except Him.

"He seeks to intimidate me," The Lord spoke with a dry chuck.

"Your Holiness, it is now time," spoke the chamberlain beside The Lord. "Your guests are waiting—"

Another gong of thunder rang them, marking the late hour, yet none were disturbed, prepared for it.

"It is a blessing, a sign that all is well with the world," crowed the chamberlain. "Let us praise His Holiness and the Most High!"

The Lord nodded, a demonic pout settling upon his downturned lips, staring out at the world He had made, appreciating its demise.

A grand flash of lightning punctuated the thought; another mighty boom from an impatient storm convinced.

Although the turret was dark, lit only by tongues of night-fire, the corridor was bright with torches.

"I shall take no humor tonight," grumbled The Lord, backing away from the rampart.

A pair of dwarves appeared in the turret in black and red uniforms, humorless harlequins, previously hidden within shadows, and stood at attention, then turned sharply and led the way out. A quartet of lithe young women in flowing red gowns, cut low enough to count ribs, heavy gold necklaces and ear rings dangling, bounded after them. Six yeomen with sabers rattling crowded into a square around The Lord and formed an escort. The chamberlain, with high collar and Book of Law in his hands, fell in with the group. An escort of thirteen guards stood stiffly in the dark corridor, waiting to follow The Lord whenever He might move out of the turret.

"Your Holiness," the chamberlain pronounced, bowing.

The Lord ignored him, staring at Kristóf.

"You! Are you not a yeoman?"

Kristóf bowed his head. Then, thinking it might not be enough, dropped to his knees, keeping his head lowered as if awaiting the fatal blow. His face touched the stone floor.

Hands grabbed him, jerked him to his feet, though his toes barely felt the stone floor the way the guards hoisted him, held him by the arms and shoulders. His eyes were tightly closed, fearing to look at His Holiness. His ears went numb, then he was hearing the bass voice of The Lord:

". . . hold him steady, for the storm demands a sacrifice."

His chin was pushed upward by a gloved hand while a large, rough, bare hand curled lovingly around his throat, and squeezed slowly until sharp sensations crackled through his body. His bones were breaking inside his skin, veins were bursting. His eyes met those of his lord and both his questions and their answers merged into a vast nothingness as he lost consciousness, becoming a bag of viscous fluid and calcified crumbs.

The skin sack slumped on the stones. A pair of guards gathered it up, heaved it from the rampart, out into the night, and no one heard it splatter on the plaza below as another round of thunder blotted out the suffering of humanity.

"You will accompany me," spake The Lord, raising a finger toward the bailiff. "What is your name?"

"I'm . . . Joshua, . . .Your Holiness."

The Lord cleared his throat, spit just past the bailiff's bowed head, down to the stone floor.

"You are one of us?"

"Vampirian, yes, Your Holiness. However, I beg you, Your Holiness, please give me any name you prefer."

The Lord's temperament burst with amusement.

"I name you Judas." He waved one of the guards to aid the chunky bailiff in rising to his feet. "Come, Judas. Let us go forth to our revelry. For tomorrow we may die again and must start over from scratch—like seeing the first dry patch appear on our skin."

○R

Opulent splendor. The words come quickly, the repeated response to the inquiry how best to describe the Great Hall dressed in its holiday finery. The cavernous room is always bathed in red. Gold establishes the form and function of the hall with the walls draped in luxurious red velvet. Black bows and ribbons adorn the moldings and lamps. The floor is polished marble from eleven different quarries, cut and fitted into a grand compass of power, a great horned façade of the Most High at the North. The audience mingles over it, casually, forgetful of its expense, delighting in their formal attire, gentlemen in long coattails and white shields, ladies in flowing gowns of red and gold, white and black, or pale pink for the virgins, as custom dictates. The Great Hall of the palace is, after all, a cathedral to the decadent.

The orchestra at the far end plays a standard repertoire of solemn holiday tunes, muted enough to allow conversation. Nothing in major keys. Soon will come the dancing, the traditional conceit to the way the world used to be: slow, dignified movements of vacuous decorum and frivolous elegance where neither men nor their women will be supplicant for more than an awkward instant. The traditions, hollow as they might be, are what keep us alive, replicating them as sincerely as possible or playing them with full open irony.

The chamberlain keeps his eye on the great clock on the wall as the hands turn. It is an ancient timepiece, a spoil of war, and must be set each day, yet, without the electric fire of days of yore, it must make do. Indeed, the lanterns in the Great Hall burn with electric fire conjured by slaves in the underground levels, pacing the panels that turn a few turbines; the process is boring to explain.

The world has changed. Is there nothing that does not change? A vampire, perhaps. However that must be all. The only exception.

Yes, indeed, *opulent splendor* it is! A perfect venue for celebration tonight: the end of one century and the start of the next.

In the throng are the famous and the infamous alike, social equals in an unequal society. Various captains of industry. A fair number of entertainers, those who follow the official line of approved jokes. The odd fashion maven or two and minor culture heroes and heroines who have enjoyed their five days of fame. The others are more notable.

For example, here are Mr. and Mrs. Orsós, Elector of the Office of Wealth Management, displaying their girth to the world, she with her auburn hair piled high atop her massive head, he with gray beard and sideburns larger than a lion's and less well-kept. And Mr. and Mrs. Halász, another banker and his personal spender; he took a shot in the face during the revolution and is missing a cheek and jaw. The prosthetic is poorly made. Here stand Mr. and Mrs. Váradi, so well-known among the entertainment set, purveyors of parties, especially drinking parties where new, exotic strains of red are sampled.

Colonel Orbán in full dress uniform of emerald and royal blue is an impressive sight, even with one arm lost in battle. Lady Boglárka, swirling her furs about her narrow bare shoulders, seems an unlikely skeleton, but she is known to be particular about her diet; she helped finance the Italian campaign so she is always invited to these functions. The Molnár twins, blonde Péter and bald Gergő, handle all manner of trade issues with the various eastern states, recently securing a deal with the Russian Empire.

Speaking of which, the ambassador to the Russias, Hunor László, is chatting politely with Spanish ambassador Alfonzo Alvarez, no doubt hatching some scheme to split up Europa between their two respective nations. For now, the border is secure, thanks to Chief Diplomat Máté Somogyi's carefully chosen words and Field Marshal Sándor Végh's carefully aimed bullets. As long as the troops feed well on the scraps of the defeated.

And there are the ladies of the Vampires of Mercy, represented by Mother Flóra and Sister Szonja. They curtsey like school girls, even in their stiff red robes.

A squad of the aged 2nd cavalry (retired) stand in an admiring semi-circle around their new matron: Princess Dzsesszika, the eldest daughter of a duke of somewhere who married well—and left Prince Zétény as a pool of pungent fluid in the center of her honeymoon boudoir, the nasty scandal quickly forgotten.

To her left is the staid Mr. and Mrs. Csonka, he the captain of the stonemason guild, she the head of nursing at the Imperial Hospice, known for their philanthropy, always invited despite his deformity (miniature head protruding from his throat) and hers (useless bat wing hanging from her right hip, generally covered by extra pleats). The medical arts are not so advanced here, as Dr. Zalán Török tries his best to reconstitute some semblance of healing, drawing upon the library headed by Professor Noémi Szóke.

The one holding court over the north point of the compass laid in the floor of the Great Hall is the nefarious Count Vass, once an unknown vampire from Timişoara claiming ancestral links to Saint Dracula, eventually dismissed as a fraud. He made back his reputation through service to the empire, negotiating the surrender treaty in Paris and arranging the capture of the French president and her family to be held for ransom—then collecting the ransom, taking his portion as commission, and returning the French first family in pieces in grocery sacks, declaring there had been no provision for returning them alive and intact. The court was amused and promoted Vass.

Now the count appears with his so-called niece, a pink-gowned waif he introduces as Dorottya. She shyly fingers her long jet curls, extending to her waist. And, if one may dare to squint at her figure, one might detect a slight curve of her belly. It is good he has managed to continue the line though it is an insult to bring her in a pink evening gown. Someone should take him aside and reprimand him. Mr. Antal sees the affront, fortunately, and tugs at the Count's sleeve, takes him away through the crowd, leaving the young lady at the mercy of Mihály Faragó and Imre Balla, two of the most notorious playboys in the capital, masters of many newly sworn servants of the empire. Dorottya seems pleased to have their company. Mr. and Mrs. Szűcs turn to keep an eye on her, this newly sworn girl.

And there is Mr. Dobos with the newest missus, a blond sprite named Kinga, he the head of Balaton Industries, makers of various armaments and suppliers to the military forces of the empire. He has garnered many awards for his service and so deserves a line of brides. Unlike Countess Alíz and her line of unfortunate husbands, the latest being Szilárd, the son of the chief millmeister in the grain industry. She flicks her vapor stick at the four diminutive men conversing with her; one moves to catch the deposit, realizes it is only smoke. She places her hand on one shoulder and he cringes, poor thing. A new husband is being chosen. The others turn gray, eyes reddening.

And Mr. and Mrs. Deák seem unduly dour this evening, as do the Budais and the Kerekes, though a bit more smug than either the Fehérs or the Kozmas. Or the Pintérs. Less so the Bartas and the Lengyels. It shall be their loss. It is a night for celebration, after all, and those not in the proper spirit should have stayed at home. Did the invitation not say to appear full of mirth and ready for merriment? Then comes the storm.

The announcements are called—interrupted by another booming of thunder. Unafraid, the guests gather, perhaps close to three hundred in the Great Hall. The lanterns flicker. The orchestra fades to silence. Staff members in smart black uniforms line the wall with trays of celebratory florets of merlot. When the chamberlain flicks his white-gloved hand, the staff moves into the crowd to distribute the florets.

Thunder shakes the Great Hall as His Holiness takes the steps up to the great throne, led by a ceremonial bailiff, chosen at random from the corridor, who clears a path then steps to the side at the bottom of the steps, head bowed.

The Emperor stands tall, mighty before the crowd, a god on earth. His long robe is a menagerie of ermine, sable, fox, and wolf, with bold red cuts of human flesh joining the collection of pelts. Beneath the robe of office, his black uniform impresses: militaristic yet stylish in civilian quarters, with medals in rows across his chest, and a wide red sash hanging diagonally shoulder to hip. A sabre hangs at his hip, and he always keeps a hand on the hilt. He has needed to use it more often than would be proper. The high collar hides the marks of his office: the welts of lust, the portions of poison shared. They are difficult to see with the wealth of black beard that fans out from his square chin. The long black moustache droops, merges with his beard, yet his fat red lips stand out in the hairy composite. A nose of regal bent supports his dark eyes, intense luminaries that bring pain to those who dare to disappoint him. A broad, pale forehead, barely wrinkled with age, shows through the drape of the tangled black locks that fall to his shoulders. He wears no crown—everyone knows him on sight—yet for this special occasion, he bears the Mongol-inspired helm, bearing four wild boar tusks and a pair of domesticated auruch horns solemnly projecting. Legend has it the helm was won in close combat with a previous leader of the Magyar clan. Many attend such official occasions solely to see the ceremonial helm.

The Emperor levels his gaze at the assembled, generous locks of his jet mane falling over his face. A servant raises a tray and he takes the floret and raises it. The audience raise theirs. A cheer goes up. And all drink to the bottom. The crashing of glass matches the splinter of the lightning as the florets are dashed against the marble floor. Thunder outside covers much of the shattering of glass.

When the process has completed, standing with regal mien, the greeting must be spoken:

"To all who fill this hall, welcome. Greetings. It has been a long year, a long century, much too long, since last we met for celebration. Tonight we gather to raise a cheer and bid farewell to a hundred years of chaos. A new century commences, opening to a full era of darkness over the land. Victory is complete. Let this new century be the era of our darkness!"

He waits for the cheering and applause to peak then subside.

"Word comes this evening from the battlelines, and it chills my heart. Our enemies have been driven to the sea. As we dine tonight, our forces press upon them, cutting them to pieces, supping on their flesh and sipping their blood. Let us raise a mighty cheer for them, the army of the undead—forever in struggle against the forces of light, the human host on the run, vanquished, doomed, written out of history!"

The gathering cheers and the noise batters the walls and jiggles the chandeliers. A great clap of thunder accentuates the moment.

"I greet you, vampire kin of Europa! Let us all enjoy the fruits of our labors! Let us praise our benefactor! Be joyful!"

With his arms lifted high, the orchestra strikes up a lively tune, half imperial march, half waltz. The horns blast their theme, trumpets the staccato stings of triumph. The guests swirl into a great dance, like umbrellas twirling under a midnight moon.

The emperor stands a moment longer, studying the exuberance in the Great Hall, as though checking that everything is as it should be, according to plans, following protocol, obeying the master whom he is bound to serve—for everyone has a master.

Yet an emperor is granted leisure in moments such as these.

He retires to the huge throne, a single piece of dark exotic wood carved from a great mahogany trunk and inlaid with gold. The cushion which supports his body accepts the folding, crumpling cloak, the crossing of thick, muscular legs, the crusty leather of knee-high boots, for the furniture is his, made especially for him, as is everything else within his sight.

The music plays—sad, decadent tunes which harbor regrets and sorrows, the emotions which are celebrated on a night such as this. From his slumped pose upon his throne, he gazes over the crowd, not seeing the revelers, not hearing the music, never a thought to their entertainment. He gazes beyond what is visible, onward to the dark netherworld of his master, the grand spirit he playfully calls Luce.

◌

It is a duty, he considered. Yes, as sure as to those he tends during the other nights of the year. This is a reprieve, a rest for the weary. His court needs their reward, he understood. And the final night of the century only comes around once in a hundred years, the final night of a millennium even rarer. He did not expect to see the next such night.

Soon the music changed and staff filed out from each side of the great hall bearing trays. Sampling the delicacies, the assembled partook of snacks seldom offered on other festive nights: ladyfingers fashioned from the fingers of ladies, pigs-in-blankets made from pork parts, roasted drumsticks torn from the hips of babies, baked blood tarts, and more. To wash down the food, more florets were delivered and gratefully lifted to greasy lips and the sloppy noise of chewing and gulping filled the Great Hall.

A staff person, approved by the ceremonial bailiff, climbed the six steps up to the dais, bowed, and offered a tray of the same delicacies.

"Your Holiness," the staff member uttered.

He waved off the food and drink. The server retreated.

"My darling," a woman's haughty voice floated over the joyful din. Ensconced in a floor-length red velvet gown, her bare shoulders like snow broken only by her dark flowing locks, her ankles beneath the gold-embossed hemline pale as bone, pressed into sandals fashioned from human leather, balancing herself upon the stiletto heels made of human vertebrae, she arrived at the dais. She had a floret in her hand, its portion of red half gone, staining the crystal. Glancing at the red a moment, she returned her gaze to her lord. "Don't be so glum."

The woman meant well, he recognized, accepted. She always strove to change his mood, yet on a night such as this it would be impossible.

He cleared his throat, as though a century of dust had accumulated there, hardening with each day's duties. A page boy with one eye sewn shut, matching his sewn lips, and a jagged scar across his bald scalp rushed to the throne, accepted the spittle into a golden basin, and as quickly disappeared.

"Be at ease, My Love," the woman continued, daring to languish aside the broad arm of the great chair, fingers tickling the red satin padding. It was difficult to pin her age; she could have been twenty or a hundred and twenty years. The rouge was likely dabbed blood from a willing pet. Deliberate black shadows surrounding her eyes accentuate her era, the nights when everyone wore smoke to signify membership in the midnight revolution.

He glared at her and she withdrew.

"My Lord," she corrected herself, then waited to see whether he would dismiss her or allow her to remain. His dark brows pinched and she relaxed, able to read his quixotic moods.

"We must celebrate," she dared to speak up. "How often does a centennial passing come, even to us, long-standing guardians of this place? What shall we do to abide our lot until the next centennial night arrives? Shall we exist so long?"

She turned to study the boisterous crowd. Half were dancing and half eating and drinking, chatting, hatching conspiracies or soliciting boudoir partners. Like every occasion in the Great Hall. None of them seemed to consider the ramifications of this night.

"And yet it seems not as exciting as I had imagined." She breathed deeply, as though detecting a strange scent. "Perhaps it is the weather. The storm draws its energy from us. The pity. Yet they dance. Dance as though they would never be asked to stop. It is much as we did many years ago. Is it not, My Love? The nights of dancing? Do you remember how we danced all those nights, slept all day, and in moments between caught our fill of premium Roman red?" She focused on his face, the black beard *sans* streaks of gray, and the blacker moustache, the dark eyes forever plotting, planning, scheming. "Do you recall?"

He pursed his lips and with a grumble spouted: "No."

"It has been a long time. I understand. How could anyone recall fifty years past? Or more. 'Twenty-eight seems so long ago. So devilish our meeting—the brutality of that night! We should need a book to recount all those years. So much mayhem has transpired since then. The revolution, the terror, the great replacement. The black storms. The years run together in my head—"

"Seventy," he grunted.

"What's that, My Lord? Seventy? Years?" She thought to laugh but, seeing his cold face, tucked away her smile. "You, of any of us, should recall that era. And be ever-proud. You led us through it. And we thank you for that. This revelry tonight is as much for you, a well-deserved thanks, as it is for all of us and our minor achievements. We now have an empire of the undead, thanks to you, My Lord."

She extended her arm, trying to brush his hair with her hand, as she had done many times before. He slapped her hand away. It hurt and she brought her hand up to her lips, licked away the sting.

"Forgive me, My Lord. I meant no disrespect."

The woman cowered, and when he failed to notice her submissive gesture, she shrank away, slinking down the steps, disappearing among the throng of revelers, lost in the stormy night, leaving him to his brooding as crackles of lightning clawed the windows.

CR

Explosions of thunder continued to rattle the Great Hall although most of the revelers ignored it.

The chamberlain bent low, pressing his lips close to The Lord's ear, to deliver a secret message, perhaps, or be better heard among the noisy throng.

"Shall Your Holiness go among your audience?" He appeared to have doubts about his choice of words. "On this rare occasion, it would be a wise gesture to greet them personally. An audience always likes to be appreciated." He saw his words affected no response from The Lord. "They will follow you to the ends of the earth if only you give them the slightest grin. Perhaps a scoff for some of them. A tap on the shoulder. A solemn glare. Something which they might call personal contact. Something to boast on. Then they will obey without any hesitation."

His Holiness moved to scratch at his thick moustache, dark eyes unblinking. "What do you think of this foolishness?"

The woman, sneaking back to the dais moments before, spun at his voice, happy to be noticed again. The woman in her red velvet dress, pale shoulders drawing envy from the polished marble of the Great Hall, acted demure.

"My lord?"

"This suggestion of his . . . ," spake The Lord. "Does it not seem . . . uncharacteristic of me? To wade among the swamp creatures?"

"Oh, My Lord, it is quite uncharacteristic of you!" She laughed. "So you must do it. To baffle them. Frighten them." A string of giggles. "It would most certainly ingratiate them to you."

"You think I should mingle." It was not a question.

"Yes, My Lord. Mingle. That's the word, what I've heard it called."

His Holiness shifted upon the mighty throne, pulled himself up straight, leaning forward, an elbow upon a knee, the other arm bent to hold up his head, chin embedded in a fist. The entire dais seemed to rock as he adjusted himself.

The chamberlain stood stiffly at attention and gave a glance at the ceremonial bailiff at the foot of the steps, the halberd resting against his broad shoulder, ready to protect the dais from those who thought to come too close.

"Your new guardsman can accompany you, if you have doubts," the woman suggested, adding a crystalline chuckle.

"Indeed." The Lord sat forward, both hands on his knees, staring at the bailiff he had dragged into the Great Hall from a side corridor.

The Lord stood.

And the audience's boisterous din immediately withered and died, swallowed in an abyss of silence as all eyes turned to regard His Holiness dismounting the dais like a god arriving for worship.

"I shall mingle," muttered The Lord.

"Yes, My Lord," said the lady in red velvet. "Go amongst them. You may absorb their energy and thus become stronger. I would welcome that in our bed upon the morn. Possibly you may grow twice the power in a single hour." She giggled.

He faced the lady and she did not glower. "If it please you, I will do it, this mingling like a party whore. Yet nothing more."

"*J'adore!*" she sang.

He turned to his chamberlain, who shrank back. "Then I will retire and let the vagabonds of the night make their merriment."

The chamberlain bowed low. "As you wish, Your Highness."

The Lord took a step down, his massive figure shaking the floor.

"He's coming down," a member of the audience declared from the center of the crowd.

"He comes down."

Others hushed, cheered, shrieked.

"He's standing."

"He stands!"

"He will join us."

Similar utterances of surprise splashed through the audience.

"It is a night of blessing."

"He will give his blessing."

"The new century will be honored."

"This one night he honors us!"

"Quick, make way!"

"Stand aside."

"Beware, if he touches you death may consume you."

"He has the devil's curse."

"The devil's touch."

A fresh crackle of lightning, another rumbling explosion from the clouds above. The Black Storm enveloped the city.

Descending the steps one heavy boot after the other, the Great Hall echoed with cries of pain from souls buried beneath the palace, growls from the starving dogs in the kennels, shrieks from the bats in the rafters, as the unsteady crowd shuffled away in three directions, as if none wished to be the first to be greeted by their lord and master.

Yet some unfortunate soul must be first. Dr. Török gave his friend, Professor Szóke, a shove forward. The professor feigned alarm then held out his hand to His Holiness. With a snicker and whispered warning from Török, Szóke withdrew his hand. One should not make physical contact with The Lord upon pain of death. His Holiness had the curse.

"Good evening," intoned The Lord with a casual grin, as though he understood the gesture was pure theatrics. He shared that assumption with his audience. "Good evening," he spoke to another and another, his voice measured. He gave a dip of his head to indicate each person he addressed. "Good evening."

As His Holiness waded through the crowd, a tall, bearded fellow seemed to step boldly forward, appareled in a black tuxedo with the prominent red badge of the judiciary. Actually, those around him had stepped back as The Lord pressed ahead.

"Ah! Borbély, you poor cuckold," The Lord spake with a chuckle. "I am surprised to see you received an invitation."

"I did, Your Holiness," he whimpered, cowering. "On behalf of my father, who is with us no longer."

"Yes, his demise was spectacular," spake The Lord. "So how is your dear wife this evening?"

With a fierce pout, the man saluted with two fingers, then shrank into the crowd, mumbling: "She's dead, and you know it."

Zsombor Biró, head of a major munitions factory, stepped up as though eager to embrace his benefactor. "Your Majesty, the night is for your blessing—"

"Curse," The Lord corrected. "It is a night for curses."

"Yes, My Lord. Curses, it is."

"And the black wave." He glanced toward the tall windows on the far side of the Great Hall, a crisp white light crackling there.

A young lady pushed through the crowd to stand at the edge of the circle surrounding The Lord, clearly excited for the chance to greet Him up close. In black evening gown, red rose over her breast, her other breast exposed by the eccentric cut of the gown, a beautifully pale mound marked by a red dual-fang tattoo, as if to indicate the proper location for a snack.

"I've waited all my life to meet you, Your Highness," she spoke with a quivering voice. "I'm Léna Szücs. I came tonight with my aunt and uncle. My father is—"

He bore no smile as he cut her off. "Doctor István Szücs."

"He worshipped you in the 'eighties."

"I remember. Sad ending."

"He was loyal to you to the end, Your Majesty. As am I."

"Yes, indeed. To the end. All are loyal at the end."

He stepped deeper into the crowd, the circle of respect moving with him, leaving the woman behind. As she watched, she realized she was now forgotten, and poked her eye to produce tears. When none came, she stabbed harder—until blood shot out instead of tears. She continued to call after him pitifully until some of her acquaintances escorted her away.

"Zoltán Király, Your Majesty," a sharply dressed military officer of general grade, announced, with a curt bow, clicking his boots together. "Thirteenth Brigade commander at the Battle of Chernobyl."

"I remember. The battle was lost, then won—"

"When we charged forward against the Russian eastern flank," he blurted excitedly.

"When the fifth brigade came to your aid at the Dnieper," The Lord corrected, moving on into the crowd.

Király was left with his mouth agape, fearful of immediate cursing.

The Lord paused, threw a hand back at Király. "The end result was satisfactory, however."

"Yes, Your Majesty," said Király, recovering. "A hundred-thousand captured and put to the bleeding farms."

The Lord gave a nod, pursed his lips.

An older woman stood her ground as The Lord pressed ahead.

"Your Holiness, so good to see you on this momentous occasion," she spoke in a sonorous alto. "Surely, you recognize me?"

"Panna Novák," he responded without hesitation, a mere teardrop of grin peeking from the corner of his mouth. He brushed back his long moustache. "The opera diva. I remember. *Hippolit the Butler* by Eismann. Were you in that?"

"Yes, I played Terka, the daughter who fell in love with a man not of her father's choosing."

"A meaty role for you."

"It was a less traditional time," she said with a sheepish bow.

"And those works by Franz Lehar, Emmerich Kalman, and Sigmund Romberg. And who could forget *Székelyfonó* by Kodály?"

Novák's chuckle was like the honking of a car horn. "My Lord, those works were all before my era. Yet I appreciate your love of them. We must preserve our heritage, even the mistakes. My most famous role, you must recall, was Isla, the vampire queen in *Fall of the West* by Julia von Gomperz and András Hamari. We toured all over Europe. That was after the fall of Paris, so it was apropos—"

"I remember," spoke The Lord softly, as though lost in thought.

"As well you should," said Novák with a lingering warm smile and a sideways glance at her neighbors in the crowd, making certain they were attentive. "We dared have a fling in, what was it, 'sixty-eight or thereabouts. Before you became emperor. Before I turned vampiric. We had three children from that affair. A boy and twin girls."

The Lord, surveying the crowd, returned his focus on the woman.

A strange statement piqued his ear. As a vampire, he could never sire children—as everyone knew. So the children this opera diva counted could not have been his.

"And where are they now, these children you claim?"

Her face reddened, full of shock. "Where are they? Why, they are dead, of course. You ordered me to kill them. And eat them."

"And did you?" The Lord inquired flatly.

"It—it was your command. I dare not disobey."

He tipped his chin. "Indeed."

"My Lord—Your Majesty—Your Holiness—"

He continued into the crowd, half-way across the floor of the Great Hall as he left her words behind, surrounded by a cloud of quickening dismay and quizzical chatter. The diva fainted.

"Greetings, Your Highness," crowed smug Mihály Faragó, offering a smart bow. The playboy's *frou-frou* dress and demeanor reminded The Lord of his early days in the capital, rubbing elbows with the elite of society, fashioning himself likewise a playboy without any care. A life which lasted only a few weeks. "A glorious night for the empire!"

"Indeed," echoed The Lord. "The empire."

"There is none greater on this world than ours."

The Lord cocked his head to the left. "The empire exists. It shall exist forevermore," mumbled The Lord, as if reciting a script. Part of a pledge school children were made to sing each evening as their classes began. "As long as the nights are deep and the daylight brief."

"Yes, My Lord." His smile was wide, toothy. "You have managed to vanquish the sun itself! Bravo!" A few around him applauded. "Fifty years of atmospheric engineering! A marvel of modern technology. We commend you!"

The Lord pursed his dry lips. "I employ competent scientists."

"Nevertheless, My Lord. It was all at your direction."

"Now we need not hide when the sunrise comes," interjected the playboy's friend, Imre Balla. He introduced himself.

"Indeed," mugged The Lord. "The sunrise is no more. No more the sunset, either. A mere line of light across a horizon, a moment's pause. Enough for us to count the nights, then go about our business at ease and in comfort."

"Engaging vampirian society as we choose," Balla finished. "The return to our glorious past, the traditions of our classical era, they are to be treasured . . . ."

The Lord stared at Balla a beat longer than decorum allowed, as though sensing something askew. He glared at Faragó, also not fixed in a sound pose. With a slight turn, The Lord bent his arm upward along his side, as if anticipating the need for defense.

"My Lord, will you . . ." Faragó spoke, then fell silent.

A commotion in the crowd, from behind The Lord, all the way from the side of the Great Hall. The audience stirred like a crocodile was slithering through the swampy waters. Ladies were pushed aside, gentlemen bumbled in confusion. The crowd gasped.

A gloved hand went heavily to The Lord's uniformed shoulder, over the armored plates. It was Balla, holding him steady.

Bursting from the wall of guests, a man dressed in serving staff garb held forward a silver knife. Before anyone could act, the blade snapped into The Lord's side, under the lowest rib. It was not the intended target, yet as The Lord twisted away from Balla that was the target that presented.

"*Sic semper tyrannis!*" cried the man.

The Lord shot out the arm he had folded along his chest, grabbed the attacker's arm and whirled him around. The Lord's grasp caused the flesh to crystalize inside the sleeve, the bone to crack, severing the limb. The Lord released him and the severed portion hit the floor and the attacker with it. The man shrieked in pain as the audience gasped.

"My Lord!" cried a woman over the crowd, a red dress pushing into the throng, thrashing her arms to swim toward him.

"Grab him!" several demanded.

The crowd gasped yet did nothing. Someone called for the guards. Others called for someone to do something, though it was not clear whether they meant to defend him or attack Him.

Before The Lord could give any command, a wide blade snapped downward between the attacker rising from the floor and The Lord, holding his wounded rib. The halberd sliced an opening in the attacker from groin to throat. Entrails bowed out, blood ran. The second swing of the blade lopped off the attacker's head, leaving the body to fold into a pile on the marble floor.

A few cheered. Others remained astonished, paralyzed.

The Lord saw the man wielding the halberd. It was his ceremonial bailiff. The age-old custom was to grant an ordinary palace functionary a chance to be involved in a high ceremonial occasion not usually part of his duties. The bailiff dipped his head, acknowledging his act and The Lord's gratitude.

Emergency personnel cut through the crowd. A guard contingent rushed after them, overtook them as the crowd scattered.

"Your Majesty," grunted a man, pushing into the circle. It was Count Vass. The knife in his hand did not hesitate but thrust forward into The Lord's chest. "Here is your dessert, sir! Chew it well—for mine and ours, for those in the empire who died for your grace, who gave their deaths to your life!"

The bailiff, startled, swung the halberd around and separated the Count's head cleanly from his shoulders—as The Lord dropped to His knees, swaying. He grabbed at the Count's knife, pulled it free from His chest, let it drop with a clang on the stone floor. No blood spotted His uniform, the organ dried and withered after so many years.

Immediately, a young man in the crowd scrambled to the floor and took the knife in his hand, jumping up and stabbing the tip inside The Lord's collar.

"For Anna!" the young man cried. "For Míra!"

Three men from the crowd restrained the young man. The knife was wrested from his hand.

"Your Holiness!" cried the captain of the guards, arriving through the crowd. He directed the squad of guards to form a protective circle around The Lord.

"No," groaned The Lord, hand to his chest. "Stand aside."

The Lord, on his knees, focused his dark eyes on the young man who had stabbed him. The men who held him immediately released their grip, leaning away. The young man glanced around, searching for assistance.

With effort, The Lord lifted his arm, palm open, and stretched his hand toward the assassin. An explosion of golden light blinded those standing there. The young man's head and chest likewise exploded into golden shards that rained down like soot. The lower half of the body, unbroken, toppled over, spilling a basin of blood.

"Your Majesty," called the court physician who had arrived.

Medical personnel grabbed at The Lord, tried to pull him onto a carrier but he slapped them away.

He turned on his knees, eyes cursing the crowd as their fear choked in their arid throats. He struggled to stand yet when he did, his mighty arms extended in opposite directions, open palms aiming at the far walls of the Great Hall. A deluge of energy shot out from his hands, burning through the crowd, destroying a dozen people, wounding a dozen more in each direction as the devil's breath quickly crystalized and shattered them.

"Your Holiness," shouted the guard captain, "be calm. We have the situation under control."

The Lord whirled around, his eyes sending the same energy against the captain. He grabbed his face, felt for his eyes, found them melting down his cheeks, and he shrieked.

The lieutenant stepped forward. "Your Holiness, we have secured the hall."

He wavered like a drunkard, a head taller than anyone, and readied himself to strike at further assassins.

"None?" he growled at the audience members around him. "Is there no one else?"

The bailiff circled around his lord and master, halberd at the ready.

"You wait for this occasion? Have you no sense of tradition? The sacred night of our legion?"

The Lord let loose a terrifying howl and the crowd cringed.

"I am the devil's prophet," he roared, plucking out the first knife from his ribs. "Left hand of the Most High. YOU CANNOT KILL ME!"

2

"WILL HE BE REPAIRED?" ASKED THE WOMAN IN THE RED DRESS, trying to push into the room. "I must see him! My Lord, are you well? Are you? Let me in!"

A guard pressed the door shut. "His Holiness must rest."

"You must update me hourly."

The guard nodded, let the door close.

The old physician, thick-set, balding, on one knee beside the chaise longue, applied the ointment using a small wooden applicator. He dipped it into an open jar of gray paste and dabbed it along the fissure like a painter on a canvas. The canvas was The Lord's bare flesh, rough and mealy with age, thrashed a hundred times over the years, flakes of skin laying like feathers across his body, hideous dry patches elsewhere.

"The silver blade did some damage, Your Majesty. Cauterized the open wound. It will leave a mark, for sure, but at least you're alive and well."

"In a manner of speaker," muttered The Lord.

"Likely the tip of the blade pierced your kidney, yet over the years that organ has calcified so no serious harm done. It's a miracle you're still alive—"

"You keep using that word."

The Lord slapped away the physician's thick hand and the wooden applicator fell to the floor, clattering on the stone.

"Speak not to me of living, of being alive, of cheating death . . . for the words hurt me and I will not be hurt. Nevermore!"

He turned to his chamberlain, standing at attention by the door, beside the ceremonial bailiff. Outside the door stood a contingent of palace guards mixed with his own squad of personal guards. They were quite safe now.

"Have you found them yet?" he addressed the chamberlain in a tone half way between anger and amusement.

"No, Your Majesty," he spoke with hesitation, then more quickly: "However, we have top people investigating as we speak. The lead investigator is Rikárdó Kozma, the best in the empire. Fear not, for they will track down the parties involved—"

"I do not fear." The Lord grunted his displeasure. "Kozma is likely the instigator of the plot."

"Your Majesty, had you no warning? No clue among words spoken? Behavior? The throng is ever restless."

"All of that I considered normal." The Lord gave a laugh, raspy and cold. "What is normal for me? Or these days? Or this institution?" The Lord pointed at the ceremonial bailiff. "You!"

The bailiff broke from his position of attention. "Your Holiness?"

"Come over."

The bailiff leaned his halberd into a crook in the wall and stepped carefully toward The Lord, half his torso naked upon the chaise longue. The physician got up and stood aside. The bailiff bowed as he arrived.

"I will thank you for protecting me," spake The Lord, rough breath wavering. "It is a fine fate that brings you to me tonight. You swung the blade well. What is your name?"

"Your Majesty, my name is whatever you wish it to be. My mother called me Joshua, yet you named me Judas when you appointed me to this event. I remain diligent to your wishes, Your Majesty."

The Lord grinned. "Well spoke. Exemplary. Then I shall continue calling you Judas. You bring me luck. Good or not, I have yet to decide. Yet you are skilled and observant, quick with the blade, and markedly accurate. I will appoint you to my personal guard."

"It is an honor, Your Majesty!" The bailiff slapped his arms to his sides, stiffening his back, goateed chin up.

"You remind me of a doctor I once knew," spake The Lord. "He had your dimensions, your voice, yet he betrayed me in the end."

"The end, Your Majesty?" asked the bailiff, wary.

The Lord looked up at him. "The end of my apprenticeship, or so I have dubbed it." A thought flittered across His face. "Oh, he was not in control of himself. You see, in the old days a vampire was usually made through the bite, not as now with mandatory inoculation at age sixteen to twenty-two. Then, it was deemed a curse, akin to catching a sexual disease, and scandal would follow—if anyone followed at all. We were underground, as it were. Now we have risen so obviously. You studied history in school, did you not?"

"Yes, Your Majesty."

"We—myself and our ilk—the last generation bred in the ancient way. For me, once upon a time an innocent worker in a far away land, it was in my family line. I had no choice. Now it is in every family's line. We make certain of the choice: to enter our dark world as soon as is humane or forever serve our kind. And from there our power grows. You see it every day, sup it with every dose of red. Indeed, I see you are one of us, Judas, a bearer of the mark of Saint Dracula. Tell us of your transition, your . . . accursèd transformation, however we may call it."

The bailiff, already stunned by the unexpected favor of his lord and master, grew pale. "Your Majesty . . . ?"

"Tell us of your death. Who is your mother?"

"My mother . . . ?"

"Even the Christ wailed for his mother at the very end. I mean the woman who pulled you from her loins. Your natural mother, not the one who pulled you into nighthood."

The Lord fought against his physician's annoying attempts to continue treating the wounds as the bailiff began his speech:

"Your Majesty, I am but a poor staff member whose only fortune was to be in a lucky place at a lucky time. Your Majesty could just as easily have chosen my friend Kristóf. He would be a better servant, for he has wit and humor."

"I'm not interested in wit or humor. I need a quick blade."

"I understand, Your Majesty. I was ranked second in my class of hussars—"

"Second? Yet you are in my place service."

"Your Majesty, I failed. Once. At one thing, so I was demoted and sent to this position by Colonel Kelemen. I owe him this job. He—"

"You owe *me* this job." The Lord sneered. "It is more than a mere job, it is the life of your lord and master. Yet you did well in your first test. You will guard me always, from this day forward—"

"Your Holiness," a captain cried, rushing in. The man immediately seized up, struck my an invisible hand.

"What belief have you of your right to interrupt?" The Lord blinked and the captain fell dumb to the floor. "You are dismissed. Back to squad corporal for you. Send in your new commander."

The former captain scrambled to his feet, found his soles numb, toes unmovable. He stumbled and recovered, bouncing from the room like a marionette, eventually regaining his legs' control.

Within a minute a lieutenant appeared, stood at attention, waiting his turn to speak. The bailiff stepped dutifully to the side.

"Your report?" spake The Lord.

The lieutenant saluted, fist to throat. "Your Holiness, the guard has captured fifty-two potential conspirators from the centennial audience in the Great Hall. It is possible others escaped yet we have personnel tracking them as we speak."

"And the chattel?"

"Your Majesty . . . ?"

"Collateral damage, I believe it was once called."

"Those deceased in the Great Hall are thirty-four. Those wounded yet still animated tally but sixteen. The tally does not include those attackers upon Your Majesty's person, the palace staff member, Count Vass, or the youth."

"What of the staff member?"

"We have determined he was not an actual member of the staff. He stole the uniform and used it to gain entry. His name is Viktor Rácz. He was a student at the university. His professors have been detained for questioning."

"The name seems familiar. Rácz?"

"We are checking references. His mother was collected in the last purge, Your Holiness."

"Which last purge?"

"In preparation for this centennial celebration, Your Holiness."

"Indeed." The Lord scratched under his thick beard. "One hundred eighty-six rabble-rousers, mostly from Óbuda. If I remember correctly. There were plans for such an episode as what occurred tonight." He chuckled like a child enjoying a new toy. "Instead of the mother and her ilk, we get the prodigal son, the wayward youth, bearing the great silver wand of salvation. How fitting!"

"It is appropriate, Your Holiness."

"What is appropriate?" snarled The Lord. "To strike down the only figure keeping you alive?"

"I humbly beg your pardon, Your Holiness," said the lieutenant, bowing deeply.

"Rise, new captain of the guards." The Lord watched the lieutenant stand tall once more. "You will please me from this day forward. When you displease me will be your final day."

The new captain bowed again.

"Count Vass!" The Lord spit upon the floor, a bloody sputum. A dwarf servant rushed to wipe it up. "We should have had him arrested long ago, yet he was useful to us, an aid to the empire. Yet even an empire can do without one such as him. How has this figure been prepared?"

"Exposure to the Black Storm is standard," the new captain began, then halted. "As Your Holiness wishes, certainly."

The Lord stared at the far wall of the room, a painting there of a woman with dark hair and almond eyes, locked in a half-smile putting to shame the *La Gioconda* portrait hanging beside it. There had not been much worth removing from the sack of Paris, but The Lord had always liked this work of art, so he took it.

"The body, yes. Exposed to the acid rain. The head, hmm . . . . Let us have an appropriate craftsman fashion it for hanging upon a wall." He turned on the chaise longue, disrupting the physician still tending to his wounds, and pointed. "To be hung there. That I might toss darts at it whenever I wish to feel amused."

The physician bent low with needle and thread.

"Must you keep annoying me?" spake The Lord.

"Your Majesty, the wound needs to be stitched to heal."

"To heal? What care I of healing? Let it rot. Let it become a plague. I care not for your medicine. Be gone!"

The old physician tottered, bowed awkwardly, and departed with his bag of tricks.

"Painful old windbag," grumbled The Lord with a shake of his head. He regarded the new captain. "And the youth?"

"Your Holiness, the youth who took up the knife of Count Vass was none other than Márton Bognár, son of—"

"Yes, yes, I know. The Bognár family has been a vile pestilence for decades. Reason enough to curb their activities by holding hostage the daughters. If only Anna had acted quicker! She could have ended this ruse and saved us all from . . . ."

The room fell silent.

"Your Holiness?" queried the new captain after a moment.

"I said if her blade had been quicker, she could have saved us." A bold guffaw erupted. "I would be forever ended and the empire saved. Whatever 'saved' should mean these days. It is all in the interpretation, certainly. Some say my very existence is the foundation of our empire. Others decry my existence as a weight upon expansion of the empire. Yet it is not for me to say, for I am hardly a trained linguist."

The new captain nodded in acknowledgement, showing he was listening.

"You think it strange I should call for my own stoppage?"

"I do not, Your Holiness."

"There are many who wish it. I wish it—more often than I care to confess. For I am weary of this evil. Always the evil. The requirement of my own Holiness—He, the Most High—who beseeches me to act on His behalf, to affect the darkness of the world, to ever-expand our influence over all that the Most High surveys."

The Lord chuckled, a cold, hollow drumming.

"Indeed, it is a wonder we have not yet conquered other worlds. The Anglos tried it, put a damned contingent upon Martian rock, left them to die when supply rockets went bad. We should have sent our own member to vampirize them. And the Russian agency! How they bungled their attempts, as well! Why colonize barren worlds when we can create a barren world of our own right here? Then the Black Wave was born! Covering the earth and bringing the empire we have today. Is it not glorious? Perpetual night! Or nearly so. And a fabulous return to the traditions of our heritage! Castles and serfs! No more electric wires of servitude! No more carbonic expulsion of mobile machines! You see what we have wrought, new captain of my palace guard? We have remade the world in our image, in our own thought and deed, and in doing so have brought our world to the brink of community in holy flesh and blood! It is glorious! It is! For here, in this the fifty-fourth Year of Our Dark Lord, the Most High—or, if you prefer, two-thousand-ninety-nine. That's for the simpletons. Yes, now twenty-one-hundred in the old calendar—and the troubadours sing well of it!"

CR

The Lord, having no need of true sleep, rested in a gold-embossed case of mahogany and ebony, fashioned by craftsmen from Milan. Inside, the box was filled with fresh black soil from a Louisiana bayou which He swore restored his flaking, boil-prone skin to youthful elasticity and official pallor. Stretched out naked within the casket, The Lord could afford some semblance of normalcy for a few hours. On rare occasion the hibernation might last days. Then He would arise to do the work of the Most High.

"As for Míra Bognár," spake The Lord upon rising on the third eve, "she had such a delightful rosé to her blood. I could sup on her essence for nights. Alas, she eventually faltered, could produce no more, and withered in my arms. It was enough that I was properly refreshed. She was honored for her duty to the empire and raised up to the rafters of Saint Istvan Basilica, adored by one and all, her bite marks exposed for all to see, throat to calves. Truly a work of art, everyone has said, and praised Petra Soós for her craftsmanship. It was only when some rats got to the suspended figure that she was lowered and placed in a glass case for countless school children to admire on educational forays into modern Europa history. Many drew their own renditions of Míra's bent body and sagging face. Contests were held. Graduates emblazoned effigies of her upon their ceremonial gowns. Indeed, she was widely remembered and praised for her noble example. So why should that youth, Márton, think to be vengeful? She received the highest honor."

As always, The Lord's ceremonial bailiff, deemed Judas, replacing his bailiff uniform for one of the personal staff, stood close at hand for bodily protection.

"Judas!" called The Lord, sitting naked on the edge of the casket, rubbing his arms and legs, flicking off granules of dirt. "What think you of this Míra fiasco?"

No matter how he tried, Judas could not keep from gazing upon the naked form of his lord. The skin did look strangely refreshed yet scars remained, etched in the flesh. Raised welts, lines of old stitching, a wart or a patch of dry skin here and there, the cool paleness of the flesh covered by the coarse black hair, thick on his chest tapering to his belly then widening once more to a thick forest there between his mighty thighs. And his member! Thick and of a length unseen on most humans. It must be true, then, how He grew in odd ways with each life taken.

"Your Holiness," Judas stammered, "it is not for such as I to offer an opinion. My thoughts count for nothing."

"I ask for your thoughts," spake The Lord. He flicked the air with his gnarled hand, stretching his fingers, yellowed talons glistening in the lamplight. "Fear not, for I give you leave to speak anything without punishment or penalty." He turned to his chamberlain. "Mark it in the register. This ceremonial bailiff, now on my personal staff, by the name of Judas, or—what was it in your former life? Joshua?"

"Yes, Your Holiness." The bailiff swallowed hard.

The Lord laughed. "We are all the same in our vampirian society, as one clan in our transformation. For in the end blood is blood, nothing more than corpuscles, red and white cells, plasma, various hormones and proteins and enzymes, too complex for anyone to manufacture from scratch. This is how God maintains the patent." Another laugh.

When The Lord noticed that no one else in the room shared his amusement, He ceased and stared once more at the portrait on the opposite wall.

"Míra . . . ," sighed The Lord, pondering for a moment. He caught himself. "No, that is not her up there on the wall. Not Míra." He jutted his chin at the painting. "That is my first love. Long ago, obviously. In my much former life. Indeed, even I have a former life—that is, a life before the transformation." He coughed, spit on the floor. A page boy rushed to wipe it up as a quartet of servants entered bearing the night's garments. The Lord again addressed Judas: "What is your opinion of Míra Bognár's fate?"

"Your Holiness, she . . . she . . ."

"Speak freely."

"She must have felt honored by the attention of Your Holiness."

"Nothing more?" asked The Lord, standing and stretching out His arms for the dressing servants to garb Him.

"Your Holiness, I do not know the story. I think she would have been happy to serve you, and gone graciously to her role in the court. Beyond that, I cannot say. I am not entitled to an opinion."

"Well spoke. And true—true enough." He continued to stare at the portrait on the wall of the other woman. "When your lord calls you, it would be an error to dismiss him or hesitate in answering the call. Perhaps she joined me out of fear. I wish it were not true. Who can say? A fine actress, let us imagine."

"Everyone seems to play a role these days," the bailiff muttered, only then noting the utterance. He gasped, afraid. "Your Holiness, I mean that society has become so well-defined that each of us has a clear role to play in it. We have no need of variance. I think I heard it called 'communization' in school. An old style of governing."

"A new society, especially one given our unique constitution, must operate smoothly," spake The Lord. "Each person, whether vampire or not, must fit in or be cut off. It is the way of the world. It is the way of the Most High." The Lord at that moment seemed to be struck dumb, perhaps swept into a silent conversation with a spirit unseen by others in the room. "It is not now as it was in the days of my youth."

Judas bowed his head, smiling. "It must have been a glorious time."

"What? Not now?" The Lord slapped the seat cushion. "Is now not a superior time?"

"Yes, Your Holiness! I thought only that . . . that the nights of one's youth are usually remembered as being glorious."

The Lord grinned. "You are a fine actor, too, Judas."

"I speak truthfully, Your Holiness."

"There is much that fails when speaking the truth."

The Lord gazed toward a small window high on the stone wall. Outside the black wave blotted out all hope.

"The nights we enjoy now, this is the way everything should be. We have suffered greatly during the past thousand years—indeed, longer. Now we have this freedom—bearing each to his role."

He scratched his black moustache, hiding a smirk.

"Perhaps you are too young to recall when citizens were monitored at all times, forced to sign their names hourly, compelled to indicate their approval or disapproval on trivial matters by pressing a finger to a painted icon on their monitors. That was not freedom. Fail to sign in and police would hunt them down, examine them for cross-thought or bio malfunction. If found disabled, they would have their amusements suspended. Likewise, if the amusements consumed too much of their nightly tasks, the amusements would be suspended. Yet we learned it was these amusements which compelled many to rise at all upon the dusk. How great the inventions of the past! How the imagination of the Most High corrals us, mends us, makes us into obedient servants despite our best efforts to rebel. How we must free ourselves from the tyranny of technologics! The answer, as we now know, is only in a determined return to the past, to our traditions, to our heritage, to a new society based on the best of the old."

"Citizens welcome the change, Your Holiness!" Judas puffed out his chest. "Many of us knew not the struggles of the old nights."

"The old nights were full of terror. So many of our school books had to be rewritten to bring the truth to the present generation. We could no longer endure the waves, perpetually injuring our citizens. The towers of power and their fingers of death! Brain damage. Cancers. So many children were suffering. Worse than the transformation itself! Even as they sought to control the populace. And the infiltration of the water with passivist chemicals—as though no one knew about or could detect the devastating effects. We removed that, though no vampirian requires bodily water. Industry needs water."

A spot of silence.

"And then the plague came . . . ."

The bailiff, lost in his thoughts, had mumbled a bit too loudly.

"I am not a monster," spake The Lord with a huff. "What I did was necessary to save us—to save all, vampirian or not—from the scourge of the yellow banner and their technologics."

"Your Majesty!" cried the new guard captain as he burst into the room. "Beg pardons, Your Majesty, but you should know the protests continue out-of-doors! It grows frightful. They do not—"

"They will always protest what they do not understand," spake The Lord with a fang-bearing yawn.

"The protests increase! Stones launched at the palace walls, broken windows, shouting through the daylight. We fear for your safety, Your Majesty."

The Lord gave a nod, his moustache hiding a grin noticed only by Judas standing to the side, seeing the bend of cheek muscles.

"I believe I am safe within these walls. I need not address them, for they are small folk who possess small minds and smaller hearts, blood thin as rainwater, no souls left to corrupt. Pity them not!"

"But, Your Majesty, we have never seen them acting so rash. Shall we discipline them? Or leave them be till they tire of the sport?"

The Lord, fully vested for the night's tasks, stood boldly, adjusting his thick belt, sweeping back his flowing black mane with one hand, combing his moustache with fingers of the other hand. "If it be three nights then discipline you must. Let them know how we disapprove of protests, for this is the best existence they could ever imagine." He glanced at the chamberlain.

"Your Majesty has been casketed three nights thus," responded the chamberlain.

"Then be about it. Separate them. The maidens to the right, the old folks to the left. Others save to the middle and discipline fully. Report at the conclusion."

"Your Majesty," the captain sought to continue, raising his gloved hand, "how shall we dispense with those of the centennial audience? Three have expired falling short of blood ration. Five have attained dire consequences. Most cry out for freedom."

"Interrogate them?"

"Yes, Your Majesty. None remaining have sworn knowledge of the conspiracy."

"Falsehoods come easy to those fearing death." He laughed. "Yet we are already dead." He shook his head slowly. "Let them go, all save the relations of the conspirators. I will ask them myself the questions they would rather not answer. I will have them choose their punishment."

"As Your Majesty commands!"

The captain snapped to attention, turned to exit.

⚮

From a high palace tower, The Lord gazed down upon the rabble in the forecourt, lit by torches and oil lamps, surveying the throng of heads bobbing outside the walls. The populace held great banners bearing declarations of hate. They raised their farm implements and factory tools, shook them vigorously. Beneath the dark overcast, only enough sunlight radiating in from the far horizon to illuminate the grounds, they shouted vehemently their anger without stoppage.

It was true what the captain had reported: the largest gathering at the palace in years. Word must have spread quickly what happened at the centennial celebration, though none should have escaped to tell of it. Perhaps a few staff members had slipped out and begun the vicious rumors. Three nights later and it seemed as though half the capital stood ranting at the palace gates.

The Lord stood in awe, counting the rabble below, measuring the troops needed to quell such a riot.

"Summon the palace brigade," spake The Lord to a lieutenant, who dashed away with the command.

"Your Holiness," Judas dared utter, "will that be the best response? Perhaps Your Majesty should—"

"I welcomed you to my staff because you bring me fare fortune. Do not ruin that opportunity with idle chatter."

"Yes, Your Holiness." He bowed from the waist, keeping his gloved hands tight around the shaft of the halberd, ready to protect.

The Lord chuckled deep within his throat yet it shook the stone walls of the battlement.

There had been attempts on him prior to that night. And there had been protests of one trivial thing or another previously. Yet these two

38

had combined into the maelstrom The Lord surveyed below. The sight agitated Him to His limits. He was about to blithely dismiss them all and return to His chambers for a quiet rest when an arrow whistled skyward and arched down to strike the battlement beside The Lord's great hand. The iron arrowhead stuck in the mortar between the stones, while the wood shaft broke, the feathered end tumbling below. He lifted his hand, saw there was no wound.

"There he is!" some of the rabble cried out below.

"Free the centennials!"

"Compensation for the dead!"

"No more a tyrant!"

He whirled around, his dark eyes scanning the crowd below, those in the forecourt packed shoulder to shoulder, seeking the archer.

There! A sniveling everyman in threadbare jerkin and torn trousers, smiling like he had gotten the better of God.

"You!" shouted The Lord, marking the man.

It was some distance, yet with a tight focus of his energy, The Lord could latch onto the figure below and raise him out of the crowd—lift him into the air, as though running a bale of hay up a taut transfer line from a wagon to a tower's open window. Half-way, suspended between the ground and the tower, The Lord waxed amusedly how the Most High granted him such powers over quantum mechanics while the fearful archer squirmed frantically, arms and legs thrashing about as the crowd below beseeched His Holiness for mercy.

Yet their words were not so soft, not so submissive—

"You strike at me? I strike at you!" shouted The Lord.

Suddenly, with a flick of His fingers, the man suspended in the air exploded into a ball of flame. Pieces of his clothing flittered away with the breeze, burnt flesh slewed off and dropped among the crowd. Bone crumbs and sinew threads fell. Then nothing remained in the air.

The crowd did not quiet, did not turn solemn; rather became more ferocious, crying out their demands and threatening His Holiness with violence.

"You dare threaten me? Who launched an arrow? Not I," spake The Lord. "I give you so much. A land of our own. An empire of riches, of blood! Blood for all! Yet you protest! That cannot continue!"

He ripped off his greatcoat and, with a sleeve torn, swept his hand across the forecourt, lighting flame wherever it might catch hold on the garments of the crowd. The people scrambled to avoid the flames but, packed in, could not wheel away. They slapped each other to quell the flames, poured water from bottle and bag over themselves despite the sting of it. They stood as one in the forecourt and undulated as a mighty ocean beyond the walls.

The chamberlain gasped at the action.

The Lord turned at the gasp. "You think me cruel? How else to deal with an unruly populace? I gave fair warning. Did they heed? No. They must learn the limits of my patience."

"Your Majesty, perhaps there is a better way. You could trick them. Pretend to hear their demands and offer them a small compromise. They will be forever grateful and obedient. Your Majesty still has need of a productive populace, legions of workers."

"The head is good, the heart weak," mugged The Lord. He returned his attention to the frantic crowd, waving his arms abruptly. The fires ceased. "There! No more the flames! Be at peace! Mend your wounds! Bother me no more!"

The crowd remained angry, shouting curses up at The Lord.

"What more can these snails and worms want?" He turned to the chamberlain again, shrugging his broad shoulders. "They pester me to no end. I want them gone."

"Your Majesty," spoke the chamberlain, alarmed, "we should be calm, perhaps, and let the pests go freely. You need not—"

"You? *Yoooou?*" raged The Lord. His hand went up, reaching out, and the chamberlain dropped to his knees, face reddening like all the blood within in him had surged into his cheeks.

"For-give me, Your Maj-est-y," the chamberlain sputtered. "I only ask—on their behalf—for you—to show—mer-cy—"

"You shall not speak of mercy, not when I am assassinated!" The Lord closed His outstretched hand, made it a fist, and as He did so, the chamberlain's eyes popped out of his skull, dangling on his cheeks, as his face swelled like a balloon to impossible dimensions and burst into a pink cloud of blood and pus. The splattering gore stained The Lord's gloved hand, some on His boots, some on the floor. The chamberlain's body collapsed with a sloppy thud. "This is mercy! A quick end!"

The Lord saw Judas take a step back.

"And you? Do you wish to speak? Offer me advice? Speak truth to power? Do you? Can you?"

Judas shook his head, face carefully frozen without expression.

"Ah, but you must," laughed The Lord. "I've lost my chamberlain, foul thing. You can learn the protocols well enough, Judas, in time. A promotion is in order for you. Now speak your mind. What say you to this outrage?"

Judas, the new chamberlain, bowed deeply. "Your Holiness, allow those whom you have selected as your governing operatives to handle this unfortunate situation. Your Holiness need not bother with these unpleasantries. It is unworthy of you. Retire to your private quarters and take your ease. Think no more of this situation. It will be taken care of by your staff. Your Holiness may rest."

"An excellent decision," spake The Lord, giving a sideways glance at the dwarves cleaning the grisly mess off The Lord's boots and the stone floor. "Only this fellow may speak in such a manner. So I command."

Judas gave a quick head bow. "I shall speak, Your Holiness, as you command, if that is what you wish."

"I wish it. Doubt me?"

"For a moment, Your Holiness."

"There is speaking truth, eh?"

"If it please Your Holiness—"

The Lord suddenly threw up his hands. "My council! Where is my council?" He sauntered away from the window in the tower. "They sit on their hands all night. Useless. Have they come to any conclusion about how to handle this centennial uprising? Let them assemble and report. It is not for me alone to govern this empire—as my new chamberlain reminds. Further foolishness will upset the Most High, and no one wishes that."

The Lord gave a quick, disapproving look at Judas.

"And get my new chamberlain a better uniform."

The Lord stalked away down the dark corridor, followed closely by His chamberlain, Judas, and a pair of dwarfs in clown costumes, sent to humor His Holiness and dissuade Him from rash action.

STEPHEN SWARTZ

CR

"I do not want your peevish recommendations!" raged His Holiness. "I do not need your whimsical suggestions! If you will not acknowledge our achievements, I must dismiss this council!"

The council of governors had been assembled, given time to debate among themselves and reach a consensus. His Holiness was escorted to the council hall. Beside him, as always, stood his chamberlain to act as attorney, and this time a lucky bailiff named Judas.

The Lord swept into the chamber bearing a costume of furs and armor, red and black, as formal a uniform as ever He had worn to address the twenty-two governing representatives of the provinces of the empire. Though limited to the capital, each governor had several surrogates who reported by courier so control was maintained both locally and dispatched from the capital—the way successful empires had been ruled for centuries, His Holiness was quick to note whenever a governor dared challenge.

"So?" bellowed His Holiness from His cushy seat at the head of the long table, one leg hanging over the armrest, one hand brushing back His black mane, like a god looking down over His angels. "Report!"

Count Sipos, topped with badly-combed thinning red hair and an equally red, well-trimmed beard, pushed his great girth up from half-way down the long table. His formal attire reflected the serious nature of the meeting. Clearing his voice, he straightened his black bow tie, flicked to life the red lapel rose.

"Your Holiness," Sipos spoke through a frown, "on this occasion we have assembled to report on the condition of the empire in this new year of ancient date twenty-one-hundred, vampire year fifty-five, and to confront the impossible acts of a restless populace."

"What do you intend to do about it?" grumbled The Lord.

"In good time, Your Holiness, we shall present our answer."

The Lord tugged at his moustache. "You can say nothing?"

"Your Holiness, if I may speak frankly . . . speaking for the entire governing body . . . we believe, we all believe . . . the consensus is . . . it seems that no matter what we do to quell anger across the empire, the

42

next act by Your Holiness always causes them to revert to rage. There are persistent calls for your removal—yes, we understand you cannot be removed from your position as emperor, granted, Your Holiness. Nor do any of us wish it. I merely report what the populace says— demands, rather. Now I must beg of you, please do not harm this poor messenger . . . Your Holiness."

His Holiness scoffed. "The messenger is excused."

Count Sipos bowed. "Thank you, Your Holiness."

With the invitation of His Holiness, each of the governors spoke in turn about the province for which they had responsibility while He languished in his throne, grimacing at will, waving his hand at random during the staid liturgy. First spoke Milan, then Paris, then Barcelona, Berlin, and Prague—the major provinces of vampirian activity. With a pause, refreshment was provided. Then representatives from Athens, Odessa, and Copenhagen spoke—at the fringes of the empire and yet well-integrated. The representative from Kiev, deemed too rude in his report, citing the famine caused by the battle lines constantly shifting, was shouted down by the other governors. Reports of insurrection in each province were uniform: in each locale the populace clamored for personal freedom at the expense of community safety.

Count Sipos rose again to condense the conclusion to one fact: the empire needed to initiate a program of suppression, to enforce the laws against sedition.

"As we fight to expand our borders in both east and west, the lower end of society incites mayhem," Sipos declared. "We will need to return troops from the Dnieper front to handle the discipline. Perhaps troops from Frisia, as well. Already the invasion of Cornwall is delayed. What harm to us if we cancel the operation, let the Anglo-American Union keep its fallow isle?"

The Lord nodded at Sipos, thick eyebrows lowered as if to hide his gaze as he contemplated the reports.

"I have fought, yes, *fought*, to make this empire in the image of the Most High." The Lord pushed his chair back, stood and placed his fists on the table. "Fifty-four years ago I made the ultimate sacrifice—and I bear it to this day. None of you have done the same. It is not enough to give up an arm or a leg, a son or a daughter—no!"

He glanced around the table and none could meet His eyes.

"You wanted freedom," spake The Lord, "freedom to be yourselves, to act without persecution. So be it. Done. Laws for equality. Then you protested a lack of tolerance. The law gave you rights yet the public did not honor the law, so I bade the law be enforced. Done. The warmlings complained of my favoritism toward vampirekind, so I bade them take their natural role as sublings to vampirian society. More laws, more enforcement. Prisons became overwhelmed. Is that what you wanted?"

The Lord raised his hand, a gloved fist, and half the representatives around the table cringed.

"As we grew, you demanded sustenance," He continued, "so our prisons were transformed into blood farms. Still you demanded more!"

With great fury His mighty fist slammed down and the table shook, the wood splintering beneath his punch. A ripple ran half-way down the table, cracking apart.

"Your Holiness," came a weak tenor from down the table. Count Péter had raised his hand. "The stability of the blood farms became unsustainable. There was a serious spike in diabetes cases among the bloodling population. That does not bode well for our sustenance."

The emperor's eyes narrowed, darkened to a frightful crimson, and all those around the great table tensed at what might be coming forth from his power. He raised a hand, finger pointing.

"Because I like sweet blood," spake The Lord.

The entire room released a sigh simultaneously.

His scowl returned. "So I moved the sun and stars for you. We developed the Black Storm to blot out the sunshine. And we saw how the remainder of the world reacted. Wars and rumors of them. Negotiations with weaklings, pretending to be fair with our sublings, little brothers and little sisters. Even now we continue fighting for our right to be who we are! Is that not the fair thing to do? And we allow our sublings to live among us. We have equality yet never can we have equal success, for the sublings are not us, can never be us save for the dark rite—and we welcome them into our society."

Count Péter, Director of Bloodling Research, again raised his hand, but, meeting the emperor's glare, he thought better and lay his hand on the table.

"Until then, we ask only for tribute. We wrote it into law, for the sublings worship laws like a good bowl of soup. Once a week—that is all we ask—a draught of red is required in offering to our reservoir. A simple and not very inconvenient task to perform at the end of the working week. And children are exempt until age thirteen, as are those who reach sixty-six. Is that not a measure of fairness? Or compassion? Am I not kind to these sublings? These inferior warmlings? And have you no level of compassion for those who sustain us? For we do not corral them in blood farms any longer but allow them independent existence—so long as they pay their weekly tribute. And still you demand more! Is our own empire not yet enough?

"Every day our factories are pumping out millions of cubic meters of dark matter to feed the Black Storm. We have managed to blot out the sunshine an average of three-hundred-seventeen days each year, days with seventy-five percent more darkness. And the wind pattern continually blows it eastward. Thus we must continually replenish it. The Russians complain instead of welcoming our efforts to contain the sunshine. Look at what we have wrought on our own soil. The empire is now sixty-two percent fallow, a great improvement over the past decade. Some of the bloodlings complain. They beg for plants, for their crops, for *pretty* flowers to *beautify* the yards. Yet fruit and vegetables do not satisfy the vampirian palate. You cannot get blood from a turnip."

"But it's true, Your Majesty—"

"I understand the scheme: the plants feed the cattle, the cattle feed the bloodlings, and the bloodlings feed us, our vampirian society. That may not seem equitable to some of you. Let me make a proposition. I propose that cattle is cattle. True? Cattle is not people, especially not vampires. Also true. Thus, we make cattle feed from the corpses of the cattle. They know not the difference—nor care about it. So let the chain continue. Yes, bloodlings complain about taste, nutrition, other mettlesome things that have no bearing on the quality of their blood donations.

"Blood is blood, many of us believe, yet like any biological product there are degrees of richness. For example, consider the waves of the invaders from Africa and the Arab lands ninety, a hundred years ago. A poorly considered policy, we have recognized for decades now, yet the result was far too many migrants and refugees for the jobs available or the funds to sustain them, and the native-born suffered increased crime and disease. This has been well-documented, and the source of much anguish and pain. In time came the plague, following the same paths of destruction from centuries before. This was both a blessing and a curse. Some of us can recall the 'thirties, years of such horror, yet by the 'forties we could declare full recovery of our lands, the creation of our empire, though it was not an empire at that time. Indeed, the old Hungarian Federation had survived. No, not until the glorious year of 'fifty-four—Year One of the Vampire Age!—could we declare us officially an empire."

"Hear! Hear!" cheered the representatives.

"And yet," spake The Lord, "as we cleared away the invaders from our land, our empire—and the other ill-mannered and unfit from the streets—we improved the portion of vampires. The data proves the blood of non-indigenous was insufficient to sustain vampirian society. We did not like the taste. We did not find it restorative. Something about the ancestral line not favoring us. Indeed, that also may have been because of the poor quality of the source, the lack of nutrients in sources of poor means. Or it was simply a different blood type which our bodies, being indigenous to Europa, could not process."

"There is scientific evidence, Your Majesty," called Doctor Pál, the Minister of Medicine, "that the blood of—"

"Many question it," Sipos responded, glancing at The Lord.

"There is no question for science. It is proven," The Lord retorted. "For the influencers of our society, however, the noble instigation of injustice requires them to foment discord among the masses."

"They accuse us of bigotry, Your Majesty," Ákos Illés cried out, to which The Lord raised his hand to silence the representative from the former state of Austria, now District 8.

"Bigotry is a confusing word. It registers only for members of one group against members of another. So it is purely subjective. If I don't like you, what you do or what you say, I claim bigotry. The truth of the situation to any objective observer may be nothing at all. We do not discriminate for any reason except biologics. Besides this explanation, bigotry is not against any law, even the laws of equality which we have introduced within the empire. No one is ever required to like anyone else. No one is required to associate with anyone else. We have never forced people of differing ethnicity to marry each other against their wishes, as was done before the birth of our empire—at the same time as the old Hungarian Federation first embarked on a blockade of the invaders from Africa and the Arab lands. Now, in hiring workers, let us say, the best person for the job will be chosen, not one of this and one of that and one of another category. We are now of only two categories: the sublings and vampirian society."

"Yet Your Majesty persists in calling them 'sublings'," retorted Illés.

"No, this way is not to be considered a form of bigotry, for we have good, biological reasons for our choices. We mean to survive—indeed, we must thrive! Vampirian society has certain needs and a very narrow range of options available to fulfill those needs. Our survival is not a cause for other people's claims of injustice. Go live in your own lands, we say! Go make your own empire. Return to your homelands! Rebuild what you do not like there, there in your native homeland. Build your own—do not steal, do not beg from others who have built their own. Consider: with plenty of funds appropriated from their welfare gifts in Europa before the empire, they have the means to make their own lands prosperous. Yet do they? Can they? Will they?"

Illés raised his hand. "There are questions, Your Majesty—"

"I said as much at the final General Assembly of the old United Nations, as well as the first assembly of the new Council of Nations in twenty-thirty-seven and at three assemblies since. Needing translation, they listened politely. The harangues were many, once they got the final words. Then the assembly disinvited me, even though I speak on behalf of the Most High. But then again, I understand they have their Christian ideology, though it has faded into a self-confident atheism. Or the Islamic ideology. And the Jewish one. The up-start Clintonians, too, and the Hindalli. And others. Ah, John Williamson and his Perth group! Complete silliness. All oppose the Most High and His prophet. I understand this arrangement, these religious groups, their propensity to oppose anything which does not follow their own singular path to, hmm, what? Let's call it 'joy'. Hedonism. That is their burden. We are all authoritarian in our own ways lest we vanish from history. Recall the names of weak kingdoms. Can you? No? Indeed, I have no choice but to press on with what must be done to assure our continued success in the world. This is our world, our only world, many have pointed out to great irony. We have our laws, our goals and they have theirs. It is inevitable that we will clash. That is the reason for wars."

Count Sipos cleared his throat, his red beard waving. "Yet wars, in general, are not the best way t—"

The Lord stared at the Count and the room suddenly grew cold. The Count seemed unaware of his existence for a moment, locked in some trance. Coming back, he sputtered, then regained his voice.

"What is that?" he begged.

"That is your heart, Count, beating once more," spake The Lord. "You had forgotten how it feels. Since you continue to interrupt me, I wish for you to take note of it." Then He raised His hand and snapped His fingers. "And how it feels when it stops."

The Count seized up, grabbing his chest, a grimace on his flushed face. When he slumped over the table, the others looked away.

Countess Natália Gál, brushing aside her jet hair and affecting an expression of boredom, after a moment dared to speak: "Should we call a physician?" A dainty laugh. "Or may we continue?"

3

"THE REASON FOR OUR WARS IS SIMPLE. Our opponents will not yield. If they would yield, surely we would cease warfare. It is a simple enough equation that our enemies should be able to solve it. On the Russian front, we have control of all lands west of the Dnieper, and fighting continues to secure that border. There is no Maxim the Cruel to lead them now. His head remains in a glass case in the Museum of Political History. On the western front we have yet to secure the Frisian coast— for some esoteric reason, I'm sure. I am not a military-minded person yet I have suggested that all we need do to conquer Holland is destroy a few dikes and let the polders flood. Yet our vampirian forces are so afraid of water and the Hollanders have so much of it. Yet they provide nothing of value to vampirian society. But for their red, of course.

"As it stands, we have pushed those pathetic forces of the Anglo-American Union to the beaches. At the same time, we are prepared to invade Cornwall to put more pressure on the Isle to sue for peace. We have no interest in actually claiming the Isle. Far too much trouble to hold it. We will then consider our treatment of Brittany and Portugal, which remain outside the empire. I have heard a plan for Ireland.

"In the southeast we continue to harass the Turks—and you know I give no quarter to Turks, who murdered my elderly parents long ago. We have done much to conquer that peninsula and raze it according to historic mores. Thus we are assured they will nevermore rise against us—or anyone. And if they should attempt to re-assert their primacy in Anatolia, we will crush them and leave them in ruins for spite, and the

Most High will be pleased!"

A few representatives clapped their hands but stopped at the glares of the others around the table.

The Lord inhaled deeply, held it longer than most would believe possible, and slowly exhaled the bitter wind down the long table.

"So we labor onward to achieve our noble goals—and our goals are always those of the Most High: to transform the world into vampirian society, under vampirian rule, following vampirian manner."

The brief pause was broken by the governor of Barcelona, Hunor Hegedűs, who produced a cough and a timidly raised hand.

"Your Majesty, there are some of us who . . . ." Hegedűs paused to look around the table but some representatives glanced down. "A few of us believe that, in order to advance our objectives and secure a grand expanse as our greater empire, the means of communication must be vastly improved. It is difficult to get messages back and forth now. We suffer for that time lag. Especially on the battlefronts."

"You wish a better means of communication?" The Lord lifted one eyebrow. "Do you mean the electro technologics?"

"There is no reason for eliminating them," said Hegedűs.

"There is reason. You are young and do not recall the troubles of the electric age. We saw how the machine overtakes a person, controls a person, makes a person act in strange ways, often foolishly. We cannot have that in our society. We have eliminated a source of confusion and pain. Nothing wrong with handwritten messages of ink on paper."

"The time it takes to deliver them is—"

The Lord laughed and the representatives were startled.

"Indeed, I recall the electric days of my youth—when everyone was monitored and conditioned and manipulated into all sorts of behavior not ordered by their own minds. The mindless youth, we called them, assembling in hordes to rain destruction upon whatever target their electric masters deemed worth destroying. A violent age. All of their petty demonstrations arranged locally by electric messaging! Yet we have extinguished the grid and freed the masses. Is that not a worthy goal? Cameras everywhere. Spying on us all. Drones flying the skies, often so thick we could not know exactly which of us they surveilled.

People deigned to stay indoors to avoid official cameras—and privately commanded drones, too, snooping into windows, reading over your shoulder from kilometers away!

"Yet even there, in our own homes, we were constantly watched, our choices on the electric venues noted, our searches for information captured and used against us in the political correction courts and re-education camps. They did not know what they had created, nor did they surmise how their lives had become not their own but merely tools in a government toolbox, each of them put to use as needed, when needed, and put aside when no longer needed—given over to pointless games, animations of birds and puppets and pieces of candy, not to mention the shooting galleries and bat games, all to satisfy an abhorrent need for constant stimulation. While I endured thirteen years with only some books.

"That was not living—meaning in the old sense of existing inside a prefabricated society that considered us as bits and bytes in a program designed by 'artificial intelligence'. Oxymoronic drivel! It was called 'A.I.' in those days. Do you understand what I say? The electric boxes we now outlaw were common fodder in those days. Ubiquitous. We used to communicate through those machines. Without a machine we could not communicate. And without a code number, we could not use those machines. Predictably, all our communications were checked and double-checked for correctness and compliance with standard norms, and when out of parameters a friendly drone would knock on your door, zap you to unconsciousness when you opened the door, and off to re-education camp you went.

"No, I mean the term 'artificial intelligence'—a machine acting like a human brain acts, the machines and the instructions to operate them independent of human thought, in essence a self-operating machine, much like the vehicles designed to carry us about our nightly tasks.

"Yet such automated machinery can also bring about our demise. Hence we outlawed them. All the A.I. machinery. You may not recall that incident—it was famous, notorious as an example—where the Anglo's prime minister sent the image of his sexual organs to the queen through this electric system—quite by accident, he insisted. It was the work of this artificial intelligence, certainly, yet the queen was not amused. That prime minister had to lose his personal parts to make amends. Pity. Yet we see what can be accomplished without our knowledge or our will. Embarrassment is the least of our concerns.

"It needs to be controlled, this world of ours. I agree. Too much and for too long the scientists and the inventors sought to expand only leisure and sloth, leaving the masses unemployed and starving. Those who could work willingly worked for the lowest possible wage. Others were slaves of sloth: no will to enter the night, to make something, no, only the attention to *divertissements*. For each man and each woman must have purpose in their existence, so we have given it to them: make good your efforts to bear children prior to your transformation, raise them to obey, honor our traditions and maintain our heritage. A logical scheme. Look how we smashed the towers of commerce, those thirty-floor skyscrapers that were not a part of our traditions and our heritage. We return to the common architecture style which represents the best of our land, the best of our history—true art! And we should continue to make works of art and beauty and sing songs that glorify the empire and praise the Most High. Diligently make your specified production each night. Enjoy a sport or celebrate music in your hibernation. Notice the world around you and your place in it. Nothing occurs in isolation. This is what we do within the span of our existence. We do not seek to advance society into some strange new world full of strange objects and stranger beliefs. This is our home. Let us keep it clean and dark."

Nods around the table, none daring to rebut His statements.

"And what about those horse things you've created?" asked Réka Dobos, Minister of Human Services, after a pause. "Are they not the work of the scientists whom you decry?"

The Lord smiled, like he knew she would fit nicely in his bed the coming night, though he would never touch her that way.

"Yes, we have those." spake The Lord. "They are needed to replace the vehicular machinery we discourage. Being biologic entities, I do not count vampire horses as something strange. With the failure of the petroleum industry, we no longer had automated vehicles. The electric grid likewise did not suffice to refuel those vehicles. Already we had trollies and carriages. Steam is plentiful. So where did people need to go? Only international politicians and corporate industrialists ever had need to venture outside their home territory—such as coming to this annual meeting, but you were here for the centennial celebration, as well—and these trips could be easily rendered with airships. It is a better world we have now. And the trains run on time!"

⚮

Outside the thick wooden doors of the council hall, the palace guard contingent stirred nervously. Word had come of a situation requiring immediate action. Yet they hemmed and hawed about who among them should break the seal and enter the council hall.

"Go in," commanded the captain of his lieutenant. "You must tell them."

"I'm not going in there," said the lieutenant. "I dare not interrupt them. You know how He deals with interrupters."

"They must be told of the breach. We are in danger."

"Then you go in and interrupt their important meeting."

"I must remain here to command the guard."

An older sergeant ambled forward, weary grimace painted over his wrinkled face.

"I'll do it. Better to get killed quick by His Majesty than be chased around by a vicious horde of bloodlings."

Straightening his uniform, he gave a confident nod and his fellow guards pulled open the double doors, sending him on stage. Exposed in the doorway, he maintained the position of attention, then saluted as crisply as he had done during his recruit days—

The Lord was bellowing on the edge of anger at the representatives around the table.

". . . thus the anarchists destroyed everything they opposed, they clamored for environmental health so we gave it to them: no more petroleum, no more drain on the electric system. And candle factories were reborn. And the *vorse* breeding industry. As we learned, the same process in which a biologic human can transform into something more suitable for our society, so too the horse could be transformed into a steady and strong variant as equally suited for our new society as the ancient ones for their time. Yes, a beast which did not tire and needed only a portion of blood for fuel. I commend our husbandrists. I have sixteen of the finest vorses myself—six of them to pull the imperial carriage, two for wolf hunting—and I am never displeased with their performance."

"It is a stupendous carriage, Your Majesty!" spouted Duke Reinholt.

"To our glorious empire!" shouted the representative from Berlin.

"To the empire!" shouted another.

"We will lead the way!"

The Lord frowned, though it was difficult to see under his massive moustache and thick beard.

"Lead the way? We do not *lead* any nation." spake The Lord. "We are self-sufficient, responsible to none." He glared harshly at several representatives. "No, it is not the same. We are not leaders in some stupid parade of mercantilism. We are winners of our own condition. Our own place in history. Our own island in the moonlight. Indeed, we possess a thriving economy, developed within our traditional means and allocations—"

"Your Holiness," the sergeant called out. He dropped his salute and took two steps further into the council hall. "I must report that the east gate has been breached. A mob has entered. The palace guard holds them yet is soon to be overrun. We must make for a safe place."

"You may pity the outer regions," The Lord continued, taking no apparent notice of the sergeant, "that is, if you have excess sympathy to spend. Take the famine in the Americas, back in 'forty-five and again in 'fifty-two, I believe, when harvests failed and the cities ran thick with blood. That was a great transformation! People sought food from each other, by the arm or the leg. The riots—the chaos nearly brought down governments. I remember hearing Washington, the capital in those days, was so red with blood they said the city had been struck by a great red wave. Thus the need to move the capital west to Denver, a city I myself visited long ago, beside the mountains. A pretty place."

The Lord broke from his momentary trance, saw the sergeant once more, red-faced and anxious.

"As for the rest of the world, we see how China now covers the Asian hemisphere, and we begrudge them nothing. We intend to cover our own hemisphere. Oceans and deserts will keep us apart. Indeed, we have few contacts and little trade with any of those nations east of India. Not much transformation to the night realm in those nations, yet in some places there is improvement so we applaud them. Let them do as they wish, from the arctic wastes to the Borneo desert, and we shall keep tight to our own hemisphere. The world is large enough for all of us, especially those of the red. We remain united under the blessings of the Most High. We need nothing further."

The sergeant stepped forward, readied himself to speak again.

"Returning to the battlefields, gentlemen, we have set and defined our boundaries and, once attained, we will be content to exist within the grand tradition we have recreated now and forever more."

"Your Holiness, the situation in the palace is now dire!" cried the sergeant of the guard. "You must all come with us to safety!" He stared at the closest few representatives, dour and convincing. "Now!"

The Lord froze in his boots, arm swinging towards the table, fist pummeling the wood. He recoiled and stood straight, then swiveled slightly to face the sergeant. His bushy black eyebrows quivered at the sergeant.

"Where is your captain? I only listen to the captain."

The sergeant did not relax, kept his chin up. "My captain, Your Holiness, is a coward who dares not sound the alarm lest you strike him down for the message."

The Lord dipped his chin. "That's fair. Now what is the message?"

As the representatives began to stir, scooting chairs conjuring a din which covered the explanation, The Lord waved them to silence and bid the sergeant repeat the account.

"Rioters have broken through the east gate of the palace. Guards hold them there yet their number are certain to overwhelm our troops. I was sent to take you to safety—all of you in this hall. Come with me, sirs and madams!"

The Lord waved his hand at the long table. "Do you believe him?"

Nods all around, then a rush of pushing chairs against the table as the representatives hurried to the doors.

The guard contingent quickly divided the stream of officials into smaller groups, leading them away from the council hall in different directions to rooms where they could be kept safe. Passing them in the opposite direction was the guard captain.

"Your Holiness," the captain called, bowing, "this way, please."

The Lord grunted disapprovingly. "Where are you leading me?"

"To your private quarters, Your Holiness. The imperial suite. You will be safe there. We have suitable guard contingent—"

"Safe? I am safe in any room I occupy. How dare the rabble think they can do me in. How many attempts this week alone? A new record, I think. Still I stand."

"If you please, Your Holiness." The captain extended his arm to show the way. "Your mistress has already been taken to your suite."

"My mistress?" The Lord laughed as though it was the only joke of the night worth hearing. "She is that, poor dear. We should pity her. Yet not so much a mistress as the tabloids have determined."

He stepped toward the open doors. The squad of guards standing there had weapons drawn. Judas followed, bearing his halberd on his shoulder. A quartet of dwarves brought up the rear of the group, the doors swinging shut too quickly for the last page to escape the council hall. He shouted at the others to let him out yet they had moved on. The doors were too heavy for the dwarf to push open by himself, so he sat at the long, polished table, pretending he himself was an official of the empire and took pleasure in sulking.

☙

Showing more confidence, the captain led The Lord and His retinue of thirteen through a winding corridor, a series of steps every few meters, lit by torches.

"What is this way?" bade The Lord, grabbing the captain's sleeve. "We must be seven levels below the surface by now."

They halted in the descent, the narrow stairwell stinking of swamp gas and decay.

"It is a secret route, so none may find you," responded the captain, taking another step down, urging they proceed. The Lord's hand held him back.

"Perhaps this odd route leads into a trap," growled The Lord, yanking the captain to the side, smashing him against the stone wall.

"No, I assure you, this is not a trap!" uttered the captain.

"You speak as though you are my long-lost cousin," spake The Lord in lowered breath. "Am I not holy? Am I not powerful? Am I not the Prophet of the Most High?"

The captain glowered, straightening himself from the toss. "Yes, sir. Your Highness! I thought only to speak quickly. To not take more time to say what directions were needed. I meant no disrespect, sir—Your Holiness." He brushed at stains on his uniform from rubbing against the slimy stone wall.

The Lord gave the captain a tap forward. "Proceed."

The group continued down the steps, which curled to the left, and soon entered a wide chamber with a low ceiling. The Lord was forced to bend his neck to pass. Stone benches projected from the walls and ran along them. Lain upon the benches were long-decayed skeletons. Gazing ahead, dozens of them could be seen before the torch light faded—kings and princes, counts and bishops, and their high-born ladies from time immemorial. A dozen rats nibbling on them scattered at the light. Worms and beetles remained, unafraid. A servant rushed forward to sweep a fallen pile of bones to the side, making way for the group. Further on, more of the same.

"This is not any route I can ever recall," spake The Lord. A flutter of wings startled Him though he did not cower. "Enough bats pass here to leave a sticky mess on the floors. Look at this."

"This way, Your Holiness," the captain called, gesturing. "The way to the suite is just beyond the next archway."

"Is it?" He grunted, checking each direction.

"Yes, sir. No one will ever think to look for you and your entourage down here. Thus, a perfect sanctuary to hide from the rioters."

The Lord slapped him on the back, causing him to lose his balance and fall on a knee.

"Beg pardons, Your Holiness!" the captain cried out. His knee hurt as he scrambled to his feet again and he winced.

"I do not like this route," spake The Lord. He looked back over his shoulder at Judas. The look was a command to take action.

Judas stepped forward, stood beside The Lord, holding the halberd at the ready.

"Your Holiness, I beg you, please," the captain began, whimpering in the torchlight glimmering off the halberd's blade, "it was never my plan—"

The blade slapped swiftly at the captain's shoulders, detaching the head cleanly. It bounded a ways down the corridor, then rolled further along the dirty floor and straight into the approaching band of fighters, dressed in rags and common clothing overlaid with make-shift leather armor. Some wore beards, others clean-cheeked, all with hate in their eyes as they rushed forward, shouting curses.

"Back!" shouted The Lord over his shoulder.

Judas stood firm, halberd ready. The attackers were limited by the narrowness of the corridor, able to send ahead only two or three at a time. The dark corridors from the right and left seemed not to be filled with any attackers, as though this was not quite the location for their kill zone.

The Lord held up his large hand, pulling energy from his soul and creating an invisible pulse which punched them back like a boxer's fist. The trusty halberd snipped and sliced, dropping the first line. A second wave rushed forward, scrambling to make a convincing mêlée, then necessarily fell back, many in pieces. Arms, legs, and heads littered the floor. Bowels lay strung out—a timid rat dared appear to take a meal. The third wave showed their fiercest faces, feigned a rush twice, yet retreated like scared little boys, disappearing into the darkness of side passages.

The Lord wrung his hands, as though shaking out the last crinkles of electricity. He breathed deeply and held the breath until long after the others regained theirs. Judas seemed fit, able to go on, The Lord noticed. He clapped his chamberlain on the shoulder.

"It was good that my new chamberlain, though low on preparation for the position, still bears the weapon of his former office. Well done! You have a skill I need. You continue to bring fare fortune."

Judas, his face solemn, bowed his head, a stream of effort trickling down from his forehead and stinging his eyes.

"I am honored to serve you, Your Holiness."

"Yes, those are the proper words." The Lord stared down along the corridor at the ripped apart bodies leaking their blood. "I suspected it was a trap. I doubt I have ever been down here, so far below the main level of this palace. There is no secret passageway! Fools . . . . I didn't wish to seem rude, however. Hah! The military boys think they can trick me, that I am old and weak. It was the same in my youth. So I hid in the library." He waved at the fallen bodies. "Go on and have a snack if you wish. Then let's go the correct way to the imperial suite. My mistress awaits."

ॐ

Eleven guards stood in full battle regalia, polished armor glistening, in formation before the mighty doors leading into the imperial suite. Ten soldiers and a lieutenant, all anxious that The Lord might not appear, knew they would be struck down next. The group gave a collective sigh of relief when The Lord, preceded by a tall, menacing shadow, rounded the corner and approached.

"You the elite of my guard?" spake The Lord.

All nodded. "We are your most loyal protectors!" the lieutenant declared, saluting crisply. His guards likewise saluted.

"You are welcome at my table anytime," spake The Lord, waving at the doors. Two of the guards moved to open the doors. "Tonight stand strong. These are troubling times."

The open doors revealed his suite, all white and pure, a defect he had never bothered to correct. Sweeping into his sight was a woman in black gown, as though she was preparing to attend a formal ball. Her pale shoulders were bare and streams of black hair rested upon them. Her lips were red like fire as she smiled, revealing flawless white fangs.

"My Love!" she cried, tearfully rushing to Him.

The Lord held up his hand to catch her, brushing her belly as she came upon Him, keeping her a hand's distance from Him.

"Remember the curse," spake The Lord in an uncharacteristically gentle voice. He curled his gloved hand around her cheek, so desiring to plant a kiss yet knowing it would be disastrous. "I am safe, and so are you." He turned to Judas, standing by the doors with his halberd against his broad shoulder. "Although we did have a bit of excitement in the bowels of this monstrous castle." He gave a wink.

"We are relieved you are safe, Your Holiness," Judas replied.

"My thanks." The Lord gave a one-finger salute.

Two guards remained in the suite as others moved to close the doors and stand guard outside. As the doors were nearly closed, a brown bat fluttered between them, entering the room. One guard raised his lance, attempting to spear the creature as it flitted about.

"Are you mad?" spake The Lord. "Dare not kill a messenger of the Most High or ye yourself shall perish."

His eyes followed the bat across the ceiling as it flew back and forth, eventually finding a suitable perch on the upper molding.

The inner guards brought down the heavy wooden bar across the doors, sealing them inside.

"Oh, my darling," cooed the woman, "I worried for you. I worried so much! Are you unharmed?"

He brushed her hair, his hand lingering.

"Worry not, Maria, for I am ever ready to defend myself and you, and the palace and our empire, and the Most High, from all invaders."

She leaned in, pressing against his chest, and his muscular arms encircled her. She enjoyed his rare displays of affection, she told him; it gave her the will to go on. Turning her head to gaze up at his dark eyes, she found his thick beard blocking her view, filling her face, yet she did not complain. Instead, she kissed the fabric of his shirt, licked a spot of blood that had bubbled to the surface there and wet the shirt.

"My Love, are you wounded?" she asked, parting from His chest yet keeping her gloved hands on Him.

"Your Holiness, I see it, too," said Judas, pointing a finger. "A spot of something wet. There—on your shirt."

"It is blood," declared Maria. It had marked her black gown, she noticed, right at the juncture of her breasts. The portion touching her pale skin was deep red.

A servant hurried to his side to check.

"I felt no injury," spake The Lord. "I stood strong against the fury of the rabble. Perhaps a blade managed to slip through despite my cloak of energy. I am falling weak. I need blood."

A trio of elderly clothiers assisted The Lord in removing his many-pelt cape, hanging it on its wooden stand in the corner of the room. Unfixing the buttons, The Lord held His arms aside as they slipped off the shirt. The wound was clear against His white flesh: a slit no bigger than a fingertip.

"So they managed it, after all," spake The Lord, gazing down at His chest. "Ordinary steel. That poor effort will mend on its own. A three-day snooze in my casket and I will be as good as newly transformed. Perhaps better. Indeed, that first moment, wrenching one's eyes open to the reality of transformation, is a moment one never forgets."

Servants urged The Lord to sit on a padded stool, bare chested, His mane flowing down His back and over His shoulders, black as soot next to His pale skin. Judas stared at the body of his lord and master once more, trying not to be noticed staring. The hideous marks of a hard existence stood out and he shuttered to think of the days they were obtained, a span numbering more than a hundred years. Yet He appeared only to be a strong, fit man of fifty in bloodling years.

Little hands tended to the wound in The Lord's chest as the woman regarded Him with equal measure of love and devotion.

"My Love," the woman named Maria spoke after some time, "would you like some red to drink? To restore your mood?"

The Lord looked up, focused on her. A long-lost smile condensed upon his countenance. "Indeed. It has been a while. The damn council meeting, then this poor drama. Death to the playwright. Let us have our pleasures. Yes, Maria, let's sup a bit. Yours?"

She seemed to giggle at His words, though each of them fell and cracked against the stone floor.

"Oh, no, My Love. We have better than my poor essence, though it is ever-always yours to drink. No, My Love, this comes in a bottle, from the vineyard, by way of the distillery, to a sacred cup."

She reached for the goblet standing tall on the golden tray held by a serving maid who appeared from nowhere, a mere functionary of the palace, nothing more—as it should be, she noted by her expression.

"Here, My Love."

She held the goblet out to Him and the smile he bore grew brighter between his black beard and his black mustache.

"Only wine?" He studied the deep red color, then took the goblet in

His hand and brought it to His nose. The bouquet delighted. "More than mere wine?" His eyes lifted, caught hers.

"You always enjoyed merlot," she said with a knowing smirk. "This has been enhanced by an infusion of prime-grade blood. It comes from Italy. Milan. They do the mixing so well there. Perfect blend of the best of both worlds, the dark and the light."

The Lord could not contain His grin, waved her to join Him. She took a seat on His knee, her hand reaching to His shoulder to steady herself. She felt the sizzle in her palm and withdrew her hand.

"A cloth," ordered The Lord.

A servant placed a small square of black cloth over The Lord's bare shoulder and the woman set her hand there once more without any ill effect.

"I have many regrets about this curse, my dear," spake The Lord. "I have been set for other purposes than making love to a woman. If there were a way, I would have you in my bed each dawn and make you a woman throughout each afternoon. The nights would die in a great fever for us, for our lust."

Her laugh was painful to hear. "As I, too, have regrets. It cannot possibly grow back each time it rips. Yet it does. I cannot be a virgin forever. Not if I should live so long."

"Each of us has a curse to endure," spake The Lord, looking away.

A flutter of black wings caught His eye. He pointed to the rafters.

"What think you of my curse? Of Maria's?" He addressed the bat. "Is it a fair thing we have as a terminal burden? Why must we endure it? Have we not pleased the Most High?" Regarding His lovely mistress with soft eyes, He continued: "I shall find a suitable partner for you. Then you won't be in any further pain. Perhaps you might conceive, as you have long wished. The tricks of the Most High are infinite."

"I understand, My Love."

Frowning, she swept back her hair from her shoulder, clearing the way to her white throat. Her fingers danced there, inviting, though she knew He would not bite. His touch always burned—like ice. Beneath her black gown marks remained of their first attempts at human union, the ancient ritual, as old as time. Yet they failed and lay wounded, each by the other.

"It is not a wish I have for you and me, My Love. Let us be together without bedding and find a measure of delight in the simple clicking of our hearts in proper rhythm. Like the bloodlings do."

The Lord let go a series of chuckles. "Ever the poet. Maria, ever the Romantic. Always the heart that feels. You feel everything yet cannot do anything about your feelings. The curse is great in you. Yet here you are, bringing me blood-infused wine to soothe me in this dark night of my soul. Indeed, you are my soul. We belong together. For all time. Yes, that is our curse: we belong together. A fate worse than life."

He released a passionate sigh that blew across the room and rattled the shutters of the small window in the far wall.

"Drink, My Love!" cried the woman. "You are safe here with me. We have the guards outside to block the way. Let us be together now."

The Lord flicked His hand at Judas, waved at other servants in the room. "We are not alone, my dear. Not truly."

Her hand went to her face like a wedding veil. "Let them turn their way around and never spy upon us. You may command them thus."

"You know we can never be together in that way. Let us drink more and dream of fairer times. Let us recall the days of . . . 'thirty-nine, that autumn in Slovenia. We stayed a while at Lake Bled. Recall?"

"Oh, yes! What a delight!"

A servant brought another goblet at Maria's finger-snap. She lifted the goblet to her lips, drank quickly. The Lord followed suit, drinking down the goblet in one long draft. His lips were stained purple when he pulled the goblet away. She signaled for more. Their goblets were again filled, again emptied. Continuously.

And the sunrise soon snuck into the imperial chamber through the small window high on the wall—until a servant properly garbed it and returned the room to a satisfying degree of Erebus.

Judas nodded his pleasure, at last a rest was available. Taking a seat by the opposite wall, halberd leaning against the wall, he stared at the royal couple, noting how they kissed with a coarse cloth between their lips so they might never touch, never hurt each other. He noticed also the quiet brown bat above in the corner, observing all, so attentive, like one of those policing drones from his childhood, the stories his father told to frighten him at night.

He recalled when his father, broken from manual labor, cursed at his citizen score being lowered. Falling below 200 meant his travel was restricted and he could not get access to most banking services. He had claimed his behavior was in line with official rules and regulations. His father was not a vampire, however. Urging his son to join the military was a way for him to advance. His score stood at 425, last he checked; no bloodling could expect to rise above 200. Only His Holiness had a perfect score of 1000.

os

Drunken amusement. The Lord and his mistress were oblivious to the turmoil outside the imperial suite as palace guards battled crowds of rioters. From time to time shouting could be heard, the clash of metal, the whiz of arrows, the cries of the wounded. Within the suite, the two guards at the doors stood at attention but constantly eyed each other, as though expecting the battle to arrive at the very doors they guarded. Outside the doors, the other nine remained at the ready.

"When will come the all-clear?" asked Judas of the two guards. One shrugged, the other tilted his head at the doors. "Your lieutenant will inform you?" A slight nod on a quizzical face.

A folding screen had been set up which separated the guards at the doors and the staff from the couple's private area. In moments when the fighting let up, coy giggles and deep rumbles of lustiness could be heard on the other side of the screen, though no one present dared interrupt them or inquire if they had need of anything.

"They clearly do not need anything more than each other," Judas muttered to himself. He glanced over at a serving maid, nearly hairless and her face badly scarred, a crisp white apron shielding her lithe body in its black staff uniform. She pursed her lips at his remark.

"More wine!" called The Lord.

The serving maid stood immediately and prepared the tray, then delivered it around the end of the privacy screen.

When the girl returned from serving them, the sudden explosion of thunder overhead caused her to drop the tray. Quickly retrieving the tray and picking up its contents, she frowned in embarrassment and dipped her head at Judas. More crackles of thunder, more flashes of lightning streaking across the window, drowning out the fighting noise. There was a male scream which stood out over all.

Judas regarded the two guards, who shook their heads. No word of the all-clear yet. The arrival of the storm would likely drive away the rioters although those committed to an assassination would fight on within the walls and corridors of the palace.

Their drunkenness seemed to have worn thin yet The Lord's voice grew louder, filled with the bravado and lust of younger days. His mistress laughed fully, unashamed of her outbursts. Judas could not help but listen as they entertained each other, though he tried not to judge them. Glancing at the staff members, the reactions they gave indicated this royal boisterousness was a normal part of their work.

The little bat winged across the room, settling on the opposite side, among the rafters, perhaps for a better view, giving a single squeak of greeting.

". . . and they were as soused as we are now," spake The Lord. "Ah, negotiations are so trifling. At least it was good to have the meetings in Barcelona, a fair clime for us. However, much better to set accords in a bedroom, I say. I had designs on her, indeed, despite her age. As a bloodling, she had an excellent appearance. You know how the French are, the women slender and fit. Like yourself, Maria. Yet I had no expectation of crossing paths with Anatoly and his wife. It was pure coincidence—although what the Most High has planned can only be guessed."

"You are such a devil!" the woman laughed.

"So here is the president, Anatoly Mikhailyevich Lermontov, who styles himself as Czar of all the Russias, as though there are thirty-six or so of the little states. He's arm in arm with his wife of twenty or so years, who can say? Dazdraperma was her name, as I recall, made from the abbreviation of the slogan 'Long Live May Day'—the ancient holy day of Russia, she liked to explain. They were strolling down the hotel corridor returning to their suite after a dinner with their diplomatic staff and the boring trade representatives, a few prostitutes, perhaps. And there am I, in my pelted robe, looking fierce and dark, chatting with *Madame* President, she in her short lace skirt and long sleeves, a decadent style in those days yet she always wished to be known as a style icon even at fifty."

"So decadent!" giggled the woman.

"We all blanched at the same time, hah! There at the intersection of corridors. Imagine we pale folks blanching!"

"How pale can you be?" The woman snickered.

"So, then, the common courtesies, naturally. Then the invitation. Diplomatic barriers aside, we are all adults. Why not have a *tête-à-tête* in my suite, which is only a few steps from my outstretched hand? Nods of agreement all around and we enter my suite, which is large, the largest of the hotel, four rooms of beds and so on. If I had found you by then, Maria, I would have had you stay with me."

"So you hammered out tough decisions—"

"Amélie-Dominique takes a seat on the sofa, casually crossing her legs so her short skirt shows off her inner sanctum, unshaven, catching the eye of Anatoly and causing a sharp elbow to the ribs from Dazdra. You had to have been there."

"I wish!"

"We talk, of course, though nothing about trade negotiations, only the personal. I make bold suggestions, rude to some, intriguing to others. Then I suggest we get comfortable and Dazdra asks what I mean by that. Her husband rises and steps up to Amélie-Dominique. She stands as if by command and they embrace like they are long-lost lovers. They kiss with passion. Dazdra is shocked, curses at Anatoly. I confess a bit of surprise, too. I reach for Dazdra and spin her into my arms—like I did with you at Lake Bled, my dear."

"I can imagine how you danced!"

"Not dancing, my dear. This was before the curse, when I could still touch a woman without her being harmed by the frostbite burns and such. Not so long ago."

"So you touched her? And no harm followed?"

"There: Amélie-Dominique and Anatoly Mikhailyevich, ravenously stripping each other in front of us, like they are struck with a spell for lust. *Madame* President, a fine looking woman, fit and unshaven. Czar of the Russias regaining his manhood, using it like he was on a phallic potion. A miracle of international relations!"

The woman cannot cease laughing.

"Then it hits me! What was I thinking? These two would suddenly want to have sex together? Indeed! Not likely! The Most High has a plan and I am the instigator of it. It is suddenly clear to me. My words, my voice, have power, I notice. I speak for the Most High. He speaks through me. I am supposed to direct this affair. And so I do."

"Was that what they called 'orgy'?"

"Perhaps. So I swing Dazdra into my arms and plant a kiss on her. She struggles at first, then accepts what is going to happen, and wants it. *'Potseluy menya, dorogaya!'* she says, tearing off her dress, tossing it to the sofa. It falls partly over her husband who is already atop Amélie-Dominique, without breaking their passion. The brassiere drops and Dazdra is full-busted like a house of bricks. Her hips are a castle, the drawbridge is lowered. My cavalry must charge in! Seconds later I am with Dazdra in bedroom number one and moments later I hear the others using bedroom number two."

"*Mon Dieu!*" the woman sang.

"Later we switch partners, Anatoly and me. Then we switch again, the women together and the men together, because there is no more to negotiate. We understand everything. When Dazdra lies exhausted, Anatoly returns to Amélie-Dominique and I . . . I sit back to watch. I pour a tall draft of brandy and sip it until they are finished. Somehow the women leave in each other's garments. Anatoly sneaks off as though he has ruined the reputation of all the Russias. Then I realize the spell has been broken. They now know the things they have done, what acts they have performed, how everything was captured on film."

"On film? Like the *cinéma*? Really!"

"Well, I don't know about that for certain. Possible. It was called 'livestream' in those days. And cameras were everywhere, public and private, often so small you never noticed them—everyone was caught on livestream in those days. Except vampires. We did not appear very clear. The surveillance drones were many in those days. You could hide nothing from the government, or employers, blackmailers, family and friends. The places on the grid, what they called internet, encouraged everyone to share whatever livestream they had access to, no matter how private it was supposed to be, and many lives were thus ruined. It made people think what they did, change their behavior. Most people became puritanical, with high collars, and low hems."

"You have always had the cameras. It's protocol, *n'est pas*? So much imagery captured of my nightly endeavors, the pitiful librarians must be exhausted—"

"So I remained in my suite, took a shower to wash off the odor of them. I slept well in the bed provided. I longed for a sturdy casket full of rich soil."

"Then you embarrassed them the next day? Was it your plan?"

"It was a crazy episode, indeed, yet trade negotiations became easy after. Whenever a question arose or point of contention was debated, I would stare at Anatoly or Amélie-Dominique and everything turned in my favor. Even Dazdra smiled at me from the outer ring of seats. At the conclusion, she blew me a kiss and Anatoly frowned at her. She could not help herself. She had been seduced by the leader of the Hungarian Empire. Amélie-Dominique sidle up to me, whispered in my ear '*Merci beaucoup*' despite the international press being there. We knew what we had done."

"What did she thank you for? The night's lust? Or more?"

"A well-placed bite and Amélie-Dominique had to wear high collar fashions at the remaining meetings. She was one of us now, a member of the dark society. Blood futures went through the roof after that. My holdings soared in value. The Hungarian Empire became richer."

"I believe it, My Love!"

"We expanded our military. Eventually we conquered France, then Catalonia and Spain. We joined them to the Empire of Europa, and the Most High was pleased. So pleased, in fact, I was granted a wonderful new curse. So it be: I cannot touch a woman without her flesh freezing. It is the touch of frostbite. From my cold heart, spake the Most High. I first believed the curse came from God, knowing Him as well as I do, yet He was not the master I served. Whenever you gain something, you must give up something. That is His rule."

"I pity you." The woman seemed to weep. "I pity us."

"The men—they survive, I have learned," spake The Lord. "Anatoly was beside himself, realizing what he had done, he and I, while the women partook of their own temptations. I shook it off. I think Dazdra never let him live it down, though. He did not run for re-election in the next year. Amélie-Dominique Roussel also did not seek another term as the French *président*. I heard later she had been meeting Anatoly in Copenhagen off and on. They were seen together in the tourist areas, then found again in their hotel room, where each lay cold with an open chest, the heart of the other in each of their hands. A strange suicide. However, the Most High has a plan and we are not to predict it or to question the motives and methods. Besides, now we must deal with *Monsieur* Bastien Archambault and the *Czarina* Valeriya Alexandrovna Stepanov, though they are today mere operatives within the empire."

"Because it is you, My Love, in charge of Europa."

"The empire, yes. The Russias are client states. And we have taken Ukraine. So you see a well-timed *ménage* can buy you domination for a half-century. It pays dividends. However, you need not worry about geopolitics, my lovely. Such worry will harm your beauty, and I will not have you looking less than perfect."

℞

The couple fell silent for some time and the noise of fighting returned, at first distant then closer. The noise waned for a while. Perhaps the palace brigade had driven the rioters from the grounds. Judas stared at the two guards; they only shook their heads. Clearly they were anxious.

The floor shook. Suddenly The Lord stood at the end of the privacy screen, bare-chested, dark trousers unlaced with a forest of black hair sprouting from the gap, His hair tussled, beard mushed to one side, looking drunk and slovenly.

"Is there to be no word on our fate?" The Lord grumbled.

Judas shot up, striking a position of attention.

"Not yet, Your Holiness!"

"The boys should have defeated the rabble by now."

"Yes, Your Holiness."

The Lord regarded Judas, studying him as if trying to remember his name. "You heard everything, I suppose." He waved Judas to sit. "It is no concern of yours. You are my chamberlain. You hear and then keep my secrets. You'll learn them in time. I've been around more than a hundred years—eighty-five among the Erebus clan. The secrets I bear are many. If you do not understand something I say, you may ask your questions. You are my chamberlain now, so I will answer you without penalty."

"Thank you, Your Holiness," said Judas, dipping his head.

"Ah! I see it now," spake The Lord, attempting to lean against the edge of the screen and feeling it give way. He stood tall on his own strength, only one hand on the screen.

"What do you see, Your Holiness?" asked Judas.

"I see the inquiry there in your eyes." The Lord flicked a finger at His chamberlain, as if sending a spark to light kindling. "To answer the inquiry I see raging in your eyes, yes: If I really wish to have that kind of pleasure—sexual—it is a man I must bring to my bed. This is not a preference, mind you; it's the only option available. They will not be harmed by my touch, it seems. Indeed, I may be more harmed by their touch—if the session goes too long. The Most High has burdened me with these limitations in exchange for the miraculous power to control the elements—when I use them on His behalf, that is, to affect the changes in the world We wish to see."

He grinned, like He had told a joke and awaited laughter.

Judas remained attentive, even as his lord and master wavered on His feet, pondering the next declaration. The Lord cleared His throat, and a servant rushed to catch the phlegm.

"Now you know. In time you may need to find a partner to satisfy me. I will let you know. But I digress . . . ."

Judas held his face as solid as stone.

"I understand, Your Holiness."

"Do you?" growled The Lord immediately. "It could be you, Judas. Have you considered that? It depends on many factors."

"I swear, Your Holiness, I take these matters seriously, and I shall do as you command always. Even in that capacity. If you so command. . . . Your Holiness."

The Lord smiled, pleased. Crossing His arms, He seemed to grow larger in the room. "Your Holiness!"

"Your Holiness?" asked Judas.

The Lord swept His black locks out of His face, a chuckle tumbling out of the corner of His mouth, apparently catching Him by surprise.

"Holiness!" He roared, throwing out His arms. "Do you know why I am deemed holy?" He punched the air like a boxer: left, right, left, then sent a kick into the air. "Do you?"

"No, Your Majesty. I do not."

"Hah! Now it's 'majesty'? I've been demoted. Then you must know why I'm considered majestic."

"No, My Lord. I do not."

"Further diminution. What's this? I must be, in my drunkenness, a lesser man, a mere lord." The laughter rang hollow and everyone in the suite seemed alarmed, concerned what might happen next. "Yet I am your lord, am I not? The lord of you—of all of you here."

"Indeed you are, My Lord."

He glared at His chamberlain. "Do you know the reason I am 'Your Holiness'?"

Judas carefully shook his head, wary of offending.

"Long, long ago, the story goes . . . ." He scratched under his beard, then squinted as though the sunrise had struck Him in an unexpected flash. "There once was a man who jumped feet first into the abyss and emerged changed—in fact, changed into a monster so hideous that he scared everyone he encountered. Thus, he hid himself away, and in time he became deathly indolent. Entering the world of humans again, this monster found he had some power over them. He made a plan he thought was good. With the right connections, he could live a life of pleasures untold. Indeed, he thought it so."

The Lord regarded His chamberlain—and the staff members who had collected around him.

"Until an angel arrived to coax him into the light. Alas, it was too late for him, this monster. And the light, this . . . this sunrise, it was much too bright. It burned. By then this angel had become a monster, too, yet for her there was a chance at some kind of redemption. For all of us seek redemption, redemption for things we do not know we have done. We spend a lifetime in puzzlement. A strange game. But I digress . . . . If only this monster, this man, would make a suitable sacrifice, the angel would be redeemed."

He swung His arm around to point at the portrait on the wall.

"This monster stood tall and called forth his Maker, cursed and threatened Him, He who had made this forlorn creature, . . . this . . . this God figure. However, much as mirrors distort the vision, trickery within the folds of light, it was not this God who provided the chances, pulled carpets out from underfoot. No, it was the Most High, the entity who I address in the darkest hours as my own lord and master, Luce." Chuckles spilled out and hit the floor hard. "A pet name. It's not much appreciated, but I've a purpose—and none can take my place in this purpose. I am the chosen one. Chosen . . . hmm. How the title clangs like beaten bronze! A shield. Yet who does it protect?"

The Lord glared at Judas, who shrugged.

"Soon, naturally—hah! naturally? It should be *un*naturally, eh? Yes, it will end and I will be free. Yet will you? Will you be free when this ends? Or will you still be yoked to this demon lover?" The Lord's finger pointed at him. "You? Any of you?"

Judas gasped, holding his expression like a painter's grim sketch, unable to add colors from the palate.

The Lord swayed at the edge of balance. "My friend and confidant, Luce. Drinking buddies. We go way back . . . ."

"My Love, sit beside me," called his lady from behind the screen.

"I'd rather stand," he called back to her. "I have words to speak."

"Please," she continued, "I beg you. Be calm and sit with me."

"I dare not be so close to you, my dear, else I succumb to a devil's desire and ravish you to the end of your existence." With a grin, The Lord waved at His chamberlain, indicating he should go ahead and ask the question which was floating across his face.

"Why do we call you 'Your Holiness'?" Judas dared ask, considering his drunk lord might not be so cruel as the sober one.

"Because I am holy." The Lord's grin broke into a full smile, white fangs gleaming. "The most holy you've got in this empire. I talk with the Most High. I am His prophet. I project His desires into the mortal world. Probably I'm only a puppet, ever-tied by metaphor to invisible energy. How's that? The scientists believe it true. Yet I know my place, what manner of punishments I endure. Indeed, I am infected by this dire holiness! The abominable kiss of death! The disease of the sacred. My only pleasure is to see it through to the end, to embrace that final moment of clarity. I will see Him, the Most High, and when I do, I will cleave Him into as many pieces as I can—and quarter each of those—for I will have earned that right."

He stammered the final words, voice weak, and dropped to the floor on his bottom, a hard sit, spilling onto his side with a coughing fit followed by a loud belch.

"Your Holiness!" exclaimed Judas, kneeling beside The Lord.

The woman jumped out from behind the screen. "My Love!"

"I'm just drunk, nothing more, my dear," spake The Lord. "It seems this time is a good time for getting drunk. It is my plan, mind you. This is it. Indeed, I am at my most honest in this state. Fear not! Judas, ask me anything. I will answer and the truth will ring in your ears."

Judas straightened himself in his kneel, measuring the degree of consciousness of his lord and master.

"If you invite me to pose a question, I shall."

Grumbling. "Pose it."

Judas pursed his lips, feeling his heart pounding, then spoke: "Why did Your Holiness choose my friend Kristóf as a sacrifice?" He focused on The Lord's closed eyes. "Instead of me?"

More grumbling, as though The Lord was lost in a dream. "Because a sacrifice must be made each night. The Most High commands it. Else my power diminishes and I am unable to devote my full capacity to performing His work."

"Yet why Kristóf . . . and not me?" asked Judas, bending lower and speaking softer so the others might not hear.

"You were the healthy one. His—your friend—hah! is not everyone we use a friend?—his was a body full of disease, unfortunately, though he knew it not. I knew as I approached. The stench of corruption stings my soul. He had at best one final painful year remaining."

"He seldom spoke of it—"

"How could he know?"

"The staff has examinations by a physician every year."

The Lord opened his eyes; they were blurry—gray, not black.

"I do not concern myself with the schedules of this household, nor the tides of the Duna, nor the rats that run through the crumbling Parliament House, nor the bats that hang in the ruins of the Church of

Matthias founded by Saint Stefan himself. Not even the nitrogen level of the soil pools in the Irgalmasok Veli Bej. My concern is the empire."

A thunderous pounding on the doors to the suite shook everyone from their lethargy. The wood splintered as an axe broke through. The inner guards took defensive positions and the staff grabbed anything that could be used as a weapon. Judas held his halberd at the ready.

4

"THE END HAS COME," ANNOUNCED THE LORD, standing with effort, one hand on the screen to steady himself, the screen wavering.

Between where He stood and the doors stood the two guards, their weapons drawn. Judas held his halberd ready beside The Lord as the chomping of the doors continued: a swing, a crunch, another swing, another crunch, but the metal braces held the door together and the bar across the doors would keep them from opening. Anguished cries told them the outer guard had failed to defend the imperial suite from the mob of angry rioters and determined assassins.

Maria peered around the screen, hands at her face, tears of blood slipping down her cheeks. "Is it truly finished for us?"

"It is now in the hands of the Most High," spake The Lord without a glance back. "The day I have longed for. Prepare yourself. There's a sturdy blade in the top drawer of the chest."

The door splintered further, enough that a long vertical window formed through which each side could see the other.

Before The Lord could determine what he saw through the gap, an arrow whizzed through it, struck him square in the chest, burrowing deep, the arrowhead lost within his flesh. The arrow's shaft and its quartet of trimmed feathers bobbed back and forth.

The woman screamed and the guards hurried to dam the gap with pieces of leather and broken wood from the frame of the screen.

Judas rushed to His lord, hanging on the screen by an arm, weight settling there, like a crucifix. "Your Holiness!"

"There it is, the holiness . . . ."

The Lord reached for the shaft of the arrow, gave it a tug.

"It's too deep," said Judas. "It must be cut out. If you pull it—"

"Where is that fat doctor?" cried The Lord.

"Elsewhere, Your Holiness."

Judas tried to move Him from where He had fallen but the body was too heavy. The Lord was two meters tall, strapped with muscle like a champion wrestler. Judas tugged on one arm, saw the motion jostle the arrow, so he stopped. The Lord never complained of pain.

Further mighty chops on the wooden door by someone wielding a huge battle axe finally broke the bar. The gang outside pulled open the heavy doors and faced the wounded Emperor of Europa and members of His personal staff.

The mob cheered as they rushed in.

"Stop!" The Lord commanded. He pushed himself up from the floor on his good arm, the one Judas had been pulling. "You have invaded my space and I will not allow it!"

"Your space, sir, is the people's space now!" shouted the first man entering the suite, bearing the axe. He was nearly as tall as The Lord himself. "We have taken the palace! And with it all Budapest! Your days are at an end!"

"You are not worthy of speaking to me! None of your ilk!"

The ruffian, garbed in torn leather over a dirty wool jerkin, like a medieval peasant, raised his axe as though threatening to swing it.

"Be gone!" grunted The Lord.

Judas whipped the halberd across the interval, nipping the ruffian's upraised arm off at the shoulder. Blood spewed out of the open artery as the arm dropped on the floor, the axe with it. Ignoring the cursing, Judas swung the halberd again but the angle and short space limited his motion and thus the blade's power, so the ruffian's head only lay over on his shoulder, not completely detached. A fountain of blood spurted into the air as the body crashed on its knees and toppled over at The Lord's boots.

Others rushed in to continue the attack and the two guards shot them with their bombards, spewing pellets into the faces and chests of the attackers, who fell to the floor, leaking blood. Members of the staff, starved during their lengthy sojourn in the imperial suite, jumped at the fresh red, lapping it off the floor and trying to guzzle the spray. Vampires among the contingent of attackers pushed through their bloodling cohort to likewise partake. The dwarf staff members stabbed the invaders in their legs and groins. The clothiers dropped to their knees, begging for mercy only to lose their heads.

The attack descended into an orgy of gluttony. The flurry of blood-eaters swept into the suite, overwhelming the two guards, batting them aside. A dozen men and women dressed as citizens in house garb or work uniforms, pressed into the suite crying for justice, shouting their demands, cursing at The Lord for his evil acts and taking what they could of the free blood. The throng of blood-lappers piled up at the entrance to the suite.

Judas hurried to pull The Lord away from the mêlée. To the chaise longue they went, the same as when The Lord's physician had treated the injuries from the centennial celebration assassination attempt a few days earlier. Judas eased Him down upon the seat. Maria lay over his body to protect him, stroking his cheek with her fingers, careful not to disturb the arrow.

"My Love! My Lord!"

"No, Maria, you mustn't risk yourself for me," spake The Lord. "It will all work out in the end. I swear it. All accounts will be settled."

"Come," the serving maid called to them. "There is a way out."

Maria's pale face grayed. "Where?"

The serving girl's scarred face showed no fear. "Follow."

Judas set down the halberd and strained to help The Lord to his feet. The movement caused the arrow to shift within his chest. The Lord grimaced.

"We must get him to safety," cried Judas. "Then try to extract the arrow."

Maria tried to hold Him up from the opposite side. She had more strength than one would have guessed by her petite size.

"Can you bear me?" grunted The Lord.

"We shall, Your Holiness," Judas replied.

"We shall save you," cried Maria. "There is hidden way."

The maid curled her hand at them. In the rear of the suite was the preparation room, where items sent up from the kitchen were made ready for serving. There was a vertical shaft, a service elevator, Judas saw, but it was too small for a normal person, impossible for The Lord's dimensions.

The girl shook her head, pointed in another direction. A door! She unlatched it, opened it.

"What's your name?" asked Judas, a grin appearing.

"Nóra," the girl whispered, her voice a mere echo of her breath.

"Thank you, Nóra."

The open doorway revealed a staircase which spiraled around a central beam, leading down to the lower levels. The girl held the door open for them like a butler.

"Come with us or you'll be killed," said Judas.

Maria took the girl's hand, urged her down the stairs after Judas hefted The Lord into the stairwell.

Judas bore The Lord against his shoulder as best he could and half-carried, half-dragged the emperor down the spiral staircase, step by narrow step, pausing every few steps to catch his breath and adjust his grip on The Lord.

Everyone suddenly cringed as something black flittered past them in the stairwell, circling downward.

"Damn bat!" Judas cursed, slapping at it.

The girl closed the door behind them and followed them down the steps. Maria held up a finger to mark silence. The stumbling down the stairs had its own noise, but Nóra nodded her understanding.

Down three levels, the secret staircase met another door, which did not yield. Judas frowned. He pressed his shoulder against the door, leaned against it with the combined weight of The Lord and himself yet it did not budge. Nóra squeezed around them, holding up a key. Into the lock went the key and the door creaked opened.

Immediately the bat fluttered out of the darkness, leading the way into the next room.

"Bless you," Judas said to the girl. He turned to Maria. "We must get Him into a casket so He may recover His health. A surgeon will be needed to remove the arrowhead."

Maria teared up, her hands to her face. "How?"

"We must find a place to rest—"

"Where are we?" grunted The Lord. "Have we descended to Hell? I'm always welcome there."

"No, Your Holiness," Judas responded. "We are on a lower level of the palace. Perhaps the ground floor."

"That is not Hell," grumbled The Lord drunkenly.

"It may be close."

"We are taking you to safety," Maria told Him.

Although they had entered a room, ahead lay darkness, another corridor it seemed by the echo. No torches lit the way. This time, Nóra did not produce any miracles.

"Where are we?" asked Judas.

"This way leads to the salons," Nóra answered. "For the guests. They are served from the same kitchen."

"Guest salons, eh? Like for the visiting dignitaries?"

Nóra nodded but in the darkness he could not see her.

Maria stepped forward, setting her eyes on the black corridor. After a moment, the blackness had grayed, showing well-enough the passage clear of obstacles. Straight ahead about 25 meters, doors on the right and on the left. The corridor continued another 25 meters with more doors. At the same interval further, more doors.

Judas stared at the light coming from the vampire woman's eyes, a trick he had never seen before.

"Sorry, that's all I can do," said Maria as they returned to blackness. "At least we could see the way is clear."

"It takes some energy, I suspect," said Judas.

"I can do it only for an instant. Then I feel weak and my eyes hurt. Like I've been reading too long. And I must rest them."

"Then I shall lead us. Follow the sound of my steps."

"Are we there yet?" muttered The Lord.

"He is failing," said Maria. "We must hurry or he will fall into the deep sleep and might never awaken."

Judas pulled The Lord ahead into the darkness, slow enough not to be taken by surprise.

"To the right," said the girl, her pointing hand lost in the dark. "We can rest in the first salon."

CR

They had entered a room decorated for guests to stay overnight at the palace, a salon complete with a grand bed and grander mirrors draped with official colors of red and black. The salon was lit by two gas lamps situated on opposite walls near the head of the bed. They gave off a faint golden glow.

"No, not there," said a woman's whimsical voice. "There!"

On the bed something in a heap was squirming.

"Oh! Your Highness!" grunted a man within the tangle of limbs. A head popped up from the fleshy mass.

"A joke!" laughed a woman's voice, slapping his bare shoulder.

"Not a joke," growled the man. "We have visitors."

Judas pulled The Lord along on his shoulder, Maria helping on the other side. Nóra found a spent torch laying on a credenza by the doorway and lit it from one of the oil lamps. It filled the room further with a golden glow.

She held the torch higher. In the circle of light they could see the two figures coupling on the bed.

"We-we-we—," the man cried fitfully. "Hiding from the fighting. We were only h-hiding from the f-fight."

The woman righted herself, gazed at the newcomers over the man's shoulder, both of them naked and no sheet to be found. The woman hid behind the man, sideways on the bed.

"Is that—His Holiness?" gasped the man.

"Yes," Judas responded.

"And He needs to rest here," Maria added.

"Is the battle won?" called the woman, her tussled hair fallen over her shoulders.

Nóra stepped closer at the urging of Judas, bringing the torch up.

"Prince Giorgio!" Judas exclaimed. "Countess Natália!"

"Please understand," begged the prince. "We-we were hiding from the uh . . . those attackers. And, umm, as we waited for the horn of the all-clear, we also found—we found some—"

"Some way to pass the time," the countess spoke in a darker voice, sounding not at all ashamed.

"We care not, Your Majesties, what actions you've taken," said Judas, lowering The Lord onto the bed beside them. "We care only that you help us deliver His Holiness to a safe casket as quickly as possible. Is there a casket in one of these salons? Do you know? For vampirian guests?"

The prince raised his hand as though he was about to point, then paused. The representative from Milan, Prince Giorgio of the House of Raguzza, had governed well, Judas recalled overhearing. Yet in bed, he fumbled around like a dead fish. Rumors. His handsome face did not bear out his prowess in amorous situations—apparently. He saw the countess frowning at the prince.

"I saw one in the next room," said the countess. "Difficult to be playful in a casket."

Countess Natália Gál was head of some industrial complex Judas had forgotten, yet she appeared as ravishing as any woman could, dark hair and dark eyes, pale skin, and a body he would die again for. She turned modest at their arrival, held her arm across her breasts as she sought her black formal gown. She had appeared so elegant in the council hall.

Maria saw an open bottle of wine, a deep red shade, and two crystal goblets on one nightstand, borrowed from the centennial celebration days before.

"Give him more wine," Maria called, "to dull the pain." She grabbed the bottle and a goblet and poured.

"Help me straighten His body," asked Judas of the prince. "Careful. There's an arrow."

He held the torch closer. The arrow's shaft had broken, doubtless as they jostled His Holiness down the stairwell. Barely any of the end of that shaft now showed outside of the flesh, the other portion lost in the darkness. He could not determine how much of it had slid further into the chest of his lord and master.

"Your Holiness," Judas called, mouth to ear, "can you hear me?"

The Lord stirred but did not speak.

"How does it feel? Has it gone very far into you? Have you strength enough to travel?"

"To travel?" begged Maria, kneeling beside the bed to look. She held up the goblet. "Here, My Love. Drink this. It is pure wine yet it will help dull the pain."

She lifted the goblet to his lips and he opened his mouth to receive the liquid, as smooth as silk down his throat.

"The Bordeaux is old," He mumbled, then waved for more. Maria refilled the goblet and helped him drink.

The amorous couple regained their clothing, stood against the bed to study The Lord.

"We must get him out of the palace," said the prince. "To a safe place, perhaps in the countryside. Where he might recover. Otherwise, these brigands will surely cut him to pieces."

"And us, as well," the countess added.

Maria set down the empty goblet as The Lord expelled a long sigh as though it were his final breath. Maria pressed her hand to his cheek, tugged his beard lovingly.

"There is another palace—actually a dreadful old place he showed me years ago." Maria stood up, pondered a moment. "More of a castle, really. Not much of one, I would say. It was in ruins when he showed it to me, yet we made it stand for a few weeks as our honeymoon suite."

"Where is it? How far?" Judas pressed.

"You actually wedded?" asked the countess.

"Oh, perhaps five days' ride by carriage," replied Maria, ignoring the countess. "All I remember was it took only a single day in the great electronic carriage which took us there. A great automobile. My Lord directed it himself. *Oui*, I said it was long ago."

"Fair enough," Judas responded, poking at the wound. "We can get away using a vorse carriage. If we can get to the stables."

"I remember it was south of the Plitvice Lakes—"

The Lord moaned. "More wine . . . ."

"Is it the final breath?" asked the prince, nonplussed, leaning over.

"There is no more, My Love," responded Maria, staring across at the empty bottle on the nightstand.

"Too much wine is not good for vampirian bodies," the countess cautioned, flicking her hand at The Lord.

"His Holiness wishes it," said Maria. "So I shall give Him as He wishes. My Lord knows what is best. He has a plan, He told me, and in all things does He know what is best."

"So be it. He has many more years of death remaining," said the countess with her dark, raspy breath. "Once you pass by your warm life-span, say, one-hundred-twenty years, everything is much simpler. In fact, people start to admire you, respect you—"

"We need a physician," Judas grumbled, anxiously. "His physician likely perished in the fighting. I have no idea where he might be now. I could try to cut out the arrowhead myself. If I had a suitable knife."

"You left your halberd in the suite," Maria noted.

The countess was about to blithely continue sharing her thoughts, but Judas rudely waved her away, his eyes on the girl's agitation.

"There is one," the serving girl spoke up.

"You have a knife?"

"No, sir. I mean a physician."

Judas turned, the torch's light painting his face gold. "You know of a physician? Where? Here?"

She bowed as though Judas was a prince himself. "I do, sir."

"In the palace? Or in the city?"

"The palace, sir."

"Where?"

Nóra frowned. "You will find him locked away."

"Locked where?"

"He is in the dungeon, sir. On the fourth level. Corridor twelve. He is in cell fifty-five." A tear popped and ran down her cheek which Judas could see in the torch light. No doubt Nóra was still a bloodling. "He is my father."

"Your father?" laughed the countess, eyebrows raised.

"Yes, Milady."

The countess crossed her arms over her bosom. "How did your father find his way into a dungeon cell?"

Nóra bowed her head. "My father displeased His Holiness."

"Oh! For what act?"

Judas waved the conversation away. "Now it does not matter. Look at His stillness. I suspect the arrowhead was silver. A vampire cannot endure much more. We need your father to removed the arrow and save His Holiness."

"The dungeon entrance is on the next level below us," the countess offered. "Shall I show you?"

Judas stared at her. "Madame, how should you know that?"

She flicked her hand as though wielding a long cigarette holder.

"I am in charge of the prisons. For the entire empire. Did you not know? Not my preferred situation, surely. I am following after my late husband, Nikolasz, who was also in charge of the prisons. And that list includes the dungeon of this palace."

"You?" queried Judas.

"My late husband was the Chief Inspector of Budapest, promoted to Director of Prisons by His Holiness. Now it is I who must inspect it from time to time, distasteful as it may be."

"I thought you had some function in the fashion industry," said the prince. "You smell so fine. Like wilted roses."

"Thank you for that," replied the countess.

"If you know it—" Judas started, hesitant to interrupt the nobles.

The prince pressed: "No, I cannot imagine you down there in your elegant attire."

"I do not mingle with them, Giorgio, only look. What fashion does that require?"

"But it's such a vile place, Natália."

"From my last inspection, I believe you will find the dungeon here to be one of the more spotless accommodations for misfits, brigands, and what we used to call prisoners of political ambition. You could eat off the floors, though you likely wouldn't want to. Much blood has been spilled on them—"

"Enough of this chatter," Judas exclaimed with a shake of his head. "Pardons, Your Majesty, Madame. I am responsible for His Holiness and His health. We must make our way quickly." He glared straight at the countess. "Madame, would you help me find this physician there? Your knowledge would be most advantageous."

"I suppose I should help," she said with a dry chuckle at the prince. "Our Holiness here may repay us with kindness at a later date."

"Then I should help, as well," said the prince.

"Let us all help!" said Judas. He pointed at Maria and Nóra. "You stay here with His Holiness." Judas glared at the prince. "You should stay, as well, Your Highness, so there's a man present. In the case of attackers. And . . . if he worsens, you can—"

"Attend him?" asked the prince, slavishly. "Am I a servant?"

"Yes, attend him." Judas regarded Maria. "If His Holiness worsens, He will likely wish to have you at his side, Milady." He turned to the countess. "Let us go find this physician." To Nóra: "The location once more?"

"Level four, corridor twelve, cell fifty-five."

"I had no idea there were so many lodged beneath the palace." He shook his head. "My duties have always been above ground."

"Then you are to be commended," said the prince.

"I serve His Holiness."

"Has the fighting ceased? I dare not get my gown torn," whined the countess. "Or, dare I say, stained by any subling's blood." She slipped on her formal shoes bearing sharp heels and a red rose decoration over the toes. "All right, then. To the dungeons, my good fellow!"

℞

The countess led the way, pinching her gown at the thigh to hold the hem off the floor. The slit in the dress showed her white leg with every step, catching the chamberlain's eyes. The stiletto heels clicked against the stone floor as they walked, as quickly as they could yet with an ear to lessening the sound. Judas's boots clomped easily over the stone.

"Here," the countess gestured.

The large wooden door with metal braces did not have the bold appearance of the entrance to such an extensive underground complex he expected. Nor were there guards outside the doors. Perhaps they had fled during the riot.

Judas grabbed the iron ring affixed to the door and pulled with all his might. It moved a little.

"I've always believed male vamps were stronger than the pre-dead," sneered the countess.

Judas frowned. "I've been schlepping His Holiness on my shoulder for a kilometer of staircase. I'm tired and sore."

"Yet you serve Him. Excellent." She stared at him in the torch light. "You need a boost?" She held out her bare arm, marked by a dozen sets of teeth indentations.

"I thank you, Madame." He was embarrassed, noting the difference in rank between them. "I can go on."

"If you feel too weak, let me give you a boost."

Judas nodded his agreement. He tried the door again and moved it sufficiently they could slip through one at a time. From the other side, he pulled the door closed again by pulling on another huge iron ring.

"Well-done, sir. You've earned your stay today," said the countess.

"I serve His Holiness," Judas reminded her.

"Of course, you do," the countess mugged.

The entrance foyer gathered the twelve corridors like the hub of a great wheel, subtly lit at irregular intervals by electric lighting, run by turbines somewhere manned by slaves stepping on geared panels. A few guards milled about the entrance while other guards strolled down the long lines, checking a cell here or there, clanging a baton against the iron bars when necessary to rouse an inmate.

A stout fellow in blue cassock and red sash turned and saw them.

"Countess Natália—Madame!" cried the portly warden, startled by the intrusion. His hand quickly swept back his unruly straw hair. "Is it time for the inspection again? So soon?"

"Not yet time," said the countess. "Another matter. A prisoner here is required above."

"Have you the order?" He held out his pudgy hand.

The countess shook her head. "There isn't time."

"But I must—"

"There's fighting in the palace. There are wounded guardsmen. The imperial physician is among the dead. Likely so. You have a physician down here, I've learned. We need him."

"Fighting above?" He looked frightened. "We heard some shouting, is all. Is it safe?"

"Not yet. Well, mostly. I'm not sure." She waved her hand at the warden then down the corridor. "Lead us to him."

"Do you have a number?" asked the warden.

"He is on level four, corridor five, cell fifty-five," Judas spoke up.

"Corridor twelve, my d*ah*ling."

"Oh, yes, correct."

"And you call yourself a bailiff."

"I was never down here, Madame." He puzzled at her. "How did you know I used to be a bailiff in the main keep?"

"Your mind is easy to read. You wish you bore your precious halberd. A symbol of your prowess, your . . . manhood. You feel like a poor eunuch without it." She turned to the warden. "Give him one of yours. I will see that your bailiff receives a bigger and better staff to bear."

"You are gracious," Judas said to the countess. To the warden: "We are the only callers you'll receive today, I suspect. Tomorrow you will have your new halberd."

"As you command, Madame."

The warden snatched away the halberd of the next bailiff, handing it over to Judas, whose strong hands wrapped around its firm shaft like he had never left his own weapon up in the imperial suite.

"What shall I use when callers come calling?" asked the guard.

"Nothing," answered the warden. "Your brethren will protect you."

"Satisfied?" asked the countess of Judas.

"Yes. Thank you." He took the halberd, laid it in the crook of his elbow, hand on his belt buckle.

"Now, lead us on," commanded the countess.

The warden led the countess, appearing out of place in her elegant black evening gown and stiletto heels, with the emperor's newest chamberlain in the black and red cassock uniform of his office. They proceeded down the levels on a manually operated platform, then down the long corridor numbered twelve.

As they passed, prisoners banged on the bars, shouting at them to be freed, some daring to address the countess directly, rudely, which caused Judas to strike at them with the butt end of the halberd, and in one instance the blade end, removing a groping hand. Other cells had occupants too old, too infirm, or too insane to make much commotion.

The countess seemed undeterred, amused at the loathsome population housed below the surface.

"It is good I only need inspect this place twice a year," she muttered coolly to Judas as they approached cell fifty-five.

The warden halted and peered inside the cell. "Prisoner! Stand! You are called forth."

Out from the darkness shuffled an old man, wearing a torn, dirty smock. As he came close to the bars, the torch light illuminated his wrinkled face and stringy gray hair. He smiled stupidly, and a nearly toothless mouth greeted the guests.

"What is your name?" asked the warden. He gave a glance to the countess with a grin, then regarded the prisoner. "Do you know it?"

"I am three seven eighteen fifty-six eleven zero two, sir," the man mumbled confidently.

"No, your surface name, old man. What is it?"

"I was László Szilágyi. I think." He coughed up some phlegm which ran down his chin. He did not wipe it away. "At your service."

"This is the man you seek?" asked the warden.

"Are you a physician?" asked the countess directly.

"I once was, yes."

"Can you perform surgery now? Or have your skills waned?"

"What need you for me to do?"

"Remove an arrowhead." said the countess. "It is silver."

"From a chest wound," Judas added. "It's deep."

"I can do that." He spit up some gray gruel which dropped on the floor at his feet. He wiped his mouth with his sleeve. "If I had a knife. Do you have a knife?"

The countess turned to Judas, lowered her voice. "Is this the one you want? Surely you could do as well removing it."

"It is His Holiness," said Judas, nervous, shifting the halberd in his hands. "What manner of death awaits me if I should fail?"

"Then do not fail," snapped the countess.

"Perhaps, you are correct, Madame." He studied the prisoner. "If he were cleaned up, we might have a better impression."

"How much time for that?" she asked the warden.

Judas grunted. "We do not have such time."

"It would be quick," the warden responded, scratching his cheek. "A dunking, soap and scrub, then a fresh robe."

"Prisoner, how long have you been here?" asked the countess.

A ragged grin crackled over the old man's forlorn face.

"I displeased His Monstrosity nine years, three months, four days ago," he spoke, then paused, eyes rolled up as he pondered. "I cannot count the hours since I know not the time in this place. They took my clock."

"He seems lucid," said the countess. With Judas' nod, she turned to the warden. "How long to clean and dress him properly?"

"Not long, Madame. However, I cannot allow his release without proper documentation."

"Documentation, *dahling*? Don't be silly." She stepped up to him, her red lips smudging against his cheek. "I am certain there is some alternative process. And we shall return him when the task is done. There is no paperwork needed to *borrow* a prisoner, I am certain. But we must hurry."

"As you say, Madame." The warden blushed. "I shall bring him up to the entrance in half an hour."

"Is that your best time?" asked Judas.

"It is likely the minimum time if you want him clean—"

"Fine," snapped the countess. "It shall have to do."

The warden collected four guards and opened the cell. Two guards removed the prisoner, grasping him by his arms. The prisoner tripped as they dragged him out of the cell. His frail arms bent back awkwardly but he did not cry out. The guards picked him up and continued.

The group headed down the corridor as other prisoners cried out to also be freed. The warden snarled at them, saying they had nothing of worth to be freed for. Judas had to slap his halberd at a few grasping hands as they traversed the corridor.

The countess and Judas trailed them, holding back so the guards' and their prisoner's scent would not reach them. The countess covered her face with one hand. She paused, letting the others proceed. Finally the correct interval was achieved and she urged Judas to go ahead.

"You may exit the ranks, Countess," said the warden at the end of the corridor. "Return to the entrance, if you please. We will bring the prisoner to you as soon as we can. You must not linger down here. It's bad for one's health."

The countess gave a nod, pursing her lips, and turned away from the warden as though he was also unhealthy.

Judas gestured for her to go ahead and she took a step onto the lift.

"You do not approve of me, do you?" asked the countess as they began the ascent to the first level, the wooden platform raised by two beefy rope pullers in loincloths who drew on the ropes hand over hand.

"It is not for me to approve or disapprove of anything about Your Majesty's words or deeds."

She smacked her lips deliciously. "'Your Majesty'! Charming. You wouldn't know it to gaze upon me but I'm as low-born as you. Do not tell this to Prince Giorgio. Yes, a milliner's daughter. Until I married the Count. I let him drink from me and he was hooked. A few nights of gritting my teeth and bearing his lust and I am now worth millions. Except I must visit the dreadful dungeon once in a while. To keep up the appearance of doing something."

"Then congratulations must be in order, Countess." Judas spoke in a serious tone but she laughed anyway.

"Ah hah! Now you disapprove of me! I hear it in your voice. I knew you would. It is easy for the females to do well post-bite. Too many men dislike being subservient to a mistress. Do they not know it is part and parcel of a new existence? and requires sacrifice?"

"His Holiness remarked on th—"

"And you too have risen in a short time to your present position. You are to be commended."

"I bear some luck, it seems. Moreover, His Holiness believes I bring Him luck, too."

"Luck is only being in a good position with good timing."

"I have always believed it."

She tilted her head, narrowed her eyes. "What then is your history, chamberlain? A comely lass snipped at thee? Or did you go the way of disease, sloth, and poor blood?"

He shrugged, fingered the shaft of the halberd.

"None to tell?" The countess tapped his arm.

"I have no such story. Not as grand as yours, Countess. As a boy I dreamed of wearing a uniform and wielding a sword, firing a bombard in His Majesty's service. Helping to expand the old Federation. It is not so unusual for a boy, eh?"

She swept her hand around as though waving a wand. "Perfectly. And then? What changed you?"

Judas smiled, unable to hide a secret. "Everyone was transforming. It was an unwritten rule in the regiment. If we longed for promotion, we needed to become vampirian. One furlough, some of us went to a local inn for a feast and some bedding."

"Ah! The bedding. Classic. And she bit you."

"Yes," he said curtly. "That is all I need say."

"Do you remember her? Dream of her, this blood-wife?"

"I cannot recall her face. Older than me, I'm sure. Only someone's mother or wife, making money."

She feigned a kiss. "What a shame!"

"Yes, there is shame in . . . in getting the infection."

"Yet it makes us stronger, cleverer, and more . . . affectatious." The countess looked away, seeming to recall some memory. "Ah, to be young again and full of someone else's blood!" She smiled to herself. "It is a type of infection, isn't it? Yet another sexual transmission. I have known those who suffered greatly from it, never recovered into this long-existing form. And others who . . . shall we say have vampirism in their blood and cannot help themselves."

He shifted the halberd to his other arm. "A poor pun, Madame."

"I'm speaking of your employer."

Judas glared hard at her, feeling an insult upon him. "His Holiness bears the ancient line, I've heard."

"We have all heard. It is the reason for his monstrous nature." She spun around, dancing. "It is the reason so many wish to stop him, end his rule. I shouldn't be telling you this, of course."

"Then do not tell me—"

"And now?" she asked, her dancing coming to a halt. "Have you a vampirian brood of your own?"

He lowered his gaze. "Once I had a wife, two daughters, a young son. It was long before the bite."

"Yes . . . ." She smiled, as though remembering a similar situation for herself, a dream perhaps. "And now?"

"All gone. Dead." His grip on the halberd tightened. "In Moldavia, my home. Attacked by Russians—the army of Maxim Azov, when he invaded the Federation back in 'twenty-eight. They . . . butchered my family." He sucked in a breath. "I wasn't there. No, I was here to defend the city. I was here at this palace, a corporal in the west wing regiment. I learned of their deaths weeks later."

The countess lay her hand on his arm. "I am sorry. It was a great loss. A terrible time for us. You must be pleased now that Europa has driven back the Russians, taken their land."

"I am." He ground his teeth and blood came to wet his lips. "It was seventy years ago. I can scarce recall now. Seventy years a vampire in the service of His Holiness." He shook his head. "I should petition for a retirement. Go to the coast and find a companion to rub my shoulders and back. I have an old wound in my leg that pains me."

"Hold on to that pain," she said with a velvet tongue. "Feeling pain is what keeps us young, chamberlain. Never discount its benefits."

He bowed his head, pondering. "The benefits never cease."

"No, they don't." Raising her hand from his arm, she brushed back her dark hair, tucking a lock behind her ear.

The lift rattled as it slowed to a halt.

"Those big boys need some help pulling, don't you think?" said the countess. She grinned at him. "You're a big, strapping fellow."

Judas frowned. "I did not notice the time—"

"It must be morning outside by now," said the countess with a shake of her hair. "The vampires in the mob will sizzle. The bloodlings will keep up the fight."

Arriving at the first level of the dungeon complex, Judas waved the countess to go ahead of him stepping off the lift. They waited there by the great door, bored guards staring at them from along the corridor. The scent of the place began to overwhelm.

"Where are they?" groaned the countess. "Much longer and I shall require a bath."

"He said at least a half-hour."

"Should've taken him as he was, dirt and all. It's only the holiness to treat, nothing more. Germs will not grow on him. It's the silver that matters. A slow poisoning, a lingering death. The best way to go for a holiness."

Judas seemed shocked. "You should address Him as 'His Holiness'."

"That's for you—if you must." She pursed her lips, released them with a smack, a faux kiss. "Of course to his face I would speak thus. Now, however, he is not in a position of domination. As innocent as a lamb now." She grinned. "Though I have heard . . . ."

The clanking of metal continued as prisoners called for mercy.

Judas turned his back to the line of cells, facing the countess.

"What have you heard?"

She laughed like broken crystal. "It's hardly a secret. The holiness moniker comes not from some divine predilection but, rather, from the rumors of his private member, it's gargantuan size?"

Judas choked. "What? His private member?"

"It is grand, isn't it? Have you seen it?" She let go a tinny, artificial chuckle. "Each day he kills someone, it grows. His entire body grows. He is a good twenty centimeters taller now than the day he died. That is the deal he has made with the devil."

"A deal with the devil? For only that? I doubt it."

"Why do you doubt? The man is full of evil. He cares not for his people. He cares for his empire, certainly, but only as it stands in for him, a symbol, a measure of his . . . his size. The larger the empire, the larger the man. Hah! Boys and their realms!"

Judas swallowed what he was about to say. "I believe he is much set-upon by circumstances," he spoke instead. "He was drunk upstairs and hence took the arrow without being able to defend himself. Also drunk, he talks wildly—honestly—humbly."

"Humbly? Him?" She shook her head, careful to hold her hair in place. "I've never met a more selfish, self-centered, self-loathing person in the entire empire—or in the Russias. He hates his position, yet he relishes it. An odd dichotomy, to be sure, yet—"

"All administrators have their quirks," said Judas like a school boy's recitation. "I do not wish them on myself but it is understandable for His Holiness. He bears it well—"

"You keep using that word: 'holiness'."

"It is His proper title."

"He is just a human—like any of us. A vampire long ago made. His elevation is only because of his birthright or lineage or impure luck. They say he is born of a line which transforms on schedule at fifty years. Bloodling years. That is a mark of the devil's children. A special clan. Others need to be taken in blood to have a chance at prosperity. Not him, not his line. He is of the dirt of this land—the blood of this land. The spilled blood. His and Saint Dracula's lines could be cousins yet they would wrestle to satisfy whose line is the older. Ten-thousand years, I'd guess. It is the reason he can endure his famous punishment so elegantly."

Judas stamped the halberd against the stone floor, testing it. "What punishment is that? A lord such as He has forged an empire from a few minor states. How could that be a punishment?"

"My *dahling*." Her fingers thumped on his shoulder as if warning him she was about to bite. "I once had the chance, years before, to measure him—if you know what I mean. After a conference. We took some time together, enjoyable enough until the union. Such a spear! Split me open. I required stitches, mind you. Now I'm fit only for that poor prince you met. Ah, Giorgio is such a fool! Though he serves well enough—a decent tongue-lasher, if I must say. Oh, he must be larger today—your holiness, I'm referring to. The more people he kills, the more . . . ." She paused to revisit a memory and her smile disappeared. "Now, however, he has the frost touch. Cannot touch a woman lest she die. And that Maria, his mistress, how he wishes he could make love to her. Oh, I see it in his eyes every time she is in the room. To desire so strongly yet be unable to obtain. What a dastardly curse! A gift from his lord and master."

"What could He have done to earn such a curse?" Judas crossed his arms around the halberd's shaft. "If the Most High were so vindictive, he—"

"I heard him say it was because he showed mercy to the French. In the Rhineland. Allowed them to gather their dead and wounded. He should have kept the bodies for his own army, let them dine fully." She chewed her lip. "Yes, yes, that was mercy. And mercy is never rewarded in kind." She gazed up at Judas. "It's a cruel existence for us. He must perform his duties, like all of us, else he is punished, given a sweet curse."

Judas shook his head, disbelieving. "I heard them discuss it, His Holiness and the woman, Maria. The frostbite which women receive from him now . . . . He can only have pleasure with men. He said the men don't die from being with him."

"Oh, that's precious!" She caught herself, not wanting to keep the guards' attention on them. "Of course, there was a time decades ago when it was not a crime. They even celebrated such partnering, waved their special flags. Anyway, when we were together, in the chatting period, he went on and on about his youth, the days before the transformation, how life was so beautiful then. How pathetic! He talked so much about his first lover, too—on and on. A woman from some Asian country. She got the infection from him, he said, yet he found treatment for her and she lost the blood-curse. Where is that stupid prisoner?"

Judas' eyes widened. "Is it true? One can lose it as easily as gain it? How?"

"There is much that is true, dear chamberlain. Yet you seldom hear of it. No, I do not know how he did it. You wish to regress?"

Judas gave a glance down the corridor, checking for the warden and the prisoner. The nearest guard snuck a glance at him and the elegantly dressed countess.

"He said as much to me, too. Showed me her portrait—"

"Yet you were not in bed with him, flesh to flesh, having supped blood together, each from the other."

"No, not that," Judas responded with a grin.

"Then you'll listen to me." She drew a finger along his jawline. "His Holiness, your dear employer, told me of his deal. At the time I did not believe it could be true, yet in the years since, I have come to accept what he said was true. The one he calls the Most High is his lord and master. All that He has achieved has been solely at the behest of this creature which lords over all."

"All? The Empire of Europa?"

She turned her palms up, raised her eyebrows. "Yes, of course—although who can say about the Russias? They are surely as evil as we are. And those Anglos! Terrible people. I wouldn't want to go to the Britain these days. They still hunt vampires, you know, and burn them on public gallows. And then claim they are progressive!"

Judas glanced back at the guards. "So . . . the deal?"

"The devil makes many deals over the millennia, always the same. 'Make me the Most High of your land and I shall give you whatever you most desire.' That is common. I was offered—thought I was offered—this same deal one time, but it was only the wind. The devil's bad air. I fell faint, awoke believing I had been offered this deal. Then nothing happened. Hah! His deal, your lord and master's, is to expand the rule of the Most High over the entire world. And other worlds, I suppose, back when they were trying to send colonists up into the void. If it wasn't a myth. Stories for children. No, that much must be obvious to you. Or me—to all low-born vampires."

"Then what must His Holiness do?"

The countess scoffed like a high-born snob. She tugged at the low collar of her formal evening gown, noting she had not in her rush to clothe herself returned her brassiere to its proper place. The garment likely had fallen on the floor, got kicked under the bed. She adjusted her necklace, found its string frayed, ready to break. Too much drama for one night. She gathered her breath.

"You are a low-born simpleton, are you not?" She tried to add a chuckle, to let him know she was jesting, but the sound of her laugh was dry, hurtful. "He must obey this Most High creature. Utterly and completely. During our episode he spoke of the requirement to kill someone each and every day. He called it a sacrifice. Yes, he must do something evil each day to keep the favor of the Most High. Your lord and master was coy about it as we drank from each other, yet I know it now to be true."

"He does kill often," said Judas, scratching his chin. "And so easily, without thought, it would seem. Before the centennial celebration, he approached me and my friend, grabbed my friend right there by the throat and apparently melted his innards, left him a bag of skin full of liquid. His retinue tossed this 'bag' over the wall, let it splatter on the courtyard below. It happened so quick I could do nothing—"

"What would you have done if you had time to act?" She laughed in a way that irritated him, she saw. "It would have been you he took as the sacrifice." She continued adjusting her gown, the long V neckline stretching lower, making sure her pale bosom caught what light there was. "Now you serve him so dutifully. It's very impressive."

"I meant only—to me—he seems to act without reason, without thought. An angry, mad monster left to his playhouse of fools and victims. If I may say." He quickly looked around. "Everyone is terrified of him."

"That is his strength. His mask, too." She shifted impatiently. "That dirty doctor! What is the delay? No, Judas, your lord and master is a well-used puppet who endures his many punishments with pomp and circumstance. I see suffering behind his eyes—his sex-drunk eyes. A woman can see. He is a pitiful creature. Like the fierce panther who must always kill the innocent fawn to survive. And so people hate him for it, for doing what the panther must do."

"I might have caught a glimpse of that as he lay with his mistress before the rioters broke into the imperial suite. He said—"

"The mistress!" She burst into cursing. "An ancient one, her. Cut at a young age. Still a perfect twenty—while I remain a decent forty forever. And clever, too. A manipulator, her. A conduit—hah! Can you see it in your lord and master? More and more he has the look of that renegade Gergely Azov, the beast who used to rule Budapest seventy years ago: all the coarse black hair, the monstrous stature. Azov fed her, and she fed your lord and master." A sigh slid from her mouth. "The quirks of blood are many. I'm told I have the look of a famous Italian actress. Sophia Lorenzo somebody. Thanks to the blood my late husband traded with me. She gave hers to someone who gave it to someone else who gave it to . . . and so on. Gave it to my husband and he gave his to me. And I became transformed, naturally—or I should say *un*naturally, hmm?" More feigned laughter. "One big family, us—vampirian society."

Judas let out a sigh, eyes closed a moment. "We are one extended family, measured by blood strains."

"That's it." She brushed his arm. "In time we will surely look alike. If we stay dead long enough. Centuries, I would think. And I have only one-hundred-sixty, warm and cold." She studied him, a smirk playing in the corner of her mouth. "You're a big, stout, strong fellow. With sensitive eyes. And a goatee which doesn't seem to fit you. Who do you resemble?"

Before he could answer, a flutter of black wings startled him and he instinctively swatted at the bat circling around the two of them.

"Damn bat!" growled Judas. "Follows us everywhere."

He raised the halberd to try to stab the creature, missed.

"There are many in this palace. It is their home, a refuge from the sunshine. Your holiness boss has put protection on them. All of them. If you kill one of them, you may be placed in here with dirty doctors."

"I wonder how many in this dungeon have such a fate. A misstep, an off-hand remark, a doubting thought revealed . . . ."

"I could check the count." She waved her hand toward the nearest guard. "The ledger is in that first office."

"No, I would rather not know." He rubbed his chin. "Thousands, I would guess by the number of cells. As you say, the warm and the cold. An eternity for many of them. A final solution to some." He regarded the countess. "Could you release them? Is it in your power?"

"Not without permission from the holiness." An awkward chuckle.

"I would want to know what the old physician did to be placed in a cell here." The bat fluttered past his head once more and he swung his halberd at it, missed again. "A mis-snip? Wrong medicine?"

"That, too, could be found in the registry."

He shook his head, glaring down the long corridor, hoping to see the warden and the physician approaching.

"To answer your question," said Judas, "some have said I resemble a certain government official from the late 'twenties. I haven't seen any portrait, yet more than one person remarked I had some resemblance to Niklós Rusza, the henchman of Budapest."

The countess pursed her lips, licked away a bead of blood. "I can see that. He was well-known to us. A hunter of vampires. Yes, the brow ridge, the beady eyes, the broad shoulders. Had you any contact with that family?"

"Perhaps there's a connection. His daughter was . . . he, umm . . . . It was a sinful relationship. The record states he committed suicide by standing in front of a machine gun. After seventy-odd years, who can say? She might have taken up prostitution, her public prospects being ruined. Strange how bloodprints can be passed down a long way before turning vampiric. So the vampire hunter's ancestors became vampires themselves."

He talked further but soon realized the countess was no longer attentive. He twisted the halberd's shaft around in his hands.

"Where are they?" the countess muttered, staring down the long, dim corridor.

⚮

The little bat flittered through the corridor, locating its destination in the darkness, settling upon a narrow perch along the upper paneling which encircled the salon containing The Lord and his helpers.

"We can do it," urged Maria. "We must. There is no telling where they went or if they will return before the wound turns worse."

"Look," Nóra said, pointing to the spot on The Lord's bare chest.

A jagged blue circle had formed around the ugly wound, a gray band which seemed to outline the area of corruption. Within the area the skin had turned blue. The wound itself, where the broken end of the arrow shaft still protruded, was bloodless and now dark gray.

"*Mon Dieu!*" said Maria. "It will spread and take him from us. If we can get him into the casket . . . ."

"I could possibly bear his weight that far, I think," said the prince. He leaned down over The Lord, examining the wound. "I've seen such an affliction once before. The arrowhead must be made of silver. If so, that will poison him, make him turn to stone in time. I've seen that happen once to a man I knew. Lost a duel. Got cut with a silver blade. It took a couple months for him to calcify completely."

Maria gasped. "Is there a way to reverse the damage?"

"Not for silver. Its corruption is permanent in vampires. Even if the injury is not severe, the silver will corrupt. I've known some who lingered weeks before they succumbed to the poison. They stiffened gradually and finally they were like statues."

"Then we must hurry!" She threw The Lord's garments over His body, making Him more streamlined on the bed. She pointed to His feet. "Let us remove His boots. That will lighten the burden."

Nóra took it as a command and moved to the end of the bed. She reached to unbuckle The Lord's boots. She tugged hard on one and felt it slip loose. The other was tighter. As the leather pulled away from the

99

skin, a vile odor leaked out and she turned her face aside. She kept pulling on the first boot and got it to come free. The bare foot was blue-green, moldy. The toes possessed claws like a wolf—yet two toes were absent. Unlike the skin of his chest, which was dry, flaky, and rash-covered, the skin of the foot was moist and mealy, a gangrenous mass she could not endure.

Jumping up, Nóra cried out: "It's horrible!"

Maria saw the cause of her distress. "Yes, the corruption has gotten to His feet. It is His weakness. The bite of rabid wolves lingers. I shall remove the other boot. You tend to His belt and trousers."

Nóra held her shock. "His trousers, Milady?"

"Yes, dear." Maria addressed the situation: "We must remove His clothing, else there is no benefit to being in the casket. The soil must embrace His flesh. Go on now. Open His trousers. We must serve Him. It is our duty. Close your eyes, if you must."

Nóra's fingers shook as she touched His belt, slipping free the end from the buckle, going next to the lacing at the front of the trousers. The lacing had been half undone when He was struck by the arrow. Thick black hair sprouted through the laces. She gazed upon His face, checking for any sign He might notice her attention and react to it. Yet The Lord seemed asleep, or fallen into a trance from the effects of the wound. Or from going so long without blood. She regarded her arms, the marks where the tubes were inserted—

"Hurry!" called Maria, getting the second boot off and wrinkling her nose at the odor. "We must hurry."

Nóra tugged on the trousers, found them hugging His muscular form, thighs like tree trunks, the trousers like rough bark. Maria slid up the bed next to the girl. Working together the women wiggled the trousers down over His hips, rolling Him onto one side then down and onto the other side. The leather resisted. Maria called the prince to help but he fumbled an excuse and stood beside the bed observing.

"Help us or His Holiness will not be giving you any favor," snapped Maria.

"Oh, where are they?" the prince grunted as he took hold of the cuffs of the trousers, down near the rotting feet with the odor of death. Face turned away, he tugged a little as he continued moaning for his companion to reappear so he might be relieved of the distasteful duty. "I shouldn't be observing His naked body. It is not proper."

"Someone must help," said Maria, trying to slip the trousers down His thick legs. "Close your eyes, if you cannot withstand the sight of His private area."

"I'd rather attempt to extract the arrowhead myself than perform this grueling exercise."

"You're a prince," Maria barked. "Take charge. Act for the benefit of your lord and master."

"I am. I offered to carry Him—help to carry Him—to the casket."

"It will take all of us." She glanced about the salon. "Get a blanket and spread it on the floor. We shall lay Him upon it and pull Him to the next salon."

The plan was set and soon the trio had stripped The Lord of the last vestiges of his office. A golden necklace, an upside-down cross bearing a horned figure, remained around his thick neck, hidden by his black beard. With effort, the prince took hold of The Lord's ankles and, despite the slimy, putrid flesh, jerked the legs toward the end of the bed. His grip left red handprints on The Lord's white flesh which were slow to fade. The women held up His shoulders. The bedsheet dragged with Him as they pulled him down the length of the bed. The prince worked his hands up to the knees as they slid The Lord off the end of the bed. The Lord hit hard on the blanket, on the floor, His back slamming against the end of the bed, His head thrown against the mattress.

"So sorry, My Love!" Maria exclaimed.

"Apologies, Your Holiness," the prince quickly added.

With further jerks of the legs and arms, they got Him flat on the blanket on the floor.

Maria directed her companions to wrap the ends of the blanket around the legs and over the feet. A sheet was placed beneath His head and shoulders to keep His body off the floor itself. A pillow from the bed was set over His private area.

Nóra gave a sigh of relief.

"Never seen that before?" the prince asked her.

She shook her head vigorously.

Together they pulled The Lord, splayed on His magic carpet, out of the salon, into the corridor, and down to the next set of doors.

"This one, she said." Maria looked back at the prince. "Right?"

"Yes, this salon has no bed, only a casket," he confirmed.

They pushed the doors open and dragged their package into the room. Nóra turned on the gas lamps and stoked them. The room was identical to the previous salon but the bed had been replaced with an ornate casket worthy of a high-ranking visitor. The lid was askew.

The prince helped the women lift the lid and set it against the wall.

Maria gazed within. It was empty of both a body and any contents such as fresh soil, like the Louisiana bayou dirt her lover enjoyed for maximum restoration.

"Here," she said, motioning with her hands. "Let's get Him into this casket and I shall find some dirt. There must be a stash of it nearby for the guests."

The prince wrapped his arms around The Lord's shoulders, roughly threading his slender arms under His well-muscled arms, clenching his hands across His chest. The prince lifted up the heavy torso, grimacing with the effort, and set Him against the casket's wide lacquered edge. The two women raised His awful bluish feet, bent His legs over the edge and into the casket. The body rested precariously on the edge of the casket as the three rested a moment. Then all three raised His broad hips and buttocks and dropped Him unceremoniously into the casket—harder than they would have liked. The Lord was more on His side than on His back.

"So sorry again," Maria cooed to Him. "You're a big man, My Love."

The Lord stirred at the clumsy treatment, mumbling something about pain, about a dark dream, and a bat that would not leave Him alone. He absently swatted the air.

"My Love," Maria whispered, her lips close to His face, "be calm, for we are mending you. A surgeon is on the way here to remove the silver arrowhead. Then you shall recover in time and rule your empire once more."

"Hmm-Mmmm," moaned The Lord.

"You're safe in a casket now, Your Holiness," announced the prince, breathing hard from his effort. "Let us pray you recover. And whenever you do, please remember Prince Giorgio and that I helped you in your hour of need. That's Giorgio Raguzza, Governor of Milan. Your favorite city after Budapest. I shall need some favors, I suspect. After all, it's been a frightful night."

"The fighting must have ended," said Maria, pausing to listen. The noise they had made in their effort had echoed in the corridor. Silence had returned to the underground.

Nóra scratched at her nearly hairless scalp, knocking free some of the flaky skin. "It's probably morning now—outside."

"The night is eternal," chanted the prince, bearing a twisted grin. Shadows from the gas lamps made him seem enormous. He stared at the girl—in a way that made her uncomfortable, he noticed.

Nóra helped straighten The Lord's body within the confines of the casket, tugging this way and that, pushing his legs and arranging his mighty arms along his sides, fitting in the great dimensions of His Holiness.

In repose, The Lord appeared almost cherubic, an innocent victim of circumstance, awaiting God's dispensation.

"His Holiness seems at peace," Nóra whispered as she scratched along her arm.

"At peace, yes," the prince confirmed. "After so many years of work building the empire. He deserves to rest now. Many think so."

"There is more to do," Maria countered. She gazed down upon His expressionless face, touching His unruly beard.

"Our fate could be sealed at this moment," the prince spoke after an awkward silence. "Either He remembers what we have done for Him and either rewards or punishes us, or He dies—and others reward us or punish us. There is no certain outcome—"

"I shall look in the cabinets of the other salons," Maria announced, stepping back from the casket and brushing off her dress. She regarded herself. "A dress does not matter. I shall not need this garment for any other night if My Love does not continue." She regarded the others, as though confirming her plan with them. "*Pardonnez-moi.*"

And she broke away from them, hurrying from the salon, her dress swishing around her legs.

Left alone with the silent emperor, the prince stared over the top of the casket at the serving girl. Nóra lowered her eyes.

"You're a frightful one," he grumbled. "So poor in health, even for a vampire. Have you any blood remaining in you? I pity you. Were you bitten by someone of low birth? Ghastly scalp you have there." He looked away to make his point.

"I am not vampirian, sir."

"But I thought . . . . As ugly as your appearance may be, I thought surely you must have the disease. No?"

Nóra pouted, her cheeks burning white.

"Well, then . . . ."

"His Holiness takes from me as He needs. His Holiness needs much new blood in a day."

The prince laughed. "So you're his cow, eh? He milks you daily? Or should I say, 'bleeds you'? No wonder you're sickly. He must be about finished with you. You're almost drained."

She sniffled back tears. "It wasn't my choice, Your Majesty."

"Never is for your kind," said the prince with a haughty chuckle. "I've seen your kind before. A young girl, poor and undefended, alone in the countryside, gets a chance to serve—"

The Lord let out a groan, as though suddenly shocked with pain, and Nóra turned to examine Him, glad to shift her attention to a new topic.

5

"YOU MOVED HIM?" JUDAS EXCLAIMED as he and the countess returned to the salon with a creepy old man in a white gown and straw sandals following them. He explained their journey to the dungeon and waved the old man forward. Two guards from the dungeon held back, standing at the edge of the shadows, there to be sure the prisoner was returned after his task was completed.

"How is he?" asked the countess, pointing to the casket.

Judas waved the man forward. "László what? Szilágyi? A physician. He claims to be."

"Him? A physician?" the prince said, throwing a hand at the man.

"Father!" cried Nóra, springing up from her tasks and rushing to him. She halted, looking the man over. He had been cleaned up yet his appearance still did not inspire confidence in his hygiene. After a second, she went ahead and hugged him.

He wrapped his white-sleeved arms around her.

"Daughter," László whimpered, teary-eyed, "I feared never seeing you again." They parted and he regarded her. "You seem to have lost some hair."

"Not enough blood in my diet, I suppose." She smiled for the first time since Judas met her. Half her teeth were missing, it seemed.

The old physician patted her shoulders. "We must get you better uh . . . better everything."

Maria barged into the salon, bearing two bags upon her shoulder.

"Look what I found," she called to Judas.

The prince took umbrage at her choice of the chamberlain as the leader of their group and scoffed at her cheerfulness.

Judas set the halberd in the corner and gathered one of the two large bags she was about to drop, much too heavy for a vampire of her lithe figure to bear yet more than many bloodling men could carry.

"Look in the casket," she said proudly, sweeping her hand to it.

"What is that?" He stared into the box. "The smell!"

"This will sustain Him for a while."

His lord and master lay in peace, covered up to the chin with black crumbles of what appeared to be dirt, though not the usual Louisiana bayou soil He imported at great expense.

"I found them down the corridor, in other salons. For those guests who prefer to sleep acasket."

"Manure?" He blanched, turned up his nose.

"It is the only soil we have. With the trade embargo, we cannot get any of the Louisiana bayou soil He prefers. No matter the war, they need to continue selling it. For humanitarian purposes. It is a human right. And vampires are human, too, don't they know? The new and improved kind. Besides, it flushes out into the ocean anyway, unused by anyone. What a waste! It's not as though it goes to the war effort. I hate those Anglo-Americans! So stodgy! Until the war is won, we must rely on locally produced soil. Besides, the nitrogen content is decent. Around three percent, the package says. A bit less than is optimal for Him, but it will keep Him alive for a while."

"You have imagination," Judas said with a chuckle. "Here is the surgeon to remove the arrowhead."

"You see the arrowhead must be silver," Maria explained. "The way the wound turns blue, spreads across his chest. The nightsoil should help halt that."

"Yet it is manure," said Judas, squinting. "His Holiness cannot be covered in manure. It is sacrilegious!" He shook his head. "No, He will blame me. He will kill me for this."

"You have nothing to worry." She touched his arm. "I shall tell him the truth. It was my idea. A way to save Him. In fact, He assures me everything will work out for the best. He always says it: 'for the best'. It is part of His plan. My Lord always has a plan."

"This plan . . . ?"

He took her by the arm over to the corner of the salon, away from the others as they mingled and muttered among themselves.

"What is the next step?" he asked her in a low voice.

She seemed surprised. "Remove the arrowhead."

"Yes, certainly. Then what shall we do?"

She pouted, pinched her eyebrows. "Is the palace clear?"

"I suspect not. We likely need to escape." He glanced back over his shoulder. The others were focused on their own proclivities. "Can we trust them?"

Maria narrowed her eyes. "Can we?"

Judas nodded ever so slightly. "Perhaps. If we must leave this palace, where can we go? We need a place of seclusion. We need to get out without drawing attention."

"I see," she said, nodding. "Can we escape undetected?"

Judas frowned. "We will need a ruse. We can put the casket on a wagon, cover it, and ride like we are a merchant and his wife."

She gave a laugh. "I can play a wife, even a merchant's wife. I was that long ago. Nearly so. I was taken on the day of my wedding, in fact, bitten quickly by *Père* Pierre, who was to officiate our wedding. Then abandoned at the parish cemetery. So I remained cursed forever." She rubbed her eyes yet no tears fell. "It is all forgiven now. As My Lord requires."

"A dreadful tale, Madame." He looked around, avoiding her gaze.

"*Oui*, it was." She regarded him. "Now I am riding with My Love, the Emperor of Europa. Quite an advancement, *n'est pas*?"

"You are to be admired, Madame." He tipped his head toward the casket. "And the others? How will they fit into our plan?"

"Plan . . . ." It seemed as though she had suddenly spied something wonderful in a shop. "You are His protector and I am His mistress. We must go with Him anywhere. You can carry Him with my assistance. We will remove from this palace, seek a hidden location until . . . ."

Judas thumbed behind him. "Do we need that doctor?"

"After he performs the surgery, perhaps not."

"And that girl? To clean up? Or serve Him?"

"No, let her go away with her father."

"And the nobles?"

Maria giggled. "The prince and the countess? I do not trust them. My Lord has spoken ill of them previously. We cannot take too many or we will be noticed and exposed."

Judas dipped his chin. "I agree."

"Will you take the lead in our escape?" Her eyes pleaded. "Please?"

"Yes, Madame." He took a moment to search within himself, trying to forget the regretful days of yore he had let loose while conversing with the countess.

"It is the east gate they broke through. The west gate likely has mobs, as well."

Maria pursed her lips. "The back gate is generally unused. Only for deliveries. No one will be watching it now, even if they have taken the palace for themselves. Yet it may take some effort to unseal it."

"I can do that." He gave his goatee a brush. "I have some experience minding gates."

"You are a blessing to His Holiness." She seemed to bow, recovered.

"As are you, Milady."

They returned to the casket, took their places around its rim with the others, everyone staring into the box at their lord and master in his soil bath. The Lord's face was sullen, frozen in an expression of disdain with a touch of amusement at the corners of his eyes. He seemed close to death, locked in solemn repose—or He had entered His vampiric hibernation of three or more days.

"His Holiness may soon pass into the dream land," Maria noted.

The prince had stepped back, taking up a position beside the two guards, unable to withstand the smell.

"Are we ready now for the surgery?" asked the countess, a little too cheerfully. "Who will be removing the pig shit from the area? Not I, as my hands are much too delicate. Get the maid girl to do it."

"You are a credit to your demure sisterhood," the prince grunted from his stand across the room.

"Be kind, Giorgio. We almost made love, remember."

"And not without difficulty, Madame. Or pleasure."

The countess chuckled. "You have no means of projection, my dear. You should see to an extension. The surgeons of Milan, are they not skilled? Can make you a man again."

"How dare you!" The prince feigned being overtaken with plague, his hands to his face. "My skills lie with my oral apparatus. And you were made to moan, Madame."

"I moaned only to encourage you—"

"I'll do it," Nóra spoke up. Before anyone could object, if they had a mind to, she began scraping back the crumbly nightsoil from over The Lord's chest with her bare hands. "It is my duty to claim the unpleasant tasks. His Holiness employed me when my father was sent away to the dungeon."

"He did?" queried the countess. "What, pray tell, did he do?"

Nóra did not look up as she worked. "He touched the Letter."

"Touched the letter?"

"With dirty hands."

"Ah!" The countess started to laugh but held it back. "What is the Letter?"

"It's a letter, obviously," said the prince. "I've heard of it." He stared at Judas, then over at Maria. "It is a specimen of an older age, a dear treasure. An actual hand-written letter—on paper—from many years before, which His Majesty keeps locked in a special box to preserve it. None may touch it, fewer may read it. He takes it out once a year to read, so I've heard. He goes into seclusion for a week or more. After, he emerges with a glimmer of hope on his face, as though he got a whole set of new ideas."

"Is the letter from the Most High?" asked Maria.

The prince grimaced. "You are closest to Him. Do you not know?"

"He never mentions the Letter to me. I did not know He had such a thing. It must be very precious to Him if He does not allow even me to know of it."

The prince grinned, having the edge on her. "Perhaps you are not so special to Him, after all." He watched her squirm. "For those of His inner circle it is only rumor. I was in a meeting when He mentioned it, thought no one paid attention."

"So not true?"

The prince turned serious, adjusting his collar. "I believe it is true, yet like everyone who hears a rumor, none can prove it true or false.

Perhaps He wishes it to remain a mystery, to keep everyone guessing about it. As though it were a pronouncement from the Most High."

Maria grew more curious, leaning toward the prince. "It is nothing to do with His reign, is it? Or regarding me?"

"A message from the Czarina, perhaps?" said the countess. "About a treaty with the Russias? That would seem important."

"Or *Madame Président* of France," added Maria.

"No, nothing amorous, no love letter would ever be so precious. I'm certain of it." The prince stood tall, regaining his nobility. "His Majesty is not sentimental in that way."

"Oh, He is!" Maria snapped. "My Lord can be quite sentimental."

"When He is drunk," Judas mumbled, then caught himself.

The soil shifted and Nóra fell back, startled.

"The Letter . . . ," spake The Lord from the midst of the dark casket, His voice was the rumbling of igneous rocks in the bowels of a volcano, aching to rise and be spewed forth into a fiery sky.

"What did He speak?" asked the prince.

"He heard you mention the l-e-t-t-e-r," the countess jabbed.

Only The Lord's lips moved as the girl return to cleaning away the nightsoil from His broad chest, exposing the bluish wound. The others huddling around the casket were alarmed that He had spoken. What else might He have heard? Their faces all showed their worries.

"My Love, we mean you always the utmost respect," Maria spoke, leaning down to Him.

"Yes, what she said is true." The countess stood smugly.

"We mean no disrespect," the prince spoke, insincerity in his voice as obvious as an elephant. Maria glared at him. "Your Holiness," he added, half-heartedly.

The soil moved again and Nóra stepped back from the casket.

"The Letter . . . ," His Holiness grumbled. "Sent by . . . my . . . son." His weak breath ceased, as though He had mustered all He had within Him to expel those few words.

They waited.

A demonstrative *harrumph* came, then: "Must . . . have . . . ."

Confused glances all around.

"Your Holiness," Judas dared to speak first, "we had no time as we escaped to retrieve it. I did not know it existed, nor where it might be located. We fled the imperial suite in a rush and are trying to save your existence even now."

"Letter . . . ," sighed THE LORD.

"I can return for it if you instruct me, Your Holiness."

The Lord tried to suck in breath. Maria dug her fingers into his chest as if to help pull in air. Nóra had swept away the dirt crumbs but the skin could not be washed with water, which would burn Him. She tore the hem of her servant's dress, wiped His skin briskly with it.

"If we must . . . flee . . . ." He shoved his elbow against the side of the casket, bracing himself, pushing his head and shoulder upward by a few centimeters. "Must . . . have it."

The Lord's eyes opened, found Judas among the ring of people around the casket. "You . . . go back, Judas, my . . . my friend, and . . . get it." He paused to take three raspy breaths. "In the small cabinet within . . . cedar chest. Adorned . . . with ivory and gold, an Arabian-style box. Inside . . . the parchment . . . rolled . . . leather tube, tied . . . red ribbon."

His Holiness expired then, falling back into the casket, knocking some of the dirt aside, crumbs spilling out, raining onto the floor.

Nóra bent to sweep up the spilled crumbs.

"I must go," said Judas, glancing around the casket at the others.

"You must," insisted Maria, placing her hand over Judas' hand.

"I wouldn't make such a journey," said the prince dryly. "You don't know what state the suite may be in by now, overrun by brigands. You could be set upon, good fellow, or killed outright. And the precious Letter stolen from your hand."

"You wouldn't run into a burning house to save your own mother," sneered the countess.

"My own mother would not be deserving of saving," he snorted back at her. "Let her burn."

"Each day that He does not sacrifice a person, He weakens further," Maria reminded them.

"He killed a few in the suite, didn't He?" asked the prince. "As they burst in. That ought to count, ought to buy Him some time."

"Yet He was drunk," said Maria. "Still may be. Yet He stood before them, bantering with them, chastising them, daring them, protecting us. And they shot Him. Their lord and master! Surely the rabble has exploded into fleshy shards by now. If only He had not been drunk." She seemed to believe she was crying yet no tears ran. She wiped her eyes nevertheless.

"Now the arrow, the silver poisoning Him." Judas looked between The Lord and Maria. "It is hard to know His condition."

"My Love, have you strength to move?" Her fingertip outlined his mouth. "We will save you."

The Lord moved, enough for Maria to notice.

"I will make my way back to the suite, by the same route," Judas explained and Maria looked up at him. "If they found the hidden door, then they might have followed us and now be ready to attack outside this salon. If not, if we got away without detection, then we are safe. Either way, I should check the route. If I can get into the suite, I will look for the treasure His Holiness wants. If I can find it, I will return. If not, or if I encounter any attackers, I may not return. If it is long on time, do what you must and do not wait for me. Take His Holiness to a safe location."

And he was gone, halberd back in his hands, brushing past the two dungeon guards. Their eyes followed him down the dark corridor.

"Now let us see what we can do," spoke the old physician, rubbing his hands as though he had washed them with soap and water even though he had not. There was no water available, they all knew. His hands still had to be covered in dungeon filth. Now he was ready to cut into The Lord, the skin bearing a sheen of nightsoil.

"Think through the steps," Maria cautioned.

"A knife, I beg of you," the old physician called. "Something extra sharp . . . to make our way into the stony heart."

Maria held out her personal dagger, an ornate-handled weapon intended only for defense when attacked. The physician stared at it a moment, then took it up in his hand, manipulating it skillfully between his fingers.

"We told you our need," spoke the countess. "It does not need to be pretty. Remove the arrowhead and stitch up the cut. That is all."

"Have you needle and thread?" asked the physician.

"No, we haven't had time to think through this episode," growled the countess. "If we had bothered to be prepared, we'd have a different physician, too."

"Easy, Madame," said the prince with unusual softness. "Are you for Him or against Him?" He dipped his chin toward The Lord.

"Neither." Her stern eyes shut him up.

"As you say," the prince intoned. "As Countess Natália says. Prince Giorgio is fully with His Holiness. Remember: Prince Giorgio supports His Holiness, while Countess Natália does not."

"You crumb of nightsoil!" the countess growled.

An arm rising over the casket stopped the banter.

"An open wound is a dangerous thing," cooed the old physician, calculating angles with the knife poised.

"There are those," spoke the prince, voice low and measured, "who would benefit from a jagged knife, a rusty blade, an awkward slip of the surgeon's art. And would we not be rewarded?"

The countess regarded the prince. "We need not have any start to conspiracy talk. I wish only to return home. I tire of palace intrigues."

"It is not our arrow," the prince simpered. "It's from the attackers. We have nothing to fear. And yet . . . ."

"And yet, who are these attackers, as you call them?" the countess demanded, crossing her arms. She glanced at the old physician, playing with the knife. "Won't you cut already?"

"They are the rabble of the city, the lowly minions, the peasants!"

"They are the citizens of the empire, come to find justice."

"Justice? What madness do you dream?"

"The dreams of many," she retorted, snatching the knife from the physician's hand. "Enough delay."

"Another peasant girl climbing the palace wall!"

"Giorgio, you used to be rather charming."

The countess wiped the blade on her elegant gown, handed the knife back to the old physician. "Do only what I have told you. Do that, and you and your daughter are free to depart. Take whatever treasure strikes your fancy as you leave. Never return here."

"I agree, ma'am." Chuckling, he accepted the knife, weighed it in his hand, found the balance point and curled his fingers around the wooden handle. "It has a good feel."

"Please be careful," Maria whispered like a prayer.

He lowered his free hand, pressed it against The Lord's chest. The blade hovered a moment then dove into the flesh, which resisted at first. The physician pressed harder and the blade entered.

The Lord lurched.

"Such a small cut," said László. "It's good there is sensation."

"Is there any more wine?" asked Maria desperately. "Something to numb the sensation. Another salon, perhaps?"

"Weren't there a few bottles in our salon, dear?" asked the countess of the prince. "Be a good lover and bring them here, will you?"

The prince grunted, trudging from the room, past the two guards who were becoming weary of standing watch and slumped against the walls as a prince passed by.

"Proceed. He has no need of wine," said the countess.

"There is no blood," Maria announced, staring down.

"For the vampire kin," muttered the physician, "what blood may be within retreats from the surface and collects at the core, forming a sea of security around the heart."

"Please be careful," Maria repeated. "He is my love."

Nodding absently, the physician continued, carefully working the blade back and forth to open a trench across The Lord's chest, half way between the sternum and nipple, His thick black hair hiding the cut. No blood seeped as the physician cut. He moved the knife deeper until he struck something metallic.

"Here it is," mumbled the physician. "Let me fashion more space in which to work."

Nóra served as her father's nurse, dabbing the cutting every few seconds to keep it clean. "Father, will He live?"

"This one has not been living for seventy years," said her father with a creaky chuckle. "Likely he will continue to exist for many more years. If we do nothing."

"What do you mean, nothing?"

"This arrowhead, silver though it be, missed the mark. It ripped through his lung well-enough yet missed the heart." He looked up at his daughter, met her eyes. "I am redirecting it." He gave the knife a twist. "Now."

Nóra gasped. "You do harm upon Him?"

"I do, daughter. As He has done harm upon us." The surgeon turned the knife at an angle and pushed it deeper. A spurt of dark red blood shot out. "Now do you understand?"

The shadows of flapping bat wings made him cringe. The knife fell from his hand, banged against his hip and clattered to the floor. The physician glanced about for the animal.

"Mind you, it's His pet," said Maria.

Nóra pressed her hands to the bleeding cut. Her father tried to jerk her hands away.

"Here we are," sang the prince, four bottles carried in his arms, his hands clasped before his chest. "The finest Hungary can produce, yet never the equal of our Italian vintages!"

"Give me one," said the countess, reaching for a bottle.

The prince set them down on the dresser at the far wall, righted them. He selected one and handed it to the countess. She examined the label, nodding and grinning.

The countess returned to the casket, twisting the cork, working it with her fingers, loosening its grip, then with her thumbs, let it pop.

"There!" she sang with a laugh. "We can celebrate now."

"Celebrate?" asked Maria.

"Why yes, my dear," said the countess, "we celebrate the successful recovery of your lover."

"Oh, yes! We can celebrate that."

"Then let us celebrate!"

At that command, the countess had signaled to the prince to act. He lifted a second bottle and swung it hard at Maria, smashing it over the back of her head. She stumbled but grabbed the edge of the casket as she fell.

"Stop shaking!" cried the physician. "I'm trying to make delicate work here."

Her knee hit the floor but as she steadied herself, head swimming, she saw who had attacked her. Her eyes reddened. A vile hiss erupted from her mouth and the prince cringed, fell back against the wall. He felt his throat tighten, losing his breath. She pulled herself up to her feet and stalked unsteadily toward him, her hands raised and held up before her like knives, fingers as claws, ready to tear him apart.

But another bottle clanged against her head and she dropped.

The prince, defending himself, raised his foot as he cowered. His boot caught Maria's belly and as she dropped the foot flipped her over, onto her back, as she slammed against the floor.

"That was not in the plan," said the prince.

"She's as much a vampire as you or I. What did you expect? She wouldn't fight back?"

"Pour some wine down her throat. If she chokes, keep it down her. The full bottle if you can."

"There," announced the physician. "Done. The arrowhead has been moved into place."

"Father!" cried Nóra, seeing the shadow come up behind them.

"Well done, sir," said the countess, her head held high, her arms out as if inviting an embrace. She reached for the old physician's head, fingers encompassing his face and crown. With a sharp twist, he faced backward, vertebrae snapped. "We thank you for your service."

"No!" shrieked Nóra. "No, no, no, no, no, no," she cried stumbling around the room, her hands raised in defense.

The countess lifted an arm, pointed a taloned finger at the girl. A spark ignited from the fingertip. The girl stood stunned for a second. Then she dropped to her knees and tumbled over onto her face.

"Done." The countess regarded the casket. "As the girl said, His Holiness always has a plan."

"Might I have her now?" asked the prince, eyes bright and tongue wagging. "She's done her part. And I've held back so long now."

"The things I do for you," moaned the countess. She spied the two guards at the edge of the shadows by the doorway. "You! Get a cart to wheel out this casket." She waved them away.

"I shall be quick with her," said the prince.

The countess turned to look for the lid to the casket.

"We must hurry."

"So may I?" begged the prince, eyeing the serving girl.

"That pitiful thing? Leave her be," growled the countess. "We have work to do. Help me get that lid up here."

The prince joined the countess in retrieving the casket's lid, lain against the side wall. With some strain they lifted it over the open box with the silent vampire in repose, the nightsoil the perfect bedding.

"Steady, steady," intoned the countess.

"I know what to do," barked the prince. "And I'll do as I please."

"Easy, boy. Be a good pet."

"I'm not a pet."

The lid fit snuggly, a small recessed flange guiding their effort.

"Good. Almost complete," cooed the countess.

The prince shook off the insults. "The plan now?"

"Certainly a plan. A situation like this does not happen by chance."

"Ah hah! I understand."

"Do you?" She frowned at him. "You are a fool who followed me. That is all. You stepped into something you thought was yours. Listen to me, Giorgio: You are not a part of this maneuver. But thanks for your help."

"You don't see the opportunity here before us?" said the prince. "It is as I suggested earlier. Now it comes to fruition, does it not? With the slip of a small, metal object, it could be me as the Emperor of Europa. And if you, Madame, were to be my gracious bride, then you could be the Empress of Europa—"

"Get the nails," commanded the countess.

"Nails? Where?"

"The drawer of that nightstand."

Suddenly a screech filled the salon as a little bat fluttered about. It swooped down at the prince as he grabbed the pack of nails from the open drawer.

The countess watched the bat thoughtfully.

"Damn bat!" cried the prince, slapping at the creature.

"Wait, don't kill it," warned the countess. "It's bad luck for sixty-six years. If you have that long."

"I hate bats!" He cringed as he brought the nails and a hammer to the casket. "That one in particular."

"Here," said the countess. She cracked the casket lid and nodded towards the gap.

The bat swooped again, attacking the interlopers. As it did so, the countess raised the lid and the prince slapped at the bat, knocking it against the side of the casket. It was stunned. The prince shoved the creature inside, breaking its wing as he did so. The countess dropped the lid shut, sealing in the bat which continued to screech its rage.

"They should make good traveling companions, you think?" She clapped her hands, satisfied. "Now where are those guardsmen with the cart?"

CR

Judas burst into the salon, breathing hard, a streak of blood down his arm, beads of red dripping off his fingertips. Not seeing the casket, he paused to check if he was in the correct salon. He noticed the fallen physician, his head twisted at an odd angle. And the serving girl, Nóra, collapsed in a heap beside the far wall. He leaned the halberd in the corner, rushed to her while still grasping the leather tube he had been sent to retrieve.

"What happened?" he demanded, crouching beside her. Dropping the leather tube at his knee, he grabbed her and held her lithe body in his big arms. "Can you hear me?"

He was aware of his blood staining her dark servant's dress and the pale flesh of her bosom. He tried to wipe it away, apologizing.

She stirred and he held her close, his heart to hers.

"Can you speak?" he asked. "What happened here?"

"She—killed—him," mumbled the girl.

Judas held her away from his chest, regarded her dismally scarred face. "Who did this?"

"Countess—prince—casket—"

She struggled to breathe.

"Where did they go?" Judas demanded.

She opened her eyes, met his. "Away—far—"

He glanced about the salon: empty wine bottles on the nightstand, the crumbles of nightsoil fallen to the floor, the parallel lines of wheels running from where the casket had rested on its stand over to the door and out into the corridor.

He lowered her on the floor and rushed to the door. The dark corridor did not show him much but he guessed they had managed to push the casket somewhere. Of course they were trying to save His Holiness. She had said there was a plan.

"You're bleeding," mumbled the girl, grabbing his arm.

Judas returned his gaze to Nóra. "I am too late."

She pulled herself up slowly, leaning on an elbow, orienting herself.

"Can you tell me what happened?" His gaze was intense and she had to look away. "Where is Lady Maria?"

"She raised her hand," said Nóra barely above a whisper, "struck me with her power. And lightning hit me. My father—"

He turned to the old physician, on his side upon the floor, his back toward Judas. The physician's surprised face was twisted around also toward him, bulges in the neck indicating vertebrae out of place. The man's eyes were open, red like cherries, and blood seeped from his mouth. Judas understood.

"It appears he is dead. I'm sorry for that." He turned back to Nóra. "Who did this?"

"Countess Natália was the one to hurt me." She fought for more breath. "Prince Giorgio, too. He hurt me. They killed my father—"

"I will kill them both," Judas growled.

He helped her sit up, back to the wall, and knelt before her. His examination found no apparent wounds. Except blood stains on the bottom of her dress he took for his own blood falling there. Streaks of dried blood marked her legs, exposed by the tearing of her dress.

"Are you hurt?" asked Judas, pointing to her legs.

Her face reddened yet her scars turned pale. She tried to cry but no tears came. Her hands covered the rip in the fabric. Seeing blood stains there, she suddenly checked herself and discovered her wound.

"Yes," she finally responded. "I was not awake—"

"Damn him!" Judas shook his head, thinking of his family long ago. "Curse them both! I will find them and serve them justice!"

He sat beside her, wrapped his arm around her and she turned her face into his shoulder. She sobbed yet no tears wet his chamberlain cassock. "I should have remained to protect you."

"You had your task," she whimpered.

"I'm a bailiff first of all. I protect my charges."

"His Holiness commanded you to go."

Goatee caked with dried blood, he combed it out with his fingers. "His Holiness . . . is gone. To where?"

"They talked . . . of travel . . . far . . . ."

"I did as His Holiness commanded," Judas spoke, thinking aloud. "Returned to the imperial suite by the same route. They made the suite an orgy of blood, each feeding on the others. A grand mess. I could not see it for the same place, but I found the treasure box He wanted and I retrieved the tube from in it, containing the Letter—as His Holiness commanded. Now He is away." He held up the tube, studying it. "Such a simple thing to be called a treasure . . . ."

"You did your duty," she muttered, shivering against him.

He gave his arm a glance. The sleeve hung in tatters like a woman's imperial ball gown, torn, cut by blade, blood-stained. The blood on his hand had dried but he could shake off a few thickening globs.

"Still there were citizenry running the corridors, knifing anyone in palace garb. I shouted at them to stand down. I told them I was the chamberlain to His Holiness. They listened not, came at me wholly. Madness commanded them. I could not wield the halberd within such a tight space, yet I managed to cut down several of them before a blade came through to me." He shook his arm. "Got me above my elbow. I might need a surgeon to remove it lest it turn blue and fall off." He studied the girl, appearing more lucid now, licking her ragged lips. "If your father lived still."

"He will be dead a long time now," she said, clawing at her face, her nails digging more scars. "As will I." Her fingers moved down to her throat, lingered over the fresh marks there yet afraid to touch them.

"Now stop that, girl," said Judas. "No matter what's happened, there's no need to claw yourself." He pulled her fingers away from her throat, and saw the twin marks of bloodlust there.

"I am now dead," she sobbed.

"Taken in your sleep . . . ."

"Not sleep, sir. She struck me dumb. I could not move yet I could see and feel everything. What he did to me."

Judas pouted, understanding, yet he had no words.

The salon darkened as the gas lamps began to use the last of their fuel, wavering, creating fantastic shadows upon the walls of a room that could serve as a crypt. Time passed without measure, as it did for all vampiric society.

"Too many of our kind hurt themselves," he said at last, "thinking we surely must have done something terrible to deserve this strange fate. Something wrong . . . when it's us who are the victims."

"Everyone is a victim," she mumbled, pressing against him.

Judas shook his head and in the wavering lamplight he seemed like a monster about to pounce. Or an angel come to save.

"Where did they go?" He pondered. "His mistress told of another place, a castle near the Plitvice Lakes. Do you remember? Perhaps they couldn't wait for me. Yes, I said to go on without me if I was delayed. And so they did. I must get this Letter to His Holiness." He breathed in the cool, moldy air, the lingering scent of the nightsoil. "Yet why hurt you? Why kill your father?" He regarded the trail of crumbs leading out the door. "To keep you from revealing their secret."

He stared at the ceiling, saw the outline of a bat in the flickering shadows, for a moment believing it was real.

"Perhaps only His Holiness's pet bat knows the answer."

He looked around the salon. Not seeing any bat, he turned to the girl huddled against him. He stretched over and kissed her forehead.

"You're a poor girl to be employed in an evil venue. How we were mistaken! How we succumbed to the evil we called progress. How we let ourselves be led into such darkness! My family was murdered for this cause. I have been wounded for this maniacal agenda. You have been ravaged at the whims of bat-lovers, and we have nothing else to grasp—nothing, Nóra. There is no love in this place, no healing for this land, nothing left but our ragged souls which have long since fled us. Corpses, mere corpses. Who are we now? What can we do?"

"We are vampires," she mumbled, scratching her throat.

He looked down at the girl, her face turned up to gaze at him.

"Vampires . . . ."

Her eyes darkened, faded red. "Can you care for me now, sir?"

Tightening his arm around the girl, he understood everything.

"Certainly, my dear. You shall be my responsibility now. For as long as it takes to reach the grand ending, I shall care for you. I swear it.

From now you shall be my daughter. My daughter named Nóra."

"Thank you, sir." She hugged him. "Thank you . . . ."

He breathed deeply a while.

"And my name is Joshua. Not Judas."

CR

To: His Excellency, The Emperor of Europa, Budapest

From: The Secretary of International Relations, The Anglo-American Union, London

RE: The Coming Conference & Delegation; arrangements and protocols (The French Contingency Project)

Excellency:

It is with the utmost Honor that I take this opportunity to address Your Highness under such auspicious circumstances; furthermore to allow myself to wish Your Highness the best of all things both here and abroad. It is with great pleasure that we are able to meet to discuss matters of importance to both our constituencies in a civil and just venue. Lisbon is lovely this time of year, a perfect setting.

Please find attached documents pertaining to the Protocols of our team and your team, what our Emissaries have agreed upon thus far. There should be no further changes to the Protocols or else the Conference could become unfruitful.

There is much to discuss with regard to the French question, what we call The French Contingency Project: the division and disposition of the territory formerly known as France. The borders established by our two respective contingents remain acceptable to our side. Members of the French delegation have expressed no impasse. We expect no further changes to the borders and trade arrangements associated with the change of those borders. In brief, all territory of the former French nation shall become annexed into the Empire of Europa with the sole exception of the Department of Brittany, which shall be annexed into the Anglo-American Union. To acknowledge this annexation, a high-ranking representative from Brittany shall take the Oath of Loyalty and offer Himself to publicly receive the Mark of Justice directly from Your Highness.

While we do not advocate Vampiric transformation generally as a political maneuver, we have agreed, as has the representative from Brittany, to this unusual ritual. We accept that what is commonly known as the "bite of domination" has great symbolic value to Your Community. However, I must strongly reiterate that only the One selected representative has agreed to submit to this ritual; no other participants are to be "bitten".

For myself, I remain wholly Human and without Vampiric attributes, a status I enjoy and wish to extend to the end of my natural life. It is the belief of a majority of residents of the Anglo-American Union that a Natural life is preferable, and the most natural means of achieving a successful existence, i.e., one which pleases He who rules in Heaven. To this end, presuming the opportunity some may take to affect an involuntary Vampiric Transformation, my associates and I shall be well-guarded at all times. Do not take these precautions as a show of disrespect. We are both aware of the involuntary nature of Vampiric mania. We wish to avoid any conflicts arising from such spontaneous action.

Furthermore, the Protocols we jointly have established shall serve as the Code of Conduct for the Proceedings. Any change to these Protocols must be agreed by both teams in advance of each side's arrival in Lisbon. Please address, or have your staff address, any situations which may alter the Protocols stated in the accompanying documents. I thank you in advance, Your Highness, for your adherence to these Protocols.

I shall take this opportunity also to express some personal

thoughts. I do not know how vivid is the Vampiric memory, considering the jumble of events across such an extended existence, so I shall not call it impolite to remind Your Highness of a significant date: 8 June 2044. At the time of the scheduled Conference opening ceremony, we shall also observe the 10th anniversary of the date upon which my mother passed away and was taken gently into the arms of God. Your Highness shall recall that my mother is the same as was for a time your wife. You called her Penny. I pray you have not forgotten her, or forgotten to mark the date. Please do something to mark the date of her passing.

As I have stated in previous correspondence, Mom loved you very much, and expressed her love often, although she acknowledged the period of her life in which she felt hate for you. Even after you abandoned us for your European pursuits, she remained steadfast, refusing to marry again. She struggled greatly for several years with the disease she always attributed to you, what she called the Vampire curse. You admitted as much in your short unfinished memoir, which I have read with some discomfort.

After you left us, when I was fifteen, she fell into a long and deep depression. Although she hated that you fled once again – she often mentioned how you used to go here or there on a moment's whim without letting her know where you were going or that you were safe – she understood that you had special duties to perform. She told me often that you were held captive by forces unknown. The spiritual realm seemed but a fantasy to her, yet she accepted that you believed it. She often explained to me that you made certain sacrifices to save her – to save myself, as well. You accepted the necessity to perform certain criminal acts in order to get proper treatment for the Vampire curse, which subsequently removed the disease from her body. For that act, Mother remained throughout her life eternally grateful to you.

Because you have chosen not to return our correspondence, I

would like to tell you now about my life choices. I recall a day when Mother explained how I must always take the righteous path in life lest I turn into an "evil creature" like you. She sent me to Catholic school and I learned everything about the Righteous Path they proposed. I spent years in Asia, in the Chinese provinces of Korea and Thailand, learning more about the Light and the Path of Righteousness as they conceived them. I then attended and graduated from the Harvard University School of Government with the intention of using my knowledge to fight against corruption and evil in the world. I did so as the Hungarian Federation continued to advance east and west, north and south to become a cancer upon your continent.

In my capacity as Secretary of International Relations for both the Estevez and now the Calloway administrations, I believe I am uniquely and perfectly positioned to negotiate with Your Highness. However, you must not take our familial relationship as something which will weaken me or my team or soften our stances on the critical issues. Rather, because of our familial relationship, I must be measurably more aggressive in our debate, more substantive in negotiations, and more strict in the Protocols. Your Highness should not presume to take this declaration as a statement of hatred.

Indeed, I do not hate you. I do not really know you, Father. I would like to know you better, even if it must be from a safe distance. The years are going quickly for us; by now you should have been long dead, like Mom. I shall soon join that realm, and I wish that one of my final efforts in life is to settle these long-standing international disputes. With your Vampiric transformation in 2014, of course, there is no way to ascertain the end of your reign – unless certain forces should work deliberately against you. However, I wish you to live; I wish your existence to continue – to continue efforts toward the common good and beneficial goals which bring prosperity and health to everyone in our world – a world we share, have long shared, and shall share forevermore.

Good day to you, Father. I look forward to greeting you in Lisbon.

I remain, as always, your faithful Son,

Stefan Székely, Jr.

P.S. – Aside from my important governmental duties, I have also managed to marry, and we have four lovely children who I pray remain beyond your reach.

26 May 2054

Part Two

6

THE TANNED, LANKY MAN WIPED SWEAT from his furrowed brow, tipping his cowboy hat back on his head, short brown matted hair sticking out from under the hat.

"Damn, it's a hot one taday," he growled, reluctantly picking up the dirt-encrusted shovel from the flatbed of the truck. He hiked up his jeans, smoothed his sleeveless work shirt, always torn and stained.

"Ain't that da truth," his short, muscular partner snorted, grabbing a pick and pulling it off the flatbed.

"Not a good day ta be diggin. Not. At. All."

"We shoulda started earlier, when it was a li'l bit less baking."

The lanky man put a towel to his neck, wiped, returned it to his hip pocket. "Long drive. We did start early."

"Gonna be a heat warning, I betcha," said the shorter man, waving his ball cap in the air and replacing it on his head, mushing his hair.

"Let's get us started then."

The two men left the rust-scarred truck, parked by the entrance to a vast field of red dirt covered with an endless array of five by ten foot glass panels, side by side, end to end, all parallel to the ground, shining under a blazing sun, reflecting eons of light. The aisle through them was only wide enough for one person to pass. The lanky man led the way, carrying a device in his hand. They went about fifty steps in, boots scuffing the dirt, small clouds of red dust rising with each step.

He halted and raised the device to his face to read the data there. He pushed a button on the screen and a set of numbers flashed by. The numbers recalibrated, locked, and he stared at them, shaking his head. He continued on a few steps, stopped and rechecked their position.

"You sure it's gotta be one goddamn spot?" asked the short guy.

"Them's th' instructions. Gotta be right. Somebody's payin an awful lot to make sure we're at th' right spot."

"Shoot, Bucky, you never been so acc'rate before." With a shirt sleeve swipe of his brow he set down the pick and looked around, the solar panels spreading out as far as he could see in every direction, blinding him. "Out here in the middle of a solar farm? That's crazy."

"That's th' order," Bucky responded, checking the device again.

"Ain't it close 'nuf?"

"Gotta be exactly th' spot."

"What's so import'nt about this spot?" asked the pick bearer.

"Josey, ya know how some people are, gotta make things diff'cult fer folks like us doin th' actual work. And them sittin their cool offices flying their drones checkin on folks actin proper. So if they want it dug out here then we're gonna dig out here. Stop yer bellyaching."

"But Bucky, nobody's gonna know if we're really at the spot."

"I'm gonna know," said Bucky, starting off again.

Twelve more steps and the numbers on the device changed and settled again. All zeros.

"Here."

The aisle was barely wide enough to swing a pick without hitting the glass panel on either side. They had to work carefully, which made it slow going, extending their effort as the sun blazed down.

Josey continued complaining—as usual—and Bucky was beginning to regret hiring the man. But he needed help as he got older. Army pension wasn't enough to live on. Bucky shook his head, full of regrets.

The surface was hard-baked and required the pick to break it up. The dirt underneath was also hard but broke apart more easily. A half-meter down the dirt was softer and a shovel worked well. Little by little the dirt gave way and the hole lengthened and deepened. If only there was space for a backhoe to be brought in, Bucky wished. After a few hours of heavy sweating they began to square the hole, shaping it for the project. Eight feet by five feet, the order stated. And seven-and-a-half feet deep.

"Must be 'n extra large coffin," Josey said with a chuckle. "Maybe some giant inside."

"Don't matter who it is, just keep diggin."

By dusk, late on this summer's evening with a cloudless sky, they had fashioned the hole nearly to spec. They still had some time the next morning to finish it before unloading the box.

"Good 'nuf," Bucky finally announced and Josey gave a cheer.

The two men packed up and drove back to the town of Edmond.

In the morning the two diggers drove by the mortuary to pick up their package. A large casket had arrived with orders to be buried at a particular location. It required GPS tracking to find the exact spot, which happened to be in the middle of one of the largest solar farms in the middle of what used to be called the United States, now designated as the western district of the Anglo-American Union, a broad territory ranging from the British Isles all the way to the Nevada desert, its capital located in Denver. But the place was still called Oklahoma by the people who lived there.

Some folks grumbled about how the government treated them as nothing more than welfare hogs, ignored them except at tax season. Most had left after the drought and the famine. Others left after the plague swept through. A few still remained, more out of laziness than conviction. There was a living to be made minding the solar farms that made power for the huge metropolises on the coasts. And people that served those people who ran the solar farms and the wind farms and the methane factories. A few people managed to raise some livestock or grow some hardy crops but more often than not they failed.

"So why this spot?" Josey asked as they drove out to the solar farm, down the long dirt road with its potholes and ruts, the truck swaying left and then right, the casket on the flatbed shifting back and forth.

"All I get is this used ta be part th' city," Bucky explained, steering around a deep pothole. "Long time ago. Yessiree, had a shoppin' place 'nd ever'thing. Guess they wanted this here coffin ta be put here for, ya know, sentiment reasons." He had the orders folded in his shirt pocket, the exact words to read after they put the casket down into the grave. "I think this person musta lived here's why they want it here."

"Makes sense," Josey said, adding a yawn. "Wish they decided to bury it in winter so it ain't so dang hot."

"Not much difference nowadays 'tween win'er 'nd summer, not since th' Black Storm lifted."

"Yeah, my family can breathe again. Kids getting sick all the time ain't no fun."

Bucky was quiet when Josey expected a response.

"Yeah," he said finally. "Lost my only boy, just a baby, during one of them storms."

Josey shook his head. "Sorry, man, I didn't know."

"No problemo. Years ago."

The truck arrived at the gate by the control shed for the solar farm and the men began preparing for their day. The sun was barely above the horizon, giving enough light that they could find their way through the rows of panels. First, they took a shovel and rake and finished squaring the grave, flattening the dirt floor seven-and-a-half feet down. They measured it again to be sure the extra large casket would fit.

"Yup, inch to spare on all sides."

Usually six strong men, the friends of the deceased, would haul the casket over to the gravesite. Times were difficult after the plague hit. Too many caskets, too few friends. Thankfully, technology provided them with an electronic gurney which unfolded smoothly and rose up to the level of the truck's flatbed.

The men worked the casket off the end of the flatbed directly onto the mechanical gurney, then walked along with it as it rolled through the forest of waist-high solar panels to the gravesite. The tight space made it difficult to position the gurney. Working the controls, Bucky got the gurney turned around but hit the corner of a solar panel, cracking it. Josey laughed that now his pay would go toward repairing the panel.

They set the straps across the hole and offloaded the casket from the gurney with the hoist, balancing it precariously over the deep hole. This was delicate work, but Bucky was a master. He finessed the levers to work the hoist, easing the casket down into the hole, inch by inch, keeping each end of the box level so it would settle in a flat position at the bottom.

Then it stopped. The casket hit an outcrop they hadn't smoothed.

"Bring it up," called Josey, peering into the hole.

Bucky worked the controls again, raising the casket with the hoist until it was flush with the surface. They had to swing the casket to the side, setting it on the ground beside the grave. Bucky jumped down into the hole and cursed as he examined it.

"It's another gyawdamn rock. Or some injun bone."

Whatever it was, it protruded from the side wall. Only a little, but it would prevent the casket from lowering cleanly.

"Awrighty, we got ta dig it out," said Bucky.

"Nobody gonna know if it's straight er not," said Josey.

"I'm gonna know. Beside, if it tilts ever'thing gets shaken up. Not a good way to go, makes'em come haunting ever'body."

"You believe that shit, man?"

"We dig graves. We got ta take some things ser'ously."

Josey suddenly held his nose, like he had been taught in school whenever the Black Storm would blow overhead. But this smell was something different. He squinted, then started to retch.

"What's th' matter with you?" asked Bucky, amused.

"You don't smell it?"

"What?"

"Something really stinky."

Bucky took a whiff. There was something weird in the air. Moldy, or mildew mixed with manure. He glanced around. Normally the only smells out there were the iron of the endless red dirt and maybe some cow farts.

"Yeah, I smell it. Gyawdamn, like somebody died."

Josey laughed, still holding his nose. He pointed to the casket.

"Looks like we done broke th' seal fuckin' with that outcrop," said Bucky, staring at the lid of the casket. "Dang corpse's rotting away inside a there."

The casket sat on the hard ground beside the open grave, its top at the height they could comfortably sit on like a bench. The lid seemed in place but it had been knocked in such a way that the seal had indeed been broken. A crack was enough to let the air outside sneak in and what was inside to leak out. The hot morning sun did not help.

"We got ta get some sealant 'nd fix this before we keep going," said

Bucky. "Why don't ya go back to th' truck 'nd get it?"

"Why me?" asked Josey.

Bucky grinned. "Cuz 'tween you 'nd me, I'm th' old man here."

Josey complained about always having to do the running but then he realized he would be away from the odor, so he was happy to take the walk out to the truck.

As he waited, Bucky squatted then decided he might as well sit on the casket. It was disrespectful, he knew, but he was tired. His knees were tired. He pulled a pack of cannabis, COLORADO HIGH, from his jeans pocket and rolled a reefer, lit it from his clicker, put it to his lips and drew in the smoke. The odor of the weed covered the scent of death leaking from the casket—

He felt a thump under his butt. Not much but something. Just his imagination. He'd been in the business twenty-five years. It was easy to get spooked. He exhaled a stream of smoke after holding it in his lungs a while. Got to relax. This job is getting to me, he thought.

Another thump, right under his leg, at the side of the casket.

"Gawdammit," Bucky snapped, standing. He turned to the casket.

The lid jiggled.

He stared. And as he stared it moved.

The lid shook, raised a fraction of an inch, shifted to the side. A small gap appeared.

Bucky threw down the reefer, stepping back from the casket.

The lid jumped, the gap widening. He could see into the darkness and something was moving inside.

"Now wait jus' a minute here," cried Bucky. "I been off th' booze fer ten year now."

The lid suddenly folded up to the side, like it was on hinges, and stayed upright. The casket lay open, black as coal inside, apparently filled with dirt. No wonder it was so heavy. Good black dirt, rich soil this land had not seen in centuries—

A hand, rising to clasp the rim of the box, still bearing flesh—rotten, moldy flesh, extremely white flesh with deep red swollen veins streaked through it, the bones visible beneath.

"No way," cried Bucky. He shouted for Josey to hurry back, keeping his eyes on the hand twitching on the rim.

The hand pulled up an arm, a shoulder. Then a head appeared, its face a lot more than a decaying skull; it had a face, black whiskers on the chin and jaw, some over the upper lip. The scalp was mostly bald but some long, black hairs trickled down over the eyes—eyes which were dark red and unblinking.

"Hey, now. You leave me alone. I didn't do nothin' ta hurt ya. I'm jus' a grave digger. You got nothin' again' me, mister."

Dead men did not look like that. Dead men didn't move, neither. Didn't climb out of the coffin, like this one was doing: legs up and over the side, caked with the black dirt. A sheaf of dirt spilled over the side of the casket as the body rose—until it sat on the rim of the box, ugly feet pressed against the red dirt of Oklahoma; pale, gnarly hands clasping the rim of the casket, and the broad chest suddenly expanding as it sucked in the hot, dry air into withered lungs. The head turned, the face staring directly at Bucky, whose hands were clasped in hopeful prayer.

"Please don't hurt me, mister. Please don't," he begged, falling on his knees before the deceased. "I got a sickly sister, gotta take care her."

But it seemed the deceased had no plan to attack him. How limber could a body be after being locked up in a box? That depended, Bucky decided.

The deceased slowly stood, testing the strength of its legs, muscles wasted thin but able to stiffen to hold up the body. Its chest had a blue circle in the center and a silvery metallic object protruded from within the circle as the chest continued to heave, inflating and deflating, as the head swiveled around, observing the barren landscape—ignoring him, Bucky was glad.

"The hell you doin'!" screamed Josey, rushing up and swinging the shovel hard at the deceased.

The blade struck the mid-section of the deceased, forcing it over double. But not hurting it—him—whatever it was—apparently.

Josey froze, seeing what effect his attack had. He held the shovel up, ready for another swing as he checked on his partner.

"You okay, man?"

"I—I—I'm okay, but I—I sure don't know how a thing like that is still alive."

"Ain't alive, man." He watched the deceased recovering. "Gotta be one them vampire creatures."

"Vampires? There ain't no vampires in Oklahoma. Too hot 'n dry fer them. Too much sun. Besides—"

The deceased straighten up, standing tall faster than Josey could react, and slapped his moldy hand at the short man, knocking him into the air, sending him flying backwards and crashing on a solar panel, shattering it. Shards of glass cut into the man's back, one protruding out his belly.

Bucky screamed in shock.

"Wait! Wait, man, jus' wait a minute, please, a minute, wait . . . ."

The deceased shook, a kind of spasm like someone loosening tight muscles. Its arms extended outward as if stretching. The head circled back and around on the neck, then in reverse direction. Hands with sagging, loose skin massaged the chest and abdomen. One hand went to the face, seemed to check for flesh tone or injuries. Most of the teeth seemed to be still intact, the creature noted. The other hand plucked the metallic object from its chest, glanced at it a long moment, then dropped it casually to the ground.

Bucky saw that each foot was missing two toes. No bones there, as though they had been cut off. He also noticed, because the deceased was unclothed, unlike most who wore their best suit, the dangling penis was surprisingly unshriveled.

The deceased shook again, knocking off the crumbs of dirt that had filled the casket. Most were not filled with anything but the deceased and possibly some small tokens or mementoes.

"How—?" was all Bucky could utter, stiff with fright.

The creature glared at him, its eyes red and penetrating. Unable to meet those eyes, Bucky turned away, cowering on the ground, glanced back at his co-worker. He knew Josey was dead.

"Wh—"

The creature spoke—a deep gravelly echo.

"Wh—ere?"

Bucky about had a heart attack. "Th-this is Oklahoma."

The creature turned away, apparently surveying the landscape.

"Home . . . ."

"Yes, Ok-la-*homa*," he pronounced carefully. Then he had to catch his breath, still on his knees, afraid to rise. "It's—here's Quail Springs." He remembered the paperwork folded in his shirt pocket, pulled it out, shaking it open. "This here—this paper says this place—what's here— it's 'Barnes and Noble'—whatever that means. I dunno. But—it's here, anyways. This spot right here. It's Barnes and Noble."

The creature actually grinned—with thin, ragged bluish lips and long, dark gray teeth. Pointy teeth. Bucky could see it clearly but he had no idea what it meant.

"It worked," the creature spoke, then was quickly overcome with a coughing fit, dispelling some of the casket's dirt from its mouth.

CR

This time he brought a gun: his grandfather's Colt 45 revolver, passed down through the family. Personal guns had long been outlawed but antiques were still allowed, and with some cleaning and oiling, Bucky could give one shot at a bottle set up on a post of his back fence. He gave only one shot since bullets were hard to come by. He found five more to load into the gun, hoping they would fire when he needed them to. Then he drove back out to the solar farm to confront the deceased again.

The deceased. Funny name. He frowned in the rearview mirror as his truck bounded down the dirt road, red dust cloud trailing behind him. What else to call the strange creature that crawled out of the coffin? A man? Seemed like a man. He couldn't shoot a man. It was like those sasquatch creatures they found over in California, whole families of them in isolated tracks, then couldn't decide if they were more like humans or animals, and then some folks decided they were animals and killed them. But this creature definitely was a man, a human, in fact. Just a dead one.

But was he really dead? He moved around, sure, but that didn't mean he was alive.

"Awrighty now," he called to the thing as he approached the site where the casket still sat beside the open grave, his words acting like an advance team—like the one he'd been on while fighting for the

AAU in Frisia. That was over there in Europa, when he was young. Got wounded and sent home before the really serious horrors began there. "I think I got it figured out."

The creature was sitting on the top of the casket, he saw, its feet flat on the ground, hands at its sides, head held high, still naked and filthy. It had closed the lid while Bucky tended to Josey, extracting him off the broken glass and dragging him out to the truck, driving into town.

"I'ma guessin you got put in there against yer will, see," he spoke as he slowed, stopped at a safe distance, about fifteen feet. "You weren't really dead then, am I right? Then ya woke on up. Ya found yerself in th' box. So nat'rally you done clawed 'nd banged 'nd tried ta get on outta there. Do I gotcha so far?"

The creature seemed to be paying attention, its red eyes focused on him. Its moldy gray skin had paled up, drying out in the heat—Bucky had left it out there the whole day and night—so it was looking more normal, starting to become pinkish. It seemed there was more black hair on its chin and scalp, too.

"I get ya was jus react'ng ta him hittin you with th' shovel." He saw the deep red ugly welt across its mid-section, a serious wound for any normal living person but only a red line on the deceased. "Ya gotta unnerstand, we don't take ta folks climbing outta coffins like ya did. Josey, he jus freaked out, ya might say."

Then its head nodded. Bucky stared: not the wind making it move but a real human-like nod of the head, like it understood what he was saying—every word.

"So ya finally gotcher chance ta get outta there," he summarized.

They stared at each other a long while. Bucky thought of lighting a reefer but didn't, wanting to keep hold of the revolver, wanting to wait to see if it was safe.

"Man, ya sure—" He stopped to wipe sweat out of his eye. "I had helluva time talkin to Josey's mama 'bout what happened. Had ta say it was accident, ya know. What am I gonna tell folks? Th' truth? Man back from th' dead jus off 'nd backhands him into some solar panels? Shee-yit." He shook his head, then reached into his back pocket for the pack of cannabis. "Yep. Had ta call in th' breakage too, 'nd hell they complaining 'bout one fuckin panel get broke. I says ta them I'm just a one-man bidness, got jus' one worker 'nd he got killt on account o' th' coffin swinging over 'nd knocking him on ta that gyawdamn panel—and they didn't believe me. Well, they comin out taday to check on it so . . . whatta we gonna do with ya, huh?"

The creature continued returning his stare, unmoving, as Bucky lit the reefer and toked. He exhaled after a while, let the plume of smoke fill the space between the creature and him.

Then an amazing thing happened.

The deceased raised its boney hand, pointing at Bucky, and curled its finger back toward itself, like it was signaling for Bucky to give him the reefer.

He got up from where he squatted and stepped carefully toward the casket. He extended his arm, holding the reefer pinched between his fingers. Right up to the extended hand of the deceased, and the open fingers. Bucky put the reefer between the fingers and they closed on the reefer. He stepped back and watched the deceased lift its hand to its face, put the reefer up to its withered, blueish lips. And it inhaled the smoke—like a regular human.

"Ain't that some good shee-yit?" Bucky called over.

The deceased exhaled. Turning its hand, it examined the reefer, put it back between its lips and sucked again. Then exhaled slowly, like he had done it all its life—and death.

"Geeyawdamn, I'm sharin a joint with a fuckin corpse," said Bucky, wanting to both laugh and cry. "So how's it? Betcha ain't had one fer a long time, am I right?"

There was a sudden croak, then some sound like the gates of Hell creaking open, a hollow echoing noise.

"Not." The deceased uttered a word. "Too." Another word. Then another: "Bad."

And Bucky about soiled his pants. His hand went to the revolver on his side, holstered to light the reefer. The deceased stood, stretching for the clear blue sky, chest expanding, shoulders squaring. The guy had to be nearly seven feet tall.

"Uh, ya gotta name, mister?" asked Bucky, hand on the gun.

The deceased looked around as if searching for a name on one of the signs telling folks to keep out of this solar farm or they would be prosecuted to the maximum extent of the law. The signs were faded now with the relentless sunshine.

"Name . . . ."

"Least ya unnerstand English. Hmm. Or yer jus' copyin me." It— he—didn't seem to know what he was saying. "Maybe ya forgot yer name being stuck in there fer so long."

The jaw opened, the croak returned: "Ye-ar?"

Bucky grabbed his bowels again. "What year is it? That what you sayin? Shee-yit, its oh-three."

"Three."

"Yessiree, twenty-one-oh-three. Is that 'bout right fer ya?"

The deceased held up three fingers, boney and blue.

"Yup, three. Oh-three is th' year, though it don't hardly matter none from last year or next year. Never changes round here. Nothin changes through th' whole year neither."

"Three. Year—s."

Bucky's eyes widened. "Whadya say?"

"In—" (He thumbed back at the casket.) "—there—three years."

His eyes stayed wide open. His mouth, too.

"Ya been in that there coffin fer three fuckin years? Gyawdamn."

They traded short sentences for another hour, and the deceased's vocabulary grew tremendously, as well as Bucky's confidence that this really was a human being somehow stuffed inside a coffin while not actually being dead. He knew mistakes sometimes were made. More often made long ago than nowadays when the doctors were better at determining true death. During the plague years, lots of people fell into comas and weren't actually dead but got buried anyway. When Bucky got into the business, he usually ran a knife into their gut— which either woke them up or made certain they were dead.

"Well, I can give ya name, if ya like. How 'bout 'Harry'?"

Bucky had to laugh. The deceased was as hairless as a damn mole-rat except for some on his chin. He used to be more hairy, he guessed. There was a meager clump between his legs, a thin patch on his chest. The jagged blue circle on his chest had faded enough that he had to squint to see it. His skin overall was more pale, more true to life.

"Seein's how yer not hairy. I'm kidding. Hey, we gotta get ya some clothes. I don't fancy keep lookin at ya all naked like that."

Bucky shook his head, took a draw on his third reefer, passed it to his new buddy.

"We're gettin . . . kinda wasted . . . ya know?"

Harry nodded. "It's. Some. Good. Shit." The croaks were softening into words, sounding more human.

"I buy th' best I kin pay for," said Bucky. He cocked his head, took a serious look at Harry. "Maybe yer one o' those vampire things we had ta fight in Europa. I spent a year there. Then I got hit in th' back by one of them bombards, shredded my back. Got sent home." He narrowed his eyes. "If'n I didn't know better, I'd surely think ya could be one o' them vampires. You're walkin 'nd talkin 'nd smellin like death—'nd ya got superhuman strength, th' way ya jus up 'nd backhanded Josey about ten feet in th' air. That's what them vampires do. But all th' sunshine out here woulda killed ya already if'n ya were one."

A cloud of red dust caught his attention, billowing in the distance. Miles away across the flat landscape. A pair of vehicles charged down the winding road. Bucky knew who they were: a black sheriff's truck and a big white van from the solar farm folks. Following the road west then south, they would be at the entrance in about fifteen minutes.

"What we gonna do with you, Harry?" Bucky tried to stand, felt it to be difficult. Gravity was sucking again. "There's some old clothes in th' truck, but they gonna be short on ya. If they guess ya came outta that fuckin coffin, no tellin what'll happen. Put ya in some hospital, I guess." He glared at the deceased. "Ya got any folks round here? Should I call somebody?"

Harry grinned—looked like a grin, if you were thinking in human terms. "Thanks."

"I'm Bucky. Bucky Denham. If they ask ya anythin, just nod at me. I'll do th' talkin. Shee-yit, obvious, man. Yew ain't no talker."

They went to the truck, hurried to dress Harry, had him sit in the cab, pretending to be sleeping, Bucky's old Stetson pulled down over Harry's red eyes. Bucky blew some smoke into the cab. Maybe they would not bother Harry, thinking he was out of sorts. It wasn't against the law to be in a dope haze but an employer would frown on it.

141

"Hey, fellas!" called Bucky as the sheriff's truck and the company van pulled up at the gate beside his rusty truck. "They told me you'd be payin a visit taday."

The deputy got out of the black truck, stood with his hands on his hips. Two men exited the van wearing white coveralls with company logo emblazoned over the chest. Bucky never understood how they could keep them so white after working in the red dirt all day. Some New Age fabric, he guessed.

"You Bucky Denham?" asked the sheriff's deputy—HOLMES on his name tag.

"Yessir."

They discussed the problem a minute, then Bucky led them to the gravesite. The company men examined the broken solar panel, took samples of the blood his partner had left. Before he had managed to lift Josey off the shard, the deceased had wiped up the spilled blood and licked it off his fingers. The rest had quickly dried in the hot sun.

They were talking at him, asking too many questions, but all Bucky could think of was Harry. If he really was one of those vampires, that is, the humans that die and then wake up again, then wasn't sunshine supposed to be deadly? Wasn't that the reason they always attacked at night when he was in Frisia? He learned in school that was the reason the Black Storm was developed: to block out the sunlight so vampires could move around all the time. And there were many more vampires than humans in Europa. They called it an empire but all he cared about was the next line of fence or ditch and the bombards from that side firing over at his side. A flash of terror struck him dumb a moment.

"You doing all right, Mister Denham?" asked Deputy Holmes.

"Huh?"

"You seemed to go spacey there." He sniffed the air. "Still using the cannabis, aren't you?"

"It's legal. 'Sides, I got a doctor card." He reached for his wallet. A piece of folded paper fell out as he retrieved his wallet and opened it to show the deputy his medical card.

One of the company men picked up the paper before the wind could blow it away, his boot trapping it.

"Here. You dropped this."

"Thanks," said Bucky, accepting the paper. He recognized it as the burial order from the previous day. He kept it in his closed fist.

"You say you were out burying someone in this solar farm?" asked Deputy Holmes.

"That's right, sir." He decided to show them the order. "Says here at this location. Used th' GPS 'nd ever'thing." He turned to the company men. "Got permission from th' Suncatcher office, too. Somebody paid for this to be put down right here."

"Really?" The deputy glanced over the paper. "Where's the body?"

"Now ya see, that's th' strangest thing." Bucky was acting surprised. "When the coffin swung over 'nd got Josey, th' lid hit one o' them dang panels. Ya see th' cracked one? That broke th' seal. I tried to reseal it but I saw it was just filled with dirt. No body."

Deputy Holmes lifted his shades, gazed at Bucky. "No body?"

"Yessir, nobody. I mean there weren't no corpse in th' coffin, jus dirt, black dirt—like good shit for growing vegetables 'nd shit."

"Is that some kind of joke?"

"I dunno, sir. Strange thing, I guess, but folks pay fer all kind o' strange things. They jus wanted it buried here, that's all. We tried to get th' job done but th' coffin was too dang heavy 'nd swung outta control 'nd knocked Josey onto that panel. That's what happened." He glared at the deputy. "I tried ta get him into town, but he—he was gone before I arrived at th' hospital."

Deputy Holmes, serious expression painted on his face, pulled out his recorder and spoke some notes into it which printed on the screen as he spoke, information automatically jumping around to different boxes and filling them in. Then he hassled Bucky about the revolver but he produced a permit, citing the need for protection working out of the town, wild animals and all.

"We need to take some measurements," said one of the company men—or woman. Couldn't be sure the way they were dressed. "Then we'll know better how to resolve this situation. But you can probably expect an invoice for the damages, Mister Denham."

"It was a gyawdamn accident!" he exclaimed. "That means nobody's responsible. It jus happens."

"The company is not responsible either," said the other company person. He/She asked for Bucky's information, collected it from his microchip with a scanner running over his wrist. "We'll be in contact."

Bucky watched them depart, muttering "Gyawdamn" over and over before finally following them out through the solar panels and back to his truck.

"By the way, Denham," said Deputy Holmes. "Your worker here is over the limit." He held up the detection device, its needle flickering, which measured the amount of cannabis someone consumed by the toxicity of the air inside the cab of his truck. "He's out now. Dope haze. Maybe better get him home."

"Yessir, he's useless. Another day payin fer no work." Bucky swept his brow with the back of his hand. "Gonna fire his sorry ass soon as we get back ta town."

"Is it permitted to remove the casket now?" asked the company person of the deputy.

"Denham?" called Holmes.

Bucky spun on his boot heel. "Its my gyawdamn bidness. I'll take it away tomorrow, okay? Gotta get this boy home, ya said."

Finally everyone was satisfied. The sheriff's deputy drove off first. The company folks sat in their van a while preparing their report. Once they left, Bucky climbing into his truck and gave the slumped person in the passenger seat a shove.

"Ya still dead?" He chuckled, but it had a sad tone. "Man, yer one lucky sonuvabee-atch. Gonna put me outta bidness. Shee-yit. Let's get outta here fast we can 'fore they change their mind."

∞

Harry studied the paper. Barnes and Noble was the name of a chain of book shops a hundred years ago. One of their shops had been located in a shopping center called Quail Springs. A lot of apartments had surrounded the shopping center, and he had lived in one of them. He had gone to the book shop often, more for a good cup of coffee than to find a book. And he had gone there one day to meet a woman he'd first met over the *electronet*—or whatever they called it back then. They were typing out their communications back and forth, then decided to meet face to face, as was the custom in those days, and the Barnes and Noble book shop was a neutral location. They had conversed a while, he recalled. His heart began to warm at the thought.

Now it had been wiped clean, like history. The shopping district razed, the suburban neighborhoods stripped bare, lives forgotten. And a solar farm was eventually built on the same acreage. According to the GPS tracking device. He was supposed to be buried at the same spot where once stood a table in the café corner of that Barnes and Noble store, the table where he and the woman who would soon become his Beloved had sat and chatted for the first time, sipping lattés.

"So ya can read that?" asked Bucky from the lounger as he gazed over at the stranger he called Harry. Kicking off his boots, Bucky sat with his bare feet on the footrest. The stranger sat upright, apparently unable to relax and slump in the chair.

A woman he called "Sis" shuffled about in the next room, which they called "kitchen". The scent of something frying wafted through the house.

"Mm-mmm." Bucky smiled. "She makes one helluva quesadilla."

Harry eyed the man, looking about his age when he'd entered the casket, then followed a line around the room: paintings hanging on the walls; a big, ugly lamp on a table; a screen flashing images of products to purchase; the long chair like his *chaise longue* he used to relax on in another life; and the round cushion some animal had slept on. The animal had been sent out of the house after too much barking at the stranger. The scents were strong with this stranger.

"I lived here," said Harry in a low voice. Bucky had to strain to make out the words. "Long time."

"Yeah, I bet it's long time." He shook his head, gave a glance at the kitchen entrance, noises of cooking there. "Listen now, Harry. No 'fence, but I been wond'ring jus how a man can live that long in a box like that, like ya did. I mean, ya got no food, no water, maybe no air. How ya do it?"

Harry didn't miss a beat. "Hiber-nation. Made sleep. Body slow down. Like drinking poison."

"Poison . . . . Yeah, I getcha. So it was jus some mistake, huh?"

"No." Harry looked around as if expecting spies. In the old country there were plenty of spies, most of them electronic and controlled from afar. "My plan. Must go away—far. Hide from—"

"It's reeeaaa-dy," called the sister.

"Let's eat," cried Bucky, pushing himself up from the lounger. "Ya can eat food can'tcha?"

"Let's see," moaned the stranger, acting not very confident.

"Well, you can eat what ya like, 'nd if'n ya don't like, she won't take no 'fense."

They went to the table in the kitchen room. The food was laid out on colorful plates. The sister, plump with a big smile, helped him sit in what she called the "guest chair". She filled a plate for him, set it before him with a cheerful comment about enjoying it.

"Bucky tells me yer in the diggin bidness too," said the sister.

He tried to work the fork, following what the others were doing but his fingers could not grasp it properly.

"Here, lemme hep ya," said the sister, coming around to him. She cut up the thing called "quesadilla" and speared pieces of it with the fork, put the fork to his mouth, between his open lips. He closed his mouth and she withdrew the fork. "Go on now, chew." She turned to Bucky. "He's like one them li'l babies, ain't he?"

"A big baby, fer shore," laughed Bucky.

Harry chewed the bread and cheese thing with the red sauce full of bits of vegetables. It had a familiar flavor. Memories were sparked. The texture was unusual, crisp on the surface and sticky inside. He liked it. He opened his mouth for more.

"He's like one them li'l baby birds sittin in a nest, ain't he?" giggled the sister.

When the meal was done—Harry kept it all down—Bucky went to another room looking for a fresh set of clothes while the sister got a shower ready for their guest.

"This the best I got," Bucky told him, coming out of a room with half his torso unclothed, carrying a set of clothing. "Belonged to my pop. He was taller than me so it maybe fits ya. Give it a try."

When Bucky turned, Harry could clearly see the mottled pattern of pockmarks marking his back, the wounds from a bombard blast. They had healed, of course, but still left a painful map of his war years.

"Oh, that?" Bucky thumbed to his shoulder. "I was o'er in Frisia for a year, fightin th' Europa vampires. Got this here wound 'nd they sent me home. Yeah, don't hurt now, but shee-yit shore did when it was still burning, I mean li'l blue flames rising from each hole, like to beggin for someone ta kill me right off. But I got ta th' hospice in time 'nd they put out th' flames 'nd bandaged me tight. Worst year of my life, lemme tell ya." He shrugged to show it didn't hurt now. "But they get me good now, takin half whatever I make diggin graves for folks no matter I did my service. My pops kicked off while I was o'er there. My baby boy had with a gal down the street, too."

Harry accepted the stack of clothes with a nod, felt him put them on his outstretched arms.

"It's reeeaaa-dy," sang the sister, stepping out of the room. "Here's a towel fer ya."

"Thanks," said Harry, stepping into a room which was only a little larger than the casket.

Water was a hazard. For a vampire, water burned the skin like acid. He wasn't sure what to do, uncertain if everything had been changed or only some things. However, he knew he needed to clean himself. Three years in a box full of manure could leave a bad smell. He wanted to apologize for that, for "funking up" his truck, as the man said, and now his home. His dog was going crazy, wouldn't stop barking outside.

So, with a stream of water dropping down from a spicket, he held out his hand. Droplets hit his palm like the pellets from a bombard. He waited for the burning sensation. Nothing. He moved his arm under the spray and felt no pain. Inch by inch he moved on into the basin catching the water, stood with the water covering him, running down his body, washing away the film of dirt, the stink of another age.

He took up the pink bottle standing in the corner of the basin and squeezed out pink liquid which spilled over his hand and ran down his abdomen. It smelled like flowers. He smoothed the gel over himself, enjoying the fragrance. He turned around, washed again. He pushed his head into the water spray and felt his scalp soothed. He lingered, thoroughly wet, covered in the lather from the liquid soap, feeling . . . alive. First shower in ninety years.

When he stepped from the water room, he forgot to wipe off the water. He also forgot to put on the set of clothing. The sister rushed to grab a towel and cover him, holding up her hand to shield her eyes. She turned her head away as she rubbed the towel up and down his body, then called for Bucky to help him get dressed.

"Well, that's a new one fer her," Bucky laughed. "She never found nobody to wed her 'nd she never goes to th' bed-n-break fer some bed fun, neither. Even tho' I told her it's permitted now, on account of th' plague wiping out lotta elig'ble men. Had ta do something keep folks going. Tried ta get ever' female around here pregger ta save th' human race, yessiree. Man cannot live by man alone, they say."

Harry stared at Bucky, understanding what had happened during his long sojourn in the east, before he was soundly casketed. Living in grand style, he had no idea the suffering the average citizen endured. He had been a different person then. He had not cared about anything but daily serving his own lord and master. But he had stepped out of the casket. He had survived water. He had eaten food and not become sick. And he had no craving for blood—after the completely automatic response to seeing it leak out of Bucky's wounded worker.

Dressed in a red and white plaid work shirt and loose-fitting brown corduroy trousers, Harry looked like one of them, a regular member of the Denham family, sitting with Bucky and Sis in the "front room" as they laughed at a set-piece drama performed on the viewing screen. He observed the scene on the screen, noted the idiocy of the people there, how they did things that made no sense, spoke strange words, and always the sound of laughter from people who were not there on the screen. Bucky and his sister laughed often, apparently understanding the jokes.

He wiggled his toes, staring at the knobs where toes had been cut off decades past.

"Yep, we need ta get ya some socks," Bucky said, nodding.

The sister popped up, disappeared and returned with a pair of gray stockings. She knelt down before him and he felt like a monarch again. But she was only slipping the stockings up his leg, giggling like it was some form of courtly entertainment.

"There ya go, ready ta dance," she laughed.

They kept staring at the screen. Another hour went by. Meanwhile,

Harry stared at the pictures of people on the walls. Young people, old people, people in military uniforms, people in white dresses with their heads covered in white veils, colored pictures, plain brown pictures, a picture of a big fish, another of a horse—a real horse, not one of those hybrid *vorse* animals. A few pictures of Bucky in his youth standing by one vehicle or another, looking happy and full of potential. He stared at the pictures for a long time, until the viewing screen clicked off with an audio message that good workers should move to the sleeping area and repose for seven hours minimum. It seemed a good message.

They got up, obedient as expected.

"I got no job lined up fer tomorrow so maybe we can getcha more clothes, better your size. We can figure out what ta do with you, Harry. You're a complete mystery."

Harry nodded, accepting the truth of the statement. Then, with a fresh croak, he spit out a string of words: "I'm sorry. Thanks you. And Sis. For all you do. For me. I don't know what to do. Now. Or next do. I got nobody. I'm good to be here. Alive."

Bucky grinned, shook his head humbly. "Well, it's good ta have ya alive, too. Heckuvalot better'n th' other choice. You're welcome ta stay til ya get yerself back on yer feet."

The sister made up the sofa for him in the front room where they had watched the screen. He put himself prone on the furniture, tugged at the old blanket until it covered most of his body. He was not cold; he saw someone do that on the screen. In the dark of the room he stared at the ceiling, examined the smells of the house, the sounds that filled the night, and recalled how he used to be awakening about this time. It used to be daylight when he would sleep. His sleep would go on for three days, his waking time for a couple weeks. Everything was backwards now.

ʒ

It wasn't so difficult to believe. The way he had come out of that coffin, that backhand swat of Josey, licking blood from the wound, the creaky words. Anybody would be stiff being stuck in a coffin for three years. And he said he was poisoned, too. Somebody really wanted him gone, it seemed.

So when he outright asked him, Bucky wasn't surprised to get a straightforward answer.

"So yer a vampire," Bucky said again, shaking his head in solemn contemplation as they sat in his truck, eating "burgers" and "fries" from a red-roofed shop. They had put in a full morning, taking Harry to the OK-Mart for clothes and hygiene products the screen told them to buy. They had gone first to the Langford store for a pair of boots.

Harry gave a slow nod, holding his burger sandwich up to his lips. A bead of ketchup had already fallen onto his shirt, a shred of lettuce in his lap.

"No, ya got ta fold th' wrapper under it ta catch anything drops," Bucky instructed.

Harry did as he was told.

Bucky sat back, watching five other vehicles get in line before the window of the store. Many of them didn't have tires, just hovered over the pavement. He grinned, thankful for his trusty Ford F-70. The truck was running fine since the year it was introduced: 2070.

"Yep, I figured it right off but, heck, ya know what happened, got a might rattled in th' moment."

"I'm sorry," Harry spoke. "I'm not know where I am."

"That's fer sure." He turned to Harry. "Listen now. We gotta go, me 'nd sister, o'er ta Josey's funeral tomorrow. You prob'ly shouldn't go with us. But yew can watch th' video screen. Lotta shows there. Sis'll leave some lunch fer ya. Hope ya don't mind, take no 'fence on it."

Harry shook his head. "No offence take." He coughed, a ring of onion flying out of his mouth.

"Yer s'posed to bite 'em not swallow 'em whole."

Harry picked up the errant ring of onion, bit off half and chewed it, holding the other half between his fingers.

"It's good, ain't it? Betcha never had this good a burger back where ya came from, ain't that right? Yeah, we been eatin burgers fer like on hunert years here. It's our home cookin."

"Okla*homa*," Harry intoned, and Bucky snorted. "I lived here many years past."

"Did ya now?"

"I ate burr-gerr many times. Drink many cups coffee—"

"I been meaning ta ask ya, what's that accent ya got? You said yer from here. Did ya forgot howda talk?"

Harry pointed to his throat. "Old throat." He frowned, not finding the right words. "Remember words . . . is very, very hard."

Bucky chuckled. "Three years, man o man. So . . . say something in vampire talk."

Harry glowered a bit.

"Go on now, say something."

"You mean like 'Good *Eeeeev*'ning'?"

"Yeah, like that. Only better. That didn't sound real."

"How is real?" He caught himself. "How is it not real?"

Harry stared out the side window.

"Ya sound like them folks on th' screen, like playin they was from Europa."

Harry shook his head and Bucky thought the man must be crying. A hundred years gone. Locked in a box. *Geeyawdamn.*

"I getcha. Shore do. All 'lone now. I jus got my sister. We ain't got nobody else. No kids ta pass on to. Maybe yer th' same. Wond'rin what ta do, where ta go, if'n ya got somebody waitin fer ya, or not. It's a dirty world out there. Lotta heartburn. I getcha, Harry. I shore do." He stared at his buddy. "Whatcha gonna do now?"

Harry recovered, blinking his moist eyes. His fingers went to them, wiped away the tears. Real tears. His eyes widened and he grabbed the rearview mirror. He stared into it, saw his moist eyes, less red, more white. He blinked more, then sat back.

"You really cryin," Bucky announced.

Harry faced him, a serious mask hiding all emotion. "What should I do? I got a son someplace. In Denver, I think."

Bucky clapped him on the knee. "Then by all means, Harry, ya better get yerself ta Denver."

Harry frowned, took hold of Bucky's hand and removed it from his knee. "I remember now. My name is Stefan. Not Harry."

7

THEY BARRELED DOWN THE HIGHWAY, BUCKY STEERING with his knees as he rolled a new reefer, lit it, and handed it to Stefan, giving a non-stop prattle about his days before the Army, when he worked on oil rigs. That was before they closed down. People complained of the pollution. And more electric vehicles meant less need for the oil, anyway, Bucky explained as they drove.

"When we get ta Col'rado, we kin get some supremo weed," he said, holding his breath. "Thank god they made it legal way back. Doctors said it had medical use 'nd that was it. Opened th' whole can o' worms, 'nd folks went fishin." He laughed heartily at his joke but the man in the passenger seat did not understand.

For two days they had been on the road, taking lesser highways to avoid any patrols looking for excuses to hassle a hard-working citizen of the Anglo-America Union. With a bag of bologna sandwiches made by the sister, they had left early the morning after the funeral of his former employee. Bucky still had papers to sign, official people to talk to about the incident. But he did get the casket off the *geeyawdamn* Suncatcher property—and found a dead bat hidden in all that manure. It likely had suffocated inside the box.

"Yeah, some message somebody was sending, ain't that right?" said Bucky. "A box full of pig shit. Like them sayin your life ain't nothing but shee-yit. 'Nd here's a dead bat, too. That's creepsy! Ya musta surely pissed on some folks back there." He turned and gave Stefan a hard stare. "So what happened?"

Smoke filled the cab of the truck and Bucky cracked the window.

"I was a government employee, a member of the staff," said Stefan, pretending he had to recall the details gradually. "It was bad times. . . . Many threats against the government. . . . People told me about a plot to kill—to assassinate the emperor."

"Zat right?"

"I was swept up in the conspiracy."

"'Nd they caughtcha."

Stefan grinned. "I was caught, yes. . . . And here I am, sent away. Exile, maybe you can call it."

"Well, if'n anybody's gonna exile yer ass anywhere, this Oklahoma ain't a very good place. I mean, shee-yit, maybe it is a good place fer it cuz it's hell on earth, ya ask me. Lots o' yer exile folks coming here in coffins, ya think?"

Stefan shook his head, received back the reefer. "Perhaps I am the only one sent here." He put the reefer to his lips.

"Then you's th' lucky sucka." Bucky perked up. "Hey, when we get to Col'rado, we can relax under some trees, real tall trees they got there, up in th' mountains, see, 'nd you can get up top o' them 'nd see real far way. I always wanted to do that, ever since I was a kid."

He exhaled. "I think I also lived under trees there."

"Well, shee-yit, where *didn't* you live?"

Stefan lay his head back against the headrest, feeling sleepy—after only twelve hours awake. So human-like, he had to laugh to himself.

"You like long story? I was born in a place called—used to be called New York. Not the big city but a small town in the north."

"Yeah, we call that North York now. They split like in 'forty-eight, sumpin like that. Lotta states split up over political rivalry. Like there's four Californias now, but used ta be one freakin state. Now it's a state called Aztlan, part of th' Mexico Republic now anyways."

"Times change," said Stefan with a weary sigh.

"So you was born in North York . . . ."

"It was called Utica. My mother and my father were doctors in a mental asylum there."

"That musta been a freaky place ta grow up."

"Yes, very *freaky*." He was relearning so many words from his host and escort. "I was a doctor, too, after going to university."

"Zat right? Yer a college boy? Never woulda guessed by th' look."

"I checked people's blood for problems."

"Oh. . . . Yeah. . . . Makes sense. . . . It's a vampire thing. I getcha. They like being close to th' blood."

"I got a job in Oklahoma."

"Yeah, ya said ya lived there. So how ya get over ta Europa?"

Stefan took a deep breath. Another. Coughed a minute.

"Yeah, that's some good shit, ain't it?"

Stefan nodded as he recovered. "I found that I had a disease. I tried everything. I went to doctors, none could help. So I went to Europa to search for help fighting the disease."

"That's some that vampire shit again, ain't that right?"

Stefan grinned sheepishly. "You are correct."

Bucky batted his eyes. "So how that shee-yit work, anyways?"

"Two kinds of people. One has it in them from birth. Then it comes out later. They transform into monsters. The other kind gets infected from a diseased person. Sharing the blood. It's the same as any disease transmission. For example, the old AIDS disease, before they cured it. You have sex with an infected person, you get the infection. Simple."

"Which kind was you?" Bucky was grinning like it was a game.

"I'm first kind. My parents had it in them. They ran away, hid in a place in Europa, died there. I was normal person—until I wasn't."

He began to choke with emotion, and Bucky turned, concerned.

"Hell, ya don't need to say no more, if'n ya don't wanna."

"So long now it's been learning to live—to *exist* with this problem."

"Yeah, it's a problem. But it makes ya so ya can stay alive in a box fer three gyawdamn years. Maybe that's a good thing, ya guess?"

Stefan smiled, tried to smile, putting on a mask. "Mixed curse."

"You mean 'mixed blessing'."

"No. Curse."

 беруться

Bucky, waiting out in the truck, got tired of the sun beating through the windows and drove it under a tree, a little farther from the door.

His buddy still walked stiff, like he had a war wound. They had found the records office for Denver, looking up the address for someone he used to know there.

"It's been how many years?" Bucky asked him as they zig-zagged through the streets to find the office.

"Too many," replied Stefan. "It's a place to start."

Eventually, he came out, looking around for the truck. Bucky gave a honk and watched the dude hobble across the parking lot.

He didn't say much, seemed a little torn up inside. A couple tears rolled down his face. He never cried much, though he had a lot of things affecting him. This was genuine tears. He gathered his words, gave directions to a residence on the west side of the city, on the way into the mountains.

It was a modest residence for the neighborhood. A house intended for a single family—for a large family, obviously. A gate and a good size yard, red brick building with white colonnade, wide veranda, older style perhaps but built only a couple decades ago. A turret on the side, with a tower, like those in some European castle. Something he had mentioned always wanting in a house. His son had listened to him, it seemed.

"He doesn't live here now," said Stefan, "but this is where he did when he . . . ."

Bucky stretched over to gaze out of Stefan's window at the large house on the large lot, a scattering of big trees providing shade and ornamental flowers brightening the property.

"Yeah? When he what?"

"When he died."

"He died? Geez, man, I'm sorry."

Stefan bowed his head, pursed his lips. "Naturally. At least he died naturally. He did not have the disease."

"Well, that's good, at least."

Stefan sighed. "I was supposed to meet him years ago. He was to come to Europa and I would meet him. It was to be in Lisbon. You know, in Portugal?"

"If'n ya say it is. I never paid 'tention much in school."

"He never arrived. I was there, but he became ill and never made the trip. He was old then. That was 'eighty-nine. I think."

"Old?" Bucky was concerned. "When was yer son born?"

"It was twenty-fifteen, but I could not be there. He was a miracle. Because I was sick with the disease, yet his mother was not. Not then. He was lucky to be born before the disease presented in her body. It almost killed her."

"That yer wife?"

"Yes. . . . . My Beloved." He wiped more tears, looking at his fingers as if the tears were something he'd never seen before. "She also has died. She had the disease but she was cured of it and died human, not vampire."

"Well, that's some trick, ain't it?"

Stefan sniffled more, seemed surprised to do so. "Yes, a trick. There are so many tricks in the world. Everyone must fall for a trick or two. I—I agreed to do some things, in exchange for her receiving the cure. Some bad things."

"Weeeeell, we all gotta make sac'fices. Don't feel bad, Steffy. Ya did whatcha had ta do. I bet she died happy, anyways. I mean, not havin th' disease no more."

Stefan nodded a long time and Bucky took it upon himself to drive away from the house. He headed south, uncertain where to go next.

"Go west," said Stefan when it seemed they were going in circles. "You wanted to see the trees, true?"

"I said I did, but we kin go anywhere ya like."

"I want to see another place. It's in the mountains."

"Awrighty! Giddy-up."

⚬⚬

The road wound up through the foothills and Stefan could see how delighted Bucky was. Oklahoma was so flat these hills excited him. He craned his neck to look out windows on both sides of the truck. They got into the trees and Bucky slowed to admire them. They stopped for lunch at a spot with a good view across a deep valley. Birds sang above, and the thick scent of pine overwhelmed the smoke of a fresh reefer. They put the wrappers from the burgers and fries in the truck.

"Don't wanna spoil any this here nature," said Bucky.

Stefan had a feeling as they continued up the road, curling around a set of cliffs and on up to the higher elevations. Excitement and fear. When they were above more of the landscape than below, he directed them to turn at a certain road junction. The gravel drive was still there, the rocks scattered over time, grass growing up through it.

Where the cabin once had stood, there was now only a concrete foundation and some burned beams and a fallen roof. Sometime there had been a fire. He remembered reading a letter about that, one he had forgotten until now. His son had written to him but he had not written back to his son. He was too busy destroying the world. His son wrote that, after he abandoned them, his mother wanted to move back to the city. They kept the cabin for a couple more years, used it on weekends and holidays, then sold it. Tried to sell it. On the day the sale was to be final, lightning struck the cabin and it caught fire. They were stuck with the loss and insurance money was not enough to rebuild it.

He stared at the structure, what remained, and felt the symbolism in its appearance. Strong foundation but load-bearing walls too weak to hold up a roof when weakened by fire. And what was fire in this metaphor? The spirit of evil? The touch of his lord and master, Luce? Now he had escaped. He had gotten drunk, taken poison, cut the link between them, and disappeared. Alcohol was poison to a vampire if it was too pure. Most beverages had a fair portion of blood mixed in to dilute the effects. And his mistress was willing to help him, adding poison, the stuff that knocked him out for three years. Until he was delivered to an address he had previously designated. But now—now everyone he had known was gone. He was alone in the world. He was free but had nothing.

"You cryin again?" called Bucky. "That's awright. Nobody's gonna think nothin of it. Ya lost yer son, so it's awright ta be bawlin."

He had lost more than his son, he suddenly realized. A century of existence was gone in the snap of fingers. His Barnes and Noble was gone. His entire neighborhood was gone. She was gone. As though none of it had ever existed. Only this cabin served to remind him of people and the moments shared with them. The day the bat alighted on his shoulder. Right here where he stood. And his wife, Penny, stood over there, next to the SUV they had. And his son, a teenager, was calling to him as he conversed with the bat. Or was he conversing with the spirit of evil, the true Angel of Death?

He suddenly ducked as something dark came too close to his head. A dropping pine cone. Not a bat.

Either way, he was home again.

"Y'awright, Steffy?"

He nodded, wiping his eyes once more. Real tears. He missed that ability of humans more than anything. The chance and the means to let out the emotions he could not contain within. The venting ports of the human soul—

My dear boy, what have you done?

Stefan froze. A breeze whistled through the pines, rattling the pine needles, disturbing the branches. A couple more pine cones dropped. He listened closer, stiff as a tree.

"What's goin on there, Steffy?" called Bucky from a few yards away, leaning on his truck.

Returning to the scene of the crime?

He glanced around—frantically. No one was there. But the world was spinning. The light was wrong somehow.

He rushed to the truck, opened the passenger-side door and dug in the cooler behind the seat.

"Whatcha doin?" asked Bucky, coming around the truck to check on him. He saw his buddy ripping a six-pack of beer from the cooler. "Ya thirsty awready?"

Stefan tore open a can, quaffed it down, went for a second can. He started to drink a third can of beer but slowed, pausing then sipping, as if checking to see what its effect was. He went ahead and finished the third can and waited, empty can in his hand.

"That's a good way ta get stone cold drunk now, fella," said Bucky.

Stefan took a step away from the truck, stumbled, caught himself. He returned to the truck and grabbed another can of beer, opened it, took a long draw, emptying half.

"Sure glad yer not drivin," Bucky laughed. "Ya really like it."

He finished the can, took a few steps, and fell over in a soft patch of moss and pine needles. He said something, but his words were now too slurred for Bucky to make them out.

"Didn't think burger 'nd fries make ya so dang thirsty, but guess'n it's been some time since ya had good beer. I like them Quartermains but they hella expensive 'nd ya done emptied four in coupla minutes."

Stefan lay as limp as a rag doll. He belched and breathed deeply. He listened to the sounds of the forest. Nothing but birds twittering, chipmunks chattering, foxes yawning, deer nibbling. But he was not satisfied. He pulled himself up, practically crawled over to the truck and hauled himself up into the seat.

"Less get outta here," he mumbled.

"Well, awrighty, whatever ya say, boss."

They turned the truck around, started down the hill, leaving the ruins of the cabin and its memories behind. The last time Stefan had been there was the last time he was free and healthy and happy. But the voice remained. It was a haunted place. Or it was all in his head. Either way, getting himself drunk was the only way to silence it.

Bucky had questions, but it was a long drive back into the city, and most of his questions went unanswered as Stefan slumped in the seat, sick to his stomach. They had to pull over twice for him to evacuate his gut. When they returned to the city, they found a cheap place to stay for the night. Stefan lay on one of the beds, his head swimming, while Bucky went to recharge the battery on the truck and get some dinner.

CR

"He said he had four children." Stefan wadded up the paper soiled with barbeque sauce, tossed it to the basket. "I wonder about them. Where they are. If they have the disease. If they will develop the disease later. If they look like their grandmother."

"Cuz yoos th' grandfather," Bucky said with a hoot. "I getcha, ya talkin bout yer wifey."

"I want to find them."

"That there's a good mission, Steffy."

"Can you continue to drive me to places? You must need to return to your home."

"My home? Shee-yit." He took a swig from his beer bottle. "That house belong ta my pops. Maw passed 'fore I went off in th' army 'nd Pops, he passed when I was in th' army, o'er Europa. Yep, me 'nd Sis, we growed up in that house. I got th' same room I got when I was a kid. Like I said, I never married nobody. Tried hooking a lady or two 'fore the army. Got a boy with one o' them. He died young. After th' war, never had no chance on account o' getting my willie bit off by some vampire fucker. Oh, ever'thing still works, jus don't look so pretty, ladies don't want it, ya know? And Sis, she got her oil sores, big black blotches on her body and legs. Not attractive fer dudes. We got no kids, so who we gonna leave it to? Ain't that right?"

"Yet you must return to your job."

"Diggin graves? That ain't no job, that's a sentence. Jus sumpin ta help pay th' bills. Army pension, dis'bility pay don't cover ever'thing. 'Nd *geeyawdamn* gub'ment take half o' ever'thing I make. I do th' work 'nd earn it 'nd they take thirty gyawdamn percent. If'n I put it in th' bank 'nd take it out later, they take twenty-five percent o' that. If'n I get it back when I'm old, they take gyawdamn fifty percent. Lemme add that all up fer ya, that's a hunert 'nd five percent they take from me. Now how's that any kinda gub'ment 'rithmetic, lemme tell ya!"

"Perhaps I could get a vehicle and drive myself."

"You? Hell, I reckon ya can. . . . You got any money?" Bucky howled with laughter. "Unless ya took it with ya—like they say ya cain't."

Bucky managed to sleep, snored up a storm, tossing and turning all night in his bed. Stefan slept silent and still, flat on his back the whole time, which was what he was used to doing in a casket. He did not sleep, though, wondering if he was still a vampire or somehow changed back to being human. His skin was cool to the touch but his heart beat. His hair was growing in, his skin attaining a rosy pink. He didn't crave blood, wasn't particularly excited by a juicy, rare steak. And he could handle his alcohol.

In the morning he stepped in front of the bathroom mirror and shaved for the first time in more than seventy years. Someone had shaved him, cut his hair. His beard and long hair were gone when he had stepped out of the casket.

"Ya sure been growin some," Bucky commented, peeking into the bathroom. "Yessiree, let's get ya lookin clean 'nd maybe ya can get a job, get some money, buy a truck 'nd go look fer yer grandkids."

Stefan nodded, wiping away the spots of foam from his face.

"It's a plan."

They returned to the records office in downtown Denver and pored through files on a computer. The local-boy-done-good had been well-known, so his children, now grown, were easy to track. An hour later he had a list of addresses of every location they lived.

The print of the list cost a lot—"on account of them saving trees," said Bucky, "which I'm all fer, even though I don't read. Yep, folks that wanna read jus stare down at a li'l screen. Ya can read th' words jus fine that way, but paper gotta be too rich fer my blood."

"It was common in my days," Stefan muttered, counting the pages.

"Ever'thing was common in yer days," said Bucky with a loud snort. "Yessiree, them trees was sumpin. Tall like giants 'nd sweet-smellin. If'n they gotta cut 'em down jus ta make some *geeyawdamn* paper fer ta make some o' them *geeyawdamn* books, then ain't worth it. I don't need ta read nothin anyhoo. I jus ask Sis cuz she know ever'thing. She used ta be a school teacher, did I ever tell ya?"

"No, you haven't mentioned that," Stefan replied absently.

"Then she up 'nd got the oil sores. Lotta folks get that, breathin too much oil smoke. She got th' dis'bility pay but she done stop teaching. Or I kin ask one o' them libberaryians. They know ever'thing, too."

When they tried to leave, a security guard at the door asked if they had paid. They didn't have any receipt. Bucky was surprised. It seemed you had to pay to use the resources of the records office.

"But there wasn't any charge the previous time I was here," Stefan argued.

"The first visit is free," the guard replied in a sour voice, like he had to say it a dozen times a day.

"How do you know this is not my first visit?" asked Stefan.

The guard pointed up to the camera overhead. "They know you visited one time already. This is your second visit."

Stefan frowned. "I see."

"And so do they." He pointed to the cashier. "Need a receipt."

Bucky stepped up. "How bout we's visitors ta th' area? Any chance we can get a break jus one time? We ain't exac'ly rolling in credits."

The guard shook his head. "It's only ten dollars. You can buy a loaf of bread for that. Wave your wrist over the scanner. You can pay with your chip."

Bucky stood thinking a moment.

"Yessiree, that's how I'd pay, awrighty. With my *geeyawdamn* chip."

He gave Stefan a look. Stefan looked back at him.

"Ruuuun!" cried Bucky and took off out the doors.

"I'm sorry," said Stefan, and hurried after him.

They piled into the truck and charged away.

ᘐ

Bucky stretched out on the bed, boots and socks off, an odor filling the room as he stared at the big screen, some drama concerning men who rode horses in ancient days, wearing big hats, twirling rope, chasing cows. He laughed every minute, called them stupid, told the people on the screen how to do everything the right way.

Stefan sat at the desk in the little room of the *motel*, reading over the information, enjoying the feel of paper between his fingers.

The show on the screen ended, something new appeared. It was a new drama about the war in Europa. Bucky perked up.

"Ya said ya was part o' some conspiracy ta 'ssassinate the emperor. Well, he was killed eventu'ly, ya know. Got stabbed by bunch o' folks at a party, I heard. Took him a week ta die. They said he was a vampire, lived fer two-hunert years."

Stefan looked over at the screen. Line after line of soldiers were on the march through the streets of Paris, most of them vampires. You could tell by the red eyes, the gaunt faces. They looked half-dead, some fully dead. Leaning against their shoulders were the bombards, a kind of shotgun designed for use against vampires but also effective against humans.

He watched for a few minutes, never before having seen a report on Europa from the other side's perspective. He always got his reports delivered on paper or spoken directly to him by an attendant of this or that department, acting quite serious and subservient. Probably they had been misinforming him from the start. Everything was always glorious on the front, except they never managed to push through. He was a figurehead anyway. The hand that pushed the buttons. Because sometimes evil has no body, cannot push buttons or stroll over the battlefields with maniacal laughter.

"Yessiree. Them vampire brigades come at us during night, firing flares 'nd shee-yit at us. Then they got th' Black Storm going 'nd they started attacking during th' day. But it weren't like no day, black clouds coverin th' sun, dark as night. They could go out then. Nothin we threw at 'em ever did much. We tried silver bullets but they just went straight through 'em. Silver's too dang 'spensive. We had ta get some sabers 'nd go fer th' heads. Lop off a head 'nd they stopped cold dead. Yep, true dead. We heard they kept 'em starved of blood then released 'em at us so they'd tear after us, ya know, ta get our blood. Ya never saw no more gore than th' battlefields of Frisia. I mean, arms 'nd legs 'nd heads laying ever'where. So many gyawdamn crows peckin at shit."

"It must have been terrible," Stefan intoned.

Bucky went on telling his war stories as the drama played on the screen, shouting corrections. The uniforms were right. The weapons didn't sound like that. They would have ducked down at that, not be looking around. And their food was not blood soup with tendons. He pointed out how on the screen version most of the soldiers were men but in reality more than half had been women or "trans-ing" soldiers, men changing to women or women to men. Others were armored up with mechanical legs and arms and eyes replacing what they had lost. The ones driving vehicles were bolted to their machines, having lost legs and arms, driving with mental commands or optic tech controls.

"That's how we was losing," Bucky growled. "They had th' undead, vampires, couldn't be killed, 'nd our side just sent anybody they could get ta fight, not th' best people, th' only people. Half my platoon was female 'nd th' other half was transers. My captain was once a man that done transed to a woman, but trans-ing back ta be a man while we was tryin ta win th' *geeyawdamn* war. He or she, or xi, or they, or we, or theta, whatever—wouldn't give th' order fer us ta retreat till we used th' right *geeyawdamn* word! That's how I done got shot in th' back."

"War is terrible for everyone," Stefan spoke up when Bucky seemed to be taking a break from complaining. "I'm sorry."

"Sawry? Fer what? Ya didn't do nothin. Them Hungryans th' ones started it all."

Stefan bowed his head, understanding. "I was in Hungary . . . when it started. The vampire rebellion. However, it's not what you think, not what they show on these screens. There was a power vacuum in the capital, Budapest. Russia took the weakness as a chance to invade. In the resistance was born the vampire juggernaut."

"The what? Juggerhoo?"

"Hungarians rose up against the Russian invaders and, when they were finally kicked out, they kept pressing. The government became infested with vampires. The army moved in every direction, to annex the neighboring nations. First was the Hungarian Federation. Then the Hungarian Empire. Then the Empire of Europa."

"Now's just Europa," Bucky said with a snort. "No more empire."

"So you say. It has been a while since I read a newspaper."

"Guess you ain't been thinkin outside th' box, Steffy." He chuckled like a circus clown. "That sucka done fall apart. Yer empire is jus li'l state now. Like Oklahoma. Shee-yit, Allied Europa occupies there now. Guess it's what goes round comes round again."

Stefan nodded, the only thing he could do to both show and hide his feelings. An era lost—thankfully. And yet . . . a moment here and there when he could forget why he was there and could simply enjoy for one brief moment a thought, a feeling, a view, something that was swept away in the next moment. The deep breath he took seemed to suck all the air from the room.

Bucky noticed, struggled to catch his breath.

Stefan exhaled and the world returned to order.

Order. And Chaos.

He remembered. Always flowing, one to the other. That was what he had learned from Luce. Never stopping, never a plateau, but always in perpetual motion, up and down, back and forth, constant.

"I have no chip in my wrist," said Stefan spoke, as calm returned to their room and the drama on the screen was coming to an end, images of flags waving and people smiling.

"They don't do th' over there in Hungrya?" Bucky yawned.

"They didn't do that to me." He sighed. "I have no record here."

"Hell ya don't. I know that. Ya come by th' postal delivery. Yer not a citizen of th' *geeyawdamn* AAU, yer a package." He yawned again. "Scuse me. No 'fense 'tended."

Stefan shrugged. "But how can I do what I need to do without any identification?"

Bucky grinned. "I getcha. Ya wanna be somebody."

"A real person."

"You's one lucky sonovabee-atch, cuz I'm exac'ly th' man ta see 'bout that. I got a drawer full o' chips from corpses. When th' body rots away there's th' chip, sitting there, 'nd I collect a whole mess o' them. Some them's gotta work. Usually they decommission th' chips when th' death certificate is filed. But sometimes they don't. Sometimes they link up with some account, too."

Stefan's face glowed and Bucky shuddered, saying he got spooked by him doing what vampires in Frisia had done, light themselves up in the dark to find their way across the battlefield. Stefan closed his eyes and the room darkened.

∞

On the road again, Stefan studied the list as Bucky drove, taking the side roads to avoid patrols. Most of them wanted to get some extra pay by stopping travelers, he said. If they were stopped and Stefan had no identification, off to jail they would go.

"His eldest child is Lily."

"That's pretty name. I'd name my daughter Lily. If'n I had one."

"She now lives in Joplin."

"Joplin. I know it. Bottom of Missoura. Bout three hours' drive."

"His eldest son is Montgomery. Monty is also listed as a name."

"That's common if'n ya got a long one."

"Montgomery Marx Kelly."

"Oh, he got named after President Marx? The worst president we ever got? Ya know he gave away California to th' Mexico for like about two dollars. Then he got tied up with fighting in Europa, got us hitched ta that Britain Yookay, way th' hell across th' seas. If'n it weren't for Marx, I'da been fighting in Arizona or someplace, not in Frisia."

Bucky cursed the former president for the next seventy miles.

"Lily married a woman named Constance."

Bucky laughed, knocked right out of his angry mood. "People do anything nowadays. We got old people marrying children. People with animals. People with themselves. Heard about a gal married a portrait of some man she never met, jus liked how he looked. Anything goes these days, 'cept yer pers'nal privacy, pers'nal freedom. Cain't say any gyawdamn anything against th' gov'ment or off ta jail ya go, but ya kin do any pers'nal shee-yit ya wanna."

Stefan flipped the page. "Monty married a woman, too. June is her name. Three children. In Pittsburgh. That's Pennsylvania. I used to live there in my youth."

"Where ain'tcha lived, Steffy?"

"China," he mugged. "Never lived in China."

"That's a good thing. Them Chinese rule half th' world now. They got some navy bases in California."

Stefan flipped to a new page, reading. "This may take a while. The younger daughter, Rose, lives in Jersey. I guess that used to be New Jersey. The younger son lives in East York. Benedict. They both have families. They have children."

"So yer a great-ol-grandpappy."

Stefan sat still as they covered the miles, feeling time slipping out of his reach. While he stood locked in one time period, life had moved on in the rest of the world. He was doing his deeds, satisfying whims, obeying his lord and master, but life went on without him. It seemed as though everything he had done had not mattered. That what he had done was mostly bad, decidedly evil, and often cruel, didn't seem to have any relationship to the basic facts of his existence: he met a woman, they made a son, and that son met a woman and they had children, and those children had their own children, and life continued unabated. As though he had not existed after that one first moment of effort.

He thought of Penny Park, ace reporter for OKC News, his Beloved, whom he had cursed with the disease, stirring such hatred for him that she had braved a dangerous journey to Hungary to find him and curse him—then became cured of the disease because of what he elected to do, what he was compelled to do. However, after two years of freedom, trying to live a normal life with wife and son in Colorado, he was called again to service at the left hand of Luce. And the world burned.

However, that was not him, not really. That wasn't Stefan Székely, phlebotomist. That was Stefan, Lord Emperor of Europa. A comic book character drawn in bright shades of crimson and black, a cold figure of pure evil. He blinked.

The Oklahoma provincial border approached and a large orange sign with black lettering stood as a warning. Possible oil hazard. Enter at your own risk. Stefan stared at it, turned his head to keep looking as they passed it.

"Now's yer chance, Steffy. It's now or never."

He faced forward. "It's home now, so . . . ."

"Don't say I didn't warn ya." Bucky drew on the reefer, held his breath. "If'n ya had more money ya could live anywheres. If'n ya had money."

Thirty-nine miles of flat red landscape.

"Where is the casket?" asked Stefan quietly.

Bucky nearly ran off the road. "The coffin?"

"Yes. Where is it now?"

Bucky started laughing. "Ya know I didn't bury it. Yeah, I dragged it off that Suncatcher farm like they demanded. Took it back th' funeral home. They's th' ones hired me ta handle it so it's theirs. They took delivery from o'er Europa."

"So it is at the funeral home?"

"I guess so. Unless they disposed of it awready. Why?"

"I want to check something."

"Check something?" Bucky had the biggest smile Stefan had ever seen. "You think there's money in it? Like you did take it with you?"

Stefan pinched his chin, bit his lip, noticed no sharp points cut it now. He was a regular guy. Just a down on his luck hobo hitching rides with grave diggers, drinking beer and smoking weed.

"It's possible."

"Th' hell yew say!"

The truck kicked into gear, speeding to maximum, Bucky anxious to make good time, no longer a sightseeing trip.

"I took it back to th' funeral home, like I said, but no telling what they do with it, maybe break it up for scrap."

Fifteen miles in seven minutes.

"If I can believe the plan was followed, there is perhaps something to find inside the casket."

"Besides a bat?"

"Definitely more than a bat."

They didn't stop for anything but traffic signals when they got into town, pulled up to the mortuary like they were robbing a bank. Bucky hopped out, rushing to the front door. Stefan followed, taking slow, deliberate steps.

By the time he entered the mortuary, Bucky was already dragging out the funeral director and starting introductions.

"That one, I remember, because it had the loveliest gold inlay," said Dr. Jenkins, looking like a corpse himself, dressed in black coveralls with the funeral home's name and logo over the chest. "I would want to see if I could extract it. Could have value. The rest, well, that's some nice timber they'd likely break up."

"That's what I told him," said Bucky, thumbing at Stefan, then he caught himself, turned down his enthusiasm. "We was jus wond'ring bout it, that's all. If'n ya got it round here, we could take a look."

"It's not here anymore."

"It ain't? Ya already sold it off?"

The mortician gave a smirk. "Oh, no. It's at my house. I poured out the dirt for my garden. That's top grade black humus. Hard to get."

"Yeah, it was might strange to find it full o' dirt," said Bucky slowly, like he was signaling to Stefan. "My friend here, he knows sumpin bout dirt. Don'tcha?"

"What I saw was, as you ascertain, top quality soil. Perhaps it was especially cultured for its nutrient value. To make the vegetables grow much better."

"I surely do hope so," said Dr. Jenkins. "I'm counting on a crop of tomatoes and squash." He turned to Bucky. "Come by in the fall and we'll see what we can give you and your sister."

"Mighty kind o' you, doc." He glanced at Stefan. "So mind if we go by and take a look?"

"We have no interest in the gold inlay," Stefan added.

The mortician brightened a shade. "Well, that'd be all right with me, I suppose."

"We'll leave it where we find it in your garden. Just wanna take another look at . . . what was that again?" he asked Stefan.

"The structure of the casket is unique. I want to take photographs, if you have no objections."

"No, nope. Go right ahead, sir."

The doctor gave a salute to send them off and Bucky knew the way: down Broadway to twenty-first, past the abandoned Whataburger and the tornado damaged Del Taco shop to the old Katy Lang Mall.

Bucky swung the truck through the residential intersections like he was on some obstacle course, pulling up along the curb of a modest ranch house with beige brick façade, sun-ravaged lawn, and a broken swingset in the front yard.

In the garden out back sat the casket. It made a lovely planter. Some kind of flowers sprouted from the dirt inside the box.

"He done made it a flower box," Bucky snorted in surprise, hands on hips. "Yer coffin. A flower box. Ain't no lilies, neither."

They approached the casket and together tilted it to pour out the dirt, making a long mound, flower bulbs included.

Stefan swept away the dirt from the interior walls. The velvet lining had been ripped out so only the wood remained. He made a fist and pounded it against the inside wall from end to end. He did not hear a convincing sound. He went to one end and knocked on the side panel. He worked his way to the other end, knocking on it like he was a door to door salesman. He went up and down the opposite side. Nothing sounded different.

"Ya think there's a secret compartment?" asked Bucky, his tongue practically hanging out of his mouth.

Stefan scooped up more dirt from the bottom and tapped on the floor panel. Where his head had been was solid oak. At his shoulders the same. Where the small of his back had lain, however, the sound was different. He clawed away more dirt stuck there. He rapped on the wood. A different sound.

Bucky was ready with a box of tools from the truck. He handed a screwdriver to Stefan who forced it into a crack between two slats. He worked the screwdriver around, deepened the penetration, leveraging it until he moved it. The panel resisted, nails popping up, but finally it came loose.

"Wuh lord amighty!" Bucky cried out.

Stefan sat back on his rear, his fingers bleeding from his effort.

In the gap beneath the floor slats were stacks of paper money. They were unable to see how much through the small opening, but more work got the slats apart and the true picture could be seen.

Stefan started pulling out ribboned bundles, handing them over to Bucky, who slipped them into the toolbox. The box filled up. He set the next bundles on the ground beside the casket. He stacked them next to the hydrangeas. When the last bundle was removed, they sat back, the afternoon sun beating down on them. And Stefan wiped his brow, felt the sweat there, and put his fingers to his lips to taste the sweetness of the salt.

◌

"I never seen so much money in my entire life," Bucky sang. "Even it's mostly foreign money. Maybe ya can change it ta dollars. Take it ta some bank 'nd convert it ta credits."

"Enough American dollars to pay for this fine dinner," Stefan said, grinning over a plate of enchiladas.

Bucky settled for a plate of tacos, beans and rice. "Best dang Mexi food I had all year. But Sis 'nd me, we cain't never afford a place like this one. Thanks, Steffy."

"You are welcome."

Back at the house, window shades lowered, they counted out the bills: the *forint* money from Hungary, Russian *rubles*, and American *dollars*. A line of gold coins added shine to the collection. Bucky watched intently as Stefan held each bundle, carefully flipping through the bills, many of them old and soft.

"Well? How much?" Bucky asked.

Stefan continued counting.

"What're you guys doin there?" asked Sis, bringing a couple glasses of lemonade.

"Now, Sis, ya know I don't drink no dang lemonwater," Bucky said, looking up. The money was spread out on the floor.

"Did y'all find the money for the Monopoly game?"

"No, Sis, it's—"

"Yes, we did. It's old enough to have some value to a collector," said Stefan, glaring at Bucky, cross-legged on the floor.

"See? A collector," said Bucky.

"Well, there's another order on the table fer ya," said Sis, handing a glass to Stefan and returning the other to the kitchen. "Body's at Smith and Sons. Tuesday funeral."

"Gyawdamn grave diggin," he grumbled, swiveling his head. "I'm getting too old fer that shee-yit, that's fer sure."

Stefan looked up from where he sat on the floor.

"I count one-hundred sixty-seven thousand and ninety-five dollars American. And forty-thousand rubles. The forint is probably worthless with the empire dissolved but there's ten-thousand of those. The gold coins number two-hundred-fifty."

He gathered several stacks and piled them up, then handed them over to Bucky. "Here."

"What?" Bucky was surprised. "It's yer money, Steffy. I'ma guessin ya died to get it. I cain't take no dead man's money. I'm th' only honest digger in th' state."

"You helped me. More than anyone could have helped. Or should have helped. Take it. What remains is more than enough for what I need."

"Ya gonna get a truck?"

"Something cheap, yes."

8

Bucky told him to save his money buying a truck. He would be happy to keep being his chauffer, now that their bills were caught up and the taxes paid so all the government folks would keep off their backs. He did one more grave, then closed his shop for a spell. Then they hit the road, churning the red dirt into clouds that trailed them all the way to Missouri.

The four-story apartment looked expensive but that was by his 2014 eyes. White stone façade with iron staircases hugging the exterior walls and a pair of big white doors leading, as they discovered, to an elevator to the upper floors. Bucky waited in the truck, saying it was Stefan's family time. He didn't need to get in the way of any reunion. He was not a hugger.

Stefan was—used to be, back in the days when he worshipped his Beloved. And this woman, the one who would greet him at the door, would be the granddaughter of his Beloved. There might even be a resemblance; he would get the chance to gaze into those dark almond eyes of his Beloved once more.

The woman had blond hair instead, had a short nose and big chin, a friendly smile but she could not be related. She inquired about his reason for waking them on a Sunday morning, and how he got inside the building, like he was a vagrant begging for loose change.

"Who is it?" a woman called from inside the apartment.

"Some man," the blond woman called back. "He says he's related to you. Want to meet him? Or I can send him away."

"Please don't send him away," Stefan muttered, loud enough for the blond woman to hear and give a smirk. "I don't mean any harm. I've been away from my son for so long, and he died before we could meet, and now Lily is my only link to him."

"Lily? You know her name." She gave him a hard look. "What's your name?"

"I'm . . . Stefan. Stefan Székely. Not the son, the father."

Something crashed behind the blond woman and she turned to see what had happened. Then she rushed away to help with it, leaving the door half-opened.

He heard them talking, too faint to make out the words, but he got the tone. Either this man was a flat-out fake or, if he was real, she had no interest in meeting him. He should have understood that would be the case before visiting. If they could believe he still lived—existed—he would be in Europa, not Missouri. More likely, if they had followed the news reports over the past seventy years, they believed he had been killed by assassins and the world saved.

"I'm sorry," said the blond woman, returning to the half-open door. She seemed to appreciate he had not taken the opportunity to enter and assault them. "My wife isn't able to see you today. She's not feeling well. I hope you understand. Good day."

She started to close the door. When it was only an inch span, he saw her purse her lips.

"Maybe try again tomorrow," she said, and shut the door.

He stood in the hallway, electricity sizzling through him. It wasn't like before, when he had control over the elements. This was plain nerves letting go. What was he thinking? He was *persona non grata*. Yet he walks up and knocks on doors of people who believe him to be dead, and are glad of it, or who would not want to see him anyway.

He breathed deeply, realizing his chest had been tight, his throat constricted—like the first time he'd met his Beloved in the bookstore.

"Well, ya have a good meeting?" asked Bucky when Stefan returned to the truck.

"It is the correct address, and she was there, I believe." He looked out the side window. "Her wife said come back tomorrow. I think she felt shock at my visit."

"Well, ya did kinda sneak up on her unexpected like."

"Yes. The whole world has been taken unawares." He thought for a moment as Bucky started up the truck and rolled out of the parking lot. "I must be careful. My name scares people."

"Yeah, I get that, too. I mean 'Stefan' sounds foreign, so natur'ly folks is scared o' ya. Maybe change yer name to Steve. Just plain ol' Steve. That'll bring a smile to folks' faces. Ever'body likes Steves."

"Yes." Stefan pointed to a turn and Bucky took it, out to the main avenue lined with shops and restaurants. "Mostly it is my family name I must change."

"Ya never did tell me that, 'nd a dude's gotta right ta some priv'cy, in my book." He steered sharply around a slow vehicle, returned to the fast lane. "So what is it, ya don't mind my askin?"

"My family name is Székely."

"Okaaaaay," Bucky responded, changing lanes.

"It means nothing to you?"

"Should it?"

Stefan shook his head. "I suppose not."

"It's strange enough seeing ya climb outta that there coffin all alive 'nd shee-yit, walkin 'nd talkin. Heck, now yer jus like some regular joe. I forget ya used ta be dead. So yer name ain't th' most inter'stin thing bout ya."

"You are very astute."

"See? You keep speaking more them big-ass words ever'day now, like yer getting yer education all back in yer head li'l by li'l."

"I should change my name." He cleared his throat. "Székely should become Kelly. Like Lily did. She changed her name to Kelly. I thought it was her married name at first, but now I understand. Nobody likes the name Székely. It has terrible associations."

"It's a foreign name, too. Folks here don't like foreign shee-yit."

"Then from this moment, I am Steve Kelly."

"Steve Kelly, grave digger—or whatever ya did 'fore yer death."

"I drew blood and tested it."

"Well, there ya go. Steve Kelly, blood doctor. Got a ring to it."

CR

He tried again to meet Lily Kelly, and again Constance answered his knock, apologized, and politely shut the door. He waited a moment, knocked again and she opened the door. He asked if he could write a note for her to give to Lily. Constance agreed, stepped away and returned with a small electronic tablet. She handed him the stylus, invited him to write what he wanted to say.

With the blond woman watching, he struggled to find the words. He apologized for bothering Lily. He said he had left his old life and that he was forced to do the things he did, regretted all of them. He meant her no harm. He only wanted to see her, long enough to see if she looked like his wife, Penny. Otherwise, he would never bother her.

The door suddenly swung open fully and a woman with short dark hair stood behind Constance.

"Do I?" she asked, holding a similar tablet she had been reading as he wrote.

A tear rolled down Stefan's face, an unexpected effect, and he let it drop to the floor.

"Yes." He could barely speak. "You do."

Her smile was the same, too, a smirk pushed into the corner, like Penny had done whenever he told a stupid joke.

She invited him in and he inched forward like a prisoner unsure if the cell door had really been left open for him.

Constance stepped aside, stood nearby, off-stage, and Lily waved him to a well-padded wing chair which nobody likely ever sat on. But it caught the bright light from the windows, perhaps as a test for him. She studied him, looking for a sign he was who he said he was.

"So you're my grandfather," she said, the hue of doubt lingering in the room like cheap perfume.

He nodded, started to speak, fell silent.

"Dad talked about you from time to time, nothing good, I'm sorry to say. So I'm surprised you're here. I thought—we all thought—aren't you supposed to be dead?"

"Yes, supposed to be." He could not conjure a smile to hang on his face. "Many have wished for it. Me included. There is nothing I can say about my fate. I seem to be, if not actually alive, then existing."

"Existing . . . . Dad used that word a lot. So did Grandma. She told us about the years she had the affliction. The difference between being alive and being dead was so . . . so difficult to discern at times. That was their way of talking about it."

"I've been both, so I can agree with that sentiment."

"Which are you now?"

"I'm not sure." He glanced at the nearest window, a full square of brightness that would have blinded him before. "I must be alive."

"You've come to . . . to ask me questions? That's what most of them want. They want to look at me and see Dad. Ask me questions about his life. Because he did some good in the world."

He turned back to her, caught Constance in the corner of his eye. A moment locking eyes with a stern Lily, his granddaughter at age fifty and looking the same age as him. He had to bow his head.

"I know what I have done. For that, I am ashamed. Believe me. I know I have a lot to answer for. Please forgive me." He choked on his words. "I have no defense, except to say I was a mere figurehead in a plan to spread evil around the world."

"That may be rather difficult—to forgive you—but I will hear you out."

He looked up. "Thank you."

"Go on," she said like a school marm. "Explain yourself."

He described meeting Penny again in Budapest, what happened there, and their escape to America. Lily had heard about that. Then he was lured back to Hungary under false pretenses to tend to apparently unfinished business by an unscrupulous entity. He became trapped there, couldn't return, forced to commit crime after crime to satisfy his boss. Through that system he rose to power, power he never wanted but which he feared losing—and with the loss of power, the loss of his ability to protect those he loved.

He told her about Lisbon, expecting to meet his son, her father, and failing to meet him. If his son had arrived, he had planned to offer concessions, offer to pull back his army from Frisia, to let the worst of his abuses dissipate. He vowed to make amends. If they could help him escape. Instead, Secretary Stefan did not arrive so Emperor Stefan had no choice: he was forced to return to Budapest without a treaty signed.

The war pressed on. Trade suffered. The world descended into chaos.

"Yes, it was chaos," she said, crossing her legs. "That is the word for what happened after Dad was killed." She crossed her arms.

"He was killed?" Stefan was puzzled. "He became ill. That is what I was told. So he couldn't attend. Later he died."

"No, he was killed." She glared at him as though he should know. "I know what happened. We were informed by a government official, someone from the Intelligence Department. He was stabbed by some men from the empire. In his hotel room. It was the first night when he arrived. Perhaps they were part of your team of diplomats in Lisbon."

"Stabbed?" He grabbed the arms of the chair.

"Assassinated." Her eyes narrowed. A finger went to the corner of one eye, wiped away a tear. "Like what happened to you—if the official reports are to be believed." She sniffled back a tear. "Yet here you are. If you are really who you say you are."

"I did not know."

"A monarch never knows what goes on under his command."

"I swear I did not order anything like that. It never even crossed my mind. My own son. Never. No matter that he represented the empire's enemy." He shook his head. "Assassinated . . . . Stabbed . . . ."

She pursed her lips, watching him grieve. "I can believe you didn't order his death, but someone did it on your behalf. Perhaps someone who would be rewarded for doing something you could not order. Your 'boss', perhaps. He knew you could never do such a thing, so it was done without your knowledge."

Stefan continued shaking his head, hoping for a fatal stroke to cut him down before he could feel further pain.

"The only other option is that you are not who you say you are." She coughed, more a polite gesture than to clear her throat. Constance tapped her back. "There have been men who came here, hoping I had some significant things to say about my father or grandfather. Connie sends them away. We've had to move often to stay away from this cruel kind of publicity. However, you have a resemblance, closer than any of the others."

"If I am not who I claim, then you cannot forgive me."

"I can't forgive you, no matter you are who you say you are or if you are only someone pretending to be my grandfather. I have not had him in my life, either way. A bad grandfather or a bad emperor. Doesn't matter, not after these many years. That doesn't make him endearing to me. From what I know, it is good he stayed away."

"I'm sorry," he muttered, then repeated in a stronger, clearer voice.

"I believe you are." She turned to Constance, took her hand. "Let's say you are a kind gentleman who only wished to ask a few questions. Let's say you're doing research on a famous person of the past century. Innocent questions, I presume. I could accept that."

He bowed his head, accepting the game. "I'll grant you that. I'm not really sure at this moment. I might be someone other than who I say I am. The past few weeks have been . . . unusual. I might be confused. I apologize for taking your time."

"It's no trouble, uh . . . what was your name again?"

Either she was offering him a face-saving exit, he decided, or the stress of being related to two notorious figures of the past century had affected her mind. She had found a way to deal with it.

"Steve . . . Kelly."

"Thank you for sharing your interest in my father."

"They were remarkable people."

"Yes, they were. For very different reasons."

"Can you . . . would you . . . tell me more about your father?"

They talked for an hour, with many moments of silence standing in for words. The women sat on the sofa, holding hands. He sat opposite in the elegantly upholstered chair. They had nice furnishings. Probably because they both were lawyers. A terrier bounded into the room and in the first instant Stefan startled. The women laughed. He recovered, no longer interested in what blood the little creature might give him. In the end they agreed the name change was best.

She liked meeting this Steve Kelly. They hugged at the door. She wished him well, as though he had the more difficult journey ahead. He promised not to bother her again but she told him he could visit again if he wanted to.

"How'd it go?" asked Bucky.

"Much better, much better." A few tears continued to roll from his eyes. He wiped them away.

"Maybe we better get us a drink if'n yer gonna bawl like that."

At the bar, three rounds of whiskey later.

"She asked me if I'm still a vampire, said I didn't look like one."

"Well, are ya?"

"I told her I wasn't sure. I don't seem to have any of the outward signs. No craving blood. No fear of sunlight. Except . . . ."

"'Cept what?"

"I'm still a hundred and thirty-five years old."

"But ya lookin a cool seventy-five," Bucky snorted.

Stefan did not share his amusement. "Barkeep, another round."

"Yessiree, keep 'em coming," Bucky cheered.

"You know, I used to be a little boy. A beautiful little boy. Once upon a time . . . ."

ʘ

The road east from Missouri was more uncertain, the highways going the wrong directions, more patrols and checkpoints. There had been an uprising in Illinois, they heard, so the whole province was locked down. Bucky turned them south, curved through Kentucky and arrived in eastern Ohio. Again he liked all the hills and the forests spreading over the landscape, everything so green.

"This my kinda place," he said, grinning, taking a welcome breath of fresh air. "None o' that oil smoke or red dust here. I should move Sis 'nd me o'er here."

"But can it be home for you?"

"Heck, yer home is where yer heart is beatin, ain't that right?"

"Indeed."

They hooked up with the highway going east. When they swooped down from the highlands to the river valley at Wheeling, the sunset hit them, the town painted in a golden glow tinged with psychedelic pink and orange. The old bridge held together. A sign stated it had been completed in 2062. Heavy trucks on wheels were not allowed.

They passed through the town, winding up through more hills and from then on everything was hilly. Bucky thought he died and went to heaven, a place of hills and woods. He swore he was in heaven, but still alive, which was the best of all possible choices. Steve agreed.

Then came Pittsburgh: coming out from the long tunnel under the mountain, right over the long bridge, with the big city skyline straight ahead, silver towers shining "like an American palace," said Bucky. Steve cringed at the mention of a palace.

The highway funneled them to a junction where they could exit onto the city streets. Bucky was a good driver, dodging other vehicles that tried to claim the shiny diode-encrusted pavement for themselves. Most of them, it seemed, didn't want his rusty wheeled truck to bang into their sleek, shiny, hovering carriages.

"Too gyawdamn rich for me," Bucky snorted at the frou-frou folks riding in their automated carriages, laughing and waving obnoxiously as they hovered over the lane lines instead of between them. "Even tho' I got some money now, thanks ta Steve Kelly, Doctor Blood."

"But continuing to drive with reckless abandon may force them to ingratiate themselves with Doctor Blood."

"If'n ya say so, Stevie."

They found a hotel which didn't turn them away because of the poor state of their vehicle. With only a couple duffel bags, they rode up from underground parking to the reception. Bucky seemed intimidated by the elegant décor, stood off to the side while Stefan slid his wrist over the scanner and almost forgot to use the name George K. Osborn III on the tablet instead of his own. Flashes of his days in Budapest before he met Luce cut into his head. The tablet, the voice commands, the pleasure robots. He dropped the stylus, caught it, finished tapping the checks on the boxes. Smiles all around.

Riding up to their room, Bucky was in awe. The view from the elevator of the provencial capital at night was magnificent. He could not keep from staring in every direction, the glass elevator blocking nothing. In the next elevator, a couple was coupling. Bucky pointed it out to Steve, laughing. The couple waved, carried on.

The room was not a suite like Stefan had enjoyed in Budapest, but it was several steps up from the fleabag motels they had stayed in using Bucky's chip. He liked the minibar most of all and soon ordered a refill from the concierge. And the view of the hills and the river—that is, the wide canyon with the stream at the bottom. And far, far below their windows, the blue swimming pool with a lot of ladies wearing nothing. Men, too. He detected another couple in love. He called Pittsburgh the 'Sin City' he always dreamed of. After all, that Vegas city was in Mexico now. You needed a visa stamp to go there.

"I remember hearing long ago that some activities were deemed human rights," said Stefan. "Couldn't be limited because it would be discrimination. For example, people have the right to talk to anyone by phone anywhere in the world. My wife told me that. And people can dress as they like or wear nothing at all, anywhere, anytime. The same for sex. Anywhere, anytime. By mutual consent. The right of a human to be a human."

"Yeah, I heard that, too, on the screen. Always announcements reminding people how to behave." He laughed, quite amused by the antics of the people he'd seen. "But didn't catch on in Oklahoma. We's the last holdout of moral'ty."

"But I do think work places can have their own rules," said Stefan, scratching his head. "Must keep workers doing their jobs. Can't have them playing around on company time. But for the public . . . ."

Bucky was staring out the windows, delighted by the lights of the city. So Stefan sat back, reviewed the information on his son, Monty, tapping back and forth on the room's complimentary tablet.

"Oh."

Bucky looked over at him. "Another human right?"

"No. I just found him in the directory."

"Your grandson?"

"He's the deputy mayor."

❦

The first stop was the shopping district, where Steve Kelly purchased what the sales robot confirmed was considered a formal suit. The high stiff collar of the dark blue, knee-length cassock didn't feel comfortable and the large white ruffles down the front seemed a bit feminine. But feminine fashion for men was the style in Pittsburgh. The black mesh trousers worn under the cassock was another decadent addition for men, a glittering white thong underneath being the only covering for one's privates. The wingtip shoes came with small wings that flapped as he walked. The sales robot confirmed he was up-to-date now.

Bucky praised the outfit, saying Steve was ready for a wedding.

"At least the cassock goes low enough."

"Don't wanna shock'em," Bucky said with a snort.

City Hall stood a few blocks from the hotel so Steve walked it while Bucky remained in the hotel room, enjoying its amenities, especially the giant screen covering the entire wall.

"His Lordship, the Deputy Mayor, will now see you," intoned the assistant dressed in a similar cassock, solid black with yellow stripes down the sides and arms. He was reminded of his everyday life in the palace back in the empire.

The doors swung open. Four guards stood in his way. No halberds but they had sidearms on their belts. He had been searched when he first applied to speak to the deputy mayor, a five minute audience only. The chip continued to scan without fail.

"George Osborn," someone called from behind the four guards.

"Yes, sir, Your Lordship."

Visitors were instructed how to address the deputy mayor. It felt odd to be on the lower end of the greetings. But this was his grandson, so he didn't mind putting on airs.

"Speak your grievance," a weary voice demanded.

The guards stepped apart so he could look between them and see the man who sat behind the huge desk at the far end of the room. The guest was not allowed to come any closer.

"Well, sir, I don't exactly have a grievance."

One guard took a step forward, hand on his sidearm.

"I mean, I've come to ask about someone we both know."

"Yes, yes, yes, who is it? What's he done?" said Deputy Mayor Kelly. "Speak the name."

"I'm doing research on your father."

"My father?" His tone seemed angry, but the man sat too far away for Steve to be sure he was. "Who wants to know about my father? He's dead now. Been dead for several years."

"Your father, it seems, was—is—my son. Stefan Székely."

A tumble of furniture and the guards closed ranks. Hands pushed between the guards and forced them apart.

The deputy mayor stood in a black cassock with a red sash, looking more like a bishop than a government official. He bore his young age well, forty-eight according to Lily. He stood tall, like all Székely men, had a black moustache, trimmed and waxed, curled, pointed at both ends. He seemed balding beneath his Hat of Office, a seven pointed cloth tam of black with gold trim.

"That name is forbidden here," said Montgomery Marx Kelly.

"Forgive me, sir. I meant no disrespect." He gave a bow, having seen many do similarly in Budapest. "I spoke with Lily a few days ago. I wanted to meet you. That's all."

"Meet me?" Again he seemed angry, his day ruined. "And how dare you bring Lily into this discussion. I trust you did not upset her."

"It seems as though your father was my son, and—"

He sneered. "You're supposed to be my grandfather?"

"I'm sorry, but it seems to be true."

"How true can that be? Aren't you George Osborn, periodontist from Tulsa, Oklahoma?"

"I beg your pardon but I had to use another name to see you."

"You know that is against protocol. You can be arrested for such deception. Get out and I'll forget this happened."

"But I am your grandfather. Stefan Székely."

"No, you're not. I don't believe you. We have gotten official word of his death. Nearly three years ago. Over in Europa. Widely reported."

Steve froze. Perhaps he hadn't thought everything through. He just wanted to meet his grandson, but he didn't want the world to know he was alive—or whatever he was now. Or where he was. Someone would be sure to come looking for him if he was discovered.

"I beg your pardon, Your Lordship. I was mistaken. Sorry. My name is Steve Kelly."

"Steve . . . ? Kelly . . . ?"

"Yes, sir. My American name. Everyone changes their names when they arrive here. I believe your father also changed his name? To . . . Steve Kelly?"

"No, he kept his birth name to the end, I'm afraid. We, his children, changed our names. Not because of our father but our grandfather. He

184

is the one we distance ourselves from."

"I completely understand, sir. I'm only doing some research . . . for a book I'm writing about that person."

"That person? Who do you mean? My father? Or his father?"

"Both, I guess."

The Deputy Mayor let go a big sigh, full of years of impatience.

"What do you want to know?" He stood confidently between his guards, shoulder to shoulder. "There have been many articles. Reports and documentaries aplenty. I suggest you review those first. I'm sure you will find the answers you're looking for. I don't—my office doesn't have the time, nor resources, to indulge every curiosity-seeking history whore such as yourself."

He stepped back and the guards closed ranks.

"But, sir—"

"I know who you are," called the deputy mayor from the other side of the wall of guards. "A fake. A charlatan. An imposter. None of the above. All of the above. Doesn't matter." He tapped a small bell on the desk and the doors opened. "Good day to you."

The four guards, shoulder to shoulder, stepped forward as one to usher him backwards through the open doors. Once the doors closed, he turned to the assistant. He wasn't sure but the assistant seemed to be amused by his plight. Maybe others had come pretending to seek information on his famous father.

He left the tall, silver monstrosity, the seat of power for the eastern district of America, and strolled at the pace of an elderly man with a busted knee down the walkway, lost in his thoughts.

You thought it would be so easy?

The voice didn't alarm him immediately. He believed it was his own thought. He stopped and played it back. The voice . . . .

Which is worse, to be forgotten or to be hated?

He glanced around, suddenly panicked, looking for a place to hide. There! A bar. The BLACK & GOLD.

Hurrying across the street, dodging a honking truck, he whirled into the bar like he was escaping a sudden downpour.

"Welcome," called the bartender, a portly man with a moustache.

"Something strong," said Steve, throwing himself on the bar stool.

"Two of them."

"Bad day at the office?"

He realized how he was dressed, something suitable for a corporate job possibly. "You could say."

He quickly drank some whiskey. And bourbon. Two martinis. Then only the vodka, no olive. And another.

"Yuh better watch yuhself, fella," the bartender cautioned.

His head dulled, the voice barely an echo.

"Hey, there," said a young man in purple cassock with a pink ruffle down the front, "we're twins."

"What?" said Stefan, a vampire from long ago.

"You and me. Same fashion, see? But you have white ruffles and I'm pink. You're blue and I'm purple."

Stefan nodded, his eyes turning gray, a good sign he was free.

"You come here often?" asked the man in purple and pink.

"Aw, leave 'im alone," said the bartender.

"Now you be a dear and leave us alone. He's exactly my type."

"Anyone in a cassock is yar type, Freddy."

"You don't know me," snapped Freddy. "You don't know my type." He turned to Stefan. "Am I your type?"

"I used to type fifty words a minute," Stefan drunkenly responded.

"That's not at all what I mean," said Freddy with a chuckle.

"Let 'im be. He came here to get drunk, not find a friend," said the bartender.

"How do you know? Friends can be anywhere. Don't need to be getting drunk to find them."

Stefan raised his hand. "I'm here to get drunk."

"See?" said the bartender.

"Let me give you my code, Mister. You can ping me anytime you're in the mood to make a friend."

Freddy held up his wrist, put his hand next to Stefan's wrist.

"Hmm, didn't click."

"He's not interested, Freddy. Leave 'im be."

"Oh you're such a pooper party, Glenn."

Stefan tried to stand up, but the room was spinning. He started to fall, grabbed the stool, both crashing to the floor.

☙

Fingernails gently stroking lines back and forth across his bare chest awoke him. The light was dim, the smell of cannabis strong. His body lay back against another man's chest, head and shoulders cradled in the lap of his host.

"You're awake," cooed the man in a soft tenor. His hands flattened against Stefan's chest but the man's sharp fingernails flicked against his nipples, intentionally, it seemed. "You have really lovely chest hair. So black and thick. Very manly. Some men shave it off but I like it."

Stefan pushed himself up, saw he still wore the mesh trousers with the glittery white thong showing beneath. This man had apparently removed his cassock and decided to nurse him out of his drunken stupor.

"Where?" asked Stefan.

"You're at my place." The man, also bare chested, saw his worried expression. "Oh, relax. Nothing happened. You're right down the street from that bar we met in. Everybody's a dramaturge."

Stefan pulled himself up to a sitting position on what he saw was a narrow bed. His companion seemed to be wearing a similar thong of pink with a purple religious symbol emblazoned on the front, over the crotch. And black boots. Stefan's wingtip shoes were still on.

"It got hot in here, so I stripped us down. Hope you don't mind."

Stefan gave a nod of thanks. Maybe thanks. He needed to get out and return to the hotel. Bucky was probably worried what happened to him. He was visiting the deputy mayor, he suddenly remembered. But he got nowhere. At least he got to see his grandson, a brief glimpse and some testy words exchanged. Can't choose our grandkids.

"What's that?" asked his host.

"I said 'We can't choose our grandchildren'."

The man snickered. "That sure is true. How many you got?"

Stefan wasn't sure he wanted to talk to this man. Maybe he needed to gain his confidence, though, so it would be easier to escape.

"I have four." He faked a smile. "In fact, I'm trying to meet them, wherever they live. They don't know me, it's been so long. They are not supposed to like me."

"I bet they're cute. I like little babies."

"They are grown up, all adults now."

The man radiated surprise. "Grown up? You don't look that old, Mister. How old are you?"

"I am the right age for today."

The other man laughed, his grin revealing a gold tooth.

"Well, aren't we all? Heck, I don't have anybody," he said, lowering his head and pouting. "Most people don't have kids. You have to get a license for that. And got to be married for the license. But accidents happen. Then you get put in an education facility." He grinned as though he was hopeful that Stefan might join him on the application. "But I get by making friends where I can."

Stefan frowned. "Picking up guests from the bar?"

"Oh, he makes it sound worse than it is. I happened to be there already when you entered."

"It must be fate." Stefan intended it as humor but his host seemed to take it seriously.

"Must be." He grinned happily. "Glenn—the bartender?—he said you came in wanting to get drunk fast. I guess you got troubles, like everybody. It's a crazy world we have."

He leaned forward toward Stefan, stretching his hand over the flower-patterned quilt, roses and lilacs, green leaves. He noticed the quilt under his hand.

"My mother gave it to me. Said I should give it to my kid. That'll never happen, I told her. She never listens. But I can share it with you. So what's your name?"

He pursed his lips, hesitant to reply. "Steve."

"Oh, hello there, Steve."

"You're Freddy, I remember from the bar."

"That's right. We were twins, remember?"

"How did I get here?"

"Well, you could walk okay if I helped, but you was heavy. You was out of your mind, too. Saying things about Europa. You must have gotten some bad juju somewhere."

"Yes, it's a curse."

"A curse, you say? I know about that, yes I do."

"What do you know? Curses are rare. And terrible."

Freddy leaned further, slid his hand to Stefan's hand. "I know how to make a curse go away. You got one you want to go away?"

Stefan chuckled at the irony of the situation.

"Let me show you." And he suddenly pressed toward Stefan, his lips against Stefan's mouth. Freddy rolled Stefan onto his back and lay over him, continuing to kiss him, sharp fingernails running down his chest, hands reaching for the top of his mesh trousers, fingers trying to roll the waistband down. "I'll make those curses go away."

Stefan got his hand between them and held Freddy away, as he continued tugging at the waistband. "Stop."

"Don't you want to make those curses go away?" Freddy remained on top of him, his mouth close to Stefan's throat. "I can do that. All it takes is one little bite."

Freddy's mouth opened wider, exposing fangs, just as he swung them down to Stefan's throat. But Stefan held up his hand and caught the open mouth with a hard chop. The fangs cut the back of his hand. Freddy switched to licking Stefan's hand.

"Stop that," Stefan grunted. "You don't know what you're doing."

"I surely do know what I'm doing, Steve. A vampire has to get some blood once in a while. And I can smell yours is top grade."

"No, you're not a vampire," said Stefan, pushing Freddy back. He got upright, holding his hands up. "There are no vampires in America."

"You think so, but you'd be wrong." He grinned, showing his fangs once more. They had cut his lower lip, which bled. "Want a taste of this?" he asked, pointing to his bleeding lip.

"No. I don't have cravings any longer."

"Cravings? You mean you're a vampire, too?"

Freddy jumped off the bed, stood with his hands on his hips, his thong askew. He looked down at his penis.

"Well, this is ridiculous. We can't both be vampires. That's not how it works."

Stefan shook his head, regaining his balance.

"Vampires can feed on other vampires, but you have to know your partner intimately, and your partner's blood especially. You must be careful whose blood you take. Not all vampires—or bloodlings—are the same. Not all are safe."

Freddy sat beside him, patted his shoulder, left his hand there.

"Yeah, I know. But you looked so handsome in your cassock, and so sweet the way you were happily drunk. I thought you must be one of the good ones, with a gentle bouquet and a strong finish. I like a strong finish." He winked deliberately. "We don't have to exchange blood. We can, you know, make some sex. Or, if you don't want to do that, then I could simply hold you in my arms until you felt your curse all gone. Would you like that?"

Stefan, Steve, whatever his name was, whoever he happened to be in the moment, remained silent, listening for the voice. It had gone, lost in the drunken stupor. He had gradually learned, on one or many nights in the empire, when he was drunk, his lord and master, Luce, could not communicate with him, could not give him commands or threaten him with punishment if he disobeyed. He tested his limits, the amount needed to overcome the voice. He was alarmed the voice found him in America. He had escaped, yes, but he was not completely free.

"Go on," said Freddy, holding him in his arms. "And then what happened?"

He had been mumbling, apparently, unable to make himself get up and leave yet not willing to indulge in a fling with a stranger. Sure, he had gathered many partners at his winsome whim in his capacity as emperor. Who could refuse him?

"I need to get drunk to stop the voice," he said more clearly.

"What voice? You mean like demons? We all have demons, honey."

"The voice of my master."

"You mean your dom? You into the domination thingy? I tried that for a while but my dominatrix didn't do it for me. Dropped her like a cat-o'-nine-tails, yes I did."

"It is a vampire thing. When you gain certain privileges, there are duties to perform or you lose those privileges. My master was very hard on me, made me do things I didn't want to do."

"Aw, baby, that's all right. You're with Freddy now. You're safe with me, poor baby."

"I'm not a poor baby," said Stefan, pushing him away, breaking out of Freddy's arms. "I'm on the run. I ran into that bar to get drunk so I could hide from the voice. From Him calling me."

"Him? Who? Your current lover?"

"No! The Most High. The God of Evil."

"Oh, that one. My lord! My god of evil is a bad boy, that's definite."

The knocking on the door broke the spell and Freddy jumped up.

"If it's Butch, just say you fell down and I was caring for you."

But it was Bucky, holding a tire iron in his hand and a mean scowl on his face.

"Steffy, there you are!" He pushed Freddy aside, though the man was taller. "I tracked ya down. Th' silver tower, then th' bar you was in. They got images o' ever'thing. Th' barkeep sent me here lookin fer ya."

"Whoa, you're a feisty boy," said Freddy. "A cowboy!"

Stefan gathered his cassock, pulled it on, fixed the magnetic snaps and straightened the ruffle. Now he was presentable in public.

"I'm sorry, I'm sorry," said Freddy as Stefan left with Bucky. "You are so lucky to have a cowboy. I envy you. But come visit me anytime. Please. Any time you want. We can exchange blood."

※

Bucky didn't do sugarcoating. "Th' hell ya doin gettin drunk 'nd goin off with a freaky stranger in a fuckin strange town?"

Stefan waved him off. "I got drunk to silence the voice."

"What voice? I thought you was meeting yer grandson."

"I did meet him. In his office, with guards. He was not thrilled to meet me. Didn't believe I was who I said I was. Besides, I'm George Osborn now. I can't even be Steve Kelly, much less Stefan Székely. The world has already forgotten me, or else they hate me, which is about the same. No one can say the name. He denied me, refused to let me ask him questions. My own grandson . . . ." He rubbed his jaw with his hand, the spot where the vampire had kissed him on the way to his throat. "He seemed to be full of stress today."

"Deputy mayor's got all kinds o' stress 'cept th' kind I guess a full mayor's got. So nothing got done."

"Sorry to worry you."

"I ain't worried, just pissed." Bucky gritted his teeth. "I got hungry 'nd don't know how ta call down fer food on th' dang machine. I was waiting fer ya ta come on back so I can get some *geeyawdamn* supper. 'Bout starving ta death."

Stefan took the tablet in the room and ordered for them and the food was delivered by robot within a few minutes. It tasted better than expected but not as good as they had hoped. Burgers and fries. They vowed to leave Pittsburgh the next morning.

Wiping his mouth, Stefan sat back in the chair. Bucky watched the huge wall screen, another war movie showing. The boys in blue were getting their asses kicked by a squad of vampire soldiers. With the screen covering the entire wall, it seemed as though they were right there in the battle.

"I used to live here when I was a teenager," Stefan spoke. "I lived with my aunt. My parents were too busy with their careers—doctors at the state hospital in Utica, up in New York—*North* York. So they had me living with a woman they called my aunt, but I don't think she was actually related. And she, my aunt, thought I had some evil touch. She took me with her to church every Sunday, but I had to wait outside. Never wanted me to contaminate the church."

"Vampire shee-yit'll do it fast." Bucky pushed his dinner plate away, reached for his beer in a tall glass.

"I found out later, of course, I actually did have an evil touch. My parents knew it but never told me. Finally, when they transformed and were hiding, my mother wrote a letter and told me the truth. About the family curse. A little too late, of course. In the end, it didn't matter. I couldn't stop it. The only thing that changed it was me going to Croatia for treatment. That treatment made me turn into a vampire immediately. I could have prolonged the suffering another ten years, if I'd wanted to."

Stefan's smirk did not register on Bucky.

"Then ya became th' gyawdamn Emperor of Europa."

An odd expression hung on Bucky's face, something wavering between boiling anger and controlled suspicion. He stared hard at the screen as bombards sprayed a squad of the AAU blue boys. The explosions were loud in the room. Bucky gripped the arms of his chair.

"That's correct." Stefan looked at the wall. "Can we turn that off?"

"Then I gotta go fight against yer gyawdamn vampire army."

"That is also correct. But I—"

"Then ya show up in a *geeyawdamn* box cuz yer evil staff jus hated ya more 'an th' people ya made go off ta fight."

Stefan bowed his head. "Yes, also correct."

"So yer jus one gyawdamn sonuvabee-atch evil demon I been drivin round these weeks, sharing my cannabis with . . . ."

"Yes. I'm sorry." He scooted to the front of the chair, hands clasped like he was about to pray. "For everything I've done."

"Fer ever'thin ya done, huh?"

"Yes, everything. I deserve a lot of punishment."

"Ya sure do, assho'e."

The screen showed an artist's drawing of the emperor in black and white, a grisly mask of pure evil. Vampiric features were accentuated. Photography had been banned in the empire; some vampires didn't appear on film. Others believed there was no point to collecting and cataloguing images of citizens.

"That you?" Bucky asked through clenched teeth, chinning at the wall screen.

Stefan gave a nod, looked away from the screen.

"I said I'm sorry. What else do you want me to do? I'm trying to make amends with my family. I'm trying to apologize—"

Bucky shot up, his hand like a knife poised at Stefan.

"I'm gonna say this jus once, kay? But anytime I give ya this here look—*this*—see?—gonna mean th' same *geeyawdamn* thing. It means —I'm thinking it again, ri' now—'nd that's a hard *Fuck You*. Got it? I'm tellin ya 'Fuck the fuck you'—'nd all yer evil shee-yit. Jus Fu-u-u-*uck* You-*u-u*! 'Nd th' blood ya rode in on!"

9

IN THE MORNING, BUCKY WAS GONE. Stefan called down to the concierge and learned he had checked out early. That is, he had announced to the reception desk person that he was "bound for the open road" and to let that "vampire sucka" pay the bill.

There was a pain in the pit of his gut, a heavy emptiness he had not felt since he thought his Beloved had died back in 2028—but she rose again. And they lived two happy years together before he was called to duty once more. Such a long period of time wasted. He had no right to come back, to continue to exist, after everything he had done. The worst acts anyone could do. Being in the same room with a war veteran and pretending there wasn't anything more to be said. And—

Did I really order the assassination of my son?

He knew this voice was his. He tried to think. How many years? What had he said? What had he implied or suggested or hinted at that would give someone on his staff the idea. Did they act on his order or alone, believing it was what he wanted? Did they know the Secretary was actually his son? Perhaps it never mattered. His son was old and could have died of natural causes—which is what he had believed all these years until Lily explained the truth.

He was so evil that evil simply happened without him ordering anything evil to be done. Evil surrounded him. Cars crashed because he was in the vicinity. People divorced because of his glance. Buildings toppled because he touched a brick. Wars started because he blinked at a meeting. Babies died at birth because he long ago had walked the same pavement as that mother did before she conceived. This was what evil does. It was a cloud that enveloped everything. This was what he had done: been a sweeping cloud of darkness.

He sat on the side of the bed and wept. The tears burned like acid on his skin. His nerves sizzled up and down his arms, his legs, and in his chest the beating slowed, then exploded in great waves of pain as he tried to suck in air, never enough, never quick enough, until he fell on the floor and in one last effort reached for the tablet and tapped the red emergency call button.

൦ൠ

Again, like so many times in his life, in his *existence*, Stefan awoke in a hospital bed. His eyes creaked open, saw the vast whiteness he at first expected was heaven, although he had no idea why he would end up there. The recessed lights overhead appeared as the Pearly Gates. And when the doctor in his white coat stood beside his bed, he was certain it must be St. Peter, determined to set the record straight, the tally of his deeds, both good and evil. But he was ready; he had memorized his excuses.

"I'm afraid you suffered a heart attack, Mister Osborn."

He winced, like he knew he was in the wrong hospital.

"I guessed as much."

The doctor smiled as though he had smiled at patients many times already that day.

"You're going to be all right. We've repaired the damage. But we'll need you to go on a strict diet and, after adequate rest, a full exercise regimen. That will improve the strength of your heart and keep you living a long, long time."

Again Stefan winced, getting the bad news. His return to normalcy hit a snag. His plan detoured. Strategy fell short. The plan was to die. Again. Not live a long, long time.

"Can't you put everything back the way it was?" he mumbled. "Let me go ahead and die."

"What's that? I couldn't understand."

He shook his head. "Never mind."

The doctor studied the information on the tablet in his hands. "You must take our advice seriously. This is your fifth heart attack, it seems. I sure don't know how you survived four others. This one was mild."

He remembered he was George Osborn, not Stefan or Steve.

"I lived an exciting life," he muttered.

The doctor grinned. "Well, it's time to shift it down a bit. You want to have more time with your family don't you?" He tapped the tablet. "Your wife, Pamela, and three children, eight grandchildren, one great-grandchild . . . ?"

"Yes," he said with a weary sigh. "The grandchildren. I want to see them."

"Then follow doctor's orders and we'll get you back home as soon as we can."

"Thank you."

He thought of Budapest in his half-sleep, both the dark years of his reign and the heady nights of his playboy lifestyle before that time, as though he were still there, again in a hospital, his second home, with his Beloved silent in a bed in a cubicle in another wing of the hospital, desperately clinging to life as he clung desperately to death. It was clear to him that what went around would continue to go around.

By day he would have technical conversations with his doctors and nurses but couldn't remember them later. The drugs kept him sedated a lot—so he could recover, they said. The room seemed like a cave, however, with a small fire burning and jumbled shadows dancing on the walls as his only entertainment. He somehow knew that outside the hospital, the sun shone brightly. And he would not be harmed by it. He asked for the blinds to be opened.

"I don't think so," he replied to doctors' questions whenever he was asked about various oddities of his health. It seemed George Osborn was a train wreck. Steve Kelly was strange in his own way, a relic of the past century when the vampire explosion brought new medicines into the world, new ways to treat afflictions, new procedures. Compassion for the suffering of vampires was popular. Until they formed armies to fight against the bloodlings. "Shit got real," he heard Bucky say in his mind. "I killt bout two thousand o' them bloodsuckers," he had said as they traveled. He missed Bucky.

When he was released, he was glad to toss his Pittsburgh fashion in the big donation bin outside the St. Nicholas Orthodox Church, the one he was not allowed to enter. He drove the rental vehicle—a basic model Hoverina sedan in gun-metal gray without fins—away from the church, circling through the streets of his old neighborhood, now about a hundred years removed, the houses remarkably the same— with more unsightly network arrays, surveillance towers, and lighting bubbles added to the roofs—repaired and renovated but presenting the same mood, the same dour attitude. Hopelessness.

He couldn't find his aunt's house and became concerned about his memory, but he calculated it likely had stood on what was a vacant lot where people had been dumping their trash for years. He hovered there, staring, for a while—

You can never go home again.

The voice had returned. But he drove on anyway, ignoring it. He had to learn to ignore it and not rush to drink it away.

He scratched his chest.

How does it feel to be alive again?

He kept his eyes fixed on the highway, maintaining his lane as he hovered over the pavement like the other upscale drivers, avoiding the *wheeled* vehicles. Focus on the road, he reminded himself. Someone had taught him the fine art of blocking out the rest of the world. Was it Maria? Or some other partner over the years?

Half-way across Pennsylvania, he realized he had lost the voice. It was like driving out from under the wireless signal bubble. His mind had concentrated on a block of ice, all its hues, the changing surface as it melted, the way the light shifted. He became an expert on ice. When he came up to the exit he wanted, he was ready to start a new life, a new existence, feeling the warm thing in his chest thumping in decent rhythm.

Then a red warning light blinked on the dashboard of the vehicle. All the gauges were different from what he was used to. He tried to read it as he veered out of his lane and back again. Something about his account coming to a zero balance. The rental period was about to expire. He had ten miles more . . . .

The engine went silent and he coasted to the side of the road.

INSUFFICIENT FUNDS blinked in yellow on the dashboard.

He cursed. Fifty minutes later he became tired of cursing and put the seat back and tried to relax. It was the same as when he returned from the chase in Hungary and his vehicle ran out of gasoline. He pulled to the side and eventually a highway patrol stopped to check on him, called for a truck to carry his damaged car into the city. And now? What was the protocol here? He was not a rich playboy. He should have paid more up-front, he realized, but he thought showing too much old money might draw suspicions.

How does it feel to be stuck in PARK?

The voice had returned.

He closed his eyes, conjuring another block of ice. Perhaps a whole glacier slowly sliding down to the sea. But the sun came out, hastening the melt, ruining his concentration.

"Leave me alone," he muttered.

You can never be free from me, Stefan. You know that.

Knowing that Luce could read his thoughts when he was sober, he focused on crinkly worms crawling through dirt, kept his mind on the wriggling creatures and the humus they shit out behind them as they crawled. He held the worms in his mind as long as he could.

You have learned some tricks. I am impressed. Yet your body and soul belong to me. They always will. Our contract is severely binding.

"I will never serve you again!" he shouted to the dashboard, adding a few hard slaps for good measure.

The echo of laughter filled the vehicle interior.

"Haven't I done enough for you? Haven't I ruined enough of this world? Can't we give it a rest now?"

There is no limit on evil. It may continue to the far reaches of time. We have had this discussion previously. Order and Chaos must exist in balance. Now is a time of Chaos.

"I've done my part. It's time for me to retire."

Again the laughter, sounding as though it was bouncing off stone walls in a dungeon, iron shackles clanging.

He sat up, adjusted the seat, firmly gripped the steering levers.

"I'm only going to say this once: Please let me go. Please."

Instead of the laughter he expected, there was only silence. Eerie silence. That unnerved him more than laughter. What would happen next? When would the final, fatal blow come? Was that heart attack in the hotel room supposed to be it? Now . . . nothing?

He says the magic word. Deep chuckles. *Because you use the magic word, I will let you go.*

"Thank you."

However, first you must perform one last task for me. If you fail, I shall not let you go.

"What is it?"

You must agree first.

"I agree, I agree. Now what the fuck is it?"

I shall tell you when the time is right.

He shook his head. "More tricks."

You have always enjoyed our tricks, haven't you?

"No, I haven't."

That hurts me, Stefan. It really does.

◌◌

In Trenton, Jersey, a few blocks from the university campus, in a quaint brown brick home set in a small yard shaded by several mature trees, a rose arbor on the side of the house, lived the woman who was his granddaughter. At forty-two, she had been a professor for ten years. Married to Frank Richardson, also a professor. Two children: a boy, age eight, named Frank after his father, and a girl, age five, named Penny— after her grandmother, he supposed. Gazing at the pretty house and trimmed lawn, he felt bad for interrupting their innocent lives, for inserting himself into their circle of bliss.

But he had to see her. At least get a look at her. Meeting might not be necessary, he told himself, getting a glimpse. Would this Rose Kelly-Richardson also resemble his Korean-American Penny? He had to see. He had spent three years in a box for this.

Standing in front of the house like some ghoul hoping for a death was not the look he was going for. When the police drone stopped next to him with a flashing warning to move on, he took a few steps down the sidewalk and the drone departed. He glanced around, wondering who watched him. Where was the camera? Perhaps it was on the house itself, a hidden security camera linked to the neighborhood monitor who would contact the police who would direct a surveillance drone to intercept him.

He walked away, thinking it was the best thing he could possibly do. Leave them alone. Let them be. Their lives had already been going along quite successfully without him, without them knowing him. But the nagging curiosity pestered him, drove him to return every day for a week, just to glance innocently at the house as he strolled by. Twice a surveillance drone approached him. Finally, it flashed a red warning: MAXIMUM WARNINGS EXCEEDED. A security patrol drove up beside him, hovering over the pavement.

"What're you up to, fella?" asked the robot in a life-like voice.

"I like the scenery on this street," he said in as calm a voice as he could conjure, imagining the robot might detect voice stress. "So I've been walking this way for my daily exercise."

"Residents have complained. Please choose another route."

"Yes, of course. Sorry. I meant no harm."

"No harm is not no harm," the robot replied like a Zen koan, eyes blinking. "Residents feel harm even if you intend no harm."

"I suppose that's true," he said with a smile.

"Please choose a different route. You are forbidden from this route from now." The robot's arm telescoped out from the hovering vehicle, a tablet attached to its hand. "Apply chip here."

He was wary of the authenticity of his chip now and stepped back from the neighborhood patrol. He turned his back to the robot and walked quickly down the slope, around the curve, back to his Hoverina parked on the street—recharged with his old paper money converted to credits at a bank, where he was advised to get a replacement chip since his was not connecting properly to the grid; he would need to visit banks in person (and walk-in locations were few and far between) to conduct further business, but he got what credits he had put on the chip he wore.

The police robot followed him to the Hoverina, flashing its red warning lights. There were no verbal commands to obey, but he knew he was being surveilled. He smiled at the robot. He had renewed his vehicle rental charge, nothing for the robot to tag him for. He pressed the button on the control pad and the door of his vehicle slid open. He dropped into the driver's seat and the door closed. He waved at the robot and started the engine.

"Bye bye, tin man," he sneered as the vehicle rose off its struts and hovered over the pavement, moving smoothly down the street.

He drove to the university and parked in the visitor lot, walked to a map board and located her building. Once inside, he strolled around until he found the Department of Modern Anthropology. The stately old building was older than him but its interior was designed in space-age everything. He couldn't sit comfortably in the triangular chairs provided. A secretary asked him who he was there to see, since he did not seem to be a student.

As he waited, he saw the secretary interacting with a dozen screens where students were voicing one concern or another, begging to be excused from class, or reciting a homework assignment. He wondered if there were any classrooms left.

Finally, a woman came out and the secretary pointed to him. He had worn an old suit—old in style, modest: brown jacket and trousers, cream-colored shirt, and the newest skinny blue necktie. He had kept the wingtip shoes.

She greeted him. With the brightest orange hair, fairly short and buxom, she definitely was not a look-a-like of Penny. Obviously she had taken after her mother, Stefan's wife. Not the Székely side of the family. She could pass for an Irish Kelly, if it were not for Kelly being a corruption of a Hungarian name.

"I'm Doctor Richardson," she spoke with a pleasantly warm smile. "How can I help you today?"

He stood, was a head taller than her, and gazed down on her with his dark eyes. He imagined her seeing a poor man not in peak health. She urged him to sit again. She took a chair and pulled it over to him, asking if he was all right.

"It's been a journey," he said, taking a deep breath.

He explained his project: researching the political figures of the past century, notably those relevant to the fall of the Empire of Europa. He understood she was the daughter of Stefan Székely, the former

Secretary of—

"I know. Believe me, I know," she said, waving him to silence. "He did a lot for the world, especially securing the treaty with the Russias. He was less successful with Europa, but that is a long story."

"Indeed, I'm trying to write that long story, which is the reason for my visit. If you have some time—I won't be long—I would appreciate asking you a few questions, if you don't mind."

She glanced at the secretary, as if noting she'd heard it all before or else indicating security should be called to remove this pest.

"I'm unclear about—I do hope you won't take any offense—about what happened in your father's final days. When he went to Lisbon."

"Yes, that story." She suddenly had a grim countenance, pausing to select her words, he supposed. "He was to attend a conference with the emperor and they would sign a treaty. I believe that the emperor had promised to ease some efforts with regard to trade and military action. I think my father was pleased to attend. Unfortunately, upon his arrival in Lisbon, in his room at the Grand Hotel Braziliana, someone broke in and stabbed him to death."

He feigned shock. Of course, it was history now, and anyone could read about it, but hearing it from the daughter was different. Knowing it was his son they were discussing made his nerves sizzle with restless energy, negative energy.

"I'm sorry." He frowned, watching her hold herself together. She had poise, he noticed, part of the training to be a professor. "You teach 'modern anthropology'? Is that the study of current civilizations?"

"Yes." She seemed happy to change the topic. "We study modern civilizations, like the Empire of Europa. We investigate in the same way we investigate ancient civilizations such as the Romans. We look at a civilization's artifacts, and people's movements, and, because we are lucky to be in a modern age, at its documents. It may seem ironic, but my specialty is Europa. The empire in particular."

"I can understand why it interests you. So you know how it began and who was involved, and everything that happened there?"

"In a manner of speaking. My Ph.D. dissertation was on the rise of vampire society in the twenty-thirties. Oh, no—I'm not a vampire. It fascinates me, this different class of people, and how their special needs could formulate a new set of laws and political ambitions. It's fascinating to me. However, we cannot know everything, so that is the reason we study it. There is always more to learn. I'm working on a new book chapter, covering the empire's annexation of Italy. I'm afraid it's due very soon, ha ha. Did you have a particular question about Europa?"

"I'm sorry to bother you. I know I could read a book or two and not be disturbing you. I only thought you may have some insight . . . on your father's death. The circumstances and . . . ."

She seemed resigned to have to tell it again and so launched right into the story. "He was there to conclude a treaty. It was a very significant act, the first agreement between the empire and the AAU ever. Someone must not have wanted that to happen, however, and killed him to be sure it didn't. That maneuver has been oft repeated throughout history. If a different person had been in that position instead of my father, the result, I think, would've been the same. It wasn't that he was my father but that it was any ambassador of the AAU. So who would have wanted the treaty to go unsigned? The powers-that-be in Europa or those in the Anglo-American Union? I have my list of suspects on both sides. Who stood to gain most from a failure of the conference? It seems as though Europa was able to advance its agenda further following the conference than the AAU did. So I believe, perhaps, someone at the highest level in Budapest had the conference sabotaged. However, I still would like to entertain the thought that whoever it may have been in Budapest may have had some arrangement with their opposite number in the AAU. I'm still researching that. The documents are slow to be collected."

He perked up. "Documents?"

"Yes, many documents. With the fall, literally tons of documents have become available. The empire produced countless paper artifacts. They avoided electronic communication. Many of the documents are priceless. For example, we have the order in his handwriting here. The actual paper document. And we have—"

"The order?" His eyes narrowed and he scratched his throat.

"Yes, the emperor's order, in his own hand. He signed the order for the assassination of my father. It's a gruesome document, of course, but it's history. My father was brave to go there, willing to do so to try to improve the world, and I will never know if he thought he would be killed or not. He always said—"

"The emperor signed an order . . . to have your father assassinated? He actually gave that order?"

"We believe so. It's written in Magyar but the translation is clear. He gave permission for his associate, whoever it might have been, to arrange the killing of my father. The order gives only the command, not the method. Presumably, whoever carried out the order was left to devise the method. Most scholars, but not me, think it was made to look like a break-in and theft. Certain items were taken to help with that view, including a broach from his mother, essentially a good luck charm."

He moved to the front corner of the triangular chair, elbows on his knees. "He ordered your father to be killed? Are you certain?"

"Yes, I told you."

"But you seem not too sad over it."

"Sad? Is that the word? I am completely heartbroken over his death but I cannot function every day if I fixate on it. I must move beyond that event. I must find a way to keep going. Yes, I know many do not. The war veterans remain traumatized fighting vampires, for example. I pity them. We have hospitals which specialize in that kind of trauma, of being savaged by vampires, or even one bite. They try to restore the veterans to some kind of a normal life. 'Once half-bitten, always a half-vampire', they say. A lot of stigma."

He could only nod absently in rhythm to her warm voice.

"I'm sorry to bother you," he said, starting to get up from the odd chair. He stumbled, the chair tipped over, and Rose—Dr. Richardson—helped him up and straightened his chair. "Sorry. Very sorry."

"I hope I've helped answer your questions."

A tear dropped from his eye, hit the carpet, a drop in the ocean.

"Thanks. I won't bother you again."

"It would be my pleasure to talk again if you have further questions or concerns. We continue to research that time period. We might find something new you'd be interested in."

He stopped his exit and turned to her. "May I—"

She paused, her hand remaining on his sleeve to steady him. "Yes?"

"May I see it? The order?"

Her face shifted. "It's locked in the archives, of course."

"Is it accessible to the public?"

"No, I'm afraid not. I could escort you to see it, if you really want to see it. But it—"

"I would. I must see—"

She held up her hand to halt him as she addressed the secretary, speaking about arrangements for clearance to the archives. It would take an hour, she explained, to get proper clearances and pass through the authentication protocol.

"We have taken images of it," she offered, "if that would do."

His face became more pale. "Yes, I suppose it would."

They walked through the large campus building, its lofty halls and tall windows making it feel like a cathedral. At the opposite end from her office they passed through a checkpoint. "He's with me." Further on, they arrived at a set of doors. Guards stood in front of the doors. She showed her badge. "He's with me."

The guards unlocked the doors with a code typed on a keypad on the wall and a full palm pressed to a screen. The doors creaked open automatically, an inch at a time.

"We must preserve these important documents for scholarship," she said as they entered and passed down the main aisle. On either side as they walked were stacks of shelving and rows of cabinets. The vast holdings of knowledge of the entire university and some research firms. The archives could withstand a nuclear blast, she informed him, and laughed that the empire never acquired nuclear weapons.

She checked her tablet, got the aisle number, shelf number, cabinet number. When they stood in front of it, she typed in a code and the cabinet unlocked. Sliding out a drawer, she set it on a table behind them. She carefully shuffled the papers in the drawer.

"We often have scholars visit to review the documents. However, we ask them to wear gloves when handling them. These images can be replaced, the originals not."

She lifted a square of paper out of the drawer, set it on the table.

He stared down at the paper, its corners curling, and immediately recognized the artistic flourishes along the borders of the page. He saw the black ink of the handwriting; nothing official was ever produced by machine in the empire. They had by design reverted to older customs, styles, methods.

A minister had dictated the words, he suddenly recalled.

"May I?" he asked, indicating he wanted to pick up the document.

"Yes, these you may handle."

He reached for the paper, took it between thumb and forefinger, lifted it off the table. He lay it over his open palm, cradling it, reading over it as he pointed at each word with a finger of his other hand. His lips moved as he read, the Magyar returning to his mind.

"Hmm, you can read Magyar?" she asked.

He got to the bottom of the page and his eyes circumscribed the curls of the signature, the extra large S and the exaggerated loop of the Y at the end. And the title: *EURÓPA CSÁSZÁRA*—Emperor of Europa.

"Is this what you were interested in?" asked Dr. Richardson.

The document dropped from his grasp, drifted down to the table as he took a step back.

"I had no idea such documents would be collected. And saved. For people to look at later. Much later. And make judgments over them."

"Judgments? What do you mean?"

"I guess you would call it scholarship. They look and decide. Make their judgments about what happened based on some marks on a page. And, maybe, human nature, certainly—whatever that is. How can they ever really know? It was a private meeting. How could they know what was said, or what may have happened next?"

"What happened next . . . ?" She turned grim, setting the document on top of the pile in the drawer. "Do you know something about this?"

He turned away so she couldn't read his face. His recently repaired heart was pounding. It no longer clicked like a vampire's did.

The soft buzz of an emergency button being pressed found its way to his ear. He saw that her hand was in her pants pocket.

The doors opened and two university security men appeared.

He had no breath but spoke anyway: "I was there."

She held up her hand to the security men. "Wait."

"I was in that room." He returned his gaze to her. "I'm from Europa and I know something. I was in that room. I saw the document written on a grand table. Five ministers stood around the table. The emperor sat in the middle, the only person sitting. It was Borbély who dictated the words. He was—was the—"

"Minister of International Affairs," she spoke, her voice strained, eyes wide, mouth agape. "He argued most vehemently for stricter trade policies with the AAU."

"The emperor . . . he wrote each word as Borbély spoke the word." He pointed to the image on the paper sitting in the drawer. "You see how every word ends like it is its own sentence. It is not a string of words but individual words written separately."

She gazed at the paper. "I see that now." She leaned closer. "I never thought of that before. Thank you. That's very insightful. Very helpful. We may need to think it over again. But what does that mean exactly? Was it written under duress?" She straightened up, continuing to gaze down at the document. "You said you were there?"

"The words were dictated, one by one." He swallowed. "Because he did not wish to write them. He hoped his personal guard detail would break into the room and save him. To keep him from signing the order. Yet, they did not. They were given furlough. An entertainment awaited them, reward for exemplary service."

"You were there? How? In what capacity?" She seemed desperate to know, the fervor of a scholar onto something big. "Were you a servant? A guard?"

He shook his head, dropping his chin to his chest. He couldn't say anything. He had said too much. But the truth of the matter carved its initials into his heart. He had to let it out, no matter who got hurt, no matter the result. His life—and his death—were already at an end.

"I was there . . . in that room." He regarded her a moment. "I was the only person sitting at that table. I was the only person with a pen in hand."

She stared, her eyes becoming teary.

"They made me write it. They made me sign it."

Suddenly her hand waved wildly and the security men surrounded them. They remained there to block him as she hurried away through the aisles. She looked back over her shoulder just before she exited.

Then the security men escorted him out of the room.

And then he was running—running as fast as he could, as fast as his heart would allow, as much as his broken feet and aged legs would bear him—until he was far from the campus, forced to stop and take a breath. He fell to his knees, crashing on the hard pavement, screamed as loudly as he could his anguish, cursing the tricks he been made to suffer for the sake of the Most High who had used him like a puppet on strings to destroy the world.

ભ

The dreams of a vampire are dark—dark red, the deepest crimson ever imaginable. The dreams of a human who once was a vampire are full of the blood he has sipped, the throats and wrists ravaged, the bodies left limp and drained. They are reminders of what could be again. Once a half-vampire, always a half-vampire, they say. Or a former vampire?

He scratched at the marks on his hand. When Freddy the Vampire had tried to bite his throat, he chopped at the man's mouth with his hand, like something learned from watching a karate movie. Freddy's fangs had scraped across the back of his hand, drawing blood. Now the lines had festered, an infection growing under the scabs. It itched, but also a dull ache spread throughout his hand. His fingers hurt when he moved them, the joints stiff. For a moment he wished he had some of Bucky's cannabis to help with that.

He needed to take the levers in his hands to operate the Hoverina. He needed to get out of town, hit the road, keep away from highways and avoid patrols like Bucky did. If his daughter thought to report the strange visitor to authorities, they could be on the lookout for him. They had enough surveillance drones available to cover the area from Pittsburgh to New York City. There would be no place he could hide.

Perhaps she believed him, took him at his word, that he really was Stefan, the assassinated Emperor of Europa, somehow visiting America and showing up at her office to discuss how he murdered her father. That would be easy to believe. No, more likely she would think he was some lunatic playing a cruel game with her, fooling her for perverse amusement. That would be more plausible. She wouldn't need to call anyone. Campus security would protect her.

Only his younger grandson remained on the list. Benedict Kelly lived in Albany. An artist, apparently. Had a gallery exhibit down in New York City a few months ago, good reviews. Wife: Katherine, Kitty for short. A girl named Bessie, aged four. Kitty stayed home, as was the custom after the Standard Wage was raised again and the Universal Basic Income was enacted in the province. He was curious what his art was about, never having much interest in painting. He thought back to the occasional sketches Penny drew on napkins in the Barnes and Noble bookstore when they would meet for lattés and conversation, portraits of the other customers around them. She wasn't very good but he liked that she did it.

The Hoverina exited the forest, sunshine hitting the windshield as the road wound through the mountains of northeastern Pennsylvania. The country roads curved, the hills rose and sank, tree-cover blocking the sun for a mile, then fields bathed in sunshine for the next mile. He crossed into New York without encountering any checkpoint.

In Albany, he located the old loft in the central business district, something with a view over the river valley and the Vermont hills. It was perfect for an artist, he considered. But no one was at home, it seemed. He asked a woman coming out of the next loft if Benedict still lived there. Yes, but he was away for an exhibit, the neighbor thought. He went down to the City every couple of weeks. Further checking helped him locate the exhibit and he decided to drive down to see it.

Being late already, Stefan drove around and found a hotel, checked in, paid with the old cash. The lady frowned but accepted it. He told her it was worth more than face value but that didn't impress her. He would need to find another money dealer and convert the paper bills and gold coins to credits put on his wrist chip before he could do any further business in town.

In his room, he examined his left hand again. It was swelling. A sizzling pain passed every few minutes. He poked at the scabs, released a glob of yellowish pus. He washed his hand with soap and hot water, felt no discomfort from the water. He seemed as close to fully human now as he had been when he was forced to leave Penny and their son in 2030.

"Seventy-three years . . . ."

He stared into the mirror and repeated the words.

Falling back on the too-soft bed, he pondered the few good things he had done in his life—and death. He saved Penny. That was about it. But he had to save her only because he had accidentally infected her with his vampire disease. That wiped out his one good deed. There were far more things he had done that were evil—pure evil. The bodies stacked up, the cries of horror raged on in his dreams. He wondered how his son had dealt with the attackers, if he fought them or went easily. If he revealed himself to authorities here in America, he would probably be arrested, put on trial as a war criminal, public execution a certainty. Perhaps that was the fate he deserved. And yet . . . .

Bucky could turn him in, if the man gave any thought to it. He had reason enough to mention him to authorities. After all, Bucky blamed him for his war wounds. As emperor, he had ordered the battle in which Bucky had been injured. However, it was not personal. "Weren't nothin pers'nal," he heard Bucky say in his head, "jus bidness." War is hell. War with vampires is a special kind of hell.

He had tried for years to extricate himself from the life he led. He hoped his son's associates could help him escape in Lisbon, whisk him away to some secret location, but that failed. Finally, his plan to escape had worked. He returned to Oklahoma in a not too bad condition. He seemed to have thrown off the vampiric effects, become human again. That was an unexpected side-effect, not anything he foresaw would happened. It would not have mattered if he had remained a vampire. He only wanted to be out from under the control of the Most High.

Then he realized just how alone he was. He had nothing—literally nothing but his flesh and bones, blood, and a box of dirt. What would he do? How would he go on *living*—using the pejorative—the next many years? He was already so old he could not be a human without dropping dead where he stood. But he didn't. The vampire years didn't count. The human count started again. He felt sixty, looked seventy.

He had some money and an idea to visit his grandchildren, scare them like any old grandfather liked to do for fun. But his way was genuinely frightening, reappearing from the dead. He was supposed to be dead. There was no question of it. But reports of his demise were seriously mistaken. The only report he was able to find had indeed confirmed his assassination in Budapest three years earlier, at the centennial celebration, stabbed by a few of his associates amidst the party. It took him six days to die. Now children could again sleep at night. No more tales of the evil emperor.

He stretched out on the bed, trying to calm his mind.

How do I spend the remaining years?

He closed his eyes and soon saw Penny running barefoot through green grass beside a large lake. He entered the scene, wearing shorts. He chased her to a tree and they embraced, kissing in the shade of the tree. A bird flew by. No, it was a bat. He awoke, shaking.

The next day he returned to the loft, saw a vehicle parked there. He went up the wrought iron staircase and knocked on the steel door, standing on the landing in the old-style brown suit again, thinning hair combed back. A stately old gentleman.

A woman answered his knock with an appearance on the screen embedded high on the door. She could see him and he her. He guessed she was the wife, Kitty. She asked what his business was and he said he came to talk with Benedict. They had a common interest. Not here, she said, adding they had a big dog. He apologized, tried to explain his purpose in coming to talk with him, mentioning Lily and Monty and Rose. When he mentioned his son Stefan, Benedict's father, as his main interest, the woman clicked off the screen without comment.

He understood. As one of those perverts and reprobates, a deviant, definitely a fake, nobody wanted to welcome him—not anyone who knew who he was. It was the same, he imagined, as those notorious leaders of Germany fleeing to South America. They hid out; then, realizing there were a lot of them there, they lived more openly, used their German names and took part in the society and government of Paraguay, Argentina, and Brazil with no one batting an eye. Here in America, he could live—keep *existing*—but no one would want to associate with him. He could only be a hermit here. He would find a hut in the woods and put himself in it, waiting for his body to break down, to crumble and become dust.

And no one would ever know he was there. None would imagine he had escaped from the clutches of his lord and master, Luce. His story would never be known. Even his grandchildren loathed him. And they would teach their children to hate him, as well. He stared at the wall for an hour, wishing he had a pistol in his hand.

He put a finger to his temple, thumb raised.

"Bang."

Rolling over on his side, he felt his eyes wet. He was human again, with human emotions, and they seeped out of him like rain, like earth-restoring rain. His tears would restore the world. His death would tie up a lot of loose ends. It would make everything right once more. He had no business existing, no reason to be in America in 2103. He should have gone easily when they tried to assassinate him. What had he been thinking?

10

HE STOPPED IN AN EMERGENCY CLINIC and had a nurse look at his hand. The nurse called a doctor over to examine it. They both agreed on the diagnosis: vampire bite. Less common now but since there were still a few of them around, such unwanted bites still happened. No, he was not likely to change into a vampire, they assured him. They gave him a spray of some anti-viral medication and cleaned his wound, sent him on his way. He wrist and forearm continued to swell.

He knew what vampirism was. Not a romantic, glittering, celebrity, playboy thing—although he had tried to be a playboy in Budapest—but an ugly, painful, miserable existence that goes on too long. It was a skin and blood disorder, not the dead rising from the grave—like he had done a few months past. It was not the fodder of teen fiction but a real syndrome, suffered by a few thousand people around the world—then millions, as they came out of the caskets and closets and walked among the living as the latest repressed minority, then equal partners, then leaders of society. He had been there.

But this—*this!*—told him the future. He was truly dying, dying in the same sense that most people died. The body decaying, withering, the day by day erosion of life. The normal, human progression. He both smiled and frowned, in mirrors which showed him his ghost and to plain walls that reflected nothing but his breath. He walked in the sunlight without fear, he hated the taste of blood, he would sleep every twelve hours or so, usually for six hours at a stretch, like a human. He had come full circle, back to human, but a hundred years too late.

Fear of identification kept him away from government institutions, like Bucky had done. The banks were the worst. Trying to convert his old cash and proving he was who he said he was—George Osborn—was a great hassle. He found a money dealer who handled antiques, who agreed to exchange what remained of his paper dollars, as well as the forints, rubles, and gold coins, for a string of numbers on a chip in his wrist. As long as the chip salvaged by Bucky continued to process, he was rich. Not rich like trillionaire Everett Custer, the man running for president. Not even rich like he had been in Budapest before the rebellion, but rich enough he could get by for a while.

After that it wouldn't matter.

Is this what you wanted? To be free? To be alone?

Stefan shook his head, aggravated the voice had found him again.

Why not visit your grandson again? I'm sure he's dying to meet you. What harm could there be in that?

He refused to answer. He'd been planning to try again but wanted to wait until he felt stronger. His hand was unsightly, could cause them alarm seeing it. Like he had a disease or something.

Back to the neighborhood of lofts he went, parking behind the same car that had been parked there before. New strategy: Ask about Benedict's art, interested in setting up an exhibit. The goal is to see him, not harangue him about his father or grandfather.

The knock went well. The screen showed him a different woman, an older and blonder woman who had a fairly nice smile, good voice. He smiled also and they chatted about Benedict's art. Stefan put on a performance, using some art terms he gleaned from reading reviews of prior exhibits. The door clicked and in he stepped.

Autumn was well past its peak, the trees bare and the wind cold, so he added an overcoat to his brown suit. He appeared grandfatherly. Or an impresario of the art world. The high school acting class returned to him.

"Greetings and salutations," he sang in mock delight. "So happy to finally meet the famous Benedict, or should I call him Maestro Kelly? I'm not too proud to address a rising star of the art world in such a way, no sir."

The woman giggled, gestured to a long, long bench he could sit on, enough length for twelve people to sit, it seemed. It was orange, artsy. The front room was the studio itself and large canvases leaned against the walls. In the center a tarp covered the floor and an easel stood with a half-finished painting on it, something in orange and blue, a horse? maybe unicorn? Hard to tell from that angle.

"It's 'Ultra-M'. Or, if you like, Ultra Modern," said the woman in response to his picture gazing. "That's what he calls his style. Bright colors, fantasy characters—playful. To counter the incessant drabness and ever-present danger of the real world."

"Yes, yes, I see that." He pretended to study the work on the easel. "I do believe I read that on one of his exhibit bios."

Beyond the easel in the center of the room was a set of three floor to ceiling windows which allowed in a bit too much of the morning light. He squinted.

"Oh, dear," said the woman, seeing his face become pale. "Sit over here."

He moved to a chair for one, well-used and soft. He sank back but felt comfortable. The windows were to his right now and he could see her clearly.

"Thank you, *Madame*."

"Madame? Hah! You can call me Julia," said the woman, about fifty in human years, he guessed. "I'm Kitty's mother. Come to help care for the baby. A new mother needs her rest."

"That is so true," he sang. "I firmly believe in the sanctity of rest." He realized he'd picked up a Southern accent somehow, but he went with it, playing the snake oil salesman. "It was always my best subject in my college days," and he laughed.

"So you wanted to discuss Benedict's work . . . ."

"Indeed, I do. I was much impressed by his exhibition in the City last month. Great use of color and texture. I cannot express just how delighted my senses were being in that hall. A true delight! Now how can I best help him—Benedict—further advance his career? I know several other exhibits we could get him into—"

His performance was interrupted by the crying of a baby.

"Oh, there she is!" cried Julia, popping up from her seat. "Excuse me. I'll be right back."

"Do take your time, Madame."

"*Madame,*" she giggled as she exited the studio for another room.

He glanced around the studio, gazed up at the high ceiling, gave a look at the three parallel windows, interested in stepping over to see what view they offered—the brick of the next building, from where he stood—but he hesitated crossing the sacred floor tarp. He wouldn't want to disturb anything.

Clearly Benedict was not at home. Probably out soliciting business, like what he was doing visiting them as some fake art promoter. He might as well leave and try another time to meet him. He could outlive his welcome and not get another chance.

"Here's our little darling," sang Julia, returning with a bundle in her arms, wrapped in a pink blanket.

She brought the bundle of baby right up to him, standing shoulder to shoulder so he could have almost the same view as she had. A pink face appeared amidst the swaddle of blanket, tiny eyes closed, mouth rooting around for a nipple. The baby had calmed, returning to sleep.

Julia nodded to the long, long bench and they took seats there, side by side. She talked about Kitty's pregnancy, a brief complication that worked out on its own, and the relatively easy labor. Only ten hours this time. She remarked they did it the natural way, as though the length of labor would not have indicated it to him. Not the new way, she explained, the two hour speedy method more people were trying. No, some things should be done the way God intended, like they had always been done, with no rushing it.

"Why, I completely agree," sang Stefan with hand gestures, the full act. "A baby is God's creation, and you can't rush it. It's a thing of beauty and thus will last forever."

"That's so beautiful," said Julia, beaming, the proud grandmother. "Is that from that old poet Byron?"

He flustered a bit. "I do believe that is Mister Keats, a far superior poet, if you don't mind me saying so."

Julia used to be an English teacher but when the subject was struck from the curriculum, she retired early. People started to think teaching English was enforcing the hegemony of the Anglo-American culture. It was discrimination to insist everyone learn and use only one language, even if it was considered the original language of the AAU. Now a vast cacophony of languages were taught in schools so students could learn in their native languages, whatever it might be. Of course, that meant every sign posted had to have at least five languages on it, more of them in some neighborhoods.

He gave his opinions as judiciously as possible, Magyar becoming dull in his head.

"Ooo, it's a bit chilly in here, don't you think?" asked Julia. "Let me turn the heat up a little." She glanced at him. "Would you like to hold the baby?"

He grimaced, came up with a suitable retort. "I must confess, I've little experience with the younger set."

"Oh, they're no bother. My other girls have five babies between them. You cradle her neck with your hand. The rest of her can lay in your lap. It's only for a minute. I'll be right back."

And the baby was suddenly in his lap, his hand cradling her head and neck. She stirred, settling into the new position. He gazed down at the pink face, the lips pursing, eyes still closed. One month old, she had said. So perfect! He had never held a baby. He missed his chance when his own son was born. He missed holding his four grandchildren, too. And this baby . . . she was his great-granddaughter. His own flesh and blood—

"Mom, what's going on?" called Kitty, coming out into the studio in purple pajamas and white slippers, rubbing her eyes like she was just waking.

"Turning up the heat," Julia replied from across the wide studio. "We have a guest. A Mister Steve . . . uh, what was your name again?"

He knew Kelly wouldn't work in this situation. That would show he was related to Benedict. So he conjured a new name: Osborn.

"Why, it's Osborn, ma'am," he said with feigned confidence. "Steve Osborn, at your service."

"Why is he here?" asked Kitty, sounding tired.

"He's here to—"

"I've come to talk with your husband about his career," said Osborn in his Southern twang. It was becoming tiring keeping it up. "There are exhibitions to set up, interviews to conduct—"

"I know him," said Kitty. "He came by last month, calling himself by the name Steve Kelly. Said he was—"

"Are you sure?" asked Julia, giving him a sharp glance.

Both women turned to regard him, the stranger holding the baby.

He didn't know what to do, what to say—

This is your chance, Stefan. That task I told you about.

He smiled as sincerely as he could. It seemed too fake, he feared.

If you want me to let you go, this is what I require.

"No," he mumbled. He meant no harm to anyone. He only wanted to meet his son. But meeting his great-granddaughter was a bonus he could not refuse. He gazed down upon her resting in his hands.

You already have your hand under her neck. Now pinch your fingers around her neck. Then twist it, slowly at first. Then give it a twist in the opposite direction. Quickly.

"No, I won't," Stefan muttered. "You can't make me."

"Give me my baby," Kitty called. She was afraid to approach him, scared what he might do.

This is what you agreed. I would tell you when to do me a favor. The time is now. Do it.

"Please, Mister Osborn, or whatever your name is," Julia insisted, holding out her hands for the baby, "hand me the baby."

"But she's my great-granddaughter," he grumbled, addressing Luce, not the two women.

"She's what?" cried Kitty, and turned to Julia. "Call the police!"

She will become an inconvenience in my future plans. Eliminate her now. As I command you. Then you are free.

"No! I won't!" he shouted.

Julia rushed to the communication box, punched the button for the police, as Kitty rush to him, arms out to grab her baby.

You must, Stefan. You agreed.

"No! I won't! I won't kill her! I can't! Get out of my head!"

Kitty screamed.

He set the gurgling baby down on the bench beside him and Kitty reached down, snatched up her baby, clenched the bundle against her chest.

Julia shouted that the police were on the way.

"Get out!" Kitty shrieked, waking the baby, who started bawling.

Stefan lumbered across the studio, tripping over the tarp, upsetting the easel, and charged straight into the middle window—smashing it, and falling, dropping, crashing down on the garbage cans and broken glass and the homeless man asleep there, as sirens echoed through the streets and the cool autumn wind blew unfettered trash through the alley, over him, like handfuls of dirt being poured over his body, inside a box, in a grave, with the prayers of people who did not know him quickly fading.

℀

The man at the end of the bar looked like hell. Had a bad smell, too. The scabs on his hand suggested he was a drug user. The swollen arm told everyone he had something worse. His face was cut up, like he had been in too many bar fights in his life, losing most of them. His coat bore the stains of the streets, his trousers ripped like a pack of dogs had harassed him, old wingtip shoes seeing better days, the wings torn off long ago. But he had enough funds in his account to buy a beer and keep them coming. The bartender always had to cut him off after a while, when he started to mumble incoherently. He left then, trudging out into a snowfall, shrugging his shoulders like he didn't believe in snow, and turned down the alley beside the bar, back to his home behind the dumpster.

He had hidden from the police until hiding became a way of life. He found he didn't need much to eat and shared what he found with the other homeless on his street. He thought of his next move, what any normal human might do in his situation. As a vampire, he might be able to resurrect a new existence, start over, build another empire, or simply resume his playboy lifestyle. If he were a vampire . . . .

No one on his block spoke much, each of them consumed by their own terrors, the horror stories, traumas and misfortune, decisions gone bad, relationships ruined. He could outdo all of them with his story, yet he kept it to himself. Yes, I once was the Emperor of Europa, he might tell them and they would have a good laugh, best joke of the night. He could tell them how he had himself shipped to Oklahoma, how he started searching for his grandchildren but made a mess of it. How he was constantly harassed by Luce and so needed to stay drunk to block the voice. They could understand that.

In time he found work in a soup kitchen, ladling out the soup to people worse off than him. It gave him a sense of purpose, like he was paying back humanity in some small way, though he knew it could never make up for the horrors he had caused. Nobody knew him, knew what he'd done. Nevertheless, he was always looking over his shoulder, expecting agents to grab him and take him to jail, then the kangaroo court would sentence him to death for his crimes. When someone thought they recognized him, he denied it, said he had been in too many fights to look the same as anybody else. Most believed him.

He wondered what Bucky Denham was doing, if he had gone back to grave digging or retired. He wondered if his only friend in the AAU had fulfilled his desire to move to some place with greenery. Perhaps Bucky and his sister were in a cabin deep in the woods outside of Albany. Or Pittsburgh. Or maybe far away in Colorado. If he could only contact him, Stefan thought, having no chip or communication node in his wrist, he would say the right words and make everything all right again. He thought often of that scenario.

If he could go back to that day in Colorado when that bat alighted on his shoulder. He would refuse the invitation, demand to be left alone, and wait to see what would happen. Maybe nothing. Maybe Luce would smile and laugh and flitter away to harass someone else. But he would never know now. His son had lived a good life and not transformed, not been lured into the world of darkness—which was the deal he had made, the deal he had delivered on for decades in order to save his son. Yet how long must a soul be taxed?

Some days, when the light was just so, he would find a park and sit on a bench under the trees and dream of days past. His heart would ache for the people he could never meet again, the ones that sat in his memory sipping lattés, and for those he had ordered killed. There was not enough pain in the world to make up for his life. So he would find a stick, break it until a sharp point resulted, and dig the point into an arm or a leg, hoping to draw blood, instead only making a mark. His existence was easy if he stayed drunk, always a little woozy, a little unbalanced, limping home to a one-cot room at the deadbeat lodge.

When Julia had summoned the police, all the vehicles on the block were instantly locked down. They scanned for his signal, found a faint marker, followed it, circled around. But he had enough time to dig it out of his wrist. And with it his only link to money. Now he earned a few credits, converted to tokens he could spend, like other people too destitute to have accounts and chips and be allowed on the grid. Not that he minded that. He slipped into a deeper level of hell with each passing week, convinced this was the way to atone for his sins.

The public propaganda screen in the bar began to show reporters discussing the changing political situation in "Europe"—not Europa, as he knew it. One after another they speculated on the sudden changes occurring. He had nothing to say, amused in the back booth, watching over the heads of the other drinkers. Another whiskey would calm his nerves, would keep the voice blocked. He watched them wonder aloud where the emperor must have gone. Who murdered him? That was the gist of the report. It was all clever fiction to his dulled head. Perhaps he had been put in a box and mailed abroad. That seemed the most likely scenario. Who wouldn't see that?

One evening, as he was digging in a dumpster outside a hole-in-the-wall café specializing in bagels and coffee, several blocks from his usual shopping area, he got into a dispute with another man over who had rights to the dumpster.

"I'll share with you," Stefan offered, holding out half a bagel fished from the dumpster. It was on top of some clean cardboard.

"It's all mine," the man grunted. "All of it."

Stefan, not yet drunk, became agitated as the argument escalated.

Then something black swooped down at him and he swatted at it, taking his eyes off the man. The man punched him in the gut and he doubled over from the motion, not from the strength of the punch. When he stood up again, the black thing was right there in front of his face, flapping furiously—a bat!

His hands shot out, grabbing the bat with both fists, pinching its shoulders. In one swift motion, he thrust his hands out in opposite directions, ripping the wings off the bat. The head and body dropped to the pavement. He immediately put his shoe over the bat and stepped hard until the body burst, blood and guts spilling out each side. He tossed the wings aside.

"Man, you must really hate bats," the man who punched him said, simultaneously shocked and amused. It all happened so fast.

An angry voice called out, a deep guttural roar like the Emperor of Europa liked to use to strike fear into his subjects.

When Stefan turned, he saw a gang of maybe ten youths, dressed for rumbling, black vests over pink t-shirts, pale blue jeans and pink sneakers, the uniform of the Midway Princes gang. He was in their territory.

"Thought we told ya dis was our street," growled the leader, the tall one with the pink Mohawk. No one dared tease their pinkness; that was the challenge designed to show their toughness. "Now it's time for yous to get yer punishment."

They came at him, a semi-circle rushing forward. The other man at the dumpster ran off. Stefan stood alone. He wished this confrontation would happen on some other day, not today. He really was not in the mood for a fight.

"Wait," he said, holding up a hand to halt them. "I'm sorry. I won't come here again. Promise."

"Yer fookin promises don't make no bits of differenz over here," growled the pink leader. He made fists, one hand with brass knuckles. His lieutenant held up an iron bar. Another wielded a knife.

Stefan held his ground. Something made the gang move slowly, like they actually feared him. Did his reputation for cruelty precede him? Did they see him kill the bat?

"Luce, I need your help," he muttered absently, keeping his eyes on his attackers.

You have it.

Energy boiled in his gut like a stoked furnace, raced to his heart, gushed into his shoulders and surged through his arms. His hands burned as he curled them into tiger claws. He crouched, turning his body away from them, but only for a second—

When he spun forward, translucent lightning shot from his fingers, as though his claws were striking directly against them. Claw marks cut their faces and chests, shirts ripped, blood bubbling. The gang members halted, not comprehending. They saw they had been cut, wounded. Yet he stood too far away to have reached out with his hands to strike them.

Some of the gang members became more angry. A couple of them ran off. The one with the knife rushed forward, stabbing at him. But Stefan twisted around, the knife avoiding him while somehow slipping effortlessly up into the throat of the man holding the knife. A fountain of red poured forth.

The one with the iron bar swung at Stefan's head but the lightning from his left hand cut the iron bar in two and, defying gravity, forced each jagged end into the youth's eye sockets. The kid dropped to his knees, grabbing at the protruding ends of the bars, pulling them out, then stumbling blindly away, bumping into garbage cans and hitting his head on the corner of the dumpster before finding his way out of the kill zone, screaming.

Stefan hurled more lightning claws at the gang members who had not yet been frightened away, giving them more cuts across their faces and bodies until they withdrew. They knew not to mess with him again. They knew his reputation for cruelty. They saw him laughing at them as they wiped blood from their cuts and slinked away, defeated.

The wailing of sirens pried him from his blood-trance. His claws returned to fingernails. His hands softened, body uncoiled. Suddenly he felt the pain of his effort. His muscles ached, nerves stung. He took a step back, sucked in a few deep breaths. It was time to run.

We are good now? Welcome back, Stefan. My associates will arrange first-class accommodations for you in Budapest.

He listened to the voice.

It is not too late. Come, Stefan. We have much to do.

Slowly shaking his head, he stepped between two dumpsters and disappeared.

Part Three

11

"I DID NOTHING WRONG!" THE WOMAN SCREAMED IN MAGYAR, poised in an ungainly stance on the accused's block. The monstrous henchman reached around, pinching her pale face between the fat thumb and forefinger of his leather-gloved hand to force her to grin.

"You served Him, did you not?" the tall prosecutor in the red robe cried out, also in the official language of the Hungarian Empire. "Why then did you murder His Holiness? Speak your confession!"

It could not matter, she realized, of which she was accused: murdering the emperor or helping Him escape. She was to be made their scapegoat either way. The audience, hovering on the edge of madness and ready to riot, seemed pleased the emperor was gone and it did not matter whether His Holiness had been assassinated or taken away by force.

"Am I tortured these months because you believe I killed Him or because you envy me?" She laughed as loudly as she could, to show them they had not broken her. "Or because you and the Court so hate that He has left you unsupervised? You are like children to Him."

"You are guilty of both terms!" shouted the prosecutor, shaking his red gloved hand at her, the red sleeve of his red cassock wavering like a waterfall of blood. "Either you murdered His Holiness or you assisted in His abduction, stealing away in the night! Which is it?"

In the cavernous High Council of Justice, the panel of nine judges sat on their thrones as the prosecutor's accusations rang out against the stone columns. The prosecutor's angry words competed with the vicious din of an impatient audience shouting their demand for the harshest punishment for the woman chained between two columns, her shift torn to her hips, blood covering her flesh—laid bare to expose her to the henchman's whip: one lash for each incorrect utterance, three for statements of defiance. In the High Council of Justice, there was only one correct response: full confession and complete acceptance of the charges, then submission to punishment: death by dismemberment.

"I did nothing wrong!" she shouted again, earning another three strokes of the whip. "I did as His Holiness requested! Only that!"

"Yet there is no proof!" retorted the prosecutor.

"You have the Prince Giorgio Raguzza and the Countess Natália Gál to confirm what I declare. They acted purposefully in removing His Holiness from the palace—"

"To a fate we do not know!" shouted the prosecutor. "We have only you to assign blame, Maria of Avignon! The prince and the countess have already welcomed their punishment. The populace has dutifully enjoyed the spectacle. How many pieces can a body be sliced into? We now know: seven-thousand-one-hundred-ninety-three. Each portion fed to a cage of starving rats as they watched, with their eyes held open by metal pins. Is that not worthy of you for your crimes? Speak the truth and perhaps a lesser punishment might be yours."

"His Holiness had many secrets," she called out, her words echoing off the stone walls and columns. "Are you privileged to know them? Only I was, as His mistress, the one He trusted, the only member of the palace He could trust."

"Trust is a two-edged sword, *mademoiselle*."

"Do not call me *mademoiselle*, for I am a citizen of the empire!"

"You are foreign-born, before the formation of the empire, thus an interloper—the obvious criminal in this case."

"I am the mistress of His Holiness, making me a true member of this imperial society—"

"No foreign-born lover can claim more rights than a whore pulled off the streets for entertainment at the whim of a noble. We do know your history, *mademoiselle*."

"I deserve no punishment! I obeyed completely His Holiness, my lord and master. In that I have no guilt. I shall submit to nothing!"

Three strokes crossed her back, already well-scored and oozing blood, cracking the congealed blood from earlier lashes. Her pain was for all to see, for all to enjoy. The crowd shouted for more.

"You can whip me as much as you like, yet His Holiness knows the truth! You—all of you here—shall feel the vengeance of the Most High, whom His Holiness serves. All that you have comes from His devotion to the Most High! Without Him, your empire will surely crumble!"

"Enough of this insolence!" the head judge cried out, standing and pointing his red gloved hand at the woman set in chains. "Silence her! Remove the tongue!"

The henchman set down the whip and grabbed the set of pincers and a large knife from the side table. He stepped upon the block her feet rested on, chained so her toes barely touched the block. He forced her mouth open as she shook her head wildly to keep away from his fingers. She bit down on a finger, with a crunch severed it, and the henchman tripped off the block with a cry of agony.

"If we remove her tongue, Your Justice," the prosecutor spoke, "she will be unable to answer our questions."

"Have we further questions?" the judge demanded. "We have heard what we need to hear to decide the sentence."

"Very well, Your Justice," the prosecutor conceded.

"Sir, the henchman is wounded," an associate called out.

"What's this outrage?" cried the prosecutor, turning to gaze at the woman. The way her breasts dripped with fresh blood running down from her shoulders, excited him. He had to grab hold of the railing of the orator's box to steady himself. The congregation rioted for blood, calling for her to be cut up and served among them. "Why, I'll whip her myself!"

He bounded from the orator's box, pushed his way through the undulating crowd, and climbed up to the accused's stand. He took up the whip, swung it behind him, and slung it forward. The leather strands struck her lower back. Surprisingly, she cursed him rather than scream in pain. He whipped her again, with all of his strength. As he set himself to throw the whip once more, he noticed how the marks on her back seemed to form the outline of a flower—a *fleur-de-lis*!

The prosecutor stepped away, breathing hard from his effort.

"Now confess!" he exhorted.

She gathered her breath, chest heaving.

"I have told you the truth. I obeyed my lord and master. I did what His Holiness asked of me. You cannot prosecute me for following His commands and doing my duty to Him, to His lord and master, to the Empire of Europa! Now you must allow me my freedom or you shall suffer greatly!"

"Suffer greatly?" The prosecutor was less offended than curious. He shook the whip to untangle the strands. "What can you do from this position of humiliation? Near a thousand citizens see you naked and wounded—shamed, if you bore any dignity. No, you cannot make us suffer. Have you special powers? A secret skill? We have guards and soldiers and a dozen more henchmen to torture you. As you well know. The Three Sisters would welcome you once more into their care." He leaned toward her, spoke softer: "You cannot survive another hour in this High Council, not without the judges' leniency."

"I can survive," she spoke firmly only to him.

He stepped up to her, her freshly-drawn blood soiling his sleeve. "No, you will not survive. That would be a waste. Let me help you. If you will give me a night of pleasure such as I have never experienced before, then I shall have you removed to your cell. Your wounds will be treated. The punishment shall be delayed. I vow this."

"And I vow that any night of pleasure for you shall be your last."

He tried to hide his grin from the Court. "Then I shall go in glory, taking the virginity of the mistress of His Holiness—as He did for my dear wife on our wedding night."

The woman, covered in blood, laughed. "He was a madman, His Holiness, yet He was my madman."

"You are perverse, *mademoiselle*." He stood a moment as the crowd roared, then leaned in to her: "Let us finish this conversation in private quarters." Hiding his grimace, he turned to the henchman: "Bring her down." To the judges panel: "She promises to confess on the morrow and in the evening submit to punishment. Let us remove her to the cell for reflection. I shall supervise her."

"So be it," the head judge pronounced, waving his hand. "Let the accused be removed from the High Council and taken to a cell for a day of solemn ponderance. We thank you for your confession."

The congregation shouted its disapproval. They wished the torture to continue. The sight and scent of her blood roused them to rage. Fangs extended, tongues wagged, blood-lust boiled—without release. The coming punishment did not assuage their anger but stoked it further. Someone must be punished.

A platoon of guards dragged her limp body from the High Council, shoves and slaps making a path through the crowd, out through the giant oaken doors and into the darkness of the corridor leading to the underground dungeon.

ଔ

"I ran after them, trying to catch up, as my lord demanded." She stared at the stone wall, her eyes tracing a trickle of brown water down a crease. "I knew the plan was going wrong when we met them in that salon. That was unexpected. I thought He had brought them into the plan. He did not tell me everything, I guessed. They seemed to go along with us for a time. The countess brought a physician to help repair His wound. Although He was heavy, we got Him into the casket and filled it full with nightsoil, as He wished. All had been ordained by His Holiness. But as I turned away, they struck a bottle upon my head. I fell into sleep for some time. When I awoke, the casket was gone. I saw the trail of dirt on the floor and followed. The corridors were dark and I had not the strength to show the way forward. I stumbled along, hands on the walls, until I found the exit. Beyond was the sunlight of day and I could not enter."

"What did you do?" asked the well-fed priest, balancing on a short stool outside the bars of the cell. "You must answer."

"I have told it more than a hundred times to twenty priests and prosecutors. It does not change with each telling."

"Repeat it then, what you have said. I must record it."

She exhaled loudly, feeling her chest ache from the beatings she had endured. Ribs had broken, yet they had mended. The rips to her skin from the whippings had healed sufficiently they did not hurt much, her gift from the dark powers.

"I threw a cloth over my head, to cover my face, and ran out. I ran down the west promenade from the Székely Keep to the Ramparts of Borbély. There I saw the crazed mob fighting among themselves, each grabbing treasures from the palace, killing each other over who would take the belongings of His Holiness. They ignored me and I ran far. Out of the palace, I followed the trail of dirt along the streets, as far as I could, but soon the streets became roads and the dirt was swept into all the trails of dirt across the world. I lost them."

She glared at the priest, who picked at a scab on his chin.

"I could not have committed a crime. I only helped His Holiness escape from the imperial suite as the brigands broke in and threatened us. We tried to save Him, to protect Him. Then I lost Him."

She threw her hands to her face, sobbing. Like a good actress, which she had been in the olden days before she was delivered to the Hungarian Federation as a gift to Gergely Azov from René Faucheux. Her pact with her lord and master assured Azov that he would always have a fresh night with her; each time she was taken, she healed and became virgin once more. Most of the time he was gentle, sometimes rough when angry. She had endured that abuse for several years while feigning affection for him, fighting for his attention against his dark mistress, that Alma Jónás creature she eventually helped His Holiness kill. They ran off in different directions that night.

"Is it not enough that I have suffered humiliation and torture? To gain nothing from confession? To hold no false word from me, nor words of truth from any conspirators? There are many who would end the existence of His Holiness. Our great emperor should be loved and adored. Everything He has done has made our world better. Some in the world do not think so; they must be the fools. Yet He is my love, my lord. How am I the one who would end Him? Tell me."

The priest yawned, doing his duty listening to the woman. "It is not for me to say. The High Council of Justice has made its ruling. All that remains is to listen to you one last time. If you have new information which may influence the verdict, speak it now."

It was the same every dawn and every dusk. One of several priests of the Dark Reign would come to hear her confession, or make up some words for her which she would recant the next visit. When the Court officials' patience grew thin, they sent her to the Three Sisters, hoping to get a more clear confession.

"They caught me as I walked the road north. I was not fleeing. I had no reason to flee. I had done nothing wrong, I told you. I walked that direction because I thought they had gone that way. I expected to arrive in Vienna eventually, following the Duna, no matter how many days it might take me. I heard them talking about Vienna being their destination."

"Someone recognized you?"

"Yes, the prince's guardsman."

"Prince Giorgio," the priest confirmed, sitting up.

"Yes, him. They were riding after the prince."

"They caught the prince up the road, where he stopped to attend to Countess Natália's carnal desires." He chuckled.

"You may believe that, yet I do not."

The priest glanced at her, as though new information was about to come forth. Yet her ghastly appearance disturbed him and he returned his eyes to the dirty stone floor.

"I am certain he had no idea what was in store for him. Countess Natália was calculating. A schemer. She likely set him up, brought him to the right place at the right time. How else could I, on foot, have met them in that space of time? They had an electro-mobile."

"True enough."

"They were the conspirators. Then she betrayed him." The prisoner modulated her voice in a certain way to elicit empathy from the priest. "I saw how she spoke to him while we were together in the salon with His Holiness. They planned to take His Holiness and hide Him, and offer Him for a ransom later. They spoke of it in the salon."

"Is that true?" The priest cleared his voice, sat up straighter. "What you say goes against what everyone already knows. Perhaps you weave a new tale to save yourself. Your soul, certainly, is beyond saving. Only He of the Dark Reign can release you from that debt."

The woman sank against the wall, her breath shallow. Her ribs hurt when she breathed. She pulled the shift tighter around her shoulders. Being torn, it would not stay up on its own. Yet it stuck to her, refusing to move, the dried blood fixing the cloth to her skin.

"Believe what you will, I speak the truth."

"There are many truths," the priest grunted. "Only the truth of the Most High can be accepted on faith alone."

"His Holiness spoke daily with the Most High. Do you and your fellow priests? I often heard Him in conversation, making their plans, and just as often His Holiness would persuade the Most High into a new course of action. There is no one who has heard more, nor seen more of His Holiness than me. I could be an excellent resource for someone's memoir. Or a history of the empire. It is not too late. I will promise to remain in whichever library they put me in and do my work with diligence. I would write down everything I heard and saw, then give it all, every page, to the highest authorities of the empire."

"Alas, maiden, we are no longer to be considered an empire," said the priest with a wheezy sigh. "Ours is the kingdom of the dark, and we do not abide by earthly boundaries. You know this from your dark catechism."

"I do, Father." She reached out through the bars, let her fingertips touch his robe. "I can be valuable to the right person, the right office, no matter whether we are an empire or something else."

"I've seen the new maps. The cartographers are always too quick. We are the Hungarian Empire now, no longer the Empire of Europa. It seems some of Europa has broken away from us. The French Republic has reconstituted. The German Union has reformed. Italy threatens to secede, as do several lands to the east and south. It is hopeless, yet we cling to our guns and religion and pray for salvation in the dark."

"Then pray on, Father, for a helpful hand given to me shall be duly rewarded twentyfold by He who has taken me unto His heart, and only Him, His Holiness, Emperor Stefan of the House Székely, wherever He may be in this world. Yet He is with me always, in my heart."

It seemed the priest was not so sure about her words. He may have heard the smallest utterance of pensive amusement emanating from within her cell. Or it could have been the squeak of a curious mouse. He was getting old, his hearing often tricking him. Still, he must have thought, if she were repressing a chuckle, it might mean she was lying. So she coughed up a string of phlegm to cover her speech.

"Dark Father," a voice spoke, interrupting the priest's thoughts.

He looked up. The squad of guards had come to take the prisoner away, as always to the prosecutor's chamber.

"Time again?" he asked, unconvinced. "Will she confess more in that favored place? Or does it count as further torture?"

The guards opened the cell door and grabbed the woman by her arms, dragging her out, her torn gown slipping low on her torso. She resisted only a little, weary of the fight. One guard fondled her as they lifted her to her feet.

"Likely both, Dark Father," said another guard. "We are to take her first to the bathing salon, then to the dressing salon, to make her presentable for His Lordship."

"As I suspected," intoned the priest.

"If only you were half a century younger, sir," laughed a guard, "you might enjoy a dalliance, eh?"

"This one's a raging wolf in a bed, they say. His Lordship best take warning," snickered a guard.

"Or does he take the pills?"

"I'd give my blood to her."

"Follow your orders," the priest chided, pushing himself with effort up from the stool. "Go in darkness, child," he spoke as the squad led her away. "Gather your strength. Pray to the Most High."

ભ

Four homely maidens tended to her wounds, bathed her, anointed her, gave her the respect she deserved, and healthy measures of blood from their wrists and throats—then dressed her in a fine, elegant dress of six streaming hues of violet dashed with flecks of white rain, appropriate for any evening party attended by nobles and government officials. Yet she knew this morning's event would not be a typical gathering of the empire's upper echelon; rather, it was to be a private meeting with her tormenter, as he had suggested: a final opportunity for him to get his pleasure before she went to her demise.

She was ready to welcome it. Too many years of sordid drama, and she finally realized how weary she had become. Born Jeanne-Marie

Poirier—changed to Maria when she entered Hungary, refusing to write the *j* in *Marija*—she was one daughter among six and four sons, a family of swine farmers outside Paris in 1778, the 11th of April, stated a piece of parchment with official church symbols adorning it. Yet that was not exactly the truth, she learned later; hers was a much more dastardly beginning.

As the maids fussed over her dress, she thought of her childhood, struggling to find memories which brought images she could recognize and deem true. Many days sitting on a hard wooden pew in an old chapel, listening to a fat old priest lecturing her on the evils of sin were the only flashes remaining. She had not been one to rebel, not at that age. When the war crossed their land and her family was forced to declare for one side then the other, then the other, she was forced to consider the possibilities of sin. Both sides could never be right.

Her thoughts of good and evil had not lasted long. Members of her family were killed in the clashes. An elder brother had taken up arms and fought for one side, died somewhere east, in another country. Plenty of horsemen in those days, charging this way and that, taking swine from the pens and slaughtering them without compensation to her family. Her only payment was the chance to flee the farm.

On the road, hiding when necessary, she made her way to the capital, knowing of some relations there and hoping they might take her in. She was a hard worker and diligent in her duties. She was also clean, pretty, and polite—as her mother had taught her. In those days, however, a girl who was pretty and polite, never mind clean, was quite an attraction. Besides, she pondered as the maids went over her dress one final time, she was going to a big city full of horror, as the Terror was underway, factions fighting each other for the right to govern the city and the country. Arriving in the capital, she found politics run amok, and *Monsieur* Guillotine's new device the talk of the town.

She had no reason to go along with either the haughty Jacobins or the more sensible Girondists; each sought out the other for execution. She begged for food, rejected those who asked for something more from her in exchange. Too soon an orphan, lost in the Terror. A scrub woman, taking pity on her, had swept her inside, making her work for crumbs. The woman had a plan to sell her to a brothel when she was another year older. Then she had watched the woman pushed up the steps to the stage; she was not an actress but a suspect. She watched the blade fall and the woman's head roll off the stage into a basket with other heads. She had fled then, smart enough to realize she should move slowly so as not to attract any attention. She slipped into a door that budged for her shoulder and found herself in the backstage area of a theater that had been shut down by order of local officials. The dramatic arts were too bourgeois for the political turn.

As the maids touched up her hair, adorning it with jeweled clips, she thought back to the days of her youth, those bucolic hours when she made her way through the theaters of Paris, a stagehand, then a chorus girl, eventually an understudy. She did have promise, many a producer told her before pushing her out of bed. With her parents and siblings killed as armies fought back and forth across her *département*, she had been on her own for years. With pretty face and innocent smile, she got food well enough. And pretty dresses, jewelry, trinkets from far away lands.

So long ago, she pondered as the girls adjusted the lace up the back of her dress. The neckline in front bowed low, an ample view of her bosom for an interested gentleman. Yet there were no more gentlemen in this city or in this empire. The Empire of Europa had collapsed; many blamed her, blamed her for taking away their leader, He who forged the empire from His sacred will. Already her caricature was paraded through the streets as warning to proper ladies. Shaking her head, she knew it would end soon. Her existence would finally be snuffed out like the pinch of a candlewick at the end of the night. And she would sleep at long last.

Ah! Sleep; if she could only dream a bit—instead of making her way down the corridors and stairwells to her destination—

A fallow wheat field flashed through her mind, the kind of memory that gets nailed to one's life. She was running, the hem of her skirt in her hands, barefoot, escaping from the gang of soldiers giving chase. She was quick, light on her feet. Then a mounted soldier raced through the foot soldiers and leaned down to grab her, swung her up over the horse's withers. As the horse slowed, the foot soldiers caught up and their sergeant threw her to the ground. There they made use of her, holding her down, taking their turns—until the man watching it all from the horse waved his wide-brimmed cavalier's hat and called them to stop.

"Enough now," he snapped when they did not cease. "There's your day's pay. Now form up and make garrison by dusk or there'll be hell to pay."

Hell to pay. The words echoed in her mind. Wounded, she vowed never to make peace with men or the countries they ruled. Taking a sharp stick from the field into her hand, she felt invincible. The next man she encountered, calling to her for favors as she hurried down the lane then following her when she dared ignore him, she stabbed in the groin, leaving the stick protruding from an artery, the fountain of red catching her attention. She stared at the arc of blood, feeling an urge she did not understand.

Then she found someone to adopt her. Rather, she adopted him; it made little difference the exact arrangement.

Monsieur René Faucheux told her she would soon crave blood and only blood, yet she must take care not to ingest too much at a feeding. She was new to the curse, he explained; if she did not restrain herself she might turn into a monster. The years' pain made her want to be a monster, to rage over the world, terrorize the citizenry, make them fear her. Pair with the right man, Faucheux told her, and she could put her hand into the political pot and stir it to her liking, perhaps toss in some poison and watch how they rolled on the floor, choking to death.

"You have a gift," *Monsieur* Faucheux always said. "You're an elven creature, both pretty and cursed. A precious bobble powerful men will wish to collect. Let them. Play their game, take on the role, and in that role work your magic."

"Magic, *monsieur*?"

"The dark arts."

She had not understood so he showed her some of his tricks. With the right words precisely spoken, the proper elements conjured, the perfect combination of rare herbs, animal bits, and gemstones, almost anything could be transformed. She observed as he turned a gray stone into a yellow frog. He made a mangy dog that kept circling the carriage at a distance burst into seven white hares. He raised his hand up to the sky and made a second moon—it appeared to be a mirror image of the moon she saw. As she watched, the second moon turned red, dripping like the blood of a fresh wound down upon the horizon until it had all flowed away. She had grinned at that illusion. Not illusion, he insisted. Then he put his hand under her skirt, found the way into her nest and told her she henceforth would forever be a virgin. She laughed like a child, disbelieving.

Oui, he was the one who changed her in that and many other ways. The bite came with permission, in a tender moment they both wanted, then a wave of pain like nothing she had ever experienced before. She resisted but his fangs remained in her throat—until she felt his hand pulling her head against his own throat. Her mouth hurt. She tasted blood; her lip had been cut, cut by her own teeth. He held her mouth to his throat and she immediately bit him, sinking the sharp eye-teeth she had grown into the vein. His blood tasted of wine he had drank, a sweet taste that made her suck more. Until he pushed her away.

"Enough for now, *mademoiselle*," he cautioned. Blood stained his face, clown-like. She giggled at the sight.

Her fingers went to her throat, felt the punctures healing already. Their eyes met, embraced, a bond formed which they both knew would last longer than a lifetime: he the older, wiser mentor, she the eager, studious protégé. In public they made an odd couple; the gentleman was surely a seducer of children, many would believe. Yet she, in her diminutive stature, was twenty, a lady by anyone's measure.

He brushed his fingers over his throat, her novice attempt at the red kiss, and a smile of delight flashed over his face.

"You have done well. You always do well. You will survive a long time. I know it."

He admitted to being more than two-hundred years in existence, a child of the Renaissance, a painter and alchemist before a fateful union with a defrocked priest led him into the dark arts. He knew of her parentage, as well. An abbot took a novice one day, producing a babe which was abandoned on the doorstep of the village church, charitably accepted into a family of swine farmers. The curse was strong in her. That was how they managed to find each other in a Parisian backstreet late at night, a winter's froth of snow around her bare feet. A heavy cloak upon her shoulders and a kind hand to her shoulder led her into her next life.

From the marching of troops in Parisian streets, the howl of guns blackening the sky, and the muddy trenches and bloody battlefields of a great war, he remained her mentor for a hundred years. On through another war and the explosion of modern technology, she had studied constantly and learned a lot. She had flirted and seduced, coaxed and cajoled, and been married away conveniently to six wealthy gentlemen, a few weeks each, turning their bodies to dust and their estates to cash, all at his beckoning.

So she was not too surprised when he introduced her to Gergely Azov when they visited Budapest in the autumn of 2006. *Monsieur* Faucheux was frail at three-hundred-sixty yet determined to find a good home for her. However, she was quite disappointed to find him leaving her there, in Azov's 'care', as though she were little more than a cute terrier transferred to a new owner. René disappeared into the night, his gnarled hand upon a gnarled white-ash cane, a black Homburg tipped in farewell, his figure silhouetted against the electric streetlamps of a modern city that had little need of dark arts.

And there she was: prepared like a birthday gift for an evening of debauchery. The first of many. Azov took her gently, amused by her child-like countenance. Yet she endured him. She endured the arrival of the witch, too. She knew her place: Gergely's pet. Not his queen of the night. Her place was to affect the role of constant admirer, so she would never be a threat to the witch. She had little to do but adore him, and in that forgotten margin she could work her magic.

Azov was content to wield his power from a comical make-shift throne, daylighting as manager of a home interior firm. None would ever suspect his true position as the top vampire in Pest and counties eastward. His veneer of ferocity covered his inner life. Over the course of her first year in Budapest, familiarizing herself walking the streets and enrolling in a Magyar night class, she realized her master of great proportions had little ambition to expand his vampiric influence or maximize evil. Rather, he preferred personal pleasures, the hedonistic, decadent mannerisms of reckless sensuality over political conquest. Then that Alma arrived! A newly turned bitch who thought she was

Queen of Hungary. The witch wooed him, made him cower to her whims. As a woman, of course she enjoyed seeing his submission, but as *his* woman she knew her status had changed.

Then He appeared: Stefan Székely, a man of—a *vampire*—of old stock, and together they killed the giant and slew the witch. She smiled at the memory. In the confusion that followed, she lost Him, then found him years later, when He had a decidedly evil gleam in his eyes. Like a moth she was drawn to His flame—yet it was a cold flame, an icy fire, so frozen, so chilling she knew He must have endured extreme hardship to turn His heart so cold—nearly as cold as the Most High.

When they found each other once more, they could join only a few times before His curse increased, a reward of the Most High, He told her, and His touch became like frostbite to her. Thus His melancholy expanded, blighting the palace, corrupting the city, rotting the nation, enveloping like a cancer this empire—until all was gloriously dark and the law of the Most High ruled supreme.

She knew then she had found a master who would help her boldly descend to the depths of Hell. He was a vampire she could work with —whom she could work on—assist Him in raising a true vampiric empire, ruling the whole of Europe if not the world, perhaps rule with Him, then alongside Him, and then, when the moment was right, in place of Him.

The two attending maids and a squad of four guards arrived at the doors of the Chief Prosecutor's suite with her in tow, ropes encircling her waist and iron bracelets clasping her wrists. One guard knocked on the door, the thud echoing down the corridor. The noise shook her from her thoughts.

12

"THERE SHE IS, MY DELICATE FRENCH FLOWER, my *fleur-de-lis*," sang the prosecutor, still wearing his official red cassock and red skullcap as though this was to be an official meeting. "You look so much more beautiful, more inviting, after they clean you up. Much better than the ravaged appearance you've previously presented—though that image does conjure a certain arousal deep in the loins, as well." He stroked his gray beard as though it were a pet. giving her a longer look, his eyebrows fluttering. "Yes, after the wounds heal, you have a unique beauty. It is a miracle."

He waved her into the chamber and she stepped carefully, not for reasons of security but her shoes were too tight and the evening gown too long, brushing the floor. He spoke to the maids and the guards, bidding them a good day. They need not remain. It was only a dinner and conversation, to perhaps arrange lesser charges which might, he muttered, enable her to be released—exiled, but free. The guards cared little for motives while the maids quietly understood too well how the daylight hours would proceed. They had been in this woman's position themselves. To work in the palace was to always be called into service by anyone with high rank.

Closing the door, the prosecutor turned to Maria. His face lit up at the sight of her.

"How lovely you look this morning. The dress suits you very well. Something lovely for this special occasion, not the pitiful, stained shift they always bring you in. Indeed, I can see now how so many have been charmed by you. Come, sit at the table. We shall dine lavishly."

He pulled a chair away from the table where a small round box wrapped in pink sat. Tilting his head at the chair, she stepped slowly to him, hesitating. Her eyes fell upon the box.

"Still feeling pain?" he asked at her pause. "I thought you healed quickly. So I heard. Read, actually, in your gynecological report. That is your gift, as they say. Does it hurt to sit on a chair? Does your *derrière* remain sore?"

She held her expression as plain as a clay mask.

"Flesh heals," she spoke softly, as though only to herself, "yet the memory of pain lingers."

"Yes—yes, I suppose it does. I'm sorry," he said with some sincerity in his voice. "I do not make the rules or establish the protocols."

Maria remained silent, her face stern.

"Ah! The pout." He tried to smile, then turned to the table. "As this, unfortunately, must be our last *rendez-vous*, I have something special for you." He gestured at the box. "Something which may improve your mood." Waiting a moment for her expression to change, he decided it might not. "Something which might yet awaken your inner demons."

He opened the pink box slowly, carefully, dramatically. Lifting the lid and setting it aside, he reached in and retrieved its contents. When he turned to face her, a fabulous necklace with a large jade amulet hung from his fingers, stretching across both hands. The strands were lined with rubies of diminishing size, the largest stones buttressing the shiny golden ring which encircled the amulet. The exuberant work of art dazzled, reflecting the lamp light.

She took in a sharp breath, her eyes wide, anxious to rush to him, to the necklace, but she held back.

"You recognize this." He studied the necklace, letting his eyes settle on the central green stone. "Your favorite possession, or so I've heard from your maids. Now it is mine, though I scarce can do it justice were it to be placed around my neck. And so, my mistress, today I wish you to wear it. The perfect addition to your elegant dress. Even if the green stone clashes with the violet. Come, let me adorn you."

Taking a step toward him, she paused, making him meet her half-way. Warily turning her back to him, she saw in shadows on the wall him raising his hands, the necklace strung between them, the effect resembling outstretched bat wings above her head. He brought his hands and the necklace over the top of her head and down in front of her face. She felt his eyes gazing over her shoulder, piercing into the crevasse between her breasts.

"Hold it while I fasten the clasp."

She pressed her palms to the necklace, held it against her chest, so tightly it dug an indentation into her skin. With her hands against the amulet, she felt its energy pulsing through her fingers, as though the green stone was a beating heart. The necklace's rubies ran up to her shoulders and behind her neck. With her hair styled up, held with pink ribbons, the nape of her neck was exposed.

His hands were dry, rough against her skin as he fumbled with the clasp. Eventually he got it fastened and lowered his arms.

He spun her around and gazed at the jade stone.

"It glows with the scent of your blood, my dear."

She thought back to the day His Holiness gave it to her, something stolen from a museum in Russia by Hungarian soldiers and presented to Him as spoils of war. He had felt its power, holding it in His hand; He had to set it down when it began to burn His palm. Before He could decide what to do with it, she had waltzed into their suite and picked it up as casually as a fork at dinner. He warned her to put it down, that it possessed special energy which might harm her. Yet she waved Him off. Fastening the clasp, she stood still a moment as though listening to a secret conversation, arms at her sides. She felt nothing, she told Him, so He appointed it her gift from the Russia campaign—

The prosecutor's hands fell upon her bare shoulders, caressing them, then slid down her neckline and cupped her breasts.

"It is fair compensation for your time under the guardianship of the Three Sisters. Is it not? A weak attempt at compensation, I dare say, yet impossible to match. However, I shall insist it be buried with you when the time comes. Until then, let us forget all of our harassments and angry words. We are out of the public eyes now. There is no need for more theater. You have served me well these many mornings, and without complaint. And your sentencing has been further delayed, as I promised. I cannot hold them off any longer. Therefore, today is for you. I wish you to fear nothing this morning, to enjoy a fine dinner. And whatever may follow."

Feeling the amulet's energy flowing into her, Maria gained some strength, felt her will to fight returning.

"Whatever may follow?" She faced him, glaring. "I suspect it is the same as always. The rape."

He frowned. "So beautifully adorned yet so full of anger." He tried to offer a chuckle but it rang hollow. "It is not a rape, my dear. You must understand the nature of the role of women in any society. The ability to reproduce is crucial to any society, except ours, and so its females are protected. It is their lot in life. In death, well . . . no. The dead, or 'undead', are also abused in order to keep them under men's control. We are devilish creatures, true: perpetually jealous of rivals, desperate to assure our offspring our truly ours, and we are quick to punish any suggestion they are not. We must have dominance over our breeders to keep them both loyal and fruitful—in a bloodling society, that is."

He glanced at her, her head bowed.

"Yet in our vampiric society, the conception and birth of children is eliminated; hence, no need to contain or control the female. We have achieved equality between the sexes in exchange for the destruction of our race. We cannot make our own, so we must rely on the bloodlings to regularly give up their brood. The emperor made a poor decision when reducing the demands on bloodling recruitment, in my opinion. Without this aspect of pregnancy and the birthing of children, female vampires have gained total emancipation. You do not need men, and we men do not need you—except, perhaps, for some sordid, symbolic nostalgia. We all need blood, however. As we now know, the female vampire is generally the more dangerous of us, full of spite and envy and bent on countless revenges born of her past human experiences. You agree?"

She dared not blink.

He glared at her, stroking his long beard. "I see it in your eyes, my dear, how you would enjoy my death. Or am I mistaken? Something more? Something of an amorous nature?"

She remained a statue, awaiting the instant he would turn violent and the morning could begin. And the quicker it would end.

Turning away, he paced the room. "This act of sexual intimidation, it is . . . an act, a fictitious thing of stagecraft, pure and simple. It is not about sex, but power—to demonstrate who is in control. And there is nothing more controlling, more dominating than to be held against your will and rammed repeatedly, even beyond physical pain; and, furthermore, implanted with an alien fluid which may or may not contain disease through which you will suffer for the rest of your life, or from which may spring a child you must tend for years. You must treat the child well, for it is this crafty being who will decide for you in your aged infirmity. Yet I never had that chance before I turned. You see, your blessèd lord and master dealt my wife and I a fatal blow in that regard, so we could never have . . . ."

He saw how she stood: demure, submissive, trying to ignore him.

A long lavender divan with gold embroidery around the borders of its rounded cushions occupied the wall opposite the table. Feeling a long string of words lining up in his throat, he waved her to sit on the divan. With a dismissive dip of her head, she took a seat, an audience of one for another pedantic speech. Better than other options for her time under his control.

With a pensive nod to an invisible courtroom, he continued: "Oh, it's a matter of perspective, I suppose. We have all kinds of words. My late wife had her own views on these matters. I call it the 'making of love' as many bloodlings do—albeit a rare act for our kind. She took the holy union as her sacred duty: the entry through the devil's door which honors the Most High." He paused as though remembering a particular instance. "No, the details conjure the names. For some, it is an unholy union, to honor our Dark Father, as you and I have done. It is natural and therefore normal for us, as vampires, to proceed thus. Let me explain: We do not have feelings—emotions, the bloodlings say—other than bloodlust, of course, which is completely biological. Once the vampiric poison fills our bodies we have no more need for such things as love or compassion or kindness or any of those other weaknesses. I hate to say it but we become automatons—"

"In the west they don't allow men to explain things to women," she interrupted.

"They also burn vampires in the west. Especially in those British Isles." He feigned laughter. "We are not in the west, my dear. It's one reason the Anglo-American Union is failing. And the Russias, too, also corrupt. As I was saying, without the role of reproducing ourselves, the only reason we might come together sexually is for physical pleasure—many of us remain in a perpetual state of erection as a side effect of our lack of motility; hence the adoption of our sweeping cassock fashion—or for the pure symbolism thrust upon us by our religious overlords. 'Go forth and multiply' the pale spirit's book declares. 'Go unto each for pleasure solely' writes our Dark Father in our catechism. You know it, I am sure."

"'Take from each as you can without regret' it says."

"Yes! Take! And have no regrets. Or apologies—a bloodling flaw."

"The Dark Father speaks of the taking of blood. Not of sex."

"The verse is subject to interpretation. I interpret it to refer to the taking of anything—everything—as each of us wishes. As I have taken from you this week. I have also given to you—"

"Against my will."

He chuckled dryly. "You are a prisoner. A condemned prisoner. A criminal. You have no rights, no will to exercise. You can be taken by anyone. If you were commonfolk, you would have a red star burned into your forehead and be turned out to the streets, at the mercy of rapists everywhere. So be glad it is I who has taken you, for I am kind and gentle—so long as you please me. Another master might be very different."

He paused, awaiting her response but she only lowered her head and kept silent—

"Like a good little prisoner."

He circled around the room, absently tugging his beard, arriving before her place on the divan. He studied her, his stern eyes falling on the V of her neckline.

"Now let me *explain* to you, my dear. The bloodlings speak highly of the front entry—presumably because they expect the conception. Yet vampirekind seem too obsessed with exchanging blood to give it a try. Perhaps they think it to be blasphemous to perform an act which celebrates the creation of life when we are about death. It is an irony.

There is a lot to be missed in not giving it a try, I think." He smiled strangely. "Let us take a kinder path to ecstasy, shall we? Let us try, for a brief respite, to become human once more, catechism or not. No one will know if we play as the bloodlings play."

Her face, so stark yet pretty, frozen at the bloodling age of twenty, gave away nothing. She waited for the session to reach its inevitable conclusion. Usually he pushed her down on the bed in the next room and stood behind her. Then she would be returned to her cell where she could slip into hibernation and forget her existence.

"As many times as you have summoned me to your chamber," she spoke, looking up from the divan, "I can hardly call it rape any longer. It seems more an unsavory duty. Like cleaning a toilet."

A horrible grin broke through his thick, gray beard. "There's the kind words. I knew you felt something. Please do not call it duty. You please me. I enjoy having you—having you here. We have had many wonderful conversations, separate from the bed chamber acts. And . . . I sense you seem to soften to my touch, to my affection. I know you have feelings, the beginning of feelings, perhaps, but everything has been difficult. If only I could keep you for myself here and not let them execute you—"

"Not kindness, sir, only an observation."

"What is?"

"Rape. Duty. Either one."

"It's only a word, my dear. There are others, and you may choose from among them. The act nevertheless remains the same. One may say our sexual motions are passionate. Others may call them barbaric, savage. If you fight me, certainly I might call it rape were I to observe our activity from across the room. And I would enjoy it all the same. However, since you lay as still as a ghost, I might as well be fornicating with a pillow."

He stood with a sour face, expecting a vigorous retort.

Nothing.

"Yes, I see. You refuse to expend a gram of emotion for me. I can understand how it must be from your perspective. Forced to comply, to take the devil's position and endure my efforts. Yet that is the price you pay for some time away from your dirty cell."

She stood automatically, wanting to refute him, yet she remained still as a statue, her breathing measured. The jade seemed to brighten against her bosom. It felt warm.

"I thought you may have developed feelings—"

"May you go to the pyre with a stake through your heart, sir."

"Ah! There she is: my sweet lady of words. *Les mots.* Ah, *les mots sont comme des flèches à mon coeur. Merci.* Thank you. I hope we shall have a delightful conversation while we dine—in Magyar or French, as you like. It should make no difference for our dinner talk whether we proceed to the passion afterwards. I have no reason to hurry. Do you? Whenever we finish, you must return to your dirty cell. So you might as well tarry here, unpleasant as you may think it to be."

He gestured again at the chair by the table, so she held the amulet tight to her bosom with one hand and placed her other hand on the table as she sat. The crisp violet dress stiffened under her thighs and the hem caught on the table leg. Pursing her lips, she shook it loose.

Although her skin had mended well, pain flickered from muscles bashed and scored by the Three Sisters. The dungeon was a forlorn place. The lowest levels held the most decrepit, the forgotten, destined to crumble to dust. Below those levels was the chamber of the Three Sisters, a set of twins and their elder sister who were devotees of the torturous arts. They took special delight working on female prisoners. Perhaps it was because they had been tortured themselves; to take on the form of that which had harmed you was therapeutic, she believed one night after enduring a water torture—

The knock on the door cut off her thoughts. For an instant she feared the prosecutor had invited his colleagues to share her—as he had threatened on previously occasions.

Instead, when the door swung open, a thin girl bearing a heavy golden tray of golden dishes stood there.

"Dinner is served, Your Lordship," the girl mumbled.

He waved her in, commenting loudly how ugly she was, the way her face was scarred and her scalp nearly devoid of hair. Her frail body was so pale and sickly he almost refused the dinner she had brought, wondering whether it was contaminated.

"If I feel even the slightest ill sensation, it is you I shall blame. And that means the dungeons, at best. Or, at worse—"

"Leave her be," spoke Maria from her seat.

He froze, pleased he had provoked her.

"As you wish." He gave the scraggly girl another glance. "One more of those walking blood bags, a servant to the thirst-crazed, opening a vein at a noble's whim. Sup for a while and return to form, eh?"

Maria watched the serving girl set the tray on the edge of the table, hands shaking. When she thought the tray was steady, she lifted the curved lid over the main course, showing it to the prosecutor while the lid hid the food from Maria's view. The prosecutor nodded approval and the girl returned the lid over the dish. Other small dishes were arranged for each of them. She placed a carafe of blood-wine in the center.

"I am certain it was prepared with the freshest ingredients and will have no ill effect," said the prosecutor with an ear toward improving Maria's mood. He regarded the serving girl. "Thank you."

The girl bowed and backed out of the chamber, closing the door after. Its weight troubled her and she struggled moving it. In the last instant, the girl's eyes locked on Maria's. She thought she recognized the girl. Quickly Maria bit her lip to block any thoughts she might have that he could detect. Blood bubbled to the surface of her lip and she licked it away.

"Shall we dine?" asked the prosecutor, picking up a golden fork. "You will note the salad course contains sweet bitterroot. Hard to get. But I enjoy it, and I thought I would share it with you. It has a sting to it when first bit, then becomes sweet. The longer one chews, however, the more bitter it becomes. A metaphor for our existence, eh? Try the blood sauce."

Taking up her fork, she recognized it as being from a set someone had absconded with from the imperial suite. It was a gift from the late Premier of the German province on the fiftieth anniversary of its union with the Hungarian Empire. Following his lead, she sampled the delicacy, unimpressed. She tasted the side dishes—blood bread, pickled hawk hearts, rat tail soup—and decided she needed no more. Her belly had shrunk during her dungeon days.

"Are you ready for the main course?" asked the prosecutor.

Before she could respond, he lifted the lid, setting it down on the credenza. There before her was a plate featuring two human breasts, topped by crisp, caramelized bits. She thought they must be breasts, turned so the nipples pointed up. She stared at the dish. Although thoroughly baked and topped with a variety of herbs and a thin, runny red sauce, she suddenly had no appetite.

"Ah! Breasts! The specialty of the female," he waxed poetic with a wry grin. "The fount of sustenance, from which death-poison flows. It amuses us to think the pale spirit claims ownership of them, declares this creation his greatest work—the artistic curvature of the female torso— while we know the sad truth. The curse of milk!"

She leveled her eyes at him. "What is that truth?"

He swept his beard to the side as he cut off the nipple of one roast breast and delivered it to his plate. He forked it and popped it into his mouth, chewing. "As the catechism of our Dark Lord states, 'Woman is ever a deceiver of Men and—'"

"'And cursed upon the Earth'—"

"'Created to be used, second only to cattle and horses, to be taken as fodder, like kindling for a fire, to be swept out like dust when the abode is cleaned'—"

"'To be forgotten thereafter, like the sunset, lost amidst the night.'"

"'Like the sup of divine essence upon the flesh.'"

His smile shone warm upon her cheeks, a disturbing sensation.

"You know your catechism well, my dear."

Her frown was cold. She felt the push of fangs from her gums, wishing she had not pleased him. The blood was warming in her chest. She breathed deeply.

"I've a long time to study, sir."

He looked down at his meal, pausing a moment before cutting into the breast with knife and fork.

"Yes. Well, you've no more time to study, my dear. The end comes too soon. Such a pity. We have only tonight for you and I to be happy, if that is your desire. It certainly is mine." He gazed across the table at her. "Not hungry?"

She flashed a grin at him, completely artificial.

"The dungeon diet has transformed me."

"You are disappointed?" He gave a *harrumph* and slid his knife into the closest breast, juices squirting out. He cut a slice. "Remarkable how they keep the nipple intact. It's the best part, in my humble opinion. Go on, try it." He set the portion upon her plate.

She shook her head, her face fighting to hide her distress.

"Would you be more interested if I told you these come from our late Countess Natália?"

She perked up. "The countess?"

"The same. I made sure of it with our chef."

"It's been so long, how can it be . . . fresh?"

"Some parts were kept frozen. She was a cold person to begin with. Not everything ended up in the baskets of the commonfolk."

"We should not consume each other," she muttered.

"We all consume each other in some fashion, my dear. Tonight it is symbolic. She betrayed you, so . . . you can have the last bite, as they say. Not so perverse, my dear. Recall how the traitor András Sándor was treated. They cut off his sacred orbs and boiled them before him, dined on them as he watched. And Eszter Szekeres, who had—"

"Stop!" She threw down her fork on the table, looked away. "Being here is worse than torture by the Three Sisters."

"I'm sure it is not." He took a bite of breast, chewed. "Not bad. I would bake it a little longer. A cream sauce might be better."

Maria watched him eat. Occasionally he would regard her and she would turn further away. She kept one hand on the amulet, felt it pulse with warmth, her only hope. Waiting for him, she finished her small glass of blood-wine, a Burgundy.

A knock on the door, though it had not closed tightly when the girl exited. In a weary voice, the prosecutor called for the visitor to enter. It was the serving girl, bearing a tray of desserts: blood tarts, by the look of them. The blood clots gracing the tops resembled cranberries.

"We are not ready for dessert," he growled. "Set them over there for now." He gestured to the credenza.

After setting down the tray, the girl took up the bottle of wine and went to refill their glasses.

Maria held her hand over the amulet to protect it from spills as the girl poured. His glass was refilled second. When Maria started to raise the glass, the serving girl bumped her hand with the back of her wrist and the wine spilled onto the table.

"Clumsy ghoul!" shouted the prosecutor.

The serving girl's eyes met Maria's. She recognized her as the one who had helped them with His Holiness. She had thought the girl was dead, splayed on the floor in the salon, clothes disheveled, bloody. Her father lay with a twisted, broken neck beside her. But Maria had more important things to tend to, hurrying after the casket which bore His Holiness—

"Beg pardons, sir," said the girl. "I'll get a towel to clean it."

She gave Maria a hard stare, dipped her forehead at the toppled glass, then shook her head. She meant for Maria not to drink it.

"Enough!" scolded the prosecutor. "Get out. We have no need of more tonight." He practically pushed the serving girl out the door and slammed it after her.

"Be easy on her," Maria cried, rising from her chair.

"Enough of you, as well!" the prosecutor shouted, returning to the table. He gave Maria a backhand slap, knocking her to the floor. "I try to be kind, to arrange a good last supper for you, and only insolence and distractions do I get. You do not appreciate my acts of kindness? Then let us proceed to the acts of depravity!"

He had slammed the door shut, but it only banged against the door jamb and stayed open a few inches as he bent down to grab Maria and jerk her to her feet. He threw her backwards against the wall next to the table. Placing his hands on the delicately embroidered neckline of her elegant dress, he ripped it open. The amulet hanging between her breasts reflected his angry face as he continued tearing the dress open, buttons falling on the floor.

"So angry you are," Maria cursed, "to destroy a well-crafted dress. Anger directed at something that does not fight with you. How can you hate the couturier so much?"

He slapped her face at that remark.

"Let us get on to the dessert, *mademoiselle*."

He noticed she did not react to the slap, no tears, no fear.

"I realize that didn't hurt you," he mugged. "I meant to stop your silly prattle. I know you are special, a creature of Hell. I am not fooled by you, as you must know by now. So you will do as I say."

With one hand pressed between her breasts, fixing her to the wall, his other hand pushed the torn dress down her body. When it bunched against her knees, he stomped it to the floor with his slippered foot. He put his hands around her slender waist, lifted her out of the crumpled clothing on the floor, and stood her up before him, now covered only by the white petticoat that hung on her hips.

"Let us see if dinner has restored your strength."

He stared at her chest, the marks of the whip still visible but healed already. White lines like worms crisscrossed her skin. Reaching out to touch her breast, he dared not gaze into her eyes, as though believing she could put a spell upon him.

"It really is remarkable . . . ."

He ran his fingers along the scars, white upon white. They crawled over her wounds. He came to her nipple, pinched it playfully.

"Remarkable . . . ."

She lifted her hand, slowly so as not to alert him, and laid it over the amulet, pressing it hard against her bosom. A weak sensation of energy expanded from the stone, filling her chest like air into lungs. It was the same experience she'd had when she had taken the necklace from His Holiness that first time.

"Yes, you appear much more beautiful with that antique jewelry on your pale breasts. I like pale—a true vampiric virtue. I'm glad you wear it. After your execution, I could probably get a great price for it. You wearing it will add value. As long as it's—"

"Thank you for letting me wear it," she cooed in a voice which had him pause suspiciously.

"Yes—you are welcome."

Taking her calloused hand in his, he led her through the doorway into the next room where a four-poster bed with a canopy occupied the entire far wall. High on each post steel chains hung down, draped on the thin mattress. Atop the pure white sheet lay a few animal pelts to use as blankets. A large pillow with red satin covering stood up against one corner of the bed, against the wooden headrest ornately carved with various mythic creatures engaged in coitus.

She stared at the Irish elk rearing back, rising over the woolly rump of the ram and remembered another time, another place.

Monsieur Aimery Bégon wanted her, drew her into his suite at the Grand Maison Hôtel in Nice, ignoring his legion of investors to dally with her. Bégon had called everyone to announce his newest product, a system for cataloguing data collected from all network platforms no matter the nation of origin, the language, or the code employed— whether or not users allowed the data to be collected, whether or not they allowed the collected data to be subsequently sold to any entity willing to pay. It was well-known how many black site operators were interested in the technology. Bégon only needed to entertain counter-offers from governments—

She saw the prosecutor's stony façade. "Please . . . ."

"Oh, now you are polite to me." He let his face turn ugly. "We shall see if you continue thus."

She had acted hesitant, then gave in. Playing her role like an Oscar hopeful, they had arrived in bed and Bégon found her delicious. She, mere arm-dressing to him, got him to boast about his new technology. He explained how it worked. Then he finished their love-making with an unfortunate accident. Rolling in pain on the floor, she offered to get help. He was too embarrassed to have anyone know, yet she insisted medical attention was necessary and he finally accepted. She ran out— and down to the lobby, took a taxi to her own small inn and divulged everything to Faucheux.

"*Monsieur,*" she addressed the prosecutor, "please allow me a small courtesy on this final night, the chance to enjoy one last embrace with a man. It would be my honor, though I deserve it not, to have you be my last partner."

He had grabbed one of the bracelets dangling from a chain at the head of the bed as she spoke. He paused, a coarse grin spreading across his face like sunlight burning vampiric cheeks.

"Let us have no chains today," she said in a soft, passionate voice. "How else might I embrace my lover?" She fixed her doe-eyes on him. "You do wish to be embraced, do you not?"

It was 2000 and Y2K fears had fallen apart. The world of computer networks would continue unabated, seducing the masses into daily connection. The technology industry eventually gathered every bit of information about everyone—then lost it to criminals and criminal governments. The population demanded action, dropping technology *en masse*, sending the industry collapsing. The Hungarian Empire was the first government to ban the use of computer networks, in 2028, although individual machines were allowed so long as they were not connected to anything but a printing unit. Even those soon fell into disrepute and abandoned. So much information was lost whenever the machines failed; better to use paper for archiving—

"Yes, my dear. I most certainly do," spoke the prosecutor in a new voice, affecting the lover's subtle cajoling. "May I? May we?"

She saw his eyes weaken as he held out his arms for her. Since the ruse had begun, she couldn't refuse, and swept up against him, sliding her arms around behind him and snuggling her cheek against his chest as her naked bosom pressed against his starched cassock. He wrapped his arms around her shoulders, gingerly, regarding the scars.

For Bégon, he lost his profits, then his investors, then his company as others took up the race to steal everyone's data. He also lost the use of his penis, broken in their passionate unification. It would not go in, he insisted, and she giggled, persuaded him to try harder. He had no idea who she was. Rosy cheeks hid her black heart. Faucheux made another tidy million in dollars, Deutsche marks, Italian lira, and francs from her night's effort. Bégon's wife, already estranged from him, divorced him, took what little he had left and sailed off on his yacht with her young Italian lover.

"The hand that moves the world," Faucheux liked to say.

"What's that, my dear?" the prosecutor asked, bringing her back.

He held her away, liquid smile as he gazed up and down her body. His hands cradled her face, one finger poking into her ear. That act irritated her yet she maintained her pleasant expression.

"Only a memory," she whispered. "I thought it long forgotten."

"As all memories are," he said softly, adding a few more verses of catechism. "Shall we make a memory?"

He threw his hand toward the bed, her signal to submit, to become his dutiful pet. But she hesitated, as though deciding which position to take, yet he did not become alarmed. This morning, he had said, was to be different. Something special.

He must believe her in her role now, she thought, adding a pout.

"Fear not, my dear, for I shall be gentle. I promise."

He watched as she turned and sat demurely on the edge of the bed.

"I understand your hesitation. A novice would be hesitant at the coming moments, like any good virgin. How will it go? Will it hurt? That is common, and normal. But you should relax. Allow me to enjoy you, and you me. I will teach you what you do not know, and what you already know we shall practice further . . . until we are perfect."

"Thank you," she replied, her voice misty. "I want it to be perfect."

With a smile breaking through his beard, he reached out, hooking his finger inside the waistband of her petticoat. She stood at his tug. Pulling the waistband away, he stepped up against her, leaning down to kiss her mouth. She shifted away, then remembered her role. His lips, greasy from the dinner, touched hers, pressed on. She parted her lips, sensing her fangs extending. His fangs were dulled, she saw.

"Let us remove our masks and lower our shields, my dear, and reveal our truths."

He tore the petticoat down and she allowed it to roll off her legs, catching on her feet. She kicked it away, taking the opportunity to test her strength and range. She resumed her innocent position upon the edge of the bed, her legs parting enough that his eyes widened, his lips reddened, and his tongue pushed out of his mouth like a snake ready to strike.

"And now me," he announced, raising a hand to unfasten the gold clasp at his collar.

His hand worked slowly, deliberately on the hooks, going down his red cassock until they were all undone. He presented a grin, nearly covered by his beard. With both hands he jerked open his cassock like the curtains of a theater stage. His body, without the usual shirt and pantaloons, was white and strung with blue veins and dark red arteries. He also was bare and his body showed the marks of his youth, fighting on one battlefield or another: saber cuts, bullet puckers. She examined them as he stood proudly, letting the cassock slip off his shoulders, falling in a clump on the floor.

"Do not be afraid, my dear. I promise to be gentle."

Below his chest, his belly had bowled out with the dinner but he was otherwise thin. His hips were boney, groin hairless, the ghostly member he swore to use gently excited and upright. In the position he usually set her, she had never been able to see his body. He showed confidence, however, believing she was impressed.

She blinked—twice.

"Forgive my appearance," he said, voice low. "I was in the war."

"A war-torn body is attractive to a lady such as me."

He smiled at her words, not caring if it was only idle flattery.

His hands shot forward, shoving her down on the bed, her face and folded arms pressed against the mattress, *derrière* upward. He admired the view: the white scars on her white flesh enticing him.

"Not this morning, my dear. The devil's door is how we honor our Dark Lord. This morning, I shall require you on your back, that we may act like missionaries stranded in some savage land. This morning, we shall honor our humankind ancestry."

She seemed confused, so he grabbed her hips, one hand on each side, and tossed her roughly upon the bed.

"I shall have your virginity this morning!"

No instant to refute his claim as he straightened her on the bed, rolling her onto her back, then climbed onto the bed. He straddled her ankles, regarding her pale figure a moment, then walked on his knees to her waist. He gazed down on her placid face, a pale masque with dark eyes, her lips cut by her fangs, he broke into a great smile full of lascivious delight. He held his long beard aside to gain the full view. *At long last*, his red eyes seemed to say.

"We shall come together as true lovers, not as blood suckers," he reminded her. "This morning shall be ours."

"I cannot help myself," she sighed, fully in the role. "It has been so long without the taste of a lover's throat."

He let loose his beard and it tumbled down over her face, nearly smothering her. She playfully slapped it to the side.

"Contain yourself, my dear, for I shall enter you forthwith."

His painted words rang in her ears and she was not certain whether they were actually spoken or were a memory from a bygone era when she went on stage. In a flash she replied, something from a medieval play she had been in, never worrying how the words sounded:

"I open my loins to you, sir, and bid you come through." It fit this occasion, coaxing her tormentor into her trap. "I welcome you."

Unable to contain his grin, the prosecutor slid himself back toward her feet, his hands pressing on her thighs and pushing them apart. He aligned himself, then charged forward like a cavalry regiment bent on breaking an infantry line. She lurched, half-way acting. He heaved with effort, as though believing he could ejaculate immediately and fill her womb with his pent-up seed. Instead, he loosed a wolfish moan and stopped.

She urged him to relax and go slower, but he could not contain himself and rammed again and again until he had to stop. As he rested, he began to feel a tightness which became more uncomfortable as his heart clicked. He tried to go again yet found the way blocked.

"So the rumors are true," he grunted, breathlessly. "You are ever the virgin. How does that feel? Never a mother then, I suspect. Does it make you sad?"

"It is my lot, sir, and I accept it in the service of our Dark Father."

"Yes, the Dark Father. You are so blissfully devoted. And so blithely ignorant. I understand now your—"

"Sir, as we proceed, may I know your name?"

The tightness gripped him further as he dug deep in his brain for a name. "What?"

"If this is to be our final tryst—if I am to be executed tomorrow and my body given to the cannibalistic masses—might I know your name? Your full name?"

"My name? What need have you of that? I am your master today. You are an entertainment. I take you as my desire dictates."

She pursed her lips seductively. "I wish to call out your name, sir, as I enter our ecstasy."

His face was illuminated by a mask of delight before the realization of the solemnity of the situation struck him. He remembered his wife, how she had struggled to survive, ravaged, her final minutes ticking by as her assailant gloated. He was not there, but he was certain how it had unfolded. The maids who found her told him.

His smile vanished like a breath upon a mirror.

"Yes, call it out. Let everyone in the palace know who takes you," he barked. "My name, *mademoiselle*, is Csanád. I am Csanád Borbély. You have not listened in the High Council of Justice? Ah, the judges do not call me by my name but by my office: Chief Prosecutor! Yes, I am the eldest son of the former Minister of International Affairs, if you wish to know. Does that name ring chimes in your head? Borbély? I wish it to ring. And loudly. It shall be my great pleasure to take all I can from you in service to the empire. For I am owed much, most of all by your lord and master—"

"Csanád . . . Csanád," she intoned as though remembering it, then whispered more words he could not understand. French? Latin? He was not sure, cocking his head as he listened. He heard her repeat the words, like a prayer.

"Enough mumbling. Let us continue," he ordered, rising up and thrusting downward, causing her to cry out. Her face burned with anguish. "There's the rupture, maiden. Once more. Yet fear not, eh? You have felt it many times before, true? It will mend. If the rumors are to be believed."

He pressed himself further, entered a steady rhythm, increasing his pace as ecstasy swept through him.

"Will you cry out my name now?"

And she did. In French. And in Latin. With her hand clasping the amulet tight against her bosom—

The pressure increased, clamping on him painfully. He chided her for her muscular exertion, then begged her to relax, to let go. Yet the pressure continued until he was crying out in agony. He attempted to withdraw but found himself unable to escape.

"Let me go!" he shouted. He grasped her throat with one hand, his thumb digging into her skin. His other hand tried to extract himself.

"I shall take from you what you most desire," she strained to speak.

He screamed—

And suddenly fell off her, tumbling to the side, released. Between his legs was a jagged bloody stump. He glanced forward, searching for what was missing. Then, between her thighs something was ejected: a crumpled clod of meat, popping into the air and bouncing off the foot of the bed and onto the floor.

He stared at his groin, saw his precious member had been pinched off by half. The rough end was white with frost and held a short icicle of blood.

Cursing her, he clambered up from the bed and swung his fist at her face. Her head slammed to the side but turned back without any apparent harm. Her cheek showed the impressions of his knuckles. Drawing back his fist for another swing, he noticed his knuckles were crystallized, whiteness spreading across his hand down to his fingertips and up to his wrist—

A knock on the door startled him.

"What foul thing disturbs me this hour?"

The serving girl had returned. She stood in the doorway of the bed chamber with another tray bearing a squat bottle of Avignon blood-sherry and two small glasses. Maria recognized the label as she sat up on the bed, pulling the leopard pelt over herself.

"Your drinks, My Lord," the girl called in a timid voice.

The chamber's doors swung open further, as if by a ghostly breeze, and she stepped into the bedroom.

"This is not a good time," he moaned, spinning away to hide his wound. As he turned, a cloud of crystallized hairs from his beard flew onto the floor. "Be gone."

The girl stepped across the room, measuring her pace, it seemed, as her eyes darted to the bed, to the woman sitting there, and back to the naked man.

"Hurry out, filthy wench!"

She bowed her head but stepped no quicker. He went to give her a shove but noticed how his injury left drops of blood on the floor that turned into hoarfrost. More of his beard dropped to the floor.

He turned to Maria. "You—icy—bitch!"

As the girl set the tray on the side table and casually arranged the glasses, Borbély became enraged. He threw her aside and grabbed the bottle, putting the cork to his teeth, unstopping it. He poured the wine into a glass, missing much of it in his fluster. He set the bottle down and took up the glass, sloshed it into his mouth, missing and spilling the liquid down his chest. He refilled the glass and dashed it against his crotch, groaning as frostbite took effect. A line of crystallization ran up his belly.

"Are you hurt, My Lord?" asked the girl, pointing at his crotch. "Do you feel the poison yet?"

Maria saw the grin hiding in the corner of the girl's mouth.

"Clean this mess," he commanded, wavering on his feet.

The glass slipped from his weak hand, shattering on the floor. He dropped to his knees, unable to stand more, and some of the shards embedded in his knees but he did not cry out.

"Do you believe what I say?" called Maria from the bed. "Today is your last day. The ice becomes you—"

"Yet I had you—"

"And the blood becomes ice."

He tumbled over onto the floor, glass fragments piercing his cheek, arm, and his ribs.

"I think rather I had you," Maria retorted, climbing off the bed. "It was never His Holiness who was imbued with the icy touch. No, it was me. And He kept his distance, believing He had the curse. And in that arrangement, we came to our arrangement—call it *amour*, if you wish."

She regarded the serving girl. "Thank you . . . mmm?"

"I'm Nóra, Milady." The girl dipped in curtsy.

Nóra went to the bed, gathered Maria's petticoat, helped her. She folded up the evening gown, slipping it into a sack she had brought.

"I've another dress for you, Milady."

"You—you planned this?" Borbély pushed himself up on one arm.

Maria snickered. "How could I do such a thing, imprisoned and alone? Only the Dark Father could plan such a thing."

"You'll pay for this."

He tried to get up, his leg bending awkwardly under him, pushing with his frozen foot, as the blood flowing inside turned to ice.

"Guards!" he cried weakly, "Guard . . . s." He broke into sobbing.

"No one will hear you," Nóra dared speak in her mousy voice. "You sent them all away."

She retrieved a set of clothing from the entrance to the suite and presented it to Maria as the whimpering Borbély groveled on the floor. The simple beige dress with pretty red lace about the high neck and around the cuffs fit her mood.

"A commonfolk garment?" she asked Nóra.

"Yes, so you won't be noticed outside the palace."

Borbély saw the jade amulet glowing against Maria's chest, bright as the sun, its green rays striping the walls of the chamber, almost like a kaleidoscope, so bright he could not look at it. Then his eyes froze, glazing over, pure white.

"You cannot go," he grumbled tearfully, bursting blindly into the dining room. He struggled to steady himself on his hands and knees. "You're already scheduled for punishment tomorrow. The execution. It has been decided by the judges—by all the Court. The dismembering has been arranged—"

"We think not!"

A great shadow fell over Borbély.

The huge man charged into the suite, bearing his halberd straight on into Borbély, gutting him from sternum to groin. Viscera spilled upon the floor and faded into wintry pallor. The ice man, face of frost, reached desperately for the nearest support—the big man's leg. But the man would have none of it and swung his gloved fist down at Borbély's crystal head, shattering it, sending a spray of ice shards everywhere. Blood bubbled out of the neck slowly, freezing as it ran, forming red icicles that stuck to the floor.

"Everyone knew he would lose his head sooner or later," Maria quipped, pressed against the wall to escape the mess.

Nóra ran to the big man, hugging him as he held the halberd aside.

"Thank you, Judas," Maria spoke to the man in the bailiff uniform as she clutched the bright green amulet. Like Nóra, she knew him from their brief interval together in the imperial suite and their escape to the underground salon.

Letting go of the girl, he wiped the halberd's blade on the white bed sheet. "My name is actually Joshua, My Lady."

"Joshua." She gave him a nod and stared down at the frozen body of Borbély. "I wish he would have suffered longer. Vampires tend to tarry too long. Waiting so long for death is a curse."

"It won't be long," said Joshua. "We must go quickly, My Lady, if we are to get you to safety—as I promised His Holiness."

13

AT FIRST, THEY DID NOT KNOW WHAT TO DO; there was no one in charge. Eventually Duke Juhász called a meeting of the Council of Ministers, but only about half attended; some were missing or were known to have been killed either in the mob's fury within the palace or while on the streets. Members who attended elected Prince Gyula of the Barta family to be *de facto* ruler until matters could be sorted out. Of course, Countess Adél Váradi objected, citing the change in protocol allowing a female ruler, but she was threatened with removal from the Council so she withdrew her objection. With the on-going terror, the time was not right. They divided duties and set about applying a steady hand to assure control of the empire.

As matters became sorted out, the Council called in Lady Maria to answer questions. She was not then suspected of wrongdoing but her answers had been flippant; in the hours afterwards, she had realized she should not have acted in that manner. It was not long before she was ordered confined to her quarters. Then, finding no other credible suspects, the Council of Ministers again called for her and, following days of interrogation, deemed her a prime suspect. With investigation, she either had murdered the emperor, likely with some assistance, and then hidden the body; or else she had helped the emperor escape to a secret location. "To what end?" she had cried. They could not fathom that His Holiness actually did not relish the daily duties of his rank and might prefer to relocate to a suitable retirement.

When Prince Giorgio and Countess Natália were caught and held for interrogation, Maria was removed from her comfortable suite and dashed into a cold, dark cell in a lower level of the dungeon. Childhood memories of the Terror returned to her. She had no more idea of the emperor's location or dispensation than the two other captives had. The prince and the countess were accused of murdering the emperor. One priest was happy to share the news with her, delighting in her reactions to every hideous detail of their public execution.

She lost count of the days in that cell but when someone finally came to let her out, she found herself transferred to a worse situation: the Three Sisters. They toyed with her, apparently instructed that all areas of her body were fair game except her face. The comely grace of her elven façade must be preserved for public display. It was the only courtesy allowed her. She was forced to endure the beatings and more imaginative tactics of torture for several weeks. And a few random visits later. Often the mere mention of visiting the Three Sisters again was enough to prompt a confession or compel her to end her stubborn silence.

She lay in her cell day after day wondering what she could have done that made them hate her so. She was a minor character in this charade. When she had awakened from unconsciousness in the salon, the emperor was already gone. The prince and the countess were gone, too. She saw the trail of nightsoil crumbs fallen from the casket as it was wheeled out of the salon. An obvious set of clues, she believed. The other two there in the room seemed dead or dying; no use to tend to them. She must hurry after the casket.

For sixty-six consecutive days she was called to the Imperium and questioned for hours. Many of the questions were the same—as were many answers. They accused her of crimes she had not committed. They put her in the accused's box and rained challenges at her. Their henchman arrived to administer punitive lashes from a whip when she displeased them. Each session left her cut and bleeding. Dragging her back to her cell left a path of blood drops rats lapped up and prisoners reached out from cells to finger and lick off. Each morning the pain was the same as the night before—except she noticed her cuts had scarred over and no longer bled. The next day's lashes would break them open. They began to order treatment for her and some prison attendants were quite happy to apply the ointment to her wounds, her body exposed in the corridor for the other prisoners' view.

She began to remember the way He had treated her with polite tolerance in public venues and with abject kindness in the imperial suite. Often they would sit together, He in His chair and she on hers, exchanging smiles, perhaps reading an ancient book or conversing in low voices, sometimes laughing at the irony of their situation. They shared twisted jokes about their fate. Despite her love for Him, she obeyed. She did what He commanded and followed dutifully His plan.

 CR

Again Nóra tried to toss the dull green shawl around Maria's shoulders and again the Lady shook it off.

"You must cover it," said Joshua, leaning back from the front bench of the carriage.

"Here, Milady," Nóra spoke, tossing the cloth around her. "It looks good over your tan dress."

"I have no wish to be a commoner," Maria insisted. "You wear it."

"People seeing your fancy jewelry will know you're a Lady and call the inspectors," Joshua grumbled. "I must ask you to cover it. Tuck it inside the dress."

"It must be set to sunlight to restore its power," Maria insisted. She pulled her low neckline further away so the fabric did not obscure the great jade amulet. The stone glowed with a dark green fire.

"Please," Joshua barked.

"If you insist." She tossed the end of the shawl over her pale bosom, blocking the view of her talisman.

The hollow clops of the vorses' hooves were the only sound in the morning. No birds dared fly or varmints scurry as they passed through the vacant streets. Maria was shocked by what had changed during her incarceration. Vehicles of all kinds sat abandoned along the streets, their batteries run down with no way to recharge them. If anyone still had a petro-mobile it was sooner left to ruin. He was correct: the vorse carriage was the only way out of the city. At the noon hour with a full sun, few were outside.

They had slipped out of Borbély's suite and down to a side stairwell which deposited them underground. At that point, Maria had insisted she needed to pay a visit to the Three Sisters, to give them what she owed them. Joshua urged her to forget them so they might escape the city, but she had to stop by, "just for a chat", to show off her new/old necklace and its fabulous talisman. Besides, they were near; it would not take long.

Before he could stop her, she hurried away, dressed in the country woman's garments and travel boots. They made noise against the stone floor. He called in a low voice they would wait only 30 minutes, then exit the palace on their own.

In twenty-nine minutes Maria had returned, looking no worse for wear, and held up the jade stone in the torchlight to wipe off a spot of blood. Her hair was disheveled and Nóra tried to fix it up but Maria waved her off. A country woman could leave her hair down.

Nóra pointed to the spots of blood on one side of Maria's dress.

"Theirs," she responded, grinning. "I used the power of the amulet to square our accounts."

Joshua eyed her suspiciously, as though he feared whatever she did would bring further alarm to a quiet palace, placing their escape plan in jeopardy.

"They were pleased to see me, the Three Sisters were. Surprised but pleased. No guard escort had tipped them and I was fully prepared. All it takes is a bit of focus, a talisman from China, and some creativity."

"They're dead?" asked Nóra.

"No, they yet exist."

"I mean . . . their vampiric lives are ended?"

"That would be too common. For the twins, I rearranged their innards. I waved a finger, their bellies opened. I flicked more fingers and their bowels sprang out. The tubes pulled apart from each of them and reattached to the other. That way one sister must from now on feed the other."

Nóra gasped, hand over her mouth.

"You never heard of conjoined twins?" asked Maria with a laugh.

"And the elder sister?" asked Joshua in serious tone, leading them onward along the dark corridor.

"She, I needed to vanquish. So I plucked out her eyes and fashioned them into the sockets of her sisters, so each twin had one of the elder sister's ways of seeing. Beyond that, she wished to scream yet she had no mouth; an old trick. I thought she might take delight in fornication so I sealed her flower, never to blossom again. I thought she may want food so I knotted her throat. And left her writhing on the floor like a blind snake."

"You are a cruel woman," Joshua muttered.

"No, I repaid in kind. You said to be quick, so I was. I would prefer they suffer longer, and I believe my actions shall provide the same."

Through the corridors they hurried, down to the garage where the carriage awaited, two vorses hitched, bored and nipping at each other like hungry dogs. Joshua helped the women into the carriage, tossed in three bags of supplies, then climbed up to the front bench to direct the vorses out into the sunlight. The beasts were already covered to protect their hairless bodies from the light, hoods to shield their eyes.

The vorse was a vampire horse, made the same way humans turned dark, and they carried their skeletal bodies like walking corpses. Easily directed, they were unsuitable for theatrical charges across battlefields or racing around a track, yet they were reliable as draft animals pulling wagons and carriages for the poor who could not afford the electric vehicles—and everyone, once the battery craze dropped off with the collapse of the power grid. Candle shops and oil lamp manufacturers did well after that. Discovered in an upper pasture in Slovenia, it was clear what the farmer's son had been doing. The vorse became useful and were bred for their tasks. The only flaw was they could get hungry and nip at any animal close by. In fact, for a longer journey, it was common to pair the animals so that, when it became necessary, one could feed the other. Once fed, the vorse could proceed for quite a while.

Crossing the Duna alone seemed suspicious and the guards at the gate on the opposite end of the new chain-link bridge stood up and got ready to confront the carriage as it approached.

"I've got a sick daughter," Joshua called down. He had changed from his bailiff's cassock to farmer's clothes. "I must get her to the farm for treatment."

The guards understood and waved them on with only a glimpse inside to confirm that two women, bundled in blankets and shawls, looking less pale than they should, rode with him. It was common to catch one of several illnesses when living in a vampiric city. A popular treatment, though not confirmed by science, was the traditional farm visit where vampiric citizens could indulge in animal blood to restore the pale.

Through the empty streets of Pest they went until they had exited the environs for the countryside. Still there were checkpoints and they held fast to their story. In the glum days of gray skies and the rare slice of sunbeams through the clouds, few were concerned about an old carriage with a pair of black-shielded vorses making its way down the road. Guards waved them through, not worth their effort as they huddled in the shadows of the gate and guard shacks, themselves avoiding the sun. Only fools and Croats went out in daylight.

❧

"I suppose I should change my name again," Maria announced the first evening when they stopped at an inn, the innkeeper happy to get some money. His wife was happy to cook blood stew for them, full of pieces of pork. Maria pointed her spoon at the big communal bowl. "This swine soup reminds me of my childhood."

Joshua looked up, spoon at his mouth. "Not so long ago, I suspect."

"Shall I feign amusement, sir?" She waited for him to finish his spoonful, then continued: "No, I got my blood cure at age twenty, if you must know. Hence my youthful vigor."

"And your magic capability," Nóra spoke meekly, eyes bright with admiration. She patted a canvas bag sitting beside her.

"That I learned from a master magician," Maria responded. "Many years of practice, certainly, yet everything is made easier when I can use this talisman. This amulet—" She took it in her fist and the stone glowed green between her fingers. "It helps focus my energy, through which I may affect what changes in atomic structure I wish. It's all very scientific—if you study it for a century, yet not easily explained to simpletons."

"We are not simpletons, My Lady," Joshua said with a grunt. "We help you because we, too, served His Holiness. We are all the same in that way. Who we serve is what unites us. It is our duty to see justice done, no matter how others may think. And . . . ."

"And what, sir?"

"What they were doing to you was the height of injustice. I could not let them destroy you."

"I do thank you, sir, for your assistance. And you, Nóra. However, I should likely have saved myself. In that moment, *Monsieur* Borbély was in the act of freezing. When he thaws, his guts shall soil the floor, thanks to your blade."

"It was my pleasure to offer you my blade." He seemed to grin, but only Nóra would notice. "Now we must flee so none might serve us as you have been served this past year."

"*Merci beaucoup, Monsieur.*" She smiled sincerely and dipped her head in thanks. "Now, my name. I was born Jeanne-Marie, then made a Magyar as Marija—with the 'j'—so now I must be Hungarian like you two. So then a name like . . . hmm. Maria becomes Míra and my old French surname Poirier becomes Pál. Easy to remember, *oui*?"

"Yes, but you must forget those French words that slip out your mouth from time to time," said Joshua, unamused. "Or, perhaps, it would be better to return to your French name, if you plan to enter Russia. They are easy on the French, I hear."

"I like it," said Nóra, giving the bag beside her a loving caress.

Joshua frowned. "What will His Holiness think?"

Maria scoffed. "His Holiness? What does it matter now? He is gone, gone to His fate."

"If He is truly holy, He will return, and in grander form than ever before," Joshua boasted.

"Much depends on His lord and master," she said with a sneer.

"My Lady," he spoke louder, "we helped you escape because we serve His Holiness. Both Nóra and me. It is our duty. He is our lord and master even when he is far removed."

"We all serve His Holiness," Maria muttered. "He infects many of us across the continent, so we all serve. We live to serve Him. We *exist* to serve His lord and master."

Nóra spoke in a mousy voice: "Do you know why He was holy?"

It was Joshua's turn to scoff. "He is prime among us. Kristóf, my friend in the palace, said so many times. His Holiness comes from the lord and master of the Dark, as personal envoy to Europa. He is high commander of vampiric forces everywhere."

Maria hid a smile with her hand. "He was made the natural way, through his family line."

"Not by the kiss?" asked Nóra timidly.

Maria placed her hand on Nóra's arm. "His is an ancient disease, passed through each generation. No bite did He receive; rather, the seeds of genetic materials condemned Him to this existence."

"Condemned?" Joshua blurted out. "It was a curse that enabled Him to rise to the pinnacle of power."

Maria pursed her lips, tightened her jaw. "He wished never to be at the pinnacle of power. He fought against it. Yet His lord and master forbade it, forced Him to go on, to be the evil the land required. Our dear Mister Holiness was forever miserable. He did not want His fate. So many hours He spoke of His former life, before the change, how much He missed His former lover, a wife He swore to save from His fate. He spoke of how He infected her and how she came to kill Him yet He managed to save her, turn her back to human, then—"

"How can He do that?" Nóra perked up.

"His powers are many. Once He had promised to serve His lord and master, the one He named 'Luce'. Then she, His true mistress, would return to human form and in full health. And they had a son, as well, who remained human. A deal with the devil, surely."

"What is the process for returning?" Nóra pressed.

"A wave of His hand, I suppose. A few words of magic. A shake of hands over an agreement. That is how He explained it. From then He could only ever complain about his fate, about her fate. They could never be together again yet she would live in peace—so long as He did His duties, which was to expand the circle of evil throughout the land."

"Seems a fate worse than true death," said Joshua.

"True death would be a peaceful respite from the daily sufferings of blood craving and the disgusting practices of vampiric society." Maria's eyes were red as her fervor rose. "I served Him as best I could, offering all of myself to Him. Yet His lord and master put a stop to our union, made His touch a frostbite unto me."

"Yet you had the icy touch for Borbély," said Joshua.

"The man had a cold heart, from which I drew out his poison. That has little to do with magic, though I used what powers I had in me, amplified by this stone." She took it out and studied it. "His Holiness claimed it came from a museum in Russia, in Moscow, stolen after the siege. Yet I know it's true origin. From China, yes, but given to me by someone I once knew. It was lost sometime during the twin wars, and found again later. I know this amulet well. Though it must need recharging now. I could barely complete my spell."

Joshua pushed his bowl aside. "Our route takes us to the border, where you will be safe. From there you may go as you please."

"And you? What will you do?" asked Maria. She glanced at Nóra, back at Joshua.

"For us, we have only one life. We will go there next. This journey is for you," he replied. "Then I will have fulfilled the final command of His Holiness: to see you safely out of the empire."

Nóra pulled the bag beside her up into her lap. "We have another one to tend to." She smiled warmly at Joshua. "I have a child."

"A child?" Maria was surprised, judging the scrawny girl's fitness for conception and pregnancy. "You left the child in Budapest?"

Nóra grinned as she opened the bag in her lap and lifted out . . . a child. The thing was the size of a newborn, frozen in a fetal position as though just delivered, and pasty gray like a statue. As she studied it, she believed it was actually a statue, perhaps something to soothe a distraught girl's agony, something upon which to put her love, a doll. The girl brushed the statue's head as though hair grew there.

"She did deliver it," Joshua explained solemnly. "Alive in the first moments. But the curse was strong in this one, and it became as you see now within a night."

"That is awful." Maria, sincerely upset, regarded Joshua. "Yours?"

He blushed, flashing a whiter pale. "Certainly not. I claimed Nóra as my daughter. After they killed her father. Remember?"

"Yes, the vile prince and that bitch of a countess."

"The prince raped me," Nóra whispered like she didn't want anyone in the inn to hear. "Then he bit my throat." She pulled away her collar to show the marks, still visible after more than a year.

"What a curse," Maria muttered, then swept away an invisible tear that she pretended ran down her cheek. A gesture of sympathy.

"They must have made the connection in the minutes before he turned her. The child was cursed in the womb. Nearly ripped her apart passing him out. She won't have another child, not as a vampire."

Maria nodded, raising her hands to her face.

"Milady? Are you well?" Nóra asked.

"Yes," she replied. "It is the curse of us who change before we can birth a child. I've heard of this: the fetus infected by the disease, born as a stone. I pity you, girl. I pity myself, never a mother—though I have existed in other ways. Not every woman must have a child, yet for us, the vampiric horde, there is little choice and even less opportunity. His Holiness had a son before His transformation was complete. And the mother of His son likewise conceived before she noted the disease was upon her. It is the sad story of our existence, meddling in the dark arts and hoping, praying for something to bless us."

ℂℛ

Maria awoke with a start, the blanket over her too warm, the room too cold. The drapery had shut out the daylight but the crack of yellow had gone as evening arrived. Beside her lay Nóra in her hoary gown; Maria had kept the blanket to herself. She pulled it away and spread it over the scraggly girl, curled up clutching her stone baby.

"Joshua," she called across the room, rising from the bed in her nightshirt. She grabbed her country dress and switched garments.

He was asleep on a cot that sagged under his weight but he stirred at her voice. His eyes flicked open.

"It's dusk." He seemed surprised. "I'm not used to sleeping so long, My Lady. Pardons."

"There are visitors outside," she whispered.

He jumped up, brushed his clothing and went to Nóra, awoke her gently and held a finger against her mouth.

Quickly they packed and slipped out the back door of the inn, to the stable where the vorses stood, buckets of blood hooked over their boney muzzles for them to lap up. He prepared the vorses, hitching them to the carriage, as Maria helped Nóra up into the carriage.

Spying through the gaps in the wall slats, Joshua saw the visitors were a plain family come for the night. That meant they were human, ready to sleep at night when they, being of vampiric society, arose at twilight.

"I think they are not dangerous," he said, "a family of bloodlings staying the night."

"Should we bleed them?" asked Nóra innocently.

"No, dear," Maria said, putting her hand over Nóra's arm to stop her from climbing out of the carriage. "We cannot make any scene. It is our right, certainly, yet someone might report us. If you can endure the fast another day . . . ."

"I can," said Nóra, "but he needs a blood ration every day."

They both gazed upon her baby, held in her arms.

"Yes, certainly," said Maria.

"Worry not, Nóra. We'll find a pig somewhere along the way." He climbed up to the bench, shook the reins. "Let us be away."

They rode on, found the next town. The rail line was out of service there so they continued, the vorses pulling their carriage without much complaint. None they passed on the country roads gave them a second look; that they had vorses made them upper-class. The workers were reduced to walking.

After another day's ride, getting only a little closer to the border, they thought to stop for the night at another rustic inn, something old and shabby enough that no official would look for them there, Joshua explained. Maria, being a Lady of the Court, took exception to the choice of accommodations, pointing to a lovely inn up the lane with flower pots on the balconies.

Joshua gave it a glance. "That is a brothel, My Lady."

She fell silent, then turned to help Nóra down from the carriage, still cradling her baby.

The inn they chose was comfortable enough for a night. Joshua kept watch, spying out the windows, curtains closed. By now, someone would have discovered Borbély's messy remains. Someone else would have known he was hosting a woman that evening, perhaps the famous prisoner, the former mistress of the emperor. Another someone would see that she had not been returned to her cell. Official people would ask questions, as he would have done if he were still in uniform in the palace, at his post.

"They questioned me after His Holiness vanished," Joshua began speaking when they were settled in their room and everyone had fallen silent for a spell. "I was his personal attendant at the time. He called me chamberlain but I had no official claim. They thought I was an idiot and dismissed me. In truth, I was still in shock for what happened. I failed to protect His Holiness."

He choked back words. A spot of blood grew in the corner of his eye and he wiped it away.

"Everyone saw the doors breached, the arrow shooting through, His Holiness fall to the floor. And I helped Him escape—with you, with Nóra. It was we three that helped Him, not those two. I don't know those others in that salon. Was that planned? The countess seemed to know something, a scheme in her head. I think fetching that physician was a ruse to get me away from His Holiness. Maybe he was drugged while I was away. Or that arrowhead, besides it being silver, could've been poisoned. He slipped away so quickly. I knew Him only a short time yet He seemed like a superbeing, strong and defiant to the end. I wish Him dark speed on His journey south."

Maria watched him, saw regret smearing his face. "I know you did your best to save Him. We cannot know what His fate is now. Once sent down the Duna, it was out of our hands."

"Down the Duna?" Joshua narrowed his eyes at her.

"The casket," she said with ironic tone. "They put it on a boat, sent it down the river. To . . . to whatever the next big city is. Then off-load it to some wagon, and onward to a postal station to have it shipped to the address His Holiness gave for delivery."

"For delivery?" Joshua sat up stock straight. "His Holiness gave the address? That was the plan?"

"I thought you knew," said Maria, flipping her hand in the air. "You were his personal assistant. I expect He told you everything. I thought you acted within His plan."

"His plan. His?" Joshua shook his head, pondering. "His plan was to be attacked? And killed? Or . . . hmm, have it appear He was killed."

"Yes, like that. What you said."

"So . . . He was not actually killed. Maybe His existence came to an end, locked inside that casket and sent down-river. If He would be discovered, surely they would end Him right there. How would we know if he arrived?"

Maria wet her lips, folded her hands in her lap, entering a role.

"Dear Joshua, do not worry about things you cannot change, nor things which never required anything of you—"

"But, My Lady, much has been required of me in my service to the emperor and to the empire. I cannot be unaccountable for what has happened to the emperor, my sacred charge!"

"I am your superior," Maria spoke in firm tone. "And I bid you relax and not feel you have failed. You acted exactly as He expected you to act. He counted on you being who you are. He needed someone who could lift Him, carry Him away when the time came. I could not bear Him, nor a handful of serving girls bear Him on. You were chosen for a special duty: to carry Him out of the imperial suite. And you performed it perfectly."

His face was a mask, gray like smoke. "He did choose me."

"You did not suspect?"

"He murdered my friend Kristóf right before my eyes. Then he ordered me to accompany Him to the centennial celebration, to be His personal guard there. It was a special honor bestowed upon a regular palace staff member. For the centennial celebration. And—and there was an assassination attempt!"

"You stopped that attempt. Yet that was not the right moment."

"The right moment?"

"Too many people." She wiped her eyes. "We could have whisked Him away, hidden Him in the imperial suite, and none would be the wiser what became of Him, what damage His wounds would incur. We could have announced His unfortunate demise soon after. Everyone would have believed it."

"Yet He defended Himself. He slaughtered dozens."

Maria frowned. "It was not yet the right time."

"How long was this trick employed?"

Maria fought back a grin, her head tilting down. "Years, perhaps. I do not know precisely. He said things which now I can understand. He wanted to die—to end His existence, to be out from under the thumb of His lord and master."

"The darkest father of all . . . ."

"He who made the dark." Maria threw her head back, flung her hand through her hair as she laughed. "When the God of the Bible cleaved the light from the dark, it was He alone who stood tall and demanded the light be returned, to be hidden, locked away, never to be seen. Humanity did not deserve light. Yet He failed and had to be satisfied with what light could, with effort, be coaxed from fire, from lightning, from luminous flowers and fish, from the eyes of cats, from the distant stars. That was all He had left, so He gathered legions of followers and vowed to make war on the light. The God of the Bible named Him thus: the bearer of light. A cruel joke."

Joshua rubbed his chin. "A twisted affair."

"He wants to reclaim the light, not exist in the dark."

"It does seem the catechism is true," Joshua muttered. He glanced at her. "You know it well, My Lady. I'm impressed. The Most High would be proud of you."

"The Most High has well enough pride for us all," she said with a sideways glance. She watched curiosity creep over his face. "Some say the God of the Bible always employs spies who work across the world, wherever needed, to sabotage His legions and obstruct His prophet."

The idea seemed to halt Joshua's thoughts. "Do you think so?"

A flash of a grin. "Who can say?"

"It does seem likely someone would work from the inside to thwart the evil of the Most High." His brow furrowed. He flicked his nose with a finger. "I wonder if the assassination attempt was such an act? Not a poor fool avenging his sisters but a higher power acting through that youth, attempting to stop His Holiness. We cannot know what forces act in the shadows."

She pursed her lips, let her eyes flutter, and leaned forward. Her gown fell away, her snowy bosom blinding him.

"Perhaps they act not in the shadows but in the sheets." Light spread upon her face. "There is a much softer means of revolution."

Joshua stared at her, eyes fixed on what showed.

She gazed up at him. "Are you afraid of me, Joshua?"

"Not much, My Lady." His voice was strained.

"'My Lady' is so old-fashioned. You were not about during the late twentieth century, were you? 'Life in the Old Days' was all the rage. Dramas shown on their electric screens told the tales of times past. Did you see me? I acted in two or five of those cinema productions. I was the stupid whore, or the silent girlfriend, or the dumb clerk behind a desk. I had one line my entire career. It was 'Stop! Don't!' I spoke it perfectly. 'Stop! Don't!' Don't you think so? Hmm? No, you did not see them. You are forgiven. Too early for you. I was not very good. That did not matter to me. I made my way among the bloodlings with little care, taking as I needed—"

"Oh! I promised you a pig," said Joshua, rising from where he sat.

Maria laughed. "I can wait till tomorrow. So can Miss Nóra."

"The border is still far off. The road is still dangerous."

"So you have a plan?" Her smirk cut through the dim light of the room like a comet's flight. "Everyone has a plan, whether or not they know it. What is your plan for me?"

He bowed from his standing position, sweeping his arm aside in full courtesy. "My Lady, I think you will be best served to leave the empire. The closest border is Russia. You're French, so they will accept you. And you know how to speak Russian."

"You have thought this out completely, I see."

"The years have made me a thinker."

"And a doer." Her smile warmed. "You have a cold cot tonight, sir. Would you like to lay beside me?"

He exhaled loudly. "I—I'd rather not."

"I do not refer to a sexual episode, sir. Only sleep."

"I mean no disrespect, but I am not able to take that role. I'm your protector. I must stay at watch. Yes, you are beautiful and any man would like that invitation. But I am on duty. For you and for Nóra."

"On duty." She scoffed, grinned. "There are other days before we reach the border. Perhaps there may be a sexual episode. Who can say? It may be the last chance for both of us."

"You have many years ahead."

"Yet we shall part at the border."

∞

The scrawny vorses took them to the next town, Szolnok, where they could be left in a stable presumably to be picked up later, after dropping off the women at the train station. Tickets were bought for the border town.

A train ride to the border, thought Maria, remembering what His Holiness had said from time to time about His other great love, how she suffered crossing the border into the Hungarian Federation in the old days. She smiled to herself; at least that one suffered to get to Him. Not like her, crossing paths in the social circles of nobility and He taking her one morning like a wild boar, rooting against her and finally letting loose his roar and rage! The only instance where she enjoyed it—though He called out *her* name, and never apologized or corrected His *faux pas*. She could forgive Him that; so much more had come to pass since that day, their fates gradually woven together, tighter and tighter. The decades when they could never touch was ever on her mind. Ah, what could have been . . . .

"What amuses you, Milady?" asked Nóra, her baby safely put away in her bag.

"Thoughts of the past, dear."

"Good thoughts, I think, to see your face glow that way."

"Mmm, good thoughts, yes."

Joshua met them onboard the train, took a seat across from Maria as Nóra moved beside her to leave the seat free for his large presence.

"This train will take us only as far as Debrecen," he said with a huff. He pulled his coat collar tighter. "We must change trains there. Guards will pour through the station so we must be cautious. Then the border. The news is not good. The Russian army has pushed east so . . . the border is now closer. Unfortunately, the rail line goes to the north. The border is now west of Lviv. Close to the city. There are celebrations of independence there, freedom from the empire."

Maria nodded thoughtfully. Freedom. Everything was serious now.

More soldiers and guards and police officers on the streets, as though word had been put out to search for them. However, with the empire's regression, electronic communication was rare; handwritten messages took time to deliver. So far they had made their way across much of the territory without anyone becoming suspicious. No one was concerned about a runaway prisoner; finding the next meal took their energy and attention. A large city like Debrecen would test their cover.

"We will part at Lviv," he continued, as though reciting the plan. He leaned forward to speak in a low voice: "I trust you will be safe from there. You'll go on to Moscow?"

She seemed to be lost in thought, already planning her new life. When he asked again, she only nodded.

"And you? Nóra?" she asked, her face showing genuine concern.

"We will go south. I will take her to my homeland in Moldavia."

"To Moldavia?" asked Nóra innocently. "Is it a beautiful place?"

"Yes, my dear. A good place for you to raise your son."

Maria smiled at the girl. "I wish you both a long existence. And a lot of peace during that time."

"Thank you, My Lady."

"You should stop using honorifics now we are among the public. You wouldn't want everyone bowing to me, would you?"

He chuckled, sitting back. "You are correct, My Lady. From now I shall call you by the name you chose: Míra Pál. You shall be my wife on this journey. And Nóra, our daughter. We are going to a spa for treatment of her poor health conditions. The story fits us."

"Yes, indeed, sir. My husband Joshua."

The train pushed slowly away from the station and soon chugged across the plain, skirting the Carpathian mountains, crossing into what once was Romania, the province of Transylvania, arriving at Satu Mare.

A line of guards stood on the platform while a squad walked the train, car to car. They did not stop for anyone as they passed through so Joshua did not worry. They had their story and were dressed for the roles. But a big fellow with two small females makes an easy target. The squad halted and returned to their pair of seats.

The sergeant asked for his papers, his identification card, and his ticket. He looked across at the two women in the opposite seat. As

Joshua fumbled in the pockets of his coat, the sergeant asked the women if the three of them were together, which Maria confirmed, then asked about their destination.

Maria shifted in the seat, let her coat open, showing her throat as she spoke to the sergeant in Russian. The man nodded, smiled briefly, and then waved his squad away.

"What did you say?" asked Joshua, settling back.

"He asked about us, so I said we were going off to a spa for our daughter's treatment. She had an ugly skin disease. They would not want to touch her or perhaps breath the air she exhaled. But we are used to it so no danger to us, her parents."

"I understand why they were so quick to depart. Oh—also . . . ." He reached into his coat pocket, retrieved a pouch. "Here."

The train lurched, began to roll out of the station.

"What is it?" she asked him.

"Some money. Enough to get you to . . . wherever you wish to go."

Her eyes brightened. "From your account?"

"I don't have money," he chuckled. "No, it was in the imperial suite, locked in the cabinet with that letter His Holiness wanted. It must be yours. Go on, take it."

She held out her hand and he lay the small bag in her palm. On the side facing up was her name, cut into the soft leather by some sharp point. Not a professional engraving but something rougher, like the emperor himself had cut her name there.

He waved his hand at the pouch. "It seems He did plan everything."

"He was meticulous," she said, caressing the leather pouch.

"Indeed." He reached into his bag and retrieved a leather cylinder, offered it to her. "The Letter he so demanded."

Accepting the cylinder, she raised her chin, batted her eyelashes.

"Should I read it? It is private, is it not?"

"I did." He shook his head. "Long time to carry it. I was curious. If it was wrong, I apologize. There's nothing too private in the letter. His son complains. That's all."

"There is much to complain about."

He had to smile. "Indeed."

"'Indeed' . . . ," she intoned. "His Holiness often said it. Hmm. 'His

Holiness.' We should not use that title. People will likely think us too religious. From now we should call him by his true name. His mother, who was Hungarian, named him Stefan. I have seldom called him by that name. I addressed him as 'my love' in our private quarters."

"And did you love him?" he asked, amused.

She stared out the window at the distant mountains, their peaks lost in the gray clouds, as she rolled the cylinder in her fingers.

"Yes, I loved him. But I have loved many."

She slipped the cylinder into her bag without a second thought and closed her eyes, drew in a long breath.

"Stefan, I shall never forget."

14

NÓRA SLEPT MOST OF THE TRIP WHILE MARIA AND JOSHUA kept up an irregular conversation punctuated by several minutes of silence before returning to the same or a new topic. It often seemed like a labor, a task to be endured, yet both seemed obligated to not let the silences go on too long.

Maria learned of his life in Moldavia before joining the army. She already knew his life at the palace after the army. She learned more about Nóra from him, a sad life as a bloodling then a worse existence as a vampire with a stone baby. She had to discount the horrors of her own life. She was quite senior to the newly born Nóra.

She remembered the moment she was caught, seduced, cajoled, bitten, sucked, and licked clean, left in a heap on the floor of the prop room of the theater in Paris. She had felt sick after, the pain of the change. She had made a plan to kill him and everyone else there who was vampiric. Her vicious goals were met for a few of them, yet others escaped punishment when she needed to hop a coach out of town. It was bound for Geneva, she learned from the other passengers. When they stopped for a lunch along the way and the coachman discovered she had no ticket, she was left to walk the muddy roads in a torn dress with a blood-streaked throat—

Joshua waved his hands sharply. "By now they are sure to find your paramour dead in his chamber and be looking for us."

Maria's angry memory twisted into the present contorted reality, and a scowl sprouted upon her face. "He was not my paramour. He was my prosecutor. He hoped to enjoy an erotic evening with me before I would be executed. His evidence would be lost then."

"We saved you from him," Nóra spoke, awaking and reaching for Joshua's arm. He moved over and she lay her head against his shoulder. "And you got that lovely jewelry."

"It is not only a piece of jewelry." Maria took a breath, not wishing to lash out at the poor girl. "It is ancient. It was made in China. I came to possess it long ago when I happened onto a traveler in Switzerland, a man named George, or possibly Gordon, some name with a 'g'. My coach was stuck in mud, a broken wheel, when his carriage appeared. He was handsome, like a prince, with a tongue full of poetry. He invited me to ride in his fine carriage and his friend had to ride outside with the coachman. Inside, we discussed the great works of literature until he fell upon me for his pleasure. The bumpy road did the rest of our exercise. In thanks he handed me the amulet, saying it was a trifle yet of sentimental value to him. Yet he would give it up for the dear time I had spent with him. Another night with him, in an inn at the next village, outside Geneva, sealed the deal. I was ready to bite him, and let him be my paramour, yet I could not bring myself to do it."

"He was not vampire?"

"No, fully human," she replied, lifting her shawl to check that the amulet remained in place around her neck. "Yet he would have made a great vampire, I believe, the way he spoke, eloquent and haughty, and his propensity for dalliance, the way he made sweet passionate love. He was passionate about all things. The way I wished to be. I was of a young age then. And now. Always. He said he had gotten the amulet in trade from a wandering Gypsy woman—or else won it in a gambling game, as his friend said."

"It sure is pretty," Nóra cooed.

"More than beautiful, dear. It had magic in it, the Gypsy woman told him, though I took his words to be mere idle prattle designed to endear me to him. It worked. Yet, as I wore the amulet, I recognized it's hold over me, a certain energy pulsing in my chest, a glow rising to my head and out to my hands. I was surprised he let it go so easily to me. Perhaps he had no idea of its powers. Or he feared its power."

"And he has since passed, this gentleman you met on the road, I presume? Being human . . . ."

"Yes, that was long ago. A distant memory. When I was newly-born into the dark. Perhaps in eighteen-sixteen—summer. Such a different time. A cold, rainy summer, I recall. Later I learned he wrote poetry so I fancied a book of his writing. I found it in a shop in Zurich eventually, but it was translated into German. It was clever, I will admit."

"Now we have only the catechism," Joshua sighed.

"Poetry is for everyone. Anyone can learn to write the things, given enough practice. Clever wordplay is all it is. The amulet, however, is the key to whatever powers I may have. Without it I am weak, like a human."

Joshua gave a smirk. "I'm sure you are strong in other ways."

"You must be the oldest of us," said Nóra.

"And the most experienced," Joshua added.

"Yet I maintain my girlish figure and am always a virgin." She gave a throaty laugh. "My curse, it seems. For more than two-hundred and eighty years. Yes, I am senior to His Holiness." She feigned shock at her error. "I mean . . . Stefan."

Joshua chuckled, partly to be polite, partly to cover his own terrible life which he had revealed to her with little sympathy in return.

CR

The train began slowing as it arrived in the outer quarters of the city. Lines of Russian soldiers in blue uniforms stood in loose formation on the streets, pending trouble. The city was recently liberated from the Hungarian Empire; new rules were in place. Continuing passengers would pass by the soldiers to enter the customs office, a gloomy place as depressing as the overcast sky. Then they would board a different train or be sent back, thought Maria with trepidation. In her bag, the one her saviors had packed for this trip, was her old French passport, expired yet a document for these desperate times which would prove her origin.

"I apologize," said Maria to Joshua after the train came to a halt. "I meant to respond in sympathetic fashion, yet those words do not come easily to me. I was not brought up to be polite that way."

Nóra turned to her, toothy grin causing Maria to cringe. The girl's cowl had slipped down on her shoulders, revealing her raggedy scalp.

"I wish I found such a man like your Mister Stefan," said the girl. "His Holiness treated me kindly."

Maria pursed her lips. "Come, girl. Let me give you something to mend your body. So many years of servitude have wasted you."

She held out her wrist, plucked a vein with a sharp fingernail and watched the red bubble up.

"Here. Drink, Nóra. Let me restore you. May your hair grow long and thick like mine. May your mottled skin be glowing and smooth. May your body grow full and healthy. I wish you to have a better life."

Joshua looked surprised. "Are you sure of this?"

"Without you and her," she spoke softly, studying her bleeding wrist, "I would be cut into thousands of pieces by yesterday's sunset. The public would dine on my flesh unto dawn."

With a nod from Maria, Nóra leaned down and lapped at her wrist as she stroked the girl's cheek. The silence of the cabin made it a holy ritual. To give some of the essence that had sustained her from before the Terror to after the collapse of the Hungarian Empire was the highest gift she could offer, more valuable than rubies or jade, gold or diamonds.

"You are generous, My Lady," said Joshua, watching intently, as though he was finding his own thirst within him.

"My name is Maria," she spoke in a flat voice. "Or, Jeanne-Marie, as we enter Russia. We are like a family now. I'm no longer nobility."

Her hand reached out for him, her fingers dabbed with her blood. He took the hint and cradled her hand, licking off her fingertips.

"A good finish," he muttered, sitting back with a satisfied grin.

"May you be restored for a long journey."

"And you," said Joshua. "A longer journey than us, I suspect."

Nóra sat up, licking her lips. She wiped her mouth with the back of her hand, leaving her cuff stained.

"Careful, Nóra," said Joshua. "Don't let people see your mouth so red. Out here there are few vampires. More persecution. We must be more alert. The age of vampiric society is coming to its end."

Maria raised her wrist, applied the tip of her tongue to the opening and after several licks it sealed. She tasted Nóra's breath on her wrist, and gazed over at the girl. With sly grin, Maria leaned over and kissed the girl full on her lips.

"You shall have a sweet life," said Maria, parting. Nóra smiled.

"If we can get to Moldavia without trouble," Joshua spoke roughly.

Maria reached across and patted his knee. "Do not worry, brave soldier. You shall be home soon. May the spirits, both good and evil, grant you both safe passage."

With a solemn nod, he glanced out the window, saw the faded billboards and unblinking electric signs, suddenly realizing they had arrived in Lviv. He muttered how the gloomy cast over the old city reminded him of battles long ago fought. It reminded him of what he had lost. He glanced across at Nóra.

"And what I've gained," he mumbled to himself.

Maria stared at the big man, the stout fellow who had wielded a sharp halberd, left behind in the palace. She wondered if he had ever disobeyed or shirked his duties. Likely not. A rare thing. He would survive, she knew. And the girl with him.

The train was finally rolling into the station.

"You continue to Moscow, I suppose?" he asked, an afterthought.

Maria turned to the window, noting the new reality outside. "It seems best. I know some people there—if they remained. Communists. They likely were executed years ago. Then I should go to China. I shall try to find a good mandarin to bless this amulet. I feel it weakening. Then my fate might be delayed once more, my existence extended. I may yet live again. Who can say?"

"Maybe you can have a baby like me," Nóra said, giggling.

Maria's lips tightened. "Perhaps so, dear."

The train rocked as it halted.

"The station." Joshua let out a long breath. "Our time is at hand."

"What time is it?" asked Nóra, looking around.

"Time for you to get your things together."

Maria tapped the girl's hand. "It is time for us to part, dear. I shall go north and you shall go south. We each have our destinations. The gods of Light and Dark have called us. To go otherwise would upset the balance of the world."

Nóra smiled brightly, like a child loving her mother.

They stood—Joshua staring out the windows at the guards on the platform, Maria and Nóra gazing at each other, a thought hovering in the air between them.

Nóra reached out with both her hands. Maria hesitated a moment, then accepted the hug. She wrapped her arms around Nóra.

Joshua dared to lay his hand on Maria's shoulder and she did not object. His hand rested heavily there as the two women parted.

"Farewell, My Lady." He sniffled, pretended to wipe a tear that did not appear, a gesture of courtesy among a society that did not cry.

"Your homely wife," she snapped.

"My pretend wife . . . ."

Maria stretched up and kissed his cheek. "Always."

"My duty is done," he spoke, stepping back.

She turned to Nóra: "Farewell, dear."

"Farewell," the girl replied, head lowered shyly.

They stepped off the train, pausing to give each other one last look, then disappeared in opposite directions, the interval quickly filled by a squad of guards. A few police craned their necks to look for suspicious passengers. After all, it was 2102 and the world was on fire, at the onset of a blustery autumn in the weary marches of a fading empire.

A gentle shower began to fall from the gray sky as Maria stood in the customs line. She looked up. Raindrops splashed against her face. They did not sting or burn her skin. She closed her eyes. The Black Storm had finally lifted.

ભ

The customs officer kept glancing up from under his bushy eyebrows, perhaps hoping to catch another angelic smile on her cherubic face. Unable to concentrate, he was going through the motions examining her travel documents so his boss wouldn't suspect he wasn't diligent in his duties. She had already explained her French passport's expiration and her inability to leave the Hungarian Empire prior to the chaos.

Two or three more sincere-looking smiles ought to do it, thought Maria, sitting with excellent posture on the hard chair across the desk from the man. His ruddy face and blonde whiskers touched by gray told her this bloodling was about fifty and disappointed with his life, a hard-drinker with cheating wife.

"I am going to join my husband," she spoke in Russian once more, trying to hurry the proceedings along. "He sent me this ticket."

The man straightened up, pen in hand over the paper form. There were no electronics in the office. No computers, no wrist scanners. The change of government was too new for Russian technology to arrive.

"Your husband's name?"

"His name?" She held her smile firm as she pulled a name from her hat of memories. "Arkady."

"Arkady what?"

"Azov," she replied instantly. "We lived in Germany for a while. He returned to Moscow on business, and I—" She started acting the role of the abandoned spouse. "I lost touch with him during the Hungarian Empire's expansion. I got trapped there. I had to work as a servant in the imperial palace. They beat me every day." With focused thought she made her forearm produce a purplish blotch, which she showed to him. "I am still recovering."

The man was nodding his head like a child's bobble toy as he fingered her passport. "Yes, I see."

"Thank you, sir."

He met her eyes, for an instant—bright, loving, yet humble—and he could not look away.

"I see no trouble with you. I will grant you entry." He stamped her passport and added a sticker marking the old document as 'refugee claim based on expired passport'; in effect, renewing her passport on the spot. There were a lot of migrants coming out of the Hungarian Empire these days, he explained to her. Because she is actually French and not Hungarian, he would let her in.

"I am so grateful to you, sir," she sang, standing with him.

"Pleasant journey," he intoned, too shy to speak up.

"A pleasant day to you, too, *comrade*," she responded, then caught herself. "I mean 'sir', not 'comrade'. Old habit."

She turned to exit the small office, her bag in hand, pulling the shawl tighter around her shoulders, covering the impressive jeweled necklace with its powerful green stone amulet.

The man shot up from his desk.

"You're not one of those vampires, are you? Lives for two hundred years, are you?"

With a girlish whirl, she turned half-way. "I hate them. Absolutely hate vampires. I hope never to see one again."

Acting fatherly, he waved her out.

She crossed through the station and out another door to enter the line for the next train.

As she waited, she had the urge to look around, to see if Joshua and Nóra might still be there, but she hesitated, believing if she looked for someone, someone might look for her. So she kept her head down and her eyes forward, yet her senses were on constant alert for events in her vicinity. She sucked in her fangs and held a grim façade for her fellow passengers.

After boarding the train, holding her breath until it started away from the station, she settled into the travel routine. Pretending to nap to avoid conversation, or staring out the window at whatever distant landscape came by. Guards passed through at each station to assure everyone's safety and proper behavior. Tickets and passports were checked, wrists scanned in some cases. She explained twice to officials the reasons she had no chip: she came from the Hungarian Empire, where they frowned on such technology. She would make her face blush and produce a tactically placed tear, moaning for her dead husband, executed in Budapest. She felt comfortable in her new role, a young widow, and her seatmates offered words of encouragement.

It was half-true, which made the acting easier. Another theater person she had lived with during the twenties—the 1920s, between the people's revolution and the end of the second great war there. When millions died defending the motherland, vampires had feasted. Thus identified as *krovososy* ['blood-suckers'], they were rounded up and executed in huge pyres. She had fled ahead of the purge, escaping to Sweden for a few years before going south to Germany in the 1960s and returning to Moscow in 1995 when she thought the vampire hysteria had settled. Back in 1932, however, she had not left any note for her lover, Comrade Kuznetsov. She had to flee too quickly for a note.

She met Yevgeni Feodorovich Kuznetsov when she auditioned for *Maiden of Midnight,* a play based on the novel by Irina Mikhailovna Popov, later hung as a counter-revolutionary. Maria hoped to be given the leading role of Alina, the novice in the Orthodox church who is raped by a priest then gets delicious revenge on everyone. She felt the allegorical drama was made for her, yet she did not get the part. She served as a villager instead and Yevgeni was the mayor of that stage village. They spent many hours together after rehearsals and after each performance, which lasted one full season before authorities shut it down. The government was becoming ever stricter, chastising any attempt at progressive art or literature. Then the next war began, right on cue—as she had been tipped off by her mentor.

This train ran smoothly, she noticed, a much better vehicle than the old one they had ridden from Budapest. Someone mentioned the train sailed over jets of compressed air. She was entering a modern world. Arriving in Moscow, she could not believe the architecture that had sprouted up like a great forest. There were the Seven Colossuses marking the old wall towers of ancient Muscovy, silver office buildings rising fifty floors, topped with great communication towers. Nothing like them existed in Budapest or anywhere else in Europe; the empire disdained anything modern. In the center of the city stood the 800-meter tall statue of Saint Vladimir, savior of the republic. Below the feet of the statue and its mountainous hill of earth and granite blocks, the walls of the Kremlin were crumbling, finally allowed to decay as an unwanted symbol of the Communist era.

She exited Okhotny Ryad station at the north end of Red Square and found the streets crisscrossed by driverless trolleys, stopping to pick up anyone who waved. After strolling the square and assuring that St. Basil's Cathedral was still as colorful as she remembered—it was, undamaged; Lenin's Tomb, however, had been occupied by the latest iconic figure—she rode to the west, then north, past the huge Bolshoi Theater extension—the arts were flourishing again, it seemed—and a grand new Orthodox cathedral on Neglinnaya Avenue dedicated to St. Vladimir. Another trolley took her past blocks of solemn gray high-rise apartments where she thought she had lived with Yevgeni. She became confused. Eventually she realized her location and stepped off.

Before her was a street of old townhouses with short stoops and iron-barred windows, tree-lined sidewalks, a formerly elegant middle-class neighborhood now lost in the vagaries of poverty. She walked a bit and found an alley between two sets of townhomes. Besides the trash cans and an old, rusted petro-mobile, a stairwell led down from the alley's pavement, set off with a wrought-iron fence to keep people from falling into it. At the top was a waist-high iron gate.

She gazed down the stairs, certain this would lead to the correct destination. She swung the gate open, wishing it did not creak so loudly. A glance around assured her that none of the neighbors were interested. She took a step down the stairs, one hand gripping her bag, the other on the railing. At the bottom, she kicked away a pile of dried leaves from the door there. It seemed no one had used the door in a while. She could see through the windows of the door that the shop was filled with old books, shelf after shelf. On the inside of the window, at the bottom edge, a small card stated the proprietor would soon return. The writing was French, not Russian, so she knew she was at the correct address.

She placed her hand on the doorknob, felt a spark and jumped. The door handle loosened, moved, and the old door opened.

Stepping inside, she was hit by the scent of old paper, parchment, glue, varnish, and dust. Surrounding her were bookshelves overflowing with unbound manuscripts, books on the edge of crumbling to dust, and a few scrolls, an archive of everything that had ever been printed, it seemed to Maria as she moved carefully through the stacks, down one narrow aisle and back up the other side. Curious, she paused to examine the items. Some manuscripts seemed a thousand years old, written in Latin or Greek or Hebrew. Other books were in Russian but an old-style script, handwritten pages with elaborate drawings.

Making her way deeper into the bookshop, she found a small office in the back with a scruffy desk and a chair with torn seat pad mended with wide swatches of tape. An old-style telephone sat there, its round dial gummed up by years of sticky fingers. Beside it sat a machine used to make printing. She remembered it was called a type-writer; it was not electronic like later inventions.

She dared reach for the desktop and using her fingertips wiped away the layer of dust that had accumulated. The chair did not look so dirty, but she shook out a handkerchief and lay it over the seat before sitting there, dropping her bag beside the chair. It was difficult for her to take any substantial breaths in the dusty place, particles floating in a haze around her.

"*Je suis ici,*" she spoke, announcing her presence in little more than a whisper.

She waited a while, head bowed, hands folded in her lap.

Looking up at the calendar on the wall—May 1962—she continued in French, with a stronger voice: "I have returned. Do you hear me? I finished many tasks. As expected. As you knew I would. And you may be pleased to know I suffered immensely during my stay there in the Hungarian Empire, the Empire of Europa, however you like to call it. I nearly did not escape. But you know everything, don't you? Master of the universe and all."

Her words seemed to echo, even in the small room, and the hollow sound unnerved her.

"Are you here? Is this the right address? Are you too busy to come here? To greet your humble servant at the end of a long journey? I am tired, and weary, thoroughly exhausted. I need to rest."

The silence after the echo died left her feeling disappointed. She stood, went to the doorway of the office and gazed out over the stacks of shelves. She almost expected to see all the paper dust fly together magically to form a person, a figure that would address her. She waited but nothing happened. Flustered, she sat on the chair again.

"I did what you asked of me. I always do." She moderated her growing irritation. "I have been your faithful servant for two hundred years. Is it not enough? I have done your dirty work, so your name would not be stained. I know my time is a drop in the ocean. Yet I destroyed the empire for you, and sent him on to his reward, left the capital in chaos. And your opponent has been once again thwarted. Now I ask for my reward, which you promised me. I want to be released. I want to be free, and never need tend to your business again. You have others who can serve you."

She pushed the typewriter aside, plopped her elbows on the desk, hands clasped, her chin resting on her hands as if in prayer.

"Please. It is a simple thing I ask in exchange for all I have done for you. Grant me my most precious wish . . . and let me go free."

This time there was no echo. The room filled with a low-pitched buzz, like an old set of electronics components had flicked on. Then, from somewhere both above and behind her, a voice, deep and rough, as though a heavy smoker had risen prematurely from a restless sleep, reaching for yesterday's cold cup of coffee:

Very well, my faithful daughter. For your long service, I shall grant you what you have requested. The great game continues, however.

"Thank you," she intoned, a whisper.

With a long exhale, she bowed her head. An eternity passed.

"Thank you, My Lord."

15

THE CABIN WAS WELL-HIDDEN FROM THE ROAD. When he parked the old sedan, the green 2088 model Yvetta, next to the cabin, the rear bumper with the faded GONZALEZ/CHANG 2096 sticker was visible, but he didn't think anyone would care enough to check on him. He lived alone, kept to himself. The nearest neighbor was three miles down the road and they never spoke. The grocery he visited once in a while was in a village out on the coast, twenty miles away. Sometimes he would spring for a lobster to celebrate an occasion such as the anniversary of his transformation—or his rebirth, his escape, or the death of someone he wished had not died. After a while they all ran together in his mind.

By the following spring—or was it autumn?—he was ready to step out again, to see what he could do to make people's lives a little better. Of course, the answer to that was to stay in the cabin and not bother anyone. But he had in time become bored. And he stayed drunk much of the time, anyway. Fearing a return of the voice, he kept the cabinet well-stocked and indulged daily in a liquid diet, maintaining a steady level of inebriation, enough to dull his mind yet not so much that he couldn't get up and chop some wood or gather berries in the woods.

However, chopping wood while inebriated had its risks. One time the axe slipped. The blade hit his shinbone. He didn't feel it at first, but when he went to take a step, he turned away with his leg and left his foot there in the snow. There wasn't much blood, not enough for a decent snack an average vampire might enjoy. He picked up his foot and limped back inside the cabin, tried to stitch it together. The ends of the bone were the hardest to mend and it never quite took. He filed it off so it wouldn't be sharp and dangerous, added a wooden support later so he could stand without leaning, so his legs were the same length. Keeping the stick strapped to his leg so tightly made his leg turn gangrenous. It discolored and stank and he wondered if he should cut it off, a little higher than where the axe had cut it. Or he could go into the town for a doctor to look at it. Another case of liquor worked just as well.

His left arm continued to calcify, becoming stiff and useless as the bone thickened and got heavier. In time he could barely lift his arm. He didn't need to use it for much, anyway. He didn't go to the grocery any longer, seldom hunted. He did set a trap once in a while, got some rodent that way, and therefore ate something to keep up his strength. Then, after he had indulged, he scolded himself for daring to keep up his strength. The goal was to lose his strength, after all. Every last ounce of it.

One summer day it rained, lightly at first, then harder. A full week of rain. The cabin roof leaked. He stepped outside, clothes-free, and let the rain wash over him, let the droplets trickle through the few strands of hair still fastened to his head, felt the streams running off his body, down his legs to the soil under his toes. And he realized it did not hurt. The rain did not burn his skin. He looked up and caught the raindrops in his mouth, swallowed them, and knew his thirst was quenched at long last.

The knock on the door was unexpected. No one ever came this far into the woods, and those who might know about him had little reason to contact him, given his reputation as the crazy wildman. It had been years since he had last wandered into town, and he doubted the Yvetta would start now.

Must be a lost hiker, he decided, hobbling to the door on his stick leg and cane, a carving knife in his hand.

"Yeah, what do you want?" he called through the crack in the door.

"Wondering if you have any food to spare," came the thin voice, like an echo on the wind. Maybe his hearing had gone already.

"I don't have any food," he grumbled.

"Could you spare some water?"

"Water?" He was angry now. Plenty of water for the taking in the stream out front, or the lake a few minutes away. "Go on. Get away. I don't need anybody."

There was a moment of silence. He thought the stranger had gone, so he hobbled back to his chair, dropped into it, picked up the book on the side table, much as his father had always done in that great room of the old villa in Croatia. Before he could think another thought about that horrible time, he picked up his glass of whiskey and finished it.

Another knock on the door.

This time he was going to get serious. He held the knife up as he opened the door.

The man had both hands out as if to halt his attack. He was maybe forty, beard grown out about a week, tall and slim, clothes like a guy out for a stroll on a Sunday afternoon, sneakers and jeans, canvas vest and a ball cap. Not a hiker. He seemed safe enough, gave a weird but disarming grin.

"I heard you were looking for me?" said the man.

He looked him over, since he had supposedly been looking for him.

"Thought you wanted food. Who are you?"

The man seemed to repress a chuckle, like he had fooled him.

"I'm Ben."

Nothing from the man in the doorway.

"Ben Kelly . . . ? I'm sorry, my name is Benedict Kelly. But we changed the family name a while back. Originally it was Székely. A Hungarian name."

His eyes widened, as much as they could given his poor health. He held fast to the door handle as he leaned forward, regarding the man.

"Benedict?"

"Yes. If you're Stefan . . . Stefan Székely . . . I need your help."

"My help?" He straightened up, still not convinced.

"Apparently, I've got some problem." He rolled up his sleeve, held out his arm, nodding at the brown, diamond-shaped patches of dry skin there. "I think it's something that . . . something you had. My father thought so. Grandma told us about you."

Stefan looked up at the man and recognized him—recognized the melding of Penny and him. His eyes pinched closed as he squeezed out two tears.

"I don't want this," said Benedict, voice shaking. "I don't want to transform into anything. I have a life to live, dammit. I'm an artist, for God's sake. I have a family now. How do I stop this from spreading? If I can't stop it, what should I do? I can't—It's better if . . . if my family doesn't know. Let them think I died."

Stefan's dry eyes blinked. "You actually have died."

∞

Years later, a group of four young people happened to find the cabin while hiking. The roof had collapsed under the weight of many snowy winters. They managed to crawl inside to escape a blizzard, and discovered a figure on a cot. They were startled. Then, stuck in the fallen cabin for several days, they became curious.

The face was little more than a skull, half the jaw gone, but the long teeth looked like fangs. They wondered if the figure could be a vampire. Beneath the blanket was a skeleton with a meager coating of flesh, viscera moldy within the rib cage and pelvis. Obviously the person had lain there starving to death, becoming bone-thin before dying. The skeleton was missing the lower half of one leg. And toes were missing from the opposite foot. The right arm had been broken in multiple places but had healed, yet at an awkward angle. Probably it was useless in that form. The left arm was more shocking, the bone much thicker than it ought to be. And the left hand's fingers were curled up tight, the bones fused together, unable to be used.

The group reported the body to authorities after the storm passed and they returned to town. Arrangements were made for a funeral and the nameless person was supposed to be buried near that cabin, with the four youths saying a few kind words about someone they never knew. Instead, when news reached a certain professor in Jersey, she signed a release form donating the remains to science and Boston University claimed them, an important addition to the Department of Vampire Studies. A memorial service was held on the campus and about fifty people attended, many only out of curiosity. The professor from Jersey did not attend.

CR

BANGOR, MAINE (AANS)—Recent discovery of possible vampire near Whiting, Maine, causes wild speculation. Forensic examination concluded the age of the skeleton found by St. Stephen, Brunswick students Lucy Fenton, Hansel James, Calvin Meissner, and Didi Emery, was approximately 168 years. According to Dr. Lawrence Ventura, a leading vampirologist at Boston University, "Vampires are just like you and me, except they tend to live about 150 to 200 years, not forever, based on a diet consisting of mostly blood, which helps stave off their painful condition." At the site, Ventura gave a detailed explanation of the genetic disease one week following the discovery. Signs of trauma on the remains suggest that the creature had been wounded in confrontations with humans or animals and apparently ran away to hide at the location where death eventually occurred, Ventura also noted.

The ultimate cause of death has been listed as starvation. "This is consistent with our long-held findings regarding vampire biometrics and their unique society," stated Ventura. "When the vampire is unable to obtain a steady blood supply, it will enter a hibernation state. However, if certain factors are present, the vampire may appear to die like any human would." Ventura also noted that the poor condition of the skeletal remains precluded the individual from ever rising from death to walk the world again. "The public need not have worries," said Ventura. A priest, Father Martin Szabo, was consulted and a special ritual of excommunication was performed to block the creature's soul from becoming active again.

Examination of the personal effects found at the location indicate the person – or vampire – had visited different cities in America and had stayed for a time in Europe. Those who knew the deceased, named in the documents found at the site, are being contacted for further information. The remains have been transferred to the Archeology Department at the Boston University for further examination. It is hoped that more details may be reconstructed from the forensic evidence, and a full history of the individual may yet come about. Dr. Victoria Kleinschmidt, Director of the Department of Vampire Studies at Boston University said the find would be an excellent addition to their museum and likely be a featured exhibit in the near future.

Fenton, James, Meissner, and Emery each received credit rewards for the find under the Body Recovery Statute of Section 5 of Maine's 2057 vampire laws. Fenton and Meissner also have been offered summer scholarships at Boston University for their discovery. James and Emery have received offers of full scholarships at Boston University's Department of Archeology. Emery has declared her interest in vampirology as a career, despite the continuing decline in vampire encounters. Warning signs have been positioned around the site and infrared motion detectors will alert local law enforcement if any vampiric activity should occur.

CR

"Yessiree, that there shore is one them vampires," said the man in his Midwestern drawl. "Lookit th' teeth on him, like right ready ta bite inta yer throat, ain't that right, Sis?"

The woman, sweeping her gray hair back, turned away.

"Don't be scared now, Sis. Ain't gonna bite cha. He's dead awready. I mean really dead not one those walkin undead creepers ya see on th' big screen."

The elderly couple stood before the nearly seven-foot tall skeleton. The figure had been posed in a menacing stance, hands raised as if to attack, mouth agape to display the fangs. In front of the creature was a plaque explaining the various aspects of the body, especially noting the flaws it obviously had. The point seemed to be how awful the genus of vampire was to humanity. You can observe how the arm and leg bones are malformed. Biologically, the creature was compelled to hunt for blood, killing often and at random, and having no sense of morality whatsoever.

"Y'ain't that da truth," the old man chuckled, one hand stuffed in his pants pocket, the other holding tightly onto his cane.

"Okee, Bucky, kin we go now?" said the woman, giving the man a shove. "I wanna get home 'fore *Vampire Island* come on. Travelin exhibit or not, I'ma ready ta leave this here moozeem."

"Awrighty now, Sis. I guess'n I'm done too. Jus wanna ta see it fer myself. Remember that fella stayed with us a while?"

"And you two go off on yer adventure—"

"Our gyawdamn adventure it was!"

His outburst echoed against the walls of the exhibit hall.

"Shhh, Bucky!" the woman chided.

"His name was Steve Kelly, ya know, 'nd this exhibit skeleton is too. 'From documents at the scene' sign says. Gotta be him."

"I thought he was a homeless man you found out the solar farm."

"No, he was . . . ."

A tall man in a trenchcoat stood beside them, staring up at the creature. Bucky glanced over at the man, got a flash of recognition. No, couldn't be. The man he knew was up on that pedestal, starved down to bones. Twisted and deformed. Yeah, he deserved it.

"Say, mister, mind my askin," he said, facing the man, "you any chance a relation t' any Steve Kelly? Used ta know fella by th' name an' ya kinda look like him."

"No, sir. My name's Benedict. Don't know any Steve Kelly."

With a polite nod, Bucky took the woman's arm and together they stepped around the side of the display, pausing so he could gaze one more time, one final time before exiting the hall.

The tall man in the trenchcoat followed them out.

When the shadow unfolded like wings against the beige wall, the elderly couple did not notice. As they passed through the archway into the next exhibit hall, a great sweep of blackness momentarily blocked the view. "Th' hell yew doin?" Then a terrifying scream echoed through the hallways. A rain of blood splashed across the marble floor and spotted the wall.

Behind the carnage, a smartly dressed woman stepped closer to the vampire skeleton on display. Her black skirt and blazer made her seem like a museum guide as she held the hand of the small boy beside her.

"And that, little Stefan, is how you feed," said the woman with a French accent, looking at the archway and into the darkness beyond. She glanced down at the boy. "You have to come up from behind. Older people make the best bloodlings, though not as sweet. When you're more mature, we shall see that you are properly transformed. They do things differently in America. We don't have a big ceremony with everyone watching you take your first bite like they do in China. Those Shanghai mandarins! Only good for crafting magical amulets."

"Mama," said the boy, tugging on her hand.

"Yes, dear?" She squatted down to meet him face to face.

"Did I really come from a green stone?"

The woman laughed, just for show. "Not really. You came from your father, who put the stone inside me. After a while, you came out. Now here you are." She kissed his cheek. "It was long ago the stone was put in me, and it sat there for quite a long time. Then, one day, after your father was long gone, I felt a pain in my belly and I had to push you out."

"Oh," said the boy. He glanced over at the blood-stained wall as frantic shouts and the noise of footsteps filled the building.

"See?" She pointed up at the skeleton on the pedestal. "That's him. That is your father. His name was Stefan. Stefan Székely. The same as you. He once was an emperor. And you can be an emperor someday, too."

Acknowledgements

Although actual places are mentioned in the novel, no disrespect is intended; nor is suggestion made of any actual impropriety by these entities. They are used fictitiously.

I always use music to assist my imagination. For this novel, I began with the playlist from the second novel's writing sessions. For the opening scene, I happened upon some orchestral music by Lucas King on the themes of *Star Wars* characters. Sometimes music from one film can inspire the writing of a totally different story. Believe it or not, aside from the few motifs we are all familiar with by now, much of the music proved helpful in setting the mood for my own writing. I also made good use of King's album *Dark Piano for Dark Thoughts*.

Later writing sessions drew inspiration from new musicians I discovered: Tracey Chattaway (albums: *Defining Moments*, *Nightsky*, and *Third Place*), Ursine Vulpine (*Respire*), and three singers: Fleurie (*Love and War*), Ruelle (*Rival*, *Madness*, and *Emerge*), and Svrcina (*Svrcina* and *Lover, Fighter*).

Thank you for your inspiration and the amazing aural support.

About the Author

Stephen Swartz grew up in Kansas City, Missouri, USA, where he was an avid reader of science-fiction and began emulating his favorite authors. Although veering away from science-fiction, his stories usually continue to feature exotic lands and foreign languages, strangers lost in familiar places, and the occasional breakfast menu.

Along the way, Swartz studied music in college and worked at a wide range of jobs: from French fry guy to soldier, tax agency clerk, and TV station writer, before heading to Japan for several years of teaching English.

Swartz is now a professor of English and has taught writing in New York, Pennsylvania, Kansas, Oklahoma, as well as China. He lives in Oklahoma, where he can be found working on his next novel most evenings and weekends.

Other books by Stephen Swartz

The Stefan Székely Trilogy

I. A Dry Patch of Skin

II. Sunrise

III. Sunset

Epic Fantasy *With Dragons

A Girl Called Wolf

A Beautiful Chill

After Ilium

Aiko

The Dream Land Trilogy

I. Long Distance Voyager

II. Dreams of Future's Past

III. Diaspora